By Genevieve Cogman

The Invisible Library series
The Invisible Library
The Masked City
The Burning Page
The Lost Plot
The Mortal Word
The Secret Chapter
The Dark Archive
The Untold Story

The Scarlet Revolution trilogy
Scarlet
Elusive

ELUSIVE

The Scarlet Revolution

BOOK TWO

GENEVIEVE COGMAN

TOR

First published 2024 by Tor
an imprint of Pan Macmillan
The Smithson, 6 Briset Street, London EC1M 5NR
EU representative: Macmillan Publishers Ireland Ltd, 1st Floor,
The Liffey Trust Centre, 117–126 Sheriff Street Upper,
Dublin 1, D01 YC43
Associated companies throughout the world
www.panmacmillan.com

ISBN 978-1-5290-8377-4

1 3 5 7 9 8 6 4 2

A CIP catalogue record for this book is available from the British Library.

Typeset in Palatino by Palimpsest Book Production Limited, Falkirk, Stirlingshire
Printed and bound by CPI Group (UK) Ltd, Croydon, CR0 4YY

Visit **www.panmacmillan.com** to read more about all our books
and to buy them. You will also find features, author interviews and
news of any author events, and you can sign up for e-newsletters
so that you're always first to hear about our new releases.

To my Aunt Elisabeth, who's always supported and encouraged me.

Thank you, Aunty Lis.

THE FRENCH REVOLUTION:
SOME MORE BRIEF NOTES

Revolutions are not tidy things. This may seem obvious, but fiction – and indeed, a lot of history books – tends to lead us to suppose that once the villains have been deposed and the 'good guys' have seized power, everything will be all right. Minor details like heads dropping into baskets or inconvenient members of the royal family being disposed of in prisons or cellars can be glossed over.

The later years of the French Revolution were absolutely not tidy.

The introduction to the previous volume (*Scarlet*) mentioned such great events as the march on Versailles, the storming of the Bastille, the overthrow of the monarchy, the installation of the National Convention (and the Committee of Public Safety), and the execution of the King. At this point (1793–1794), France was at war with Austria, Prussia, England, Spain, the Dutch Republic, Naples, and various other powers. But more than that, France was dealing with continued internal strife. In 1793 there were armed uprisings against the new government in Vendée, Maine and Brittany. In May, the leaders of Lyon rebelled against the National Convention. Soldiers were sent to put down these rebellions, and national conscription required all able-bodied single men aged between eighteen and twenty-five to serve in the army.

In the halls of power, the political parties were pursuing their own struggles over the future of France. The fall of one of the main parties (the Girondins) was followed closely by their most important members going to the guillotine, on accusations of treason and counter-revolutionary activities. Others were executed after being accused of sympathizing with these now-defunct Girondins. Marat was stabbed in his bath by Charlotte Corday. Marie Antoinette was tried and sent to the guillotine. Prisoners were executed by mass drownings at Nantes. The Hébertists (another political party) followed the Girondins to imprisonment and execution. Robespierre declared: 'The foundations of a popular government in a revolution are virtue and terror; terror without virtue is disastrous; and virtue without terror is powerless . . . The Government of the Revolution is the despotism of liberty over tyranny.'

Yet France was growing and changing in other ways. The National Convention instituted the newly created Republican Calendar (no longer in use) and the metric system (which is still in use), developed the optical telegraph, rededicated Notre-Dame as a temple of reason, and voted to abolish slavery in French colonies. Some politicians urged 'indulgence' towards opponents, and 'national reconciliation'. The National Museum of Natural History and the Louvre Museum were opened in Paris. Many people supported the Revolution because it had made – and was making – changes for the better.

The summary of events above is a gross over-simplification, an attempt to demonstrate just how much was *happening*. France was in a state of change – and so was the rest of the world. Talk of concepts such as 'enlightenment' was spreading, bringing unease to the leaders of other European countries who'd seen what had happened in France and could feel the cold wind of the guillotine blade on the backs of their own necks. Repression frequently followed. After all, in 1792 the National Convention had claimed the right to intervene in any country 'where people desire to recover their freedom' . . .

Perhaps the best word for the situation would be *unstable*, both in France and outside it. And while people who benefit from the status quo may dislike instability, others may see profit in it . . .

DRAMATIS PERSONAE

The Blakeney household:

Sir Percy Blakeney and Lady Marguerite
 Blakeney, aristocrats

Mrs Bann, housekeeper

Mr Sturn, butler

Alice and Rebecca, maids

The League of the Scarlet Pimpernel:

Sir Andrew Ffoulkes, aristocrat

Lord Anthony Dewhurst, aristocrat

Lord Charles Bathurst, aristocrat and scholar

Other gentlemen of noble birth and leisure

Eleanor Dalton, maid

Anima, ancient ghost, member by association with
 Eleanor

Genevieve Cogman

Inhabitants of London:

JOSEPH, an unfortunate valet

MRS CARTERSLEIGH, society hostess

CHARLES-MAURICE DE TALLEYRAND-PÉRIGORD, also known as TALLEYRAND, an exile

Inhabitants of Mont-Saint-Michel:

GUILLAUME DUQUESNE, Warden

MONSIEUR AND MADAME THIERS, prisoners

FLEURETTE CHAUVELIN, daughter of Armand Chauvelin

BERNARD, a person of great age and even greater concealment

Inhabitants of Paris:

ARMAND CHAUVELIN, agent of the Committee of Public Safety

DESGAS, secretary to Chauvelin

ARMAND SAINT-JUST, brother of Marguerite Blakeney

LOUIS-ANTOINE DE SAINT-JUST, member of the Committee of Public Safety

MAXIMILIEN ROBESPIERRE, President of the National Convention, member of the Committee of Public Safety

Elusive

Vampires:

Lady Sophie, Baroness of Basing

De Courcis, French gentleman vampire

Castleton, English gentleman vampire

Charles de Valois, of royal blood

Marie Antoinette or 'Widow Capet', previously
Queen of France and presumed dead

PROLOGUE

It wasn't yet dawn, but Portsmouth was already busy. The night trade – vampires, criminals, whores, aristocrats out late partying, and poor fellows who had no choice but to work those hours – was drawing to a close, and the business of morning had begun. The sky was pale and a thin light etched the horizon, glinting off the sea and gleaming on the brass fittings of the boats which filled Portsmouth Harbour. Carts of food creaked through the streets, on their way to supply inns and shops for the day. Beggars, many injured and deformed – or at least apparently so – crawled out from their nocturnal hiding-places, ready to call on the sympathies of workers heading to their jobs. A troop of freshly recruited (or possibly pressed) soldiers marched down the road to the harbour to take ship, the cadence of their boots stumbling in their newness. And in the Admiral Inn, Joseph took a jug of hot water up to his master's room so that he might shave.

Monsieur Talleyrand had his head in one of his books, but he smiled politely enough as Joseph brought the water in. None of that throwing boots at his head the way some of Joseph's previous masters had done, or damning him for a fool, or swearing that if the water was cool then he'd have his wages docked. If all the French lords and ladies were like

Monsieur Talleyrand, he couldn't understand why they'd been run out of France or executed. But that was politics for you, and as Monsieur had said, no doubt Joseph was a better and happier man for staying out of such things.

'Thank you, Joseph,' Monsieur said. He took the jug of hot water and went about the process of shaving in front of the room's small, faded mirror. The inn was cheap, and its furnishings even cheaper. They'd had better lodgings in the previous few months Joseph had been in service as Monsieur's valet, but that was before the money ran out, and Monsieur's friendships with it. A lot of the noble Frenchies held grudges against Monsieur for things which had happened in France, and like so many of the upper classes, they chose the most painful moment to put the boot in. They'd pulled strings and Monsieur had been told to leave England. He was off to America this very day on the *William Penn*.

Monsieur finished shaving, and stood back to allow Joseph to remove the jug and basin. While he looked as calm as a bishop – Joseph had heard he'd actually *been* a bishop before the Revolution in France – there was a cold light in his eye, sharper than the March air outside and enough to freeze any Christian charity right down to the bone. Monsieur might be going quietly, but he certainly wasn't going to forget this forced exile.

As Joseph opened the door, he was startled to see two men standing in the corridor on the other side. No, two *vampires*, in the hats and topcoats of gentlemen with plenty of money, their skin white as bone where it showed. They were both wrapped up against the morning light, because while vampires *could* walk in the daylight, none of them ever liked it. And while they'd both added a splash of perfume, like any gentlemen, Joseph could smell an edge of fresh blood beneath it.

'Monsieur Talleyrand!' the larger of them declared, striding

2

into the room. 'Please forgive this intrusion, but we couldn't bear to let you leave without a few last words.'

'Ah,' Monsieur said, 'de Courcis. I'd thought from the last time we spoke that the only words you'd want to say to me would be *adieu*, not *au revoir*. And . . .' He frowned, looking at the second vampire. 'Castleton. I hadn't realized . . .'

'I daresay you won't be used to hearing me speak without a cough,' the second, thinner man replied, following his friend in. Joseph had thought his hair was powdered, but it was actually white, in stark contrast to the youthfulness of his face. 'De Courcis here was kind enough to pull some strings with ladies and gentlemen of his acquaintance. As a result, I'll be around for a great deal longer than anticipated.'

Monsieur shrugged. 'There was a time when I might have argued the theology of it with you, but that was a while ago. So, how may I be of service to you gentlemen?'

'You don't believe we're here out of the goodness of our hearts?' the first vampire asked.

'It would certainly be a novelty if you were, de Courcis,' Monsieur answered. 'My bedroom is neither a gaming hell nor a fashionable salon, and as such, you are distinctly out of place. I would gladly offer you refreshments, but . . . well, neither of you take tea any longer, and my ship departs with the tide.'

De Courcis cocked his head, as though listening to someone, then flashed a gleaming smile. He had charm, Joseph would give him that, but it was the sort of charm which coaxed a man's pockets open or a woman's skirt up. 'Indeed it does, monsieur – but I fear you won't be going with it.'

'And what do you mean by that?' Monsieur demanded, one hand slipping inside his coat to the pistol Joseph knew he kept there.

Joseph tensed, aware that he should probably try to defend

Monsieur, though heaven only knew what he could do against the two vampires, but de Courcis didn't make any sudden moves. 'I mean that your presence is earnestly required elsewhere, and we simply can't let you leave our company,' he said. 'Fortunately, your place on the ship won't go to waste . . .'

Footsteps came creaking up the stairs, and two further figures appeared in the corridor. Joseph gawped to see the men standing there. One was a close likeness of Monsieur, while the other might have been taken for Joseph himself. Well, in a dim light and if the person involved wasn't looking too closely. He opened his mouth to say something, but Castleton, who had somehow moved closer to him while he was watching Monsieur and de Courcis, set his hand on Joseph's shoulder. 'Not one word,' he instructed.

Monsieur inspected the two new arrivals with a flat, unimpressed calmness. 'I take it these two gentlemen will be boarding the *William Penn* instead of us?'

'You have it precisely right,' de Courcis agreed. 'And you will be leaving with Castleton and myself.'

'And if I were to make a disturbance?'

'I fear that nobody would arrive here in time, and the only result would be your leaving here wrapped up in a blanket, rather than on your own two feet,' de Courcis said merrily. 'Come now, Monsieur Talleyrand – surely an old fox like yourself knows how to wait for a later opportunity?'

Monsieur nodded, as though he'd expected that answer. 'Your manners are no better than before, but your point is fair. So, where are we to go?'

'Sadly, that is not a matter which we can discuss in front of witnesses.' De Courcis glanced at Joseph. 'How sensible a man are you?'

Joseph swallowed. This wasn't something he'd bargained for, even knowing that Frenchies could be dangerous folk.

4

But Monsieur had been a generous master, and he owed him something. It struck him that his best course of action might be to play along with these vampires, swear he'd say nothing, then go to Bow Street and inform the officers there the moment they turned their backs. 'I'm a man as wants to get out of here alive and in one piece,' he replied. 'Milord.'

'There, I knew it!' De Courcis reached into a pocket and brought out a guinea. He flipped it between two fingers, the heavy gold catching the light, then tossed it to Joseph. 'I think it's time you took a vacation to the countryside. That should pay your bills for a while. Just remember, you know nothing, you saw nothing, you, ah – Castleton, can you think of anything else?'

'Only that he's going to *say* nothing,' Castleton said, releasing Joseph's shoulder and stepping away. 'Easy enough to remember.'

Joseph clutched the guinea and nodded fervently. 'I swear, milords, I won't say nothing.'

'You clearly inspire the same loyalty as always in your servants,' de Courcis said to Monsieur.

Monsieur shrugged. 'I'm not cruel enough to demand loyalty under these circumstances. Joseph served me for pay; I don't blame him for wanting to stay well out of this.' His frosty eyes met Joseph's for a moment, and Joseph indeed saw no blame in them, no accusation. He was speaking the absolute truth.

'That's the sad thing,' de Courcis said regretfully. 'Castleton—'

'No!' Monsieur shouted, and at the same moment Joseph felt an impact as though he'd been punched in the chest. He looked down to see the blade of a long knife standing out from the front of his coat.

He'd been stabbed in the back, his reason informed him, and stabbed so hard that the knife had gone all the way through him, to come out between the ribs at the front. It must have been something to see, he thought dazedly. You'd need a vampire to do something like that, strong enough to put a knife right through a man's body.

The floor came up to meet him. His own blood gurgled in his lungs.

'A man who'd take money to keep his mouth shut would also take it to talk afterwards,' de Courcis said, his words seeming to float down on Joseph as he lay there. 'Pray don't make a fuss, Monsieur Talleyrand, or I'm afraid it'll be the blanket after all.'

There was a muffled interjection from Monsieur.

'Oh, come now, he'd heard our names. Blame yourself for that, if you're going to blame anyone. Beamish, deal with the body after we've left but before you board the ship – there must be dozens of places round here where one can dispose of a body.'

'And given that we're being so free with names,' Monsieur said coldly, 'who are *you* working for?'

'Oh, I don't think you'd know him. You've never met.' De Courcis's voice was growing more and more distant, like a thread on the breeze.

'Nevertheless, I insist.'

'The Prince of Paris . . .'

Joseph's eyes closed, and he was gone.

CHAPTER ONE

Eleanor's tray was heavy with glasses. The party had eddied through the Blakeney mansion, from room to room, leaving behind a detritus of empty plates and drained glasses, abandoned decks of cards and pairs of dice from games of hazard. As soon as all the guests had departed, the servants had crept out from the kitchen and down from the attics to clear up the worst of the debris. At least the fires were still burning in the fireplaces, hot enough to keep all the visiting ladies warm in the March chill, despite the thinness of their elegant silk gowns. Everyone at the party tonight had been human rather than vampire, and the Blakeneys were never inhospitable. Eleanor was grateful for that. Her previous mistress had been more prone to entertaining vampire guests than human ones, and while Lady Sophie wouldn't have allowed her servants to *freeze*, there was a difference between chill and comfort.

She put down her tray and stretched, knuckling the small of her back. She hadn't been serving above stairs this evening. A party like this for the Quality had meant the Blakeney footmen – all six feet tall and matched as well as teams of carriage-horses – were the ones doing the public fetching and carrying, while the less spotless of the Blakeney servants were run off their feet in the kitchen. At least it was warm down there too. Winter this year had been bitterly cold.

Not that the weather, or the temperature, or anything else had stopped the guillotine in France from doing its bloody work.

Eleanor shivered, imagining for a moment the brush of cold steel against her own neck. Of course she was in England, not in France, and certainly no revolution like the one in France could ever touch England today. Murdering their King and Queen, and half the people of rank? Turning the entire country upside down, putting a new parliament in power and declaring themselves a republic, sending all vampires to the guillotine, even rewriting the calendar? England might have had her own civil war a hundred and fifty years ago – Eleanor was vaguely aware of the details, involving King Charles being executed by Parliament – but it was preposterous to think that anything as dramatic as *France's* revolution could take place here, in her homeland.

The problem was, she'd been to France in the last year, and she'd seen just how much people were *people*, whether they were French or English. If you pushed anyone far enough, you could have a revolution on your hands, and once a revolution started, nobody could be sure where it would stop. You set off with noble principles and reasonable demands for the aristocrats to share some of the power and food and legal privilege, and somehow ended up breaking into the Bastille to save unjustly detained prisoners, or marching heroically to assert one's rights, and even creating a new constitution and set of laws. Yet, inexplicably, things then slipped from executing a few guilty people to executing *anyone* who'd been an aristocrat, or had worked for an aristocrat, or had spoken in favour of aristocrats or against the Revolution, or . . .

That was if you were human, of course. If you were a vampire, then none of the above steps were necessary – the only steps in question were those up to the scaffold where the guillotine stood. Vampires were generally aristocrats, after all – old money, old families, old blood. You never found any who were *poor*. As a result, the only vampires currently in France were deep in hiding.

The Revolution had said other things about vampires too . . . but Eleanor had yet to decide whether or not she believed them.

You should, you know, a voice spoke in the depths of her mind. *They're quite correct. And if you have the time to stand around doing nothing in particular, might we have another look at those bookshelves?*

I need to get my work done, Eleanor answered quickly, picking up her tray again. The voice belonged – well, claimed to belong – to Anima, the ghost of an ancient mage who'd lived over five hundred years ago. She'd told Eleanor that she'd been the victim of a great war between vampires and mages which had concluded with the vampires victorious, and the mages comprehensively erased from recorded history. While Eleanor had conceded the existence of Anima's magic (Anima had proven this quite definitively), she wasn't entirely sure about the rest of it. But she'd promised Anima to keep silent about her presence for the moment.

To be fair, it was as much for her own safety as Anima's. Saying that she was possessed by the ghost of a sorceress from centuries ago would have seen Eleanor sent to Bedlam, which would suit neither of them.

Anima wasn't afraid of being dubbed a madwoman; she was afraid of being utterly destroyed. She'd told Eleanor, more than once, that if the vampires suspected a mage still survived, they'd do anything to dispose of her permanently. Which, by implication, would mean disposing of Eleanor as well. Anima also claimed that vampires could make humans obey them by feeding their blood to their victims, and that they were secretly pulling the strings behind all the kings and governments across Europe. (She admitted to not knowing anything about Africa or the Orient, still less America.)

Sadly, all these wild claims went entirely against everything Eleanor had ever known. Vampires might exercise power and influence in society, but that was because they were usually wealthy landowners and arbiters of fashion. There were laws – all the way back to Magna Carta, or so Eleanor had been told – which kept them out of Parliament in England, and prevented them from holding military rank. Eleanor herself had spent most of her life in service to a vampire, Lady Sophie, the Baroness of Basing, and it had been no worse than working for any other woman of rank. Perhaps Eleanor had needed to open a vein regularly, but Lady Sophie had always been a good mistress who paid a fair wage. Eleanor knew other women who'd endured far worse as maidservants. If it wasn't for their dislike of garlic, their lack of reflections, a hatred of sunlight as they grew older and a few other details, vampires would be just like ordinary people. Except perhaps richer.

But then again . . . when she'd been in France, Eleanor had heard talk of how the vampires there *had* controlled people through what could only be described as mystical, supernatural means. These and many other accusations had led to vampires being among the first to lose their heads to the guillotine – after having a stake rammed through their heart. (She'd seen it, once, and still had occasional nightmares.) Such rumours hadn't reached England – perhaps because the French already accused vampires of every crime in their legal code and every unnatural behaviour imaginable. But the National Committee which now ruled France claimed it was true . . .

It is, Anima commented, following Eleanor's train of thought.

And Eleanor herself had met vampires in France who'd been less than perfectly amiable, ethical or even fashionable.

One had tried to kill her. Others had attempted to kidnap the Dauphin just after the Scarlet Pimpernel (with Eleanor's assistance) had rescued him. Perhaps it was unfair to expect vampires who were being hunted for execution to maintain proper standards of behaviour, but Eleanor was no longer quite as certain as she had been.

Certain of what? Anima asked. It was like having an elderly aunt watching while she sewed, commenting on every stitch.

Everything, Eleanor replied. Last year she'd expected nothing more from life than working as a maidservant, sewing and embroidering in what little spare time she had. And maybe, if she was very lucky, becoming one of Lady Sophie's private maids, or even gaining employment at a modiste's shop. But now? She was a member of the League of the Scarlet Pimpernel, and she'd helped rescue the Dauphin from the Temple prison in Paris. The Pimpernel himself had promised that he'd help her towards employment as a modiste. Once this was all over . . .

The far door swung open, and Sir Percy Blakeney wandered into the library. Despite the hour, his cravat was still perfectly tied, an ornament on his throat as crisp and elegant as any Alpine mountain. He was in dark green tonight, but the gold embroidery on his coat and waistcoat gleamed in the light from the new-fangled Argand lamps along the walls. For all his height and his muscle – though his coat did a good job of concealing it – he looked the perfect dandy, concerned with nothing but his appearance, his clothing and his audience.

One would never have thought that he was the secret mastermind who'd saved hundreds of innocent French citizens – both human and vampires – from the guillotine, tweaked the nose of the fuming Committee of Public Safety, and a personal nightmare for the Revolution. No, this was just Sir Percy Blakeney, a man of noble blood and absolute laziness, whose primary interests were his wardrobe and his horses.

11

And nobody would ever have thought that Eleanor – a common maidservant, whose only notable attributes were a gift for sewing and embroidering, and a physical likeness to the late Queen of France, Marie Antoinette – might herself be a member of the League of the Scarlet Pimpernel.

Eleanor automatically curtsied, lowering her eyes. She had no idea who might be accompanying him, and while certain people in the household were aware of his secret, not all of them were. To be fair, practically all of them would have kept their mouths shut, whatever he might have been up to. The Blakeney household was loyal and close knit – and well paid. She'd been here for months and was still only slowly gaining acceptance.

'Still busy, Eleanor?' Sir Percy asked, closing the door behind him and dropping into a chair. 'Deuce take it, I've been eaten quite out of house and home by these ravenous vultures called Society.'

'I'm sure the staff would die of mortification before seeing you go hungry, milord,' Eleanor answered, reassured of their privacy. 'And there are still the grapes from the forcing-houses, if you want to try the diet that Sir Andrew was recommending the other day.'

Sir Percy snorted. 'He was recommending it to his mother-in-law, not to me! And what are you doing loitering in here?'

Eleanor lifted her tray in explanation. 'Work, milord. Your friends may be Society, but it seems a fair number of them chose to bring their drinks in here, to your library.'

'There's only one of them who'd have come in to actually be near the books.'

Eleanor dared a joke. 'Nobody would believe what you say about yourself if they actually looked at your bookshelves, milord.' Anima, at the back of Eleanor's mind, had frequently railed at the lack of time and access which prevented the ancient mage from studying Sir Percy's books to discover how much the world had changed. The mere fact that Eleanor, a servant, could hardly abandon her duties to illicitly consult her employer's books was quite beside the point.

'Lud, I'd just tell them I buy my shelving by the yard in fashionable colours, m'dear.' He beckoned to her. 'Let me see that tray a moment, will you?'

He inspected the glasses on it. 'The Armagnac, that'd be Ffoulkes, and he had Grimms and Arthur with him. And the lip paint on *that* one must be Madame de Chagny, I recognize the shade, and she was accompanying de Berthand. Not sure who these two last glasses belong to. That's the problem with large parties.'

'Was this party a . . . special one, Chief?' Eleanor deliberately used the form of address which she and the rest of the League were allowed to use for their leader, the Scarlet Pimpernel.

Sir Percy shook his head and yawned. 'Nothing but the usual social amenities, m'dear. If I was looking for information, it was to do with matters here in England rather than over in France.'

'To do with the war?' So far the war between France and England – not to mention Austria, Prussia and Spain – hadn't noticeably affected Eleanor's daily life. Nobody she knew had gone off to fight as a soldier, and the League of the Scarlet Pimpernel took care to stay well away from battle lines where possible. Though being disguised as a travelling group of soldiers *did* make it easier to cross France without too many questions asked . . .

'In a way.' He frowned, his mobile face assuming an unusual air of seriousness, quite unlike his habitual attitude of boredom and stupidity. 'Does the term *habeas corpus* mean anything to you, Eleanor?'

It means, let you have the body, Anima prompted silently. Apparently, being a mage centuries ago had involved learning Latin, as well as subjects such as astrology, herbalism and anatomy. Some of these were more useful in Eleanor's daily life than others. Anima didn't usually put herself forward when Eleanor was talking to Sir Percy, though. She didn't want him – or anyone else – to suspect her existence through Eleanor behaving strangely, or knowing things she shouldn't.

Eleanor let her brow furrow. 'Something about you having a body, Chief?' she suggested. She knew Sir Percy didn't *really* expect her to understand Latin.

'Not bad, m'dear,' he praised her. 'In this case it's a legal term. Basically, it means that the courts – or the government – can't just arrest a fellow and lock him up in prison without charges or witnesses. Even the King or the Privy Council can't get away with it. There've been Acts of Parliament about it, but I'm told it goes back further than that.'

'What, for everyone?' Eleanor asked in astonishment. The concept didn't precisely square with what she knew of how courts operated, and how prisoners were treated. Penniless prisoners, at least.

Sir Percy waved a vague, long-fingered white hand. 'Well, sometimes it's more in principle than in practice, but it's a deuced important principle. Precisely the sort of thing they *haven't* got in France at the moment, as you know.'

His eyes met hers, and she suppressed a shiver. She'd seen in person how easy it was in France for an accusation to turn into imprisonment, and from there direct to the guillotine, with only the barest hope of a fair trial.

'Anyway,' he went on, 'there's a great deal of talk at the moment about spies.'

'Oh, like us,' Eleanor said drily. She'd finished collecting the glasses now, and she put the tray down. 'Are they still trying to find you, Chief?'

'Without a doubt, but it's the other direction that the English government's more concerned about. Pitt – you know Pitt, or rather you no doubt know *of* him? Thin fellow, very persuasive, Prime Minister, sad tendency towards gout. Cambridge man, unlike our friend Charles, who was at Oxford. In any case, he's worrying about spies from France, and about the current talk in favour of political change. Strange thing, but once a man gets into government he's never that keen on change, whatever he may have said beforehand.'

Eleanor nodded, not quite sure where this was going. She suspected that he was talking more to put his own thoughts in order than out of any desire to inform her of current events. Still, she wasn't going to open her mouth and stop this flow of information. Other members of the League – aristocrats, wealthy, and all male except for Lady Marguerite – could pick up this sort of information by reading the newspaper or from discussions at their clubs. Eleanor, being female and poor, was limited to whatever fragments of current affairs might be casually dropped by the upper classes around her.

For most of her life, this had simply been something she accepted. More recently, perhaps due to her visits to France as much as the ghost inside her head, she'd begun to question her place in the world – and her future.

'It's in all the papers,' Sir Percy went on dreamily, 'order versus anarchy, a proper society such as ours being infiltrated – note the word *infiltrated*, Eleanor. It has a subtle sneakiness about it which infuriates any proper Englishman when applied to his own nation, however much he thinks it appropriate to the rest of the world. Every radical meeting's being held up as an example of French corruption and foreign spies. The word "denounce" has come into play, and when did we last hear that?'

'France, I imagine.' The far door swung open, revealing Lady Marguerite Blakeney. The light caught on her gleaming red-gold curls, a shade that made Eleanor privately sigh with envy over her own flaxen-pale hair as she curtsied. Lady Marguerite's light green silk gown was of the very latest cut, unpanniered and practically indecent in its lack of volume and ornament, and she had chosen to flout fashion by wearing her hair unpowdered. A beryl necklace and bracelets circled her neck and wrists, the same dark green as her husband's clothing. She could have stepped out of the pages of any ladies' magazine, but her eyes were far brighter, and her smile much kinder.

'Our guests are all safely gone, Percy,' she said. 'I've just been bidding farewell to Tony and Yvonne. I did offer to let them stay the night, but I fancy he'd rather enjoy a night drive with his new wife, even in this weather.' She held her hands to the fire to warm them, then seated herself beside her husband.

'Ah, newlyweds.' Sir Percy smiled, his eyes softening. 'Dear heart, you must allow them some time together. It's only been a month since their marriage.'

'That didn't stop you running off to France with him just after the new year,' Lady Marguerite teased him.

'And I came back with a bevy of rescued aristocrats to show for it,' Sir Percy returned. 'A happy little trip there and back, as Eleanor can tell you.'

Eleanor had been swept along in Sir Percy's wake – her third mission for the League and her third time in France. She hadn't been required to do anything particularly dangerous that time; just enter Charenton-le-Pont as a woman looking for work and infiltrate the mayor's household for information. An impoverished girl looking for work was below most people's notice, and by now her French was good enough to not arouse any suspicions. 'Happy is as happy does, Chief,' she answered, a touch pertly, 'and I for one don't like sailing through January storms.'

Anima *had* liked it, though. She had watched the St Elmo's fire, as the sailors called it, dancing on the masts and rigging, and breathed in the rising gale as though she was about to burst out singing. Through Anima's vision, Eleanor had perceived the twisting pattern of the winds like an embroidery design, and had felt how much Anima yearned for the days of her life and power, when she could have plucked out a single wind and tamed it to her whims. Sometimes – very deeply, and when she was sure Anima couldn't hear her thoughts – Eleanor wondered just how long Anima would be content to remain as a ghost in her head.

'The storms drove off pursuit,' Sir Percy countered, 'and that's the important thing.' He shrugged; the matter was closed, and there was nothing more to be said.

He can't keep doing this forever, Anima commented silently. *The risks he takes – you all take – are increasingly large.*

The Chief knows what he's doing, Eleanor answered with stubborn loyalty, stifling any traitorous thoughts she might occasionally have considered. *Besides, it's not just our lives at stake, it's the people in France who we're rescuing from the guillotine.*

It's my life at stake as well, as long as I'm bound to you, Anima countered.

Then give me a good reason to stop, that I can give the Chief, or talk to him yourself!

I'm not speaking to him and I forbid you to tell him about me, Anima said coldly. *The man's far too close to some of the vampires here in England, and his wife's worse.*

It was infuriating. There was so much Anima could do to help the League's operations – she was able to alter the weather, and she'd hinted that she could do more – but she still utterly refused to let Eleanor inform Sir Percy of her presence. And if there really was some sort of unexpected danger from the vampires, then Eleanor *needed* to talk to Sir Percy about it. Or to Lady Marguerite, or one of the other members of the League, like Sir Andrew Ffoulkes, Lord Tony Dewhurst, or Lord Charles Bathurst, the only one she would actually call a friend . . .

Eleanor suppressed a sigh and turned towards the door as

Lady Marguerite sank down into a chair beside her husband. They'd be wanting to talk in private.

To her surprise, Sir Percy raised a hand to bid her wait. 'Have you heard from Charles lately, Eleanor?' he asked.

'Not since the party at the new year, Chief,' she said, unable to suppress a smile at the memory. Charles had actually given her a *present* for Christmas – a sketchbook full of drawings of embroidery designs from his family's ancestral seat. She didn't have the spare time or resources to work on any of them for the moment, but she'd happily put it on one side for later.

When compared to his fellow members of the League, Lord Charles Bathurst might not be the strongest, the fastest, or the quickest with a lie in an emergency, but he was devoted to its ideals, and his talent for art made him an expert forger. At the moment, France was awash with official papers – passports, permits, certificates of residence, copies of orders, and more – so having someone who could supply such papers for the League was an absolute necessity. Eleanor and Charles had . . . well, not quite an *understanding*, as it would have been unthinkable for an aristocrat to have an *understanding* with a common maid, but certainly an interest in closer acquaintance, and an appreciation for each other's company. Even if nothing could possibly ever come of it, as Eleanor had to frequently remind herself, it was a joy while it lasted.

Eleanor saw Lord Percy and Lady Marguerite exchange a knowing glance at her smile, and she flushed with embarrassment, and more than a little anger. If they were going to make assumptions, she could play along with them. 'It's always nice to see him,' she said, as innocently as she could, doing her best to look doe-eyed and adoring. 'He's such a pleasant young man, and so very helpful and sympathetic.'

The Blakeneys looked at each other, and then laughed. Lady Marguerite's laugh was as sweet as her voice, while Sir Percy's was a more annoying bray, perfectly fitting his image of a brainless dandy. 'It's not that we're *trying* to push you together, Eleanor dear,' Lady Marguerite said. 'But you're such a sweet pair, and you understand each other perfectly. Forgive us; we happy couples do want to see everyone else matched as well. Who knows what may happen? The world is in a constant ferment of change, and though matters may be complicated, perhaps a solution can be found. I'm sure that Charles will still be your friend, whatever the future holds.'

Sir Percy kissed the tips of his fingers to Marguerite. 'Many more years, I trust.'

Eleanor refrained from rolling her eyes. Really, the two of them were sickeningly sweet sometimes. One wouldn't have thought they'd been married for years; they were as devoted as a courting couple. 'With all respect, sir, milady, I should be getting back to my duties. If I stay talking to you much longer, Mrs Bann will have a few words to say to me.' The Blakeneys' housekeeper was a reasonable and understanding woman, but had no tolerance for laziness. While Eleanor was known to be a favourite of Lady Marguerite on account of her sewing and embroidering skills, that didn't buy her any favours from the rest of the household. She cleaned and scrubbed just like all the other maids.

'Before you go,' Sir Percy said, suddenly serious, 'I'd like you to keep your ears particularly open, Eleanor, for any rumours you may hear about conspiracies, however frivolous you may consider them. Whether it's among your fellow servants, or among guests in this house – and even the people we've brought back from France. Pitt may or may not be right, or there may be more going on than even he knows.'

'You mean the word from France?' Lady Marguerite asked. 'Armand said it was only hearsay when he was here last month—'

'My love, your brother is a good man, but remarkably poor at judging his safety or his gossip. Some of the circles he's moving in are talking about a malicious conspiracy here in England, Eleanor.'

'We're already at war with France, sir,' Eleanor said. She'd been briefly introduced to Lady Marguerite's brother Armand, in case she'd ever need to know his face for the future. He'd made the usual comments about her likeness to Marie Antoinette and then ignored her. 'What *more* could we be conspiring to do?'

'Well, that's the interesting thing, isn't it?' Sir Percy sat back with the air of one who'd made an unassailable point.

'Is that why you didn't want me to invite Thomas Walsingham tonight?' Lady Marguerite asked shrewdly.

Lord Percy nodded. 'The fellow's always reported everything to his great-uncle. Since he turned vampire, he's been all the more enthusiastic about picking up random bits of gossip, ones I'd rather not share yet. And with Talleyrand ordered to leave England . . .'

He shook his head. 'No matter. I may need to take another trip to France soon, but we need more information before that. At least that fellow Chauvelin's not here to bother us.' He patted Marguerite's hand as she pursed her lips in dislike. 'If Mrs Bann takes issue with your work, Eleanor, feel free to tell the lady that I had you dancing attendance on me while I complained about my waistcoat. I'll have more to say later, when Andrew and some of the others have reported. Take care, m'dear, and don't stay up too late. You're not working for a vampire any more, after all.'

Eleanor nodded, dipping a curtsey – the Blakeneys might tolerate private pertness from another member of the League, but it'd be a bad idea to lose the habit of respect – and left the room.

As she returned to her duties, she couldn't help thinking about how casually the guests and the Blakeneys had spent the evening drinking, dancing and gambling, while in France

English soldiers were fighting, and French aristocrats and commoners alike were dying on the guillotine. In a way it felt . . . obscene. Travelling to France and working with the League had changed her; she'd started to wonder if things would always be the way they had been. If things *should* always be the way they'd been.

Yet the people of France had felt the same way, hadn't they? And one could hardly call the Revolution a satisfactory outcome. It had begun in courage and brotherhood and anger, and now it was awash with blood.

Sometimes there is no good answer, Anima murmured, her voice gentler than usual. *Sometimes one has no choice but to take action, and then abide by the consequences. There were those among my brothers and sisters who advocated for giving up our craft and no longer teaching new apprentices, in the hopes that the vampires would let us be. I don't believe it would have worked, though. Vampires are as thirsty for power as they are for blood. They'd never have allowed us to exist, however much we claimed we were harmless. Better to take what chances we had . . . whatever the cost.*

Maybe vampires have changed, Eleanor answered. *It's been over five hundred years.*

Anima snorted. *Humanity hasn't changed, and therefore neither have vampires.*

Then what do you call the Revolution in France, if not a change in humanity? Eleanor remembered ruined chateaus, empty rooms, shattered furniture, and above it all the looming shadow of the guillotine. *What if the entire world is changing?*

Then we must change with it, Anima answered flatly. *Ride the wave – or drown.*

CHAPTER TWO

When Alice slipped on the stairs and fell, the crash was, metaphorically, heard through the entire house. Usually it was a minor thing for one of the servants to sprain her ankle, and shouldn't have disrupted the proper running of the Blakeney household. Alice was Lady Marguerite's personal maid, however, with responsibility for all duties from bringing her morning chocolate to helping her dress and being at her beck and call for anything and everything that might be required. A lady's life was a busy one, which was why God – or their husband – provided maids to do the running around for them.

To compound it all, Lady Marguerite had accepted an invitation to a salon that evening, for which, in the absence of her husband (away on business – at least, that was the public explanation for anyone who didn't belong to the League), or any other suitable escort, she required a maid in attendance. Clearly Alice couldn't provide the proper degree of attention, with her ankle bound up and gasping in pain whenever she put weight on her foot.

Eleanor wasn't entirely sure why *she* had been chosen to fill Alice's place, and she was aware that other maids were feeling slighted that *they*, who'd been serving the household for far longer, hadn't been requested for the task. She'd have to pay for that later . . . but here and now, she was delighted at this chance to see a little more of London than she had done so far.

Alice had cornered Eleanor earlier while she'd been running an errand up to the attics where the servants slept. 'There are some things you need to understand,' she said ominously.

'Yes, Alice,' Eleanor agreed, nodding enthusiastically. It was difficult to stop herself from bouncing up and down on her toes with enthusiasm. 'Certainly. I'm listening. Ah, would you like to sit down first?'

'Kind of you to notice.' Alice lowered herself with a grunt. Her face was drawn with pain; she'd been given a dose of something earlier, but apparently it wasn't doing much good. 'I'll say this for milady, she understands that I can't be running around with my foot like this for at least another week or more . . . but in any case, it's milady I want to talk about. You must understand that it's your duty to take care of her tonight.'

Eleanor blinked. 'Milady's a grown woman,' she hazarded. And as a full member of her husband's League, Lady Marguerite was hardly the sort of woman who needed 'taking care of'. Alice wasn't stupid, though. Surely she wasn't going to suggest that Sir Percy would disapprove of the salon?

'You haven't *been* to one of these affairs before,' Alice said, in tones of deepest condemnation. 'Full of people from all levels of society. While I'm not the sort of person who'd say that everyone should know their place and never try to step outside it, my own dear mother wouldn't have approved. Now I'm also not saying milady's *wrong* to attend, but no doubt it's because she's from France that she doesn't always know how this sort of thing might be taken in England. People might *say* things.'

'The sort of people who wouldn't go to such a salon?' Eleanor hazarded.

'I knew you'd understand.' Alice leaned in closer, confidentially. 'There are some lords and ladies out there who are so high in the instep they'd cut anyone less than a baronet dead in the street. Even though, when *they're* short on money, they're the ones who'd marry a midden for its muck, as they say. Now milord's family goes back about as far as it can do, and his father, well, *his* wife, milord's mother, was noble enough blood, but she didn't finish well, between the two of us. And then milord himself went and married a lady who'd been on the *stage* – not just pays for an apartment for her, if you know what I mean, but out and out weds her. And I know milady's from a good family over there, but even so! There are people who'd be glad to hold her up as a shocking example, if only they could find some way to do it. And her being French means they might try to trap her into doing something which looks . . .' She waved a hand vaguely. 'Improper.'

This was the first time Eleanor had been admitted into so high a level of household gossip. She resolved to prove worthy of it. 'You think that milord and milady have enemies?'

Alice pursed her lips. 'Well, not so as you'd call them *enemies* in the way that all them young society hellions go round fighting duels with each other. It's nice that milord and all his friends don't behave so riotously, even if they have their heads in the clouds half the time and in their wardrobes the other half. A man can do worse than look after his appearance, if you know what I mean. But no, it's more that there are lords and ladies and honourables and whatnot who've nothing better to do with their time than to stick pins where they're not wanted and try to bring other people down. And they go to church on Sunday!' she added indignantly. 'Shame on them.'

'I've known people like that,' Eleanor agreed. 'They don't feel happy unless they're putting someone else down.'

'Right!' Alice smacked her hand against the arm of her chair. 'So it's your duty, as I can't manage it, to go with milady and be sure that she doesn't say or do anything which could be held against her. Make sure she doesn't spend too much time talking with them abolitionists and freethinkers. If there's anyone over from France who's too fond of revolutionary talk, then you need to divert her before she agrees too publicly with whatever they're saying. If that Wollstonecraft woman's there – no, wait, she's in France now, you don't need to worry about her. You can let milady talk about novels if you want,' she added graciously. 'Or maybe anything that's on at the theatre. Her having been an actress, it's not as bad her talking about it as it would be a young lady from a more discreet household.'

'But . . .' Eleanor could see one glaring problem with this course of action. 'I'll do my best, of course, but how precisely am I going to stop milady doing anything she wants to?'

There was an uncomfortable silence.

'That's the tricky part,' Alice admitted. 'But if you just stay right next to her, then there's not much as can go wrong.'

'And this is Eleanor Dalton, one of my employees,' Lady Marguerite introduced Eleanor to their hostess. 'She may soon be leaving us to join Madame Elise's staff, but for the moment we take advantage of her services. I brought her because she takes a strong interest in the enlightened spirit of the age. As you always tell me, my dear, everyone is welcome here if they're willing to converse and *think*.'

'Indeed.' Their hostess, the Honourable Mrs Cartersleigh, was a woman with formidably powdered hair, though with sadly noticeable inserts. She was wearing the new style of dress in a bright robin's-egg blue, and had painted and powdered her face so as not to appear washed out against its colour. The looser style really didn't suit her: she'd have looked better in a more rigid bodice and panniers. Eleanor would have liked to think the woman had a virtuous, friendly, charitable nature to counterweigh all these failures in style, but the manner in which she was looking down her nose at Eleanor argued against it.

Lady Marguerite herself was in a charming blue-grey silk which set her red-gold hair off perfectly. Eleanor had to admit that since going into service with the Blakeneys she had become far more observant of the details of current fashion. On the one hand, it could be vitally useful for her in her hoped-for career as a modiste, but on the other hand she had to face facts: her customers would likely be women who required a great deal of tailoring and even more tact to look half as good as Lady Marguerite. Too much honesty was not a shopkeeper's best friend.

Eleanor herself was in her best dress – a decent brown wool, just made up a couple of months ago – and new shoes. She was as neatly turned out as she could hope to be, as a maid. She dropped a curtsey to the Honourable Mrs Cartersleigh and murmured, 'I'm honoured to be here, ma'am. I'm very grateful this salon is open even to people like myself, who just want to *learn*.' It was perhaps a little too much butter on the bread, but Eleanor needed to be tolerated here, even if she wasn't loved, in order to follow Alice's instructions and stay close to Lady Marguerite.

Mrs Cartersleigh thawed a little. 'Of course, my dear. I can see at a glance that you're not one of those dreadful Republican types who go round calling for all manner of impossible things. We're more believers in the Enlightenment here – in Reason, understanding, and the advancement of Society as a whole.'

'Indeed, ma'am,' Eleanor said, keeping her eyes modestly

low. She wondered just how Mrs Cartersleigh would react if the Revolution did come to England. Would she go to the guillotine claiming that they hadn't done things properly and demand a retrial? The mere ability to spout high-minded nonsense wouldn't save her.

Still, perhaps she was being too harsh. Lady Marguerite came to her salons, after all, so Mrs Cartersleigh must have *something* to recommend her.

As the hostess prepared to greet another couple of arrivals, Eleanor quickly followed Lady Marguerite inside, determined to ensure that nobody found an opportunity to take advantage of milady.

She lasted about five seconds.

The salon was spread across several rooms of Mrs Cartersleigh's town house: elegantly adorned in jade green, ebony and ash wood, they'd very recently been redecorated by the look of them, and the furnishings were all definitely imported from France. (Eleanor had seen enough of those dainty chairs and tables by now to recognize the style.) Men and women stood round in clusters, talking noisily to each other until the ceilings echoed. Eleanor was interested to note that there were some men and women, like herself, who were clearly dressed on a moderate budget, rather than having patronized the best tailors and modistes in London. And they even seemed to be holding their own in conversations and being listened to as equals. Perhaps Mrs Cartersleigh wasn't just talk.

'My dear Luke!' Lady Marguerite swooped on three men standing together, sipping from wine glasses and discussing an article in the newspaper. 'It's been far too long. Pray introduce me to your friends.'

'Excuse me,' someone said behind Eleanor, tapping her shoulder. She turned to see another woman, in stern bottle-green and grey, squinting slightly in the way that Charles

did when forced to do without his eye-glasses. 'Do you know
if Mrs Wollstonecraft is here?'

'I don't think so,' Eleanor apologized. 'I heard she was in
Paris.'

'Oh, drat it all . . .' The woman rubbed at the bridge of
her nose. Now that Eleanor was closer, she could see faint
lines where previously worn eye-glasses had cut into the
powder on her face. *Of course a woman couldn't wear them to
a polite event like this* . . . 'I had dared to hope she'd be here.
I don't suppose you've read any of her work?'

Eleanor shook her head. 'What has she written?'

'The first work of hers I read was *Thoughts on the Education
of Daughters*,' the woman confided, 'but of course the one
that *everyone's* talking about now is *A Vindication of the Rights
of Women*. Are you sure you haven't read it? I must lend you
one of Maud's copies. She has two, you know, and never
even touched the one I gave her last year. The most absolutely
sincere and forward-thinking perspective, you know – a
response to that speech Talleyrand gave to the National
Assembly three years ago, when he said that women should
only receive domestic education.'

'Talleyrand?' Eleanor asked, fixing on the one point in the
cavalcade of words which she felt she'd heard before.

'Oh, that was before he fled France, of course, which *just
goes to show*. Forgive me, I haven't even asked your name
yet.'

'Eleanor Dalton,' Eleanor said. She cast an eye over her
shoulder, but saw that Lady Marguerite had already vanished
into the throng. *Drat.* 'This is my first time at one of these
salons.'

'Justine Atkinson.' She extended her hand to be clasped.
It was soft in Eleanor's grasp, without the callouses of work
which marked her own fingers, but there were ink-stains
under the fingernails, ground in despite what must have been

heroic scrubbing to cleanse the hand. Apparently Justine Atkinson had her own area of work.

Eleanor realized that she was on a fool's errand if she thought she had any chance of influencing Lady Marguerite's behaviour. But she might as well try to learn something from this woman. Something about Talleyrand she could report back to the Chief. He'd told her to keep her ears open, after all. 'Please tell me some more about the *Vindication of the Rights of Women*,' she said. 'It sounds fascinating.'

Justine was delighted to oblige.

Perhaps half an hour had passed before Eleanor realized she was actually enjoying herself. Oh, she had entirely lost track of Lady Marguerite, but really, how much trouble could milady get into at a polite salon? Even if there were a great many modern thinkers present? She had every faith that milady was as competent as her husband in evading trouble, and *he* was the Scarlet Pimpernel.

People drifted between the several rooms of the salon, changing conversational partners as they went, while servants flitted around the edges fetching glasses of wine, or negus, or ratafia, or other drinks on command. Quite a number of guests were willing to draw her into discussion. Her accent had developed a few steps above the servants' quarters, due to efforts from the Blakeneys and the League – and even before then, Lady Sophie had always preferred her servants to speak 'nicely'. Even if she couldn't impersonate a lady of quality, she could at least sound vaguely like someone from the middle classes. She might only have trailed along like a rowboat in milady's wake, but now that she was here, she appeared to have been accepted.

A nagging inner part of her still felt that she should be carrying the drinks, though, rather than behaving like an equal to the other guests.

Fragments of conversation swirled around her, some more comprehensible than others. '. . . the suspension of *habeas corpus* . . .' '. . . Jefferson was working with them before he left Paris, and one can only assume he's influencing the American policy even now . . .' '. . . these rumours of Pitt and secret agents . . .' '. . . the proclamation against seditious writings may have been two years ago, but nothing's got any better, and now they're talking of a Seditious Meetings Act as well . . .' '. . . the revolt in Haiti, and Pitt's expedition last year to restore slavery in Saint Domingue . . .' '. . . Thomas Hardy and John Horne Tooke are to be tried for high treason, merely for being radicals . . .'

Eleanor edged backwards while trying to overhear more of the last conversation, and bumped into someone else. She quickly turned to apologize, and found the other person doing the same.

He was a young man – about her own age, if she was any judge – and of African heritage. He wasn't the first man or woman she'd met with a skin darker than her own, in England or France, but it was still a surprise. 'I do apologize, sir,' she said.

'No, no, the fault was entirely mine.' He gave her a polite half-bow. 'Hercules Sanson, at your service.'

'Eleanor Dalton. I work for Lady Marguerite Blakeney . . .'

'Ah, another person who works for a living.' His quick smile made a joke of it. His clothing was slightly better quality than hers, but only slightly, with his neat cravat tied soberly rather than attempting the multiple folds of someone like Sir Percy, and the buttons on his coat and waistcoat brass rather than gilt. She couldn't place his accent. 'I'm secretary to Sir Luke Saunders, over there.' He tilted his head towards the group by the nearest table. As if guessing what Eleanor wanted to ask, he went on, 'He hired me in New Orleans when he was visiting there last year.'

Ah, so he was American. She hadn't had the chance to speak to an American before. In fact—

Yes, I've wanted to know about this for a while, Anima commented. *Ask him about vampires and magi in America.*

'I would like to visit New Orleans some day,' Eleanor started. It wasn't a lie. She'd love the chance to see American fashions, American needlework, American embroidery . . . 'In fact, there's a matter about which I'm curious, if I might trouble you for answers.'

'But of course,' Mr Sanson said cheerfully. Yet his eyes narrowed, and his face settled into lines of resignation, as though expecting a question which he'd heard so many times that he was weary of answering it.

'Tell me . . . are there vampires in America? Or any stories about people who use magic?'

This took him by surprise, and his chuckle sounded genuine. 'Well, I'm afraid we do have some vampires, but historically they would all seem to have travelled from Europe to reach us. As for magic, America is an extremely large place, Miss Dalton. I've been told there are different sorts of magic in different areas, not to mention what's been brought there by visitors from other countries. Pure superstition, of course, but I think we can honestly say there are more types of superstition in America than anywhere else in the world by now.'

Suggestive, Anima said thoughtfully.

Eleanor was about to ask for further details, given that the man appeared to be in a talkative mood, when a gloved hand tapped her shoulder, and she turned to see Lady Marguerite.

'Ah, Eleanor!' Lady Marguerite said with a brilliant smile, as though she hadn't been avoiding Eleanor for the last hour. She was trailed by several other men and women, and she had a large package in her arms. It was wrapped in brown paper, tied up neatly with string and sealed with wax. 'I have a highly important item to entrust to you, which you must guard with your life. I assure you that many other people here are desperate to claim it for their own.'

'Certainly, milady,' Eleanor said automatically, reaching out to take the package. It was heavier than it looked and felt like paper or books, although she couldn't be sure. 'May I ask . . .'

The people standing around laughed, and one of the women rapped Lady Marguerite on the wrist with her fan. 'Cruel woman! You're going to gloat now, aren't you?'

'It is my pleasure to do so,' Lady Marguerite said, her smile almost breaking into a full-blown smirk. 'Eleanor, what you hold in your hands is – are – the four volumes of *The Mysteries of Udolpho* by Ann Radcliffe.'

Eleanor gasped. 'Not the lady who wrote *The Romance of the Forest*?' A copy of that was current among the Blakeney servants, and she'd taken her turn at reading it with great pleasure. It was terribly dramatic – a truly splendid romance. She wished real life could be so easily dealt with by confessions, poisonings and convenient deaths.

'The very same. I believe it will be in bookshops and circulating libraries soon enough, but for the moment . . .' Lady Marguerite flicked out her own fan and posed with it flirtatiously. 'I have an early copy, courtesy of the publisher. I entrust it to you, Eleanor, before any of these *ravening wolves* here can snatch it from my hands to read it themselves.'

'Fie!' exclaimed one of the men. 'We have better manners than that, I trust!'

'I will not lead you into temptation,' Lady Marguerite retorted. 'Now, returning to our conversation . . .'

She was interrupted by a thunderous knocking at the front door, audible even in this inner room. Heads pricked up at the unexpected diversion. Darkness had closed in outside, and shadowy fog lapped at the windows. The butler soon entered the room, his pace brisker than the usual smooth glide, and murmured to his mistress.

'It's *who?*' Mrs Cartersleigh's voice rose above the noise of the crowd, then fell again. Eleanor strained to overhear. 'Well, have them come round to the kitchen entrance and I'll speak to them once this is over . . .'

While a few people endeavoured to continue normal conversation, most of the room had now fallen silent, following the unenlightened but very human impulse to find out what would happen next. Thus everyone heard the heavy tread of booted feet entering the house and the loud statement: 'I want to speak directly to your mistress, not you, and don't push me or I'll have you up on charges while I'm at it.'

'What is the meaning of this intrusion!' Mrs Cartersleigh sailed through the crowd in a billow of bright blue silk, head held high and voice honed to a cutting edge. 'I demand to know what is going on here!'

'Bow Street, ma'am.' Eleanor had edged around enough that she could now see the confrontation going on in the doorway. The man standing there was a heavy-set fellow in plain buff jacket and breeches, and he hadn't even removed his hat! He held an official-looking document out in Mrs Cartersleigh's direction. 'Under the Middlesex Justices Act, we're here to search the premises and question all present on the grounds of possible seditious activity.'

'This is outrageous!' Mrs Cartersleigh visibly inflated. 'Monstrous! I have friends among the judiciary, and I assure you they will hear of this!'

'Yes, ma'am, quite so.' The Bow Street Runner had a weary air to him. Clearly he'd heard it all before. 'Now, if it wouldn't be an inconvenience for you and your friends to stay here, I'd appreciate it if you could give me a list of everyone present.'

'Eleanor.' Lady Marguerite drew Eleanor aside quietly. 'Do you remember that church we passed on the way here, about ten minutes before we arrived? St Paul's, by Covent Garden? Can you find your way back there on your own?'

Eleanor blinked. 'I think so, milady.' This request boded poorly, but she trusted Lady Marguerite enough to obey first and ask questions later.

'Good girl.' Lady Marguerite flicked a glance at Mrs Cartersleigh, who was now claiming her guest list was the pick of London's society and therefore instantly recognizable and not to be offended, while at the same time declaring she couldn't possibly remember everyone present. 'Go round to the back. Wait ten minutes for everyone who's going to try to make an escape to do so, and let them draw off the Runners who'll be waiting there. Then slip out yourself and make your way to the church. I'll collect you from there in a couple of hours, once this is all dealt with and my carriage has arrived. And take that parcel with you.' Her eyes glinted in the candlelight. 'You can handle yourself in Paris: I'm sure you'll manage on your own in London. But do be careful. You have some money on you for emergencies?' Eleanor nodded. 'Good.'

Eleanor looked at the package in her arms with wild surmise. She wanted to ask what was really inside it – seditious documents? Secret letters? Information for the Scarlet Pimpernel? But this wasn't the place to say anything which might be overheard. 'I'll see it done, milady,' she muttered, and sidled towards the room's rear door, slipping through it into the next room along. This was largely empty, as everyone had thronged to overhear the disturbance.

She wasn't the only one trying to slip out, though. A few other men and women were moving away from the Bow Street Runners, while adopting the air of merely wishing to powder their nose or adjust stained cuffs. Yet beyond this,

34

there would be the back passages of the mansion to navigate, and the need to explain herself to the servants, and . . .

Of course. The package wasn't *that* large, and her gown wasn't *that* good. One of the servants who'd been providing glasses of wine had left their tray on a side table, probably due to the accelerating argument at the front, where Mrs Cartersleigh was now declaring shrilly that she'd order her servants to bar the doors to all invading Bow Street Runners if necessary. Eleanor removed the glasses and put the package on the tray, then began to walk out with calm rectitude, eyes modestly lowered, the picture of a maidservant on an errand. Another servant retreating with a trayful of glasses gave her a path to follow.

She heard the scuffling by the back door before she reached the kitchen. A couple of maids were leaning round the kitchen door to watch, wincing every time a cudgel hit home, and someone female was screeching about how dare they, how dare they . . .

Eleanor tapped the closest maid on the arm. She turned reluctantly, and her eyes narrowed as she looked Eleanor up and down. 'You don't work here,' she said.

'I don't,' Eleanor agreed. 'What's going on out there?'

'Treason,' the other maid contributed. 'Least, that's what them Runners said when they started cracking skulls. Wouldn't have thought the mistress had such a thing under her roof. Right shocking,' she added belatedly.

Eleanor wished there was some way to hide the parcel, but its bulk made it impossible for her to conceal it in her skirts, or slip it into her bodice. 'I have a problem,' she said, 'and if you can help me solve it then there's a shilling in it for you two to share.'

The first maid looked at Eleanor's parcel suspiciously. 'Are you trying to smuggle out treasonous documents?'

Eleanor rolled her eyes. 'What sort of treasonous documents

get handed over in a parcel this size at a public salon like this?'

'She's not wrong there,' the second maid agreed.

'It's a present,' Eleanor invented, 'from a milord to milady, except that milady isn't actually married to milord, and so she wants me to get it out of here before the Runners start taking down everyone's name and what's going on. Because milord's wife reads the newspapers and journals every morning like they're the Bible, and who knows what's going to be published in them?' She shrugged. 'And now it's my problem because milady's made it my problem, after she dragged me all the way here to have a proper maid by her side, not that my company was actually wanted once she *got* here . . . if you know what I mean?' She was rather proud of her innuendo: her reading of novels had proved itself useful.

The maids both nodded. 'Half a crown each,' the first one said, eyes avaricious.

'A shilling each,' Eleanor countered. It was extravagant, but she knew Lady Marguerite would recompense her – and she couldn't afford to be caught. 'You show me a safe way out and one of you takes a quick look first to make sure there aren't any Runners watching.'

The maids exchanged glances. 'It's a bargain,' the first one said.

A few minutes later, Eleanor was picking her way down a dark side alley, the package heavy in her arms.

CHAPTER THREE

Eleanor wasn't stupid. She knew that a woman on her own, carrying a large parcel, scurrying down dark side streets, was practically wearing a sign on her back inviting assault, robbery, or worse. The most sensible thing would have been to walk down the wide main street in a purposeful manner, like a perfectly normal woman out on a late-night errand. Though since no normal woman would be out on a late-night errand by herself, and if she had, then she'd be wearing a proper cap or bonnet and cape or coat – well, she'd be conspicuous in any case. Still, the street lights and passing carriages might have caused robbers to look elsewhere for prey.

The problem was that the Bow Street Runners were still scuttling around the front of the house like woodlice erupting from under an upturned stone. Apparently they weren't content to invade the place (through the front door!) and question the guests impertinently: they were stopping passers-by to inquire about their names, places of residence, reasons for taking an interest (and honestly, who wouldn't take an interest in an affair like this?), as well as any seditious goings-on that they might have noticed in the area.

Eleanor would have found it funny if she hadn't been reminded of France and the Revolutionary Guard. She knew that even if the Bow Street Runners waved law and justice like a banner, they didn't poke their noses into crime unless they were paid – which meant that someone high up must be paying for all this. She didn't want to be questioned by people in authority ever again. Reluctantly she turned back down the side alley and into one of the minor streets which ran between the main blocks of houses, their backs facing each other, just as the house fronts faced each other on the wide main street. She picked her way daintily down the pavement, avoiding the mud, the puddles and the shadows, but didn't let her pace slow. It wouldn't take much for the Runners to check down this way, or for one of the maids she'd bribed to tip them off . . .

She remembered that the church Lady Marguerite had mentioned was to the east, about ten minutes by carriage, so probably a walk of about fifteen minutes. Had the driver been allowed to let out the horses, the carriage would have been going much faster, but, well . . . London traffic. At some points on their journey to Mrs Cartersleigh's house the men and women strolling on the pavements had been going faster than they were. The slowness of their journey had prompted Lady Marguerite to point out the church, as an interesting sight en route. Eleanor had thought it pretty enough, though not very much like a normal church: comforting red brick at the back, but pale stone with pillars at the front, like one of those old pagan temples, and the whole thing looking like a huge barn, with no proper bell tower or spire. Lady Marguerite had said it was built by someone called Inigo Jones, and that a lot of actors went there. She'd sounded regretful when she mentioned this. Sometimes Eleanor wondered just how much she missed being on the stage in Paris – her life before she'd married Sir Percy.

Conveniently, the street she was on now bent towards the east, and Eleanor followed it, grateful for her training in Lady

Sophie's household. When one's mistress was a vampire and often spent all night up and about, the servants had to learn to work in the dark. There were no street lights here, no overhanging lanterns, and the clouds and fog covered the moon and stars. Lights flickered in the windows above her and through cracks in the shutters. One coal cellar stood open: half a dozen men were gathered just inside it, around a lantern, playing cards and sharing bottles. She deliberately didn't let her eyes linger on them as she passed, in case they took it as an invitation.

Someone behind her chuckled. The sound carried unpleasantly, sending a shiver down her back. She wished again that she was wearing her cape, or even a shawl – something to cover her hair and shoulders. She wished that the street was shorter. And she wished that Lady Marguerite had thought her a little less capable and found some other way of disposing of this parcel. Ahead of her, she finally saw the end of the street, with an opening onto a wider main street where there were lights and people. She quickened her pace.

Then she heard the sound of running feet behind her – more than one person, approaching *fast*.

She'd never make it to the main street in time. She'd be run down like a hare by hounds. This was a pretty pickle. *Wake up, Anima!* she ordered as she turned to face her pursuers, shifting the weight of the package in her hands. It was four volumes, after all. That was enough to put a great many people to sleep, if applied strategically.

There is no need to shout, Anima answered, unamused. *I can hardly leave you.*

I thought you might wish to know we have a problem on our doorstep, Eleanor answered. The three men who'd come running after her slowed as they realized there was no need for haste now. In the barely lit alley she could make out little of their expressions or clothing, but what she could see didn't inspire confidence. They looked *precisely* the sort of men one didn't want to meet down a dark alley.

'What do you think?' one of them said to another.

The second man, the smallest of the three, stroked his chin. 'Question is, is she going to be a good girl or not?'

'I don't want to be hurt,' Eleanor said quietly. She knew that even if she screamed, nobody from the main street would arrive in time to help her – assuming they came at all. And rich people whose houses backed onto dark alleys certainly didn't take an interest in what *happened* in those dark alleys. *Anima, I know these men aren't vampires, but . . .*

Oh, trust me, I have a few things I can do to living men which will teach them some respect for women, Anima answered. *I'm rather disappointed in you, though. You don't usually permit yourself to be put in this sort of situation.*

I couldn't have predicted these men, Eleanor answered, stung.

I'm not talking about the men. Anima paused. *But it can wait.*

'Sensible,' the man allowed. 'What's in the package?'

'Books,' Eleanor admitted. Perhaps they had unexpected religious sensibilities? 'I'm taking them to St Paul's in Covent Garden.'

'Can't get much for books,' the third man said, picking his teeth.

'The books aren't important,' the first man said. 'It's blood that's the going thing these days. You're healthy, girl? Good household? Eat plenty of meat? We know some people who'll pay well for what you have in your veins.'

Eleanor flinched a step back. It wasn't acting. There was a difference between having given blood in the past for her mistress, neatly bleeding into a cup and seeing it reflected in her wages, and what these men were suggesting. 'No,' she said firmly.

I thought for a moment you might agree, Anima commented, *just in order to get away from them.*

Are you joking? They'd never let me go. Eleanor didn't have Anima's bone-deep distrust and hate for vampires, but the sort of vampire who paid back-alley thugs to force young women into providing their blood was not the sort of vampire with whom she desired closer acquaintance.

Further down the alley, behind them, she saw more figures approaching. More ruffians? No, they were moving with a firm, definite stride rather than a saunter, and now that she had a better view of them, they looked like the Bow Street Runners she'd hoped to avoid. This might be a catastrophe on the one hand, but on the other an opportunity . . .

'I'm not going with you,' Eleanor declared, raising her voice. 'I'm not going to let you take me away for immoral purposes! I'm a decent woman and I'm—'

She was cut off by the small man grabbing her and trying to put his hand over her mouth. Eleanor bit down on his fingers, hard: she might not be a vampire, but even human teeth could hurt. As he howled in pain and pulled his hand back, she hit him in the ribs with her parcel, taking full advantage of its weight.

As she'd hoped, the Bow Street men came on at a run to intervene. What had been a simple accosting of a helpless woman turned into a brawl, giving her the chance to sidle away while the men were all caught up with each other.

Unfortunately the man whom she'd bitten didn't forget about her so easily. He dropped his opponent with a punch to the stomach, then came after Eleanor with a nasty snarl as she backed away, his expression suggesting that this time he wouldn't limit himself to simply a hand across her mouth.

When you said you had something in store which would teach him respect for women . . . Eleanor reminded Anima.

Give me control, and slap him. There was a tinge of anticipation to Anima's voice. *Trust me.*

Letting the weight of the package fall onto her left arm,

Eleanor slapped the man squarely across the face in the best manner of theatrical melodramas. At this, Anima became abruptly present in Eleanor's skull in a way that she hadn't been before, and Eleanor looked out at a world which sparkled with new threads of light and changed perspectives. As her hand moved, it seemed to slow down, as though the air was weaving itself into a new pattern around her skin like a glove. She thought she could smell sulphur. It was almost like the time before, in the sewers of Paris, when she'd hit the vampire Marie Antoinette – except then she'd been full of panic and terror, and now it was anger and exasperation driving her, flavoured by solid justification.

How pleasant it feels to be absolutely certain about what one is doing . . .

Light crackled and spat around her fingers, like lard in a hot pan, or sparks shooting out around the cover of a dark lantern. She jerked her hand back reflexively: it stung, as though she'd slept with her arm trapped under her and the feeling was now flooding back into it again. The man, on the other hand, keeled over as though a vigorous member of the League had applied a blackjack to his head from behind.

There are times to stand around inspecting the outcome of an experiment, and times to remove one's self from the area, Anima said tartly. *Get out of here before I have to do that again.*

She didn't need to be told twice. Eleanor ran down the dark side street, skirts caught up in her free hand, her soft indoor shoes barely audible on the filthy cobbles and paving stones. She'd had no chance to don pattens before leaving the salon, and it was a *crying shame* to do this to her nice new shoes. All she could say about people who went round preaching that you should discard luxuries in the face of a life-or-death situation was that such people probably had the money to buy their luxuries again afterwards. But *she didn't.* As she nearly slipped on something rotten which squished and slid beneath her foot, her resentment was quickly replaced by panic. She had to reach the main street and lights, she *had to . . .*

Eleanor stumbled out of the alley, gasping for air. Even though fear still pumped through her, she had the common sense to step to one side and mingle with a group of people who were peering at some prints and caricatures that filled every pane of a print shop window. Yet she was still far too obvious with her lack of a hat or bonnet, as well as no outer wear of any sort. *This would be easier in Paris,* she thought, and almost laughed at how ridiculous an idea it was. *I know Paris – well, a little, at least. I don't know London.*

Nevertheless, she did at least know where Covent Garden lay from here: she could see lamps and hear the calls of street barkers and food vendors. As she drew closer, the city seemed to reach out to take her into its arms, reassuring, welcoming. These were *ordinary* people here, not aristocrats – English or French – and not Bow Street Runners. They were like her, simply trying to make a living. They were selling the sort of things she'd buy, or at least, that she'd like to buy if she wasn't putting every penny aside in the hopes of eventually working in a modiste's shop. Ribbons, sweets, dainties, books and pamphlets, toys . . .

Blood?

'Guaranteed from healthy young men and women!' a skinny man with a voice out of proportion to his size declared to her right. A heavy coat with multiple shoulder-capes made for a larger man weighed him down, and the powder on his face didn't quite conceal the sores near his mouth. 'Do you have a master or mistress who's not entirely happy with what your household can produce? For just half a crown we'll provide you with a half-pint bottle which will satisfy them! Sealed under the most cleanly conditions and guaranteed not to have been taken from cattle or pigs! If they don't like it, then on my oath we'll give you your money back *and* an extra bottle!'

'Don't you listen to him,' a woman on Eleanor's left stepped in. 'What you want is a way to keep giving good blood. Just one spoonful of this tonic a day, made with real ginseng all the way from China, will do as much for you as a week's rest in the countryside. You'll see the roses in your cheeks and the hair on your head growing twice as thick within a fortnight! You'll have them raising your pay to twice what they're giving you now – no, three times – because you'll be quality, my lads and lasses, pure quality! Just give it a good shake, and swallow it down every morning, and . . .'

Eleanor lowered her head and focused on pushing her way through the crowd. A couple of times she felt hands fumbling at her skirts, but her inner pocket was well concealed: no pickpocket was going to get her few coins. As she heard more and more of the sellers offering blood, or ways of procuring blood, a chill rose up her spine. Had matters grown worse in the last few months, or last few years? Was providing blood to vampires really so much of an industry?

Eleanor hadn't had the opportunity to wander round London before. She'd grown up and spent her life on Lady Sophie's estates. She'd never had any excuse to leave them, however much she might have wanted to. Matters had been so much *simpler* there – an occasional cup of blood for the mistress, and a few extra pence in her salary for that week. She'd never thought twice about things being different elsewhere.

She'd never *had* to think about it.

As the church came into view (and she *still* thought it looked like a barn rather than a proper church), she forced herself to face the other possibility. Perhaps it wasn't so much that things had grown worse, but that they'd *always* been like this.

I told you, Anima said unhelpfully.

Yes, but surely if it should be fair wages for fair service, then what could be wrong with that? Eleanor argued, conscious that she was trying to convince herself just as much as the old mage.

By the same argument, it's no shame for a whore to earn her money on her back, Anima replied.

Eleanor certainly wouldn't have associated with prostitutes, but she knew how thin the line was for a maidservant between paid employment and a good character, and the gutter and doing whatever it took to feed herself and stay alive. *Blame the man who put her there and everything that keeps her there*, she snapped.

Oh, I do. Anima's voice had a smugness which suggested that Eleanor had walked directly into her conversational trap. *So tell me, child . . . what do you think the vampires who buy this blood would do if it was no longer conveniently available for sale? If they could no longer obtain it for fair wages, then what steps do you think they might undertake to keep themselves fed?*

No worse than a living person, I'm sure, Eleanor retorted stoutly, but the idea nestled deep within her heart, an uncomforting seed that would bring later nightmares.

After all, she reflected as she walked into the church, both Paris and London had shown her just how far living people would go to stay alive . . .

CHAPTER FOUR

April had kissed England and the country blossomed; the grass was a green so bright that Eleanor sighed for a silk that would match it in her embroidery, flowers filled the garden and clustered in vases throughout the great house, and the footmen were constantly trying to coax the maids behind hedges. The weather was beautiful enough to make Eleanor hum to herself as she dusted. Sunlight blazed brilliantly outside, turning the old diamond-shaped panes of the windows into gems that sparkled as brightly as Lady Marguerite's jewels.

It was eleven o'clock, but Lady Marguerite herself was still in bed, lounging with a cup of chocolate (her third so far this morning) and a copy of the latest issue of *The Lady's Magazine*. Alice, back on her feet again, had promised to pass the magazine on to the other maids once Lady Marguerite had finished with it – another cause for cheerfulness. The rest of the household didn't get to lie in, though; they were about their daily duties, from the housekeeper and butler to the lowest scullery maids and stable boys. The whole house felt to Eleanor as though it was buzzing with the vigour of spring's return, where even the dirtiest and most unwelcome jobs were made that bit more tolerable by the sunshine and the fresh breezes.

Sir Percy himself was . . . elsewhere. In France, presumably, but only he and the members of the League accompanying him knew precisely where, or under what identity. The Committee of Public Safety might search for him here, there, or everywhere, but the Scarlet Pimpernel was still as elusive as ever. This particular mission was, she'd been told, a quest for information rather than a specific rescue, though no doubt the *Daydream* – the Blakeney yacht – would return with a few extra passengers.

From outside came the sound of horses rapidly approaching the house. Giving way to temptation, Eleanor peered out to see who was visiting at this early hour. She was surprised to recognize the curricle of Sir Andrew Ffoulkes, another member of the League and Sir Percy's acknowledged lieu-tenant, and his pair of matched greys. She strained to see if anyone else was in the curricle with him – Sir Andrew always drove his own horses – but couldn't make it out. A thrill of excitement twitched through her. If this was League business, then perhaps it might involve her.

But of course she couldn't leave her work half done and rush off to ask questions. She was simply a maid in the household, after all, not a family member or a guest. With a sigh she resumed her dusting. *I wish that your magic allowed me to see things from a distance,* she told Anima. *Witches and sorcerers do that in the stories.*

As I have repeatedly informed you, I am not a witch, Anima replied wearily. *Witches are folk tales. Magic is real. It would have taken the power of a dozen sorcerers like myself to scry on a distant location, or a hundred willing friends to provide their strength to assist me. On my own I can call storms or prevent assaults, or drive off vampires and cleanse others of their blood-induced influence, but I cannot do the impossible.*

Sir Andrew jumped out of the curricle, throwing the reins to one of the grooms who'd come running up, and stalked towards the Blakeney house's front doors in a flurry of capes and great-coat. (Four shoulder-capes, even. Sir Percy would need to add a new extra layer to his own to outdo his friend.) Behind him, pausing to adjust his eye-glasses in the bright sunlight, came Lord Charles Bathurst, thinner and gawkier, wearing the same style of clothing but without quite the same grace. Eleanor felt a little flutter of happiness at the thought of seeing him again – and if it was League business, out of the hearing of the other servants. It had been a good few weeks since they last met. He looked healthy enough, they both did, but their urgency was visible even through the thick glass of the window.

Further inside the house, Eleanor could hear shouts and running footsteps. Mr Sturn, the butler, would be hastily organizing a reception, sending a maid up to Lady Marguerite, having food and drink prepared and all the other polite necessities.

Normally the household wouldn't have displayed such internal signs of stress while preparing to receive visitors. Everything would already have been in place, with a mere murmur bringing the footmen to the door, and Lady Marguerite already in proper morning dress, lounging in a room other than her bedroom. But normal visitors – of the gentry, at least – signalled their arrival well in advance. They didn't drop by at this hour out in Richmond, with it not even being midday yet.

Have you considered any further how we might visit Oxford for me to investigate certain matters? Anima asked.

I can't just leave here and travel to Oxford, Eleanor protested wearily. Anima's suggestions had been growing more pointed over the last few weeks. *And even if I did go there, what could I actually do? What man of learning is going to answer the sort of questions you want to ask – especially when they come from a common housemaid?*

I need answers. Anima's voice in Eleanor's mind was

uncompromising. *I have to know what happened, and what action to take now. My time with you won't last for ever. Our link grows weaker. I refuse to pass away with my work incomplete, with the vampires still controlling all Europe, and with you still claiming that this state of affairs is somehow normal . . .*

It's going to have to wait, Eleanor replied firmly, ignoring Anima's aggrieved sigh. *Even if I could ask for leave, I can't do it now. Andrew and Charles wouldn't arrive like this unless there was a problem. I may be needed.*

Although Eleanor was excited at the possibility of League work, she knew that an unexpected visit like this, without a word of warning, was far more likely to be bad news than good.

Something was wrong.

Eleanor hurried through the rest of her duties, skimping what could be skimped and avoiding what could be put off, buying herself a little extra time before she'd be needed in the kitchen. Still clutching the duster tightly in her hand, she pressed her ear against the door of Lady Blakeney's study.

'. . . no word for a week now.' Sir Andrew's voice rang with controlled anger.

'And Jerry is still in France?' That was Lady Marguerite's voice.

'Indeed. He's checking the local prisons, using the papers Charles gave him from last time, but . . .' Eleanor could imagine Sir Andrew's shrug. 'If the fellow were in a normal prison, I'd expect that the news would have spread across Paris. But if the circumstances are abnormal, then heaven knows where we stand.'

Cold fear curdled in Eleanor's throat. One of the League missing? Captured, even? She frequently doubted her own abilities, but never the rest of the League. If some disaster had struck their organization in France, though . . .

She had to know more. Forcing calmness on herself, she tapped on the door.

The sudden dead silence on the other side indicated just how secret a meeting this was. Then footsteps, and Charles pulled the door open, glaring down at her. 'Your mistress is busy – oh, Eleanor! Come in, m'dear. That is . . .' He looked to Sir Andrew and Lady Marguerite. 'It seems half the League knows already, so we might as well share our information. When it comes to rescues, as the Chief says, beggars can't be choosers.'

Sir Andrew gave a weary laugh. He hadn't bothered to sit down, or even remove his greatcoat. His blond hair was disordered from its normal glossy elegance, and shadows showed under his eyes. 'I'm sure that we'd have asked you to join us if we could think of an excuse to do with embroidery, Eleanor. A pity that I haven't come with better news.'

Lady Marguerite gave Eleanor a nod of acceptance, then turned back to Andrew. Despite having dressed at short notice, she looked elegant enough to attend a first night at the theatre. The only sign of haste on her part was that her hair was still down, falling in red-gold waves over her shoulders and nearly to her waist. 'Why don't you tell us the whole business again from the beginning, Andrew? Eleanor doesn't know anything about it, except for Percy going to France. Perhaps explaining it to her will help the rest of us find some clue to the matter.'

'But what's happened?' Eleanor asked, hoping against hope that she'd overheard wrongly. 'Is someone . . . missing?'

Andrew finally took a seat, gesturing for Charles and Eleanor to do the same. 'That's the sum and total of the matter, m'dear. What makes it more difficult is that none of us are quite sure what might be going on, even the Chief – and you know the Chief's somewhat prone to keep his own counsel.'

The man would make a mystery of the weather, Anima said

sourly. She was as curious as Eleanor, though; Eleanor could sense her impatience for Sir Andrew to continue.

Eleanor nodded. 'I know the Chief left England a few weeks ago,' she said. 'All the servants were saying that he'd gone up to Scotland to review some holdings up there?' She didn't sit down. If any of the other servants came in, she shouldn't be caught seated in the presence of her superiors. She did stand next to Charles, however, and he briefly squeezed her hand.

Andrew nodded. 'Very important thing to have a good cover story. It hides a multitude of sins . . .' He yawned, covering his mouth. 'Sorry, m'dear. I didn't get any sleep last night; we dropped anchor in Portsmouth, and I came up here directly, collecting Charles on the way.'

'And worrying Charles vastly on the way,' Charles put in.

'Lud, if worrying's the worst we do, then I think we'll have come out of this better than we dare hope for,' Andrew said. 'I was trusting that you might have some idea of what's going on, given all the permits and other forgeries you prepared for Percy.'

'I fear not,' Charles admitted. He rubbed the bridge of his nose – a habit he was prone to even when not wearing eye-glasses. 'The most I can tell you is that he wanted papers which would allow him to claim he was an emissary of the Committee of Public Safety, sent to examine local dock records – Marseille, Lyon, Le Havre, and so forth. He visited me at my London house. Good thing my father wasn't around; you know what he thinks of the Chief.'

'Percy does a great deal to cultivate the impression of an all-round good-for-nothing,' Lady Marguerite said reassuringly. 'You shouldn't blame your father for taking him at his word. But he didn't tell you any more than that?'

Charles frowned. 'Only that he'd been down to Portsmouth just before.'

'But who's missing?' Eleanor broke in. 'Is it one of the League?'

'No, thank heavens.' Andrew seemed to relax. 'Thank you for that, m'dear – you've reminded me how much worse things could be. No, the missing fellow's a chap named Talleyrand. It's a long story . . .'

Eleanor saw the little lines of concern around the corners of Lady Marguerite's eyes. 'Percy told me he was going to Portsmouth, and then to France. Andrew, for the love of pity, tell us your part of the story *from the beginning*. You were supposed to be enjoying a few months of peace with Suzanne?'

Andrew sighed. 'As ever, there's no such thing as peace when we're needed in France, and the Revolution claims yet more innocent heads. Suzanne understood that when she took my hand in marriage.'

'Details, Andrew my sweet, some details, I pray,' Lady Marguerite prompted through what Eleanor suspected were gritted teeth.

Andrew coloured with embarrassment, and took a hearty swig of the coffee. 'A few weeks back, Percy arrived on my doorstep and commanded my assistance. He said that he'd lost track of a playing piece, by which he meant Talleyrand – you know how deucedly vague he can be – and that he needed myself and others to track a certain ship, confirming whether or not she had arrived in France. We were travelling in pairs, of course – safer that way. If one should be caught up by the Guard, the other can help him to escape.'

Eleanor knew that Lady Marguerite was aware of this sort of detail – she'd been assisting the League's operations before Eleanor herself had joined, after all. But the older woman displayed all her skill as a noted actress by nodding as though this was some new piece of information, and smiling gently for Andrew to continue.

'The ship's name was *La Surveillante*,' Andrew went on.

'The problem, of course, was that she might have landed somewhere quiet along the coast, much as Percy likes doing with his *Daydream*. Nevertheless, we had information that she'd been in poor condition when she left port. Percy thought she'd need proper attention, and you can't procure that when you're hiding in a cove somewhere with only smugglers to scrape off the barnacles.'

'Not to mention the movements of the army divisions and the increase in patrols,' Charles added. 'It's not as easy to hide out as it used to be.'

Andrew nodded. 'The Chief thought that Calais, Dieppe or Le Havre – Hâvre-Marat these days – were the most likely options. Probably not Saint-Malo – *La Surveillante* didn't go through the Channel Islands – or Cherbourg. The whole thing was guesswork.' He drained his cup and held it for Lady Marguerite to refill. 'Forgive me, milady, you know I have the greatest respect for the Chief, but sometimes it'd be helpful if he'd share a few of his confounded hunches.'

Lady Marguerite shrugged. 'And yet they are so frequently right, are they not? How can his wife contradict him?'

Eleanor rather thought that Lady Marguerite did say quite a few things to contradict him, but took care to say them in private. She herself was trying to visualize the situation. She recognized the names of three major French ports, but her grasp of French geography was sadly lacking. 'Are those three places very far apart?' she asked. 'And which one did the Chief go to?'

'It's a hundred miles from Calais to Dieppe,' Andrew said, 'and another seventy-five from Dieppe to Le Havre. Quicker by sea than road, if one's lucky with the wind, but you can see why the Chief had us travel in separate groups. We were to meet at Dieppe. The Chief went to Le Havre with Jerry, while I took Dieppe with Philip Glynde, and Fanshawe and Hastings stopped off at Calais.'

'With that much distance to cover, I can see why you travelled concurrently rather than consecutively.' Charles hesitated, waiting for a laugh that didn't come, then went on. 'Did you find what you were looking for?'

'No.' Andrew set the empty coffee-cup down with a click that was almost more emphatic than a thump in its desperate self-control. 'It was a wasted mission. None of us found a single piece of useful information. The ship might as well have vanished into thin air. At which point the Chief sent me back here to conduct further investigations.'

'I think I may be able to give you a piece of the puzzle,' Lady Marguerite said slowly. 'I know what was exercising Percy's thoughts shortly before he left, though he told me little more than he did you. How much do you know *about* Talleyrand?'

'A deuced twisty type,' Andrew replied. 'A priest, wasn't he, before he was excommunicated? Sent over here as deputy to the Ambassador while France was still trying to avoid war with us, then after he'd gone back, he had to leave France again just ahead of an arrest warrant, and took harbour here. Then he was ordered to leave England back in early March.'

'Calling him a deuced twisty type's understating the matter,' Charles said with some heat. 'The fellow used to be a bishop, but he resigned the position. He was in with the Revolutionaries from the beginning – helped write their Declaration of the Rights of Man, proposed nationalizing the Church and having all the priests swear to the government rather than the Pope, and even favoured the appropriation of Church properties!' He caught sight of Eleanor's rather lost stare, and explained, 'That means the State confiscates all Church property and sells it, m'dear. More than a bit scandalous for someone who'd once been a bishop.'

'He sounds a complete and utter hypocrite!' Eleanor said, rather shocked.

' 'But a splendid conversationalist,' Lady Marguerite said wistfully, 'and so charming. Highly gifted at persuading people that their interests aligned with his, and I do believe that he was sympathetic to the *idea* of recreating France . . . even if he's currently on the outs with the National Committee. That was why he was due to take ship to America.'

Eleanor shivered at the very thought. She'd been told that journey would mean a month at sea, or more, and the idea chilled her to the bones, and unsettled her stomach too. She didn't like sea travel. Crossing the English Channel to France had been bad enough. 'If he was considered an enemy of the Republic, then why didn't he stay in England, milady?' she asked. 'Why was he ordered to leave?'

'Oh, he was considered . . . dangerous.' Lady Marguerite pursed her lips in a little moue. 'Not that I disagree! It was Pitt's Alien Bill, I think?'

'Might have been drawn up with the fellow in mind,' Charles said. 'Eleanor, earlier this year the Prime Minister had a bill drawn up and passed by Parliament which let him expel any foreigners who were thought to be a threat to England's security. Talleyrand was ordered to leave England in January, but he managed to get it put off till March. Wrote letters to all and sundry, even His Majesty the King, but Pitt had his way.'

'He booked passage to Philadelphia,' Andrew agreed. 'That's in America,' he added in clarification.

Eleanor frowned. 'Does this Alien Bill mean they're going to start sending the aristocrats whom we rescued from France back again? That seems rather cruel.'

'Anyone whom we've rescued isn't going to be helping the Republic, so there'd be no worry there,' Andrew said. 'Quite the opposite. Talleyrand, however . . . nobody could be certain what he'd do, and there are enough Royalists in England now who carry a serious grudge against the fellow. Some of them lost family and friends because he was supporting the Republic at the time. I'd lay good money that they were putting pressure on Pitt.'

He held out his newly emptied cup for more coffee. 'Pitt may have hit the mark better than he knew. What if Talleyrand didn't leave for America as planned, but slipped off back to France instead to take up the cause of Revolution again, eh? It wouldn't be the first time he'd turned his coat.'

Charles nodded. 'And if the fellow was travelling on the *Surveillante* . . .'

'But could a French ship have landed in Britain to pick him up?' Eleanor asked.

'Not *legally*, no,' Charles said. 'Then again, the Chief's *Daydream* doesn't precisely make legal port in France. Besides that, there are smugglers up and down the coast who could have picked the fellow up and transferred him.'

Eleanor chewed her lower lip. She had the feeling they were missing something here. 'But how did the Chief *know* the French ship's name?'

'I can answer that one,' Lady Marguerite said. 'It was in the papers which Eleanor saved for me a few weeks ago. The *Surveillante* was one of a few ships which had raised official suspicion, but then the only one that'd been allowed to proceed with business as normal – which in itself signals strangeness, given how *any* suspicion in France these days is grounds for arrest. One of the contacts I have in France sent me the information by means of a friend who's now working for George Robinson, the publisher. The friend saw to it that the letters were hidden inside my copy of *The Mysteries of Udolpho*. Thanks to Eleanor's quick wits, they didn't fall into the hands of the Bow Street Runners.' She smiled at Eleanor, and Eleanor couldn't help but be warmed by the compliment.

'Was that why the Runners were there in the first place, milady?' she asked.

'I wouldn't have thought it, but who can tell?' She shrugged gracefully. 'And Percy has his own set of friends, gossips and correspondents. Even more people pass information to him than Citizen Chauvelin of the Revolutionary Committee has informers. Then again, people like talking to my beloved Percy, and I've yet to meet anyone who likes talking to Citizen Chauvelin.'

Charles twitched slightly, looking away. Eleanor suspected it wasn't just the thought of Chauvelin, with whom they'd both had unpleasant experiences, but Chauvelin's *daughter*, Fleurette. The last time they'd seen her, she'd just discovered that the two of them were part of the League, and had been . . . upset. She was a nice girl – no, to be fair, a truly generous, sincere and *good* woman – but she believed in the Revolution just as strongly as her father did. Eleanor *liked* her. She just wished there was some way they could have been on the same side.

Lady Marguerite's frown had deepened. 'I fear we're missing the full potential danger of the situation,' she said. 'Talleyrand moved among some of the highest circles while he was here in England. If he's slipped back to France, then who knows what information he's taken with him? Indeed, was he ever truly a defector from their regime, or might he have been a spy for them all along?'

The room was silent. Then Andrew said, 'We can't keep this to ourselves within the League. If what you suggest is true, milady, then England's security may depend upon it.'

'Nor can we run to Pitt's spies with it now, not with Percy still investigating in France,' Lady Marguerite retorted.

Charles coughed. 'I . . . might know someone who might know someone, milady. I could claim that I'd come across some rumour that Talleyrand didn't sail to America after all, and ask for their advice?'

Eleanor reminded herself that she *was* a member of the

League, she *had* a right to speak her piece, even if everyone else in the room was by far her social superior, and that *someone* had to be the advocate of common sense in the group. 'But for that, surely, we'll need more information about how he didn't sail there – assuming that he truly didn't, of course – or what ship he actually sailed on, if not the *Surveillante*. Isn't that why the Chief sent Andrew back here – to find out?'

Charles shot her a slightly betrayed look, then shrugged. 'You have a point, m'dear. But I think we should reserve the possibility of informing Pitt's men, if we don't hear from the Chief soon. This is not some light-hearted hypothesis; as Lady Marguerite says, this may be a threat to England herself.'

'You are both right,' Lady Marguerite said, bestowing a smile on them. 'We cannot keep silent if this is truly a matter of national interest. But until we have more evidence than Percy's comments to me and his private investigations . . . well, how would we explain to Pitt's spies our *own* frequent travels to France? As my love has said, the political climate is touchy and there are people out there who'd be glad to seize on suspicions of treason. Perhaps it really was my papers that the Runners were after.'

Silence fell on the room again. It was broken by Lady Marguerite rising to cross to her desk and open one of the dainty lacquered drawers. She withdrew a sheaf of letters and invitations and began to sort through them. Eleanor repressed the urge to lean over and peer, even though some of them looked interestingly scandalous. 'I believe I can be of some assistance. I can seek out word of Talleyrand and other rumours from the current French ambassador, as well as the cream of exiled aristocrats at Court.'

Now it was Andrew's turn to frown. 'The Chief wouldn't care for you to risk yourself, milady.'

'Bah,' Lady Marguerite said lightly. 'If you're going to tell me that you can do such a thing better than I can, Andrew—'

'No, no!' he objected hastily. 'But to endanger yourself alone . . . it's not to be thought of.'

'I certainly won't be doing so *alone*.' Lady Marguerite put down one of the invitations she'd selected. 'See, this is for a gathering at Lord St Clare's house in two days' time. I'll attend by myself in Percy's absence, but it'll be a crowd – worse, a sad crush. Nobody will be walking out with me in a bag over their shoulder, Andrew!'

She made a joke of it, but it was clear from Andrew's face that he was indeed concerned about such a possibility. 'If Eleanor were with you . . .' he suggested, then broke off.

'No, perhaps not. You may be able to impersonate Marie Antoinette, but I fear you would be unable to pass for an English lady of rank at such an event,' Lady Marguerite said.

Eleanor knew this only too well, but there was something about the way she put it that made her wish she could throw coffee-cups at every aristocrat present. At least at the previous salon people had treated her with a degree of equality. Yet this was the problem with living between two worlds, as she was doing. She could pass for a serving-maid or housemaid anywhere, but not a woman of the upper classes. The moment anybody saw her face in a good light without cosmetics, or her hands with all the marks of frequent housework, or the scars on her forearms from where she'd drawn blood for her previous mistress, or heard her speak . . .

'It's true,' she said, schooling herself to resignation and forcing a smile. 'I'm going to need a great deal more education before I can impersonate an *Englishwoman* of the upper classes.'

'Ah, but I have a more dangerous mission for Eleanor and Charles than that!' Lady Marguerite flashed a brilliant smile at them all. 'If anyone at the reception *does* wish to speak to me privately, they certainly won't do it there, nor will they wish to call at my husband's town house. No, they'll hope for a secret word with me later. Which means I must give them the opportunity.' She plucked out another invitation. 'At the opera, for instance. To be more precise, this production of Gluck's *Echo and Narcissus* which I'd intended to avoid. As does everyone else, I hear. A sad waste of time and talent. But it'll be taking place the same evening as the reception, so I'll drop a word in every appropriate ear that I plan to attend afterwards. Then if anybody *does* want to speak with me in private, what's more private than a box at the opera?'

'And us?' Charles asked eagerly. 'What's our mission?'

'Why,' Lady Marguerite said, a mischievous sparkle in her eye, 'the two of you will be in the next box, and I'll be counting on you to listen, and to defend me, should it be necessary. The two of you will be my hidden cards.'

Eleanor found a grin creeping to her lips. This would work – and it would let her *help*. Alongside Charles, which was even better. 'Count me in, milady,' she said happily. 'I've always wanted to go to the opera.'

CHAPTER FIVE

As a child, Eleanor had daydreamed about going to the theatre in London. And since it was a daydream, she'd imagined herself in a beautiful silk dress, accompanied by a handsome and romantic beau. They'd sit in the finest box in the theatre, the envy of all who saw them, and everyone would gasp in admiration at the way she handled her fan and quipped wittily to her partner.

No doubt it was good for her character to have such romantic dreams punctured and destroyed, but it still stung. The theatre was mostly empty, and when she and Charles had arrived, Charles had done an effective job of convincing the usher that he was entertaining an inappropriate liaison and wished to avoid attention. They were in the box next to Lady Marguerite's – who, to be fair, must be even more bored than they were, having nobody to talk to – but seated well back, out of public view. The few people in the stalls below were either devoted enthusiasts who didn't take their eyes off the stage, or couples like Charles and herself who only had eyes for each other.

'When I first heard about opera,' Eleanor murmured – not that anyone could have heard her over the soprano's voice – 'I thought that perhaps I wouldn't like it because I had no experience with the more refined sorts of music. But after sitting through half an hour of this . . .'

'Yes?' Charles said.

'I've come to the conclusion that I don't like this because it is simply *awful*.'

'Can't disagree with you, m'dear.' Charles was slouching in his seat like a discarded anatomical skeleton from some doctor's surgery, arms dangling and legs stretched out in front of him. He'd subsided further and further into the chair as the opera had continued, as though he hoped to sink through the floor and deafen himself that way. 'Not that I'm precisely a connoisseur, but I'd say that anyone who wasn't tone-deaf would agree this is simply rank bad. Goes to show that just because the lady's a vampire and doesn't need to breathe, doesn't necessarily mean she can sing.'

Eleanor winced as the soprano hit a full high note and the glasses of wine on the table beside them trembled in sympathy. 'Also, the story's *wrong*. I thought Narcissus died of starvation and Echo wasted away.'

'True enough.' Charles slanted a sideways eye at her. 'I'm surprised you know it, though. Did they tell you that sort of story at dame school? I thought they restricted themselves to the Bible, with a bit of Bunyan's *Pilgrim's Progress* for variety.'

It had been Anima who'd passed on the original myth, but Eleanor couldn't confess that, even if she wished more and more that she could. Charles was one of the few people who might believe her story rather than consider her a lunatic. And it was becoming increasingly difficult not to slip up. Anima kept telling her things which Eleanor, as a housemaid who'd never been taught such things as Latin or Greek, couldn't justify knowing.

'I think it was the vicar who told us the fable, to warn us against vanity,' she finally said, hating herself for lying. But what else could she say? That she was haunted by a ghost who shared this sort of information as a way of pointing out just how ignorant Eleanor was? Anima had never hidden the fact that she would far rather have had an educated host – one who would catch her references and appreciate her witticisms.

'Oh well, that explains it. Our vicar loved to use the old myths to scare people into good behaviour,' Charles said, sounding almost grateful for the explanation. He slumped further into his gilt chair, practically horizontal. The candle-light in the box glinted on his shoe-buckles.

'Charles . . .' Eleanor hesitated before asking, aware how fragile their friendship was, and how easily he might recoil from a sensitive question by declaring that it was none of her business. But it *was* friendship, and she *did* care about him, even if it couldn't possibly go beyond that. 'Is something troubling you?'

'A few matters,' he admitted unwillingly. 'Nothing compared to the risk of Talleyrand being a spy, of course, or Lady Marguerite's concerns . . .'

Eleanor daringly patted his hand. 'You know you can trust me.'

'And would you tell me your own problems?' he asked, annoyingly perceptively.

Because of course, no, she wasn't going to share the issues of Anima possessing her, or her loneliness, or the manner in which it was becoming increasingly difficult to balance her duties to the League with her work around the Blakeney mansion, or simply wondering where it was all going to end . . .

'I have hope that mine will be resolved by time and persis-tence,' she said. After all, the League couldn't go on like this for ever – sooner or later England must win the war with France, and then the Revolution would surely no longer be an issue. And then she'd be free – able to find a job and become a skilled professional in London, with the Blakeneys' backing. Lady Sophie, her previous employer, must have long forgotten her existence – what was one more maid to an aristocrat? As for Anima . . .

I like the current situation no better than you do, Anima whispered in her head. *If only we can find another sorcerer, a living one, then I'm sure we can be separated. Failing that, my brothers and sisters must have left books and records behind. I refuse to believe that the vampires destroyed them all; they're avaricious creatures, hoarders who cling to anything which might be of use.*

Even information about magic and spells which they could never cast? Eleanor asked. She knew from Anima's previous diatribes that the dead couldn't use magic; and according to the ancient mage's ghost, vampires were most emphatically dead.

Even then. They live in fear. Their hands are clenched tight on everything they own – money, property, treasures, people – and they will not release them.

'Time and persistence.' Charles sighed. ''Tis true that those may amend the problems with my own estates – my father's, rather, as he never misses the opportunity to remind me. Many young men have gone as soldiers, volunteers or pressed, and we're already feeling their loss. My uncle, who made his money in India, in trade . . .' He turned his gaze to his feet, embarrassed to have mentioned such a thing as making money rather than earning it. 'His understanding of the trade routes is better than my own, and he claims that if the current move to free slaves should go ahead, then it will drastically impact Great Britain's wealth and prosperity. As matters stand, the recent bread riots are causing many to check their pockets and feel the pinch.'

'France is talking about freeing slaves as well,' Eleanor put in. 'And I know you don't approve of that cruel trade – you were positively stirred up when you showed me the pamphlet of Wilberforce's speech.'

Charles looked increasingly uneasy. 'That's perfectly true, m'dear, but it doesn't make it any more comfortable at the family dinner table. What's more, friends of mine from the days when I was at Oxford have encouraged me to join Pitt's informers, saying it's the best thing for our country's security. One of them has even suggested that I should turn vampire, though my whole family would cry out against it, leaving my father with no living heir. And most of all . . .'

Eleanor tilted her head questioningly.

He rubbed the bridge of his nose. 'Eleanor, do you think less of me if you see me wearing my eye-glasses?'

Eleanor gritted her teeth for a moment in exasperation. 'Charles . . .' Then she saw the smirk he was repressing, and sighed affectionately. 'I think you have greater problems than *that*.'

A conversation from earlier that day drifted back to her.

She and two of the other maids had been arranging their belongings in the attics of the Blakeney town house in St James's Square. Lady Marguerite had declared that if she was going to attend London parties without Sir Percy to escort her, she refused to be driven back to Richmond every night. As a result, half the household had been required to pack up and move with barely half a day's notice. Eleanor and the other maids had been run ragged with cleaning, tidying and managing Lady Blakeney's wardrobe. The footmen had fared no better, with all the furniture and cases that needed carrying. Even though Lady Marguerite had sweetened it with promises of an extra half-day's leave here and there, the household was simmering like a boiling pot of stew, with murmurs of how she wouldn't have done this if his lordship had been there popping up like angry bubbles.

'You're one of the staff with leave later today, Eleanor, aren't you?' Alice asked. As Lady Marguerite's personal maid, she was sadly the person *least* likely to be granted time off. After all, the whole purpose of this little jaunt was for Lady Marguerite to interact with Society – which meant that she had to be dressed properly, and have her hair suitably arranged, and all the other tasks that an aristocrat couldn't be expected to do for herself.

'I am,' Eleanor said cheerfully. 'Can I look for anything for you in the shops?'

Alice exchanged glances with the other maid sharing the room with them – Rebecca, a steady sort not prone to drama. 'We were thinking that it might not be so much the *shops* you were planning to go to,' Rebecca said.

'Oh?' Eleanor said, as innocently as she could. In the back of her mind she was panicking. Had the two of them somehow been suborned and turned into spies?

Don't be ridiculous, Anima said sourly. *It's probably some petty household jealousy.*

Alice nodded. 'We were wondering if you were planning to meet Lord Charles Bathurst.'

They did know too much. Eleanor contemplated making a run for the door and down to Lady Marguerite. She had to be warned.

Rebecca sighed. She put a hand on Eleanor's shoulder, forcing her to sit down on her bed, then plopped down beside her. 'You don't have to answer. Your face says it all.'

Alice folded her arms, looking down at Eleanor, but she didn't look gleeful or threatening, simply weary. 'Eleanor, you're a good girl. I've worked next to you for months now. You don't try to shirk your tasks or take advantage. But I know that you've spent most of your life on the Basing estates, not in London or Bath or any of the big towns.'

'And?' Eleanor demanded. This wasn't going quite the way she'd expected. 'What's wrong with that?'

'Because whatever Charles Bathurst may tell you, sweeting,

he's not going to marry you,' Rebecca said. Her arm went sympathetically round Eleanor's shoulders. 'There's only one thing you'll get from those games, and that's a big belly and a journey home to your parents.'

That's two things, Anima said smugly.

'But it's not like that,' Eleanor protested feebly.

'Isn't it? We know he always takes time to see you when he comes to visit milord and milady,' Alice said.

'He even gave you a Christmas present, didn't he?' Rebecca prodded.

Eleanor *knew* she should have been more careful, but there was only so much she could hide from all the other servants in the household. 'He's never been anything other than an utter gentleman with me,' she tried. 'I think he must have had some sort of younger sister whom I resemble. Or maybe a cousin? Besides, milord and milady don't seem to mind.'

Alice frowned. 'Milady's a sweet, generous woman, and I wouldn't have anyone think otherwise, but she doesn't always look on these things in a practical way.'

'Well, she was a French actress, and she married an English lord,' Rebecca said. 'Stands to reason she might have inflated expectations about how other people could do the same thing. But we here all know different, don't we?' There was kindness in her eyes, but her face was stern as iron. 'He's not going to marry you. If your mother was here, she'd say the same thing.'

'Have you actually told her about him?' Alice asked.

'I didn't like to worry her,' Eleanor made a quick excuse. 'What with her being so ill . . .'

'And that's another thing,' Alice said. 'Milord and milady have been proper generous to you, giving you time off to go and nurse her, and even paying the stagecoach fare. What sort of behaviour do you think it is, to go round playing fast and loose with one of their friends? It's not just improper, it's *ungrateful.*'

Eleanor couldn't really admit that her mother's 'illness' was just an excuse for when she was sent on League missions. As far as she knew, her mother was still in the prime of health – she only wished she *could* visit Lady Sophie's estates and see her, rather than going to France. She lowered her eyes and did her best to sound humble. 'I'm truly sorry. I don't mean to be ungrateful to milord and milady after they've been so kind to me. And I do understand you're both saying this to help me, but I think you're mistaken about Lord Charles's character. I've heard about the sort of well-born young men who think we're nothing but lightskirts . . . but he's not like that, really he isn't. He just likes talking to me about his studies from when he was at Oxford, and things like that. I think he doesn't have many friends.'

Alice rapped her head with a knuckle. 'Well, that's not your problem! If he needs someone to confide in, then he can go and talk to one of milord's friends. *Not you.* If he has any real regard for your good name, then he should be leaving you alone to get on with your work. Now I'm not saying that you don't finish your work around the house, or that you're not a dab hand at sewing, but if you keep on spending your time with him like that, you're going to be in trouble.'

'Alice is right,' Rebecca agreed. 'You need to tell him so, and do it the next time you see him. Be gentle about it, but make it nice and clear that he can't expect you to . . .' She looked for words. 'To be the plaything of his idle hours,' she finished proudly.

'I still feel you're being unfair to him,' Eleanor said rebelliously. 'He's a nice young man.'

'If he's a nice young man, then he'll understand and not pester you any longer,' Alice said firmly. 'A man of his position should know full well how society works. This isn't *France.*'

'If it was, he'd probably have had his head cut off by now,' Eleanor sighed.

As the opera music swirled around her, Eleanor wondered what Fleurette would have said on the subject. After all, Fleurette was the daughter of a confirmed Republican – it would, indeed, be difficult to be any more thoroughly Republican than Citizen Chauvelin. Perhaps she'd think that Charles, as a man of noble birth, was unworthy of Eleanor? The thought made her bite back a giggle. But common sense intruded, as ever an unwelcome visitor. Marrying her would mean Charles giving up everything – family, Society, friends.

No. It would never do. And Charles would surely be fully aware of this as well.

'Have you considered—' she started, then broke off as the door of the box next door creaked open, then closed again with a click – barely audible over the music, but they'd both been listening for it.

Someone was paying a visit to Lady Blakeney. Someone had taken the bait.

Eleanor and Charles both hurried to put their ears against the thin wooden partition which separated the boxes. They were just in time to hear Lady Marguerite say coldly, '. . . did not expect to see you here.'

'Really? I was quite certain from your remarks at the reception that you would be entertaining guests. I wonder who.'

The voice was none other than that of Citizen Chauvelin himself – agent of the French Republic's Committee for Public Safety, and absolute enemy of the Scarlet Pimpernel. For a moment Eleanor's stomach clenched with fear, remembering previous encounters in France, when he'd had the power of life or death over her and she could have been sent to the guillotine without a chance of reprieve.

But that was then, she reminded herself, *and this is now, and we're not in France. He can't have us all condemned to death.*

The thought wasn't as comforting as it should have been. While Chauvelin wasn't in direct danger in England, it was hardly safe for him; he must have some pressing reason to be here, and to be talking to Lady Marguerite. Life or death for someone – but who?

'I merely said that I intended to attend the opera,' Lady Marguerite replied. 'I was not inviting guests to my box.' She would have deliberately seated herself next to the partition between boxes on her side, to give Charles and Eleanor the best possible chance of overhearing.

'And yet I am here.' There was the faint creak of someone sitting down. 'Spending your time reading, Lady Blakeney? *A Vindication of the Rights of Women.* Perhaps you still nurture some republican sympathies.'

'I heard that the author has been arrested,' Lady Marguerite replied. 'Like so many others of *truly* republican sympathies, she has suffered at the hands of the Republic.'

Before Chauvelin could answer, the woman singing Echo hit a tone so painful that the very chandelier chimed in seeming protest. 'What a dreadful voice that woman has,' he remarked. 'You should be grateful to the Republic that she no longer sings in Paris.'

'Her patrons here are much like her patrons there – less concerned with her voice and more concerned with her body.' Lady Marguerite sighed. 'Ah me, how easily you make me fall back into the days when you were just one of the crowd at my soirées!'

'Indeed,' Chauvelin said. Did he, Eleanor wondered, actually sound almost nostalgic? 'You were the darling of Paris society, then. We all believed that you would be with us for ever.'

'The world turns more swiftly than any of us expected, mon petit Chauvelin.' Without a change of tone, she added, 'So why are you here?'

'I? I merely thought you might wish to speak with me about your brother Armand's safety.'

She snorted. 'You tried to blackmail me once before—'

'And you accepted my bargain. I remember that at the time you were quite ready to betray the Scarlet Pimpernel to me.'

Charles and Eleanor exchanged shocked glances. 'From his perspective, no doubt,' Charles whispered in her ear.

'Yes, I remember precisely what happened,' Lady Marguerite said, her tone needle-sharp. 'Tell me, just how many times has the Pimpernel slipped through your fingers? What do your superiors have to say about that?'

'Did you know,' Chauvelin said lazily, and Eleanor could almost imagine his thin-lipped smile, 'that your brother has fallen in love?'

'It is quite possible,' Lady Marguerite said. 'He's a young man. I have observed that young men frequently commit such follies.' Yet behind the casual tone of her voice, Eleanor could sense wariness.

'Sadly true,' Chauvelin allowed. 'His latest passion, then, is for Jeanne Lange. She is an actress at the Comédie-Française – after your time, I fear. They call her the brightest star in the world of art in Paris. She is only twenty,' he added, as though it was an afterthought.

'And?'

'She has been . . . unwise, I fear. Doubly unwise, in not only nurturing counter-revolutionary thoughts, but expressing them in letters which have come into my hands. And which also implicate your dear brother. You must know, Lady Blakeney, how dangerous Paris is these days.'

For a moment there was silence in the box next door, coinciding with a moment of silence on the stage. Eleanor's hand tightened on Charles's arm, and the whole theatre was still, holding its breath.

Then the orchestra struck up again as Zeus descended onto the stage on the end of a rope, and Lady Marguerite said flatly, 'What do you want?'

'I? I want so many things, madame. But out of a possibly misguided, generous impulse, I thought that I would give you – now what *is* the term? Ah, yes. The first refusal.'

'Pray explain yourself more clearly.' Eleanor could almost sense the way that Lady Marguerite's hand would be clenched on her fan.

'Was it not simple enough for the premier wit of Paris? I do apologize. I will permit you, madame, to make me an offer for the letters. If this offer fails to satisfy me, then I will return to Paris and bargain with your brother Armand instead. I have no doubt *he* will be willing to come to terms.'

Eleanor knew nothing about Lady Marguerite's brother Armand, but the way that Chauvelin was dangling the offer like bait above a fish's mouth suggested that Armand could be expected to react . . . unwisely.

'The devil,' Charles whispered. 'The cruel, smiling devil. Surely he can't expect her to trust him . . .'

He fell silent as Lady Marguerite spoke again. 'The fact that you've come crawling to me about this first, Citizen Chauvelin, indicates that there's something in particular you want from me. Pray tell me what it is – I've never been good at guessing games.'

'I would be interested in your husband's current where-abouts, and what he's up to,' Chauvelin replied smoothly. 'Since the Dauphin's kidnapping last year—'

'His rescue,' she contradicted him.

'His cage in Austria is just as much a cage as the Temple prison in Paris was, though I'll allow that it may be far more gilded,' Chauvelin said. 'In any case, it has made the

Pimpernel even more sought after than he was before. You could make your life and that of your brother a great deal easier and safer, in return for a mere few words . . .'

There was no answer. After a moment, he sighed. 'It seems you are as obstinate as ever, madame.'

'And it seems you bargain like a Paris fishwife, Citizen Chauvelin. First you ask me for a price I cannot—'

'Will not,' he corrected her.

'*Cannot* give,' she went on. 'Tell me what you *actually* have in mind, and perhaps I will listen. Otherwise you may as well leave me to this pathetic opera. The principals may be an offence to the ears, but even so I find them less wearying than your society.'

Another pause, and Eleanor and Charles pressed themselves even closer to the panelling, unwilling to miss a single word.

'There is another matter which interests me,' Chauvelin said slowly. 'I – we – have reason to believe that there is a conspiracy afoot in Paris, consisting largely of certain vampires who have managed to avoid arrest and execution. These blood-drinkers are conniving with some of their fellows who have escaped here to England. Bring me information about their plans, and I will be . . . grateful.'

Lady Marguerite snorted. 'Have you any idea how many refugees from the guillotine who've found shelter here plot vengeance against the Committee? There were probably a dozen of them at the very reception we left earlier.'

'The ones in whom I take an interest refer to the "Prince of Paris", and their plans involve Monsieur Talleyrand. You now know almost as much as I do.'

'The Prince of Paris?' Lady Marguerite sounded genuinely surprised. 'What sort of title is that? It wouldn't even be appropriate for the Dauphin. As for Monsieur Talleyrand, the last I heard he was on his way to America.'

'Nevertheless,' Chauvelin said thinly, 'that is all the information I have.'

Chair legs scraped against the ground. 'Are you leaving so soon?' Lady Marguerite asked.

'I have other calls to make before I return to the Embassy. Till later . . . citizen.'

The box door creaked open, then paused, whining on its hinges. 'Oh, one final word. I will be asking other people for information, as I'm sure you appreciate. If one of them can help me – why, I will have no further need of information from *you*, or your brother, and will dispose of Citizen Lange's letters in whatever way I consider most convenient. Do I make myself clear?'

'Very clear, Citizen Chauvelin,' Lady Marguerite replied, and she didn't trouble herself to conceal the detestation in her voice.

The door clicked shut, and footsteps ticked away down the corridor. After a moment Lady Marguerite spoke again. 'Follow him.'

'I'll go. You should join milady, m'dear,' Charles said, pressing Eleanor's hand. 'I'll be back with you as soon as I may.' He opened the door a fraction, peering through, and slipped out into the corridor, making for the stairs down to the foyer.

Eleanor was about to do as he'd directed, and her hand was actually on the door to Lady Marguerite's box when a worrying realization struck her. *Chauvelin is not stupid – nor does he expect milady to be stupid. He was aware she was making herself available for a meeting. He said as much. What if he expected someone else to be present, and to try to follow him? Could Charles be walking into a trap?*

Her heart leapt into her mouth. She hurried for the stairs, aware that Charles was a few crucial seconds ahead of her, yet hoping she could somehow catch up to him without alerting Chauvelin. A thread of caution made her pull up the hood of her cloak to hide her face. Chauvelin knew what she looked like, and if he saw her, then . . . well, she wasn't sure what might happen, but it wouldn't improve the situation.

She ran through the empty foyer and out into the street, pausing on the steps to look round for Charles. The crowd was thick – London was busy even at this time of night. Under the harsh glare of the lanterns which dangled from the lamp posts, the street was a moving sea of men and women, rich silk and brocade contrasted with tattered coats and cheap rags. This was no place for a woman on her own; she'd be assumed to be one of the whores touting for trade.

Then, over to one side, she caught sight of Charles's hat, its high crown catching a momentary gleam of light. He was moving briskly, heading east along the main street. And pushing through the crowd close behind him was someone else – a man, not clearly visible, but his path evident through the reactions of the people around him.

Eleanor took a deep breath, pulled her cloak tight around her, and dived into the crowd after them.

CHAPTER SIX

The crowd buffeted Eleanor from all directions, making it impossible to follow a direct path. She had to slip through wherever she could, her eyes fixed on Charles's fashionable hat. So far he was still moving in a straight line, northwards, but she had no idea what lay in that direction or what she'd do if he turned a corner and she lost sight of him.

This hadn't been one of her better ideas. As she elbowed someone who'd tried to slip a hand into her cloak, and forced her way past a vigorous dispute over a dog fight, she couldn't help wondering just how much use she'd be if Charles *was* in trouble. If Chauvelin had arranged for his own men to waylay attempted pursuers, what would she be able to *do*?

She gritted her teeth. Well, if all else failed, she could always scream her head off and draw attention. Spies never liked attention. Of course, that depended on Chauvelin, Charles, and everyone trailing behind them – like Eleanor herself – staying in the safer areas of London, rather than the unlit back alleys. At night. Where nobody would come to help if they heard screams, and where any attention they might draw would be strictly that of curs hoping to pick over the wreckage. Her own recent experience was proof of that.

A well-bred couple clove their way through the throng on the pavement, the woman's gloved hand on his velvet-sleeved arm, and the resultant wave of shoving and edging nearly knocked Eleanor into the gutter. Bare inches from her face, a hackney carriage drove past. The street was too crowded for it to be going fast, but it still outpaced the pedestrians, and the horse snorted and tossed its head as though in mockery of Eleanor's efforts.

Eleanor had every reason to be angry and frightened. Yet why was she feeling so . . . terrified? She looked from side to side for a moment, trying to determine what had rattled her. She couldn't see anything out of place – at least, nothing more than one might expect from a crowded street in London at night. A couple of men called out to her, taking her glance as an invitation and offering a drink or demanding her price, but that was normal enough for any city, English or French. So what was wrong?

Don't look, Anima said sharply. *Listen.*

Then she heard it. The noise was coming from somewhere ahead of her, vaguely north-west. It was mostly drowned out by the hubbub of a busy street, but still perceptible, and rising with every passing minute. The sound of angry men and women, the stamping of feet, the pulse of shouted demands, the hot and heady throb of fury becoming vocal and released to indulge itself. She'd heard it before, in France, when men and women were being dragged to the guillotine; when the mob was demanding blood and calling it justice.

But what was it doing in England?

Get off the street, Anima said urgently. *Go back to the theatre or take shelter somewhere. You don't have your League with you this time – you should find a safe place.*

The noise was much louder now, audible over the normal racket of the London street, and people were turning to each other in confusion. There were shouts of 'Bread! Bread for the people!' and 'Down with Pitt!'; 'Kill all the vampires!' and 'Cursed Whig republicans!' and other yelling which blended into an incoherent fog of noise.

Charles's hat – the only thing she could see of him – had paused, as though he was taking stock of something he could see but she couldn't. Then it turned, reversing course, rapidly retreating from the oncoming mob.

Eleanor knew that the Scarlet Pimpernel, Sir Percy Blakeney himself, would have met the mob courageously, and probably even have infiltrated it to gather information while masquerading as one of the crowd, but she wasn't the Pimpernel. She was a woman on her own, and right now her common sense, as well as Anima, was telling her to get away from here.

That was why she was backing into a side alley when it happened. She couldn't see exactly what was going on – lanterns threw streaks of light across the churning crowd – but she heard the sudden surge like the breaking of a wave. The mob had turned into the street. The people currently there flowed backwards, like the regurgitation of a sewer swelled by a spring tide, flooding up through all its drains. Horses neighed and stamped as their drivers tried to keep them steady, or to guide them out of danger, and fist-fights broke out in all directions. There was no hope of trying to keep sight of Charles in this confusion; it was all she could do to keep from panicking and running herself.

Another woman collided with her, and as the two of them lurched against the wall Eleanor felt the woman's hand groping for her purse. She grabbed the woman's wrist with one hand and slapped her across the face with the other, shoving her back and into the swell of people. For a moment the woman's face seemed to float in the darkness, a painted mask of powder and rouge, and then she was gone, swallowed up in the yelling mass.

78

'Down with Pitt!' someone screamed. 'Warmonger! Villain! Profiteer! He steals bread from our mouths and sends our men to France as soldiers while we starve!'

Eleanor pressed herself back against the wall, almost trying not to breathe, hoping to go unnoticed. No constables would be foolish enough to venture into the centre of this. They'd end up in the gutters or dangling from the lamp posts. The best she could do was keep herself safe until it was over, and hope that Charles had done the same. Chauvelin would have to wait, as would his spy . . .

Then, through the halos of light and darkness, she recognized a face, one she knew from France. Desgas. Chauvelin's secretary. He was a rabbity little man, with small sharp eyes that were currently wide with panic, as he struggled between two large men who were knocking him around in a playful way, like idle cats with a mouse, demanding that he tell them something. It wasn't clear what they wanted him to tell them, but it was obvious he was panicking. The swirling of the crowd had brought them near her, close enough for her to see and hear. But most importantly, she could see that his coat matched the one that the man following Charles had been wearing. *He* was Chauvelin's spy.

Her first thought was, *Serve him right,* but her second was, *He knows something, and I want to know what it is.*

Not allowing herself time to reconsider, Eleanor darted out from shelter and shoved through the crowd to reach Desgas. She caught him by the shoulder and pulled him towards her just as one of the men had been about to hit him again. 'Leave my brother alone!' she screamed at them.

She could almost track the slow progress of thought across the man's face. He was drunk enough that it took him several seconds to remember exactly what a brother *was.* His expression settled into a nightmarish smirk. 'Give us a kiss, love,' he slurred, reaching for her.

'Look!' she said, pointing over his shoulder as she backed away, dragging Desgas with her. 'The Bow Street Runners!'

He turned to see, far more interested by the prospect of another brawl than by a woman, and Eleanor managed to back away, Desgas in tow. He was wiping blood from his face – a nosebleed, nothing more, though no doubt it was painful – and had enough sense to go along with her, the person saving him, without pausing to ask who was doing this and why.

Then he *did* see her clearly, and stiffened, arm going rigid in her grasp. Even with her hair its natural flaxen colour rather than the light brown it had been a few months ago, he recognized her. 'Anne Dupont,' he snarled.

'The same,' Eleanor replied. That was the alias she'd been using when they'd first met, posing as a French peasant, and she certainly wasn't going to correct him if he didn't already know better. 'Here, by the wall . . .' She tugged him towards the niche where she'd been sheltering. 'We can wait until the mob has passed.'

Desgas tolerated her direction, though she could feel him drawing away from her touch as though she was contaminated. The niche forced them to stand as close as cousins, but every line of his body spoke of his distrust and dislike. 'Are you English, then?' he demanded. 'You know that you look like—'

'The late Queen of France, yes.' There seemed little point denying it now. 'But since she's dead, I don't imagine anyone will be confusing me with her in the near future.'

'Dead? I suppose you could call her that. Certainly the vampire which now prowls the streets of Paris is no longer a living woman.'

'She's still . . .' Eleanor hesitated, trying to think of the right words. She'd seen Marie Antoinette as a vampire – had fled from her, pursued into the River Seine and out onto its

banks, and had almost died at her hands. When a patrol of
the Revolutionary Guard had fired at the vampire, and she'd
fallen back into the river, Eleanor had assumed that was the
end of her. Apparently not.

Desgas gave a brief nod, and she guessed that Chauvelin
would be receiving a full report later. 'Amateurs,' he sneered,
glancing at the crowd. He wisely kept to English, though his
speech had a betraying French accent. This was no time or
place to indicate that he was from an enemy nation with
whom England was at war. 'All show and no substance.'

'I suppose if this had been Paris, you'd already have a
dozen aristocrats dangling from the lamp posts,' Eleanor
answered.

'These days it's harder to find the aristocrats,' Desgas said.
'But that doesn't stop us from looking.'

Eleanor shrugged. 'This is England, Citizen Desgas. They
have yet to build guillotines over here.'

'And what are *you* doing here?' He glanced meaningfully
down the street towards the theatre. 'Are you working for
Lady Blakeney now?'

Chauvelin might know that Sir Percy was the Scarlet
Pimpernel . . . but his subordinate probably didn't. Even if
Desgas was a loyal secretary, that didn't mean Chauvelin
shared everything with him – particularly when it was a
piece of knowledge which made Chauvelin indispensable to
his own superiors. 'Perhaps I have a reason to be watching
her,' Eleanor parried. 'She has some very important visitors
these days, doesn't she?'

'Working for the sanguinocrats, then,' Desgas said with
disgust, using one of the French insults for vampire aristocrats. 'Feeding them your blood, no doubt. A woman who'd
sell her body will sell anything.'

'Some of us haven't always had a choice about our lives,'
Eleanor said coldly. Blood for money was a simple enough

transaction. Thousands of servants did it. It didn't entitle him to treat her like a whore. 'Have you condemned every peasant in France who ever opened a vein for their superiors?'

'Only if they're still doing it.' His eyes, in the lantern-light, were flat and cold and utterly judgemental.

A scream rang out from somewhere in the mob beyond. It was a frightened one, panicking, rather than the sort of cheerful drunken cry that Eleanor had heard earlier. Things were turning nasty. She could hear glass being smashed, and smell smoke. Something was on fire. Many things were on fire.

'Are you going to try to convince me that I should be grateful to you for saving me from those men?' Desgas asked.

Eleanor sighed. 'What would the point be? I'll be honest with you, citizen. It was a spur-of-the-moment reaction. I didn't want to see someone I knew knocked around like that in front of me. Blame a woman's sentimental nature.'

'Because I can assure you that I feel no debt towards you whatever,' he went on, as though she hadn't spoken. 'If I saw you in Paris in the middle of a mob, I certainly wouldn't pull you out of it.'

'Thank you for your charming sentiments,' Eleanor retorted. So much for any sort of gratitude – even the most pathetic, debased, self-justifying sort. 'I thought no better of you, and I'm unsurprised to see that I'm correct. However, if you have any sense, you'll endure my company a little longer. The streets aren't safe tonight, and this street particularly so.'

'Kill all the French spies!' someone shouted, on cue. 'The vampires, the revolutionaries, the alien scum!'

'Revolutionaries are *not* vampires,' Desgas hissed, affronted.

'You're welcome to go out there and explain his errors to him in person,' Eleanor said. 'Or blame the British press, if you will. There's a lot going on that doesn't seem to be mentioned in the newspapers.'

For some reason that made Desgas pause. 'You admit that the British public's view of things may not be entirely accurate?'

'No more than the French public's view of things.' Eleanor shrugged. 'I've become a cynic, citizen. Both sides control what gets printed.'

'Then why do you give your loyalty to this country, a place which never gave you a choice about your life, and never *will*?' He gestured angrily. 'There are Englishmen who've seen the light of reason, who recognize the truth of what France has done . . .'

'You killed your king!' Eleanor interrupted. 'How can any nation who's done something like *that* hope to be accepted?'

'Louis Capet was a fool, a traitor, and an enemy of France,' Desgas said flatly. 'Merely being born into a position doesn't make a man fit to occupy it. France has demonstrated that it does not need kings. Other nations will follow. And you have little room to sneer at me – didn't your own king face the scaffold a hundred and fifty years ago?' A smirk stole across his face. 'But I suppose having a madman for a king proves that one isn't necessary to a country's good functioning. Perhaps I can agree that England's progressing.'

Eleanor's hand itched to slap him, but she restrained herself. 'His Majesty's doing very well, thank you!' She'd heard the rumours that King George had been . . . unstable, but that had been years ago.

'For the moment,' Desgas said, clearly pleased to have got a rise out of her. 'I wonder how long it'll last?'

Eleanor didn't want to give him the satisfaction of losing her temper any further. She turned to assess the crowd instead. 'I think we might be able to edge our way out of here in a few minutes; they're moving south.'

Desgas nodded. 'And then what? You'll try to follow me across London?'

'Good god, no!' Eleanor exclaimed. 'I'm not that reckless. Besides, you'd be watching for me now, wouldn't you?'

'Of course.' He appeared to be meditating something. 'Tell me, what is your relationship with Lady Blakeney? Do you have any sort of influence over her? It's clear enough that there's something between you, with my master meeting her here and you loitering nearby.'

'Very little,' Eleanor said. She was quite sure that if Lady Marguerite had a strong desire to do something, Eleanor's influence would be worth about as much as a few grains of sand in the balance. Any woman who'd made a career for herself as the star in the world of Paris theatre, been a crowning light in society, and involved herself in the League no doubt had a will which could cut diamonds. Cautiously she added, 'Though she might listen to me if I had some actual information for her, rather than just threats or warnings.'

'This is worth listening to.' Desgas drew Eleanor closer. 'Tell her to cooperate with Citizen Chauvelin – for everyone's sake.'

Eleanor looked into his cold eyes, and saw sincerity. It might be a sincerity which would gladly send Eleanor to the guillotine, but that didn't mean it was a lie. 'It'll make it easier for me to offer her that advice if I have a reason to give her along with it.'

He chewed his lower lip for a moment. 'Citizen Chauvelin has to satisfy the orders of his superiors – not just for his own sake, but for his daughter's. You remember her?'

Eleanor blinked. 'Yes. I remember Fleurette.' The one soft spot in Chauvelin's heart, and the one weak point in his armour. Sweet, sincere, honest, and all too vulnerable in this time of revolution. 'Is she . . . safe?'

'It's good to see you can feel *some* guilt,' Desgas said sourly.

'She's been taken into protective custody, like a number of other relatives of important men. They're kept at the old abbey at Mont-Michel . . . for their own safety.' His gaze dared her to call it anything else, such as official kidnapping to force obedience from the people who loved them. 'If the Citizen succeeds in his current work, she'll probably be released.'

Eleanor did indeed experience a pang of guilt, like a rough needle working its way in and catching on every sensitive feeling. Chauvelin had tried to use his daughter to persuade Eleanor to betray the League, but Eleanor herself had brought the League to Chauvelin's door and put Fleurette in danger. Fleurette was a sincere believer in France, the Republic and the new laws, but that wouldn't save her if she was suspected of treason. 'I hear you,' she began carefully, 'but—'

'You may hear me, but you don't *understand*,' Desgas snarled. 'Citizen Chauvelin will do anything to keep her safe – no matter what the consequences may be to others. If you want to help Lady Blakeney, then you'll give him what he wants. Citizen Chauvelin has very little patience at the moment, and though he may have shown you some of the cards in his hand, believe me, *he has more*. Have I convinced you?'

'You have,' Eleanor said slowly. Chauvelin operating under normal circumstances was a deadly threat. Chauvelin turned vicious and desperate to save his daughter might do anything. Desgas himself could also be just a pawn to be sacrificed in a battle of this kind. Was that why he was passing the information on to her? In the hopes of saving his own skin, as well as Chauvelin's? Lady Marguerite had to be warned, though, and so did the rest of the League. 'We should go.'

'Stay out of my way in future,' Desgas said coldly. 'I'm not interested in seeing you again.'

'Believe me, that makes two of us,' Eleanor answered. Out

of habit, she tried querying the mage's ghost – she'd been more silent than usual over the last couple of weeks, but maybe she'd have some useful opinion to offer. *Anima? Do you think he was speaking the truth?*

But Anima didn't answer.

CHAPTER SEVEN

Eleanor was in disgrace.

Nobody was feeling overly charitable towards her. Lady Marguerite blamed her for not accompanying Charles properly, staying with him; Charles accused her of throwing herself into danger by not staying with Lady Marguerite; Mr Sturn, the butler, was unimpressed by her late return from leave; the other maids were angry that her behaviour had endangered their general liberty (misbehaviour by one implying misbehaviour by all, after all); and even Andrew felt that she had, as he put it, 'risked herself unduly'.

And for some reason Anima had fallen entirely silent at the back of Eleanor's mind, so she didn't even have the opportunity to complain to the ghost about everyone's unfair judgements. It would almost have been an improvement if Anima had been present to complain as well. At least then Eleanor could have argued back and had a target for her temper, rather than having to bite her tongue and apologize to everyone.

If I'd been one of the men in the League then I wouldn't be in so much trouble, she thought bitterly as she scrubbed the floor. Usually that was someone else's job, but today it was all hers. *I'd probably have been commended for my initiative and for managing to bring back valuable information. I wouldn't have been told that I was foolish, or careless, or reckless, or that they'd thought better of me.* Those comments from Charles had really hurt. She'd been trying to help.

But – the cold thought stole into her mind like filth spreading in a bowl of water – this was her future. She depended on the Blakeneys for employment, unless she was forced to go back to Lady Sophie and depend on her instead. Any attempt to find another job would mean begging for a good reference – after all, who'd employ a woman without one? And while she might be a trusted member of the League – well, a member of the League, at least – she didn't have the money, social rank or independence that all the men did. She had to live with the responsibilities and duties of a housemaid, and she couldn't even explain it to any of the other maids. Anima was the only person she could talk to honestly . . . and even then, Eleanor knew that Anima thought she was just a stupid little servant who went around risking her life for foolish reasons, and would probably end up in an early grave from scrubbing floors. If she wasn't guillotined first.

Bitter thoughts whirled through her mind like a spinning top, more painful with every revolution. It wasn't *fair*. Tears stung her eyes.

Her only consolation was that at least it wasn't washing-day today, or for another week. If so, she would certainly have spent all day doing scut-work for the laundry-maids: washing, rinsing, wringing, hanging out to dry, and all the other tasks that gravitated to the bottom of the household. In comparison with that, the floors were almost bearable.

Eleanor heard feet approaching – a woman running, the quick slap of a maid's shoes rather than the softer sound of milady's slippers. She sat back on her feet, dropping the cloth into the tub. To her surprise, it was Alice who entered the room.

'Is something the matter?' Eleanor asked nervously.

For a moment Alice just looked down at her, arms folded angrily. She was twenty years older than Eleanor, though the grey in her hair barely showed, yet at this precise moment Eleanor could feel every one of those years as an additional note of disapproval. 'I did *tell* you,' she said, though not as angrily as Eleanor had feared. 'I did *warn* you to keep yourself careful and your nose clean.'

'It all seemed like a good idea at the time,' Eleanor offered, not expecting it to do much good.

'Which bit of it?'

It wasn't clear exactly what Alice was referring to, and Eleanor was afraid that giving the wrong answer might be far too much information. 'Well . . . all the separate parts. At different times. Is Lady Marguerite still angry with me?'

'Forget milady, *I'm* still angry with you,' Alice snapped. 'I thought you had enough sense not to be caught like that!'

Eleanor reshuffled her thinking. 'That wasn't what you were saying to me yesterday.'

'Well, it wouldn't have been, would it? Rebecca was there. I couldn't let her hear anything she shouldn't be hearing.'

But Alice wasn't one of the League, or even aware of it . . . was she? Eleanor took a sharp look at her own judgements, and didn't like what she saw. She'd been making assumptions just as much as she'd accused the men in the League of doing, believing that naturally Alice had no idea about what was going on. Which was not only careless thinking, it was rank stupidity. How could milady's personal maid, the person who was closest to her in the household beside her husband, *not* have noticed anything strange?

She swallowed the unpleasant taste of her own smugness, and simply said, 'I'm sorry. I didn't think and I didn't understand.'

Alice sniffed. 'I'll give you credit for honesty. Not that I suppose you need honesty that much, with what you might be doing.'

'And . . . what do you think I'm doing?' Eleanor tried to interpret Alice's face, but the older woman gave nothing away.

'It's not my business to think about what milady's doing,' Alice said flatly. 'Nor to know or talk about it, especially the last. What *is* my business is taking care of milady, keeping her safe, and making sure she's dressed as she should be. A *proper* household takes care of that sort of thing without anyone having to know or think or talk about what's going on.'

'Then I wish I was a part of this household,' Eleanor said, the words spilling out, 'because you know I'm not. Not in *that* way.' She had far too many secrets for that.

Alice sighed. She bent down and picked up the basin and cloth. 'True enough. Milord does as he will do, and maybe it's for the best, but I'm not saying it's always the right thing. And you and I know there's a difference between the two. Now I've come here to tell you you're to go up to milady; she's in her study at the moment, with Sir Andrew, Lord Anthony and Lord Charles. When you're done, come on down to the kitchen and tell them you've been tidying the boxroom on my orders. Unless milady gives you something *else* to do, that is.'

'Such as?' Eleanor asked, hoping she could push this limited understanding a little further.

'How should I know?' Alice sniffed again. 'Like I said, it's not my place to think about it or know about it. Milady's business is her business. Now get a move on. She'll be waiting.'

Eleanor scuttled up the back stairs and scraped on the study door to be let in. When she stepped inside there was a deathly silence, which suggested an argument had been in progress a few seconds before. Pages of the newspaper were strewn across the table, the modern newsprint grimy against the polished beechwood.

'Ah, Eleanor!' Andrew said, with a good attempt at cheerfulness. 'What are you doing here?' He and the other two men weren't in high fashion this morning, but in more casual clothing: buckskin breeches rather than satin or velvet ones, and cravats more like normal wear than white muslin fortifications for the neck. Though their boots were perfectly polished, of course.

Eleanor blinked. 'I was told milady wanted to see me, sir.'

Andrew gave Lady Marguerite a sidelong glance. 'I thought we'd agreed—'

Lady Marguerite impatiently gestured for Eleanor to sit down on a spare footstool. She was dressed, for her, positively primly, as though the neatly styled blue muslin was an armour against the world. 'Either Eleanor is a member of this League – which my husband said she *was* – or she isn't. And if she *is*, then her thoughts may be useful. We've already had enough reproaches this morning. Let us consider how to fight back. What can we actively *do* from here? Tony? Andrew? Charles?'

Tony – Lord Anthony Dewsbury – sat perched on the edge of his chair as though ready to launch himself into action, his amiable face firmly set in lines of determination. Charles was seated at Lady Marguerite's desk, going through a sheaf of papers. Given that they were in private, he was wearing his brass-rimmed eye-glasses balanced on the end of his nose. Both of them turned to Andrew for his opinion.

Andrew gave Lady Marguerite another sidelong glance. 'We did consider burgling Chauvelin's lodgings while he was here – take out those letters he claims to have and his leverage in one fell swoop, so to speak. But he's probably considered the possibility of that himself. After all, he knows that we know that he knows who we are.'

Lady Marguerite nodded reluctantly. 'Yes, he will expect me to have told you.'

'But on the wider problem of this conspiracy Chauvelin is investigating, from what he said we can assume the disappearance of Talleyrand is connected. And regarding that, I've had word from Everingham. The *William Penn* sailed from Portsmouth on schedule, and apparently Talleyrand was on it. But—'

'But?' Lady Marguerite enquired.

'There was some sort of confusion about the fellow's embarkation,' Andrew said slowly. 'Turned up on the dock at the last minute, just before sailing, so wrapped up in a coat and scarves that you'd think a single breath of fresh air would blow him away. Claimed he had a rheumatic fever and that he desired to be left to frowst in the warmth of his cabin once he was aboard. He had a manservant with him, of course, but Everingham told me that one of his men had been on the dock that day, and it was a *different* manservant.' He paused, sorting through his words. 'That is, not the lackey he'd seen Talleyrand with before. Who has also vanished, inasmuch as can be traced. Though given that everyone thought he was on the *William Penn*, they didn't try very hard.' Besides, he didn't bother adding, the fellow was just a manservant, and of no real importance to the League.

Eleanor tried to get all this straight in her head. 'You think he was replaced by an impostor on the dock at the last minute?'

Andrew nodded. 'I can certainly see how it could have been done. The Chief's managed similar last-minute exchanges himself.'

'But then what happens if the impostor is found out halfway to America?'

Tony reached over to pat her hand reassuringly. 'Don't

fret. I'm sure they wouldn't toss him overboard into the Atlantic. Likely they'll just put him ashore at the other end.'

That wasn't exactly what Eleanor had meant, but it wasn't worth arguing. Tony was the sort of generous-hearted person who *would* think the best of everyone – much like Fleurette, really, except more prone to hunting, shooting, fishing and rescuing aristocrats from the guillotine. Instead she nodded, and turned back to Sir Andrew. 'So Talleyrand could still be here in England, if the Chief has found no trace of him in France either?'

Andrew and Lady Marguerite both nodded. 'But as yet,' Lady Marguerite said, 'we have no idea why.'

'And who is this Prince of Paris Chauvelin mentioned?' Charles added. 'Could it all have something to do with the Church in France?'

'Faith, we'll need to wait a while if we have to work someone into *those* corridors of power!' Tony said. 'Do you suppose the Pope might give us exemptions if we promise to observe Lent and only eat fish on Fridays?'

Lady Marguerite lowered her head for a moment. 'It is my husband's life at stake on the one hand in France,' she said, her voice as edged as a razor, 'and my brother's life on the other. Pray restrain your English sense of humour, my friends, I beg you, and give me something I can work with. I have already spoken with many of my contacts in society, but I fear I am looking in the wrong quarter. If there *is* more information to be gained, then I'm sure it lies amongst the Royalists – and I'm hardly welcome there.'

The question *Why?* hung on Eleanor's lips, but she had the sense to bite it back. Another idea had come to her, triggered by one of the invitations she'd seen the other day when Lady Marguerite went through the contents of her desk. The older woman hadn't seemed overly proud of that particular document, so Eleanor might need to approach the topic very carefully. Hesitantly she said, 'Milady . . . what about the next Victims' Ball?'

There was a combined intake of breath.

Then Charles said, 'What an excellent idea!' He paused mid-enthusiasm, noticing the glares the other two men were giving him. 'Well, it is, isn't it?' he continued less brightly.

Lady Marguerite, on the other hand, was focusing on Eleanor, her eyes glittering like frost. 'Eleanor, my dear, whatever gave you *that* idea?'

Eleanor bit her lip. 'Because I saw the other day that you had an invitation for it. I know it's only for people who escaped the guillotine . . . but if they sent you an invitation, then—'

'They did *not* send me an invitation,' Lady Marguerite corrected her, each word doled out like a piece of ice. 'It was given to me by another person who had no intention of attending and was asking me for advice. I don't know why you're raising the topic, but—'

Eleanor interrupted, going against all rules of courtesy and common sense. 'Milady, even I know about the Victims' Balls, and who attends them! Surely there couldn't be a better place to go for information?'

It was true – from the servants to the impoverished on the streets of London, everyone knew about the gaudy, dramatic, morbid, *tasteless* events which were the Victims' Balls. They were held by members of the French aristocracy who'd avoided the kiss of Madame Guillotine, or who'd lost a relative to the Reign of Terror. Some were living humans, but many of them were vampires. Those attending wore the full clothing of the *ancien régime*, heavy embroidered silk and velvet. The women were usually in low-necked gowns worn over petticoats with panniers and wide skirts, stomachers and trains, while the men's costume might have changed less but was thick with embroidery, decoration and lace.

Alternatively, the guests sometimes came in threadbare black clothing, mocking severity and morbidity alike. Above all, the ball-goers made sure to wear red ribbons tied around their necks – the line that the guillotine had missed.

There were all sorts of stories about the gatherings. The words 'orgiastic debauchery' were thundered from pulpits by red-faced preachers, and the newspapers – the scandal sheets, mostly – were full of gossip and rumours about what went on towards the end of the night. If the public hadn't had more important things to deal with, such as the war with France or the shortages of bread, these balls would no doubt have been even more widely condemned. As it was, the fact that attendees were restricted to refugees from the guillotine together with their guests – and that generally society could believe *anything* of the French – kept them just barely permissible.

Eleanor couldn't understand why Lady Marguerite hadn't thought of trying them before, despite her disdain. In retrospect, perhaps she should have considered that there would be a good reason why milady hadn't . . .

'None of us can attend,' Lady Marguerite said firmly. 'I am distinctly *persona non grata*, and the rest of the League would be outsiders too, even if they could secure an invitation. And you, my dear Eleanor – impossible.' She softened slightly. 'I know that I've trained you in a few airs and graces to mimic the late Queen of France, but you must understand that everyone with a right to be there will know everyone else. Even if we disguised you, dyed your hair, whatever, you still couldn't claim you were the daughter of some dissolute poverty-stricken baron from the provincial middle of nowhere. People would ask how you'd reached England, discuss politics and literature with you, all that manner of thing . . . And I know I'm not an aristocrat myself – by birth, at least – but kindly note that I have *not* been invited. Even without the matter of Saint-Cyr and his family—'

She broke off, clearly having said more than she intended. Yet behind her kind words, Eleanor could hear the bitter truth of something far more overarching and definite. *We may have allowed you into our League, our circle, but you will never truly be one of us.*

'It's still not a bad idea,' Tony said slowly. 'I mean, dash it, there are good reasons why milady and Eleanor can't go, but what about the rest of us? We might be outsiders there, but that doesn't mean we couldn't pick up a few rumours. There has to be a lady in the town with an invitation who could be persuaded to bring one of us along as her cavalier, surely?'

'Who was your one from, milady?' Andrew asked Lady Marguerite. 'Perhaps they can be persuaded?'

'It belonged to your wife, Suzanne,' Lady Marguerite said reluctantly. 'She was asking my advice about it, as an older woman and a lifelong friend. Naturally she knew that you wouldn't want her to go . . .'

'Well, of course,' Andrew agreed firmly. 'Something like that? Certainly not.'

'And you certainly couldn't masquerade as her either, Eleanor,' Lady Marguerite added, 'so don't even consider it.'

True enough. Suzanne Ffoulkes – once Suzanne de Tournay, before she had to flee from France and fell in love with one of her rescuers – was dainty and winsome, with a wealth of dark brown curls. It would take a very dark night for Eleanor (or Lady Marguerite) to pass for her, together with a cloak, a mask, and somehow losing several inches from her height. Then again, Suzanne hadn't come over from France alone . . .

'If she received an invitation, milady, then did the rest of her family?' Eleanor asked.

'Probably,' Lady Marguerite said reluctantly, 'but her parents, the old Comte and Comtesse, would certainly refuse to attend, and would forbid her brother to do so as well. These affairs have an unfortunate reputation.'

Eleanor still thought that it sounded *exactly* where they needed to go. She cudgelled her brains as the others argued, trying to recall anything in the whispered stories and scandals she'd heard which might offer a possible route to their attending. Perhaps she was looking at this the wrong way by considering invitations. Servants needed to be there too, after all – who else would serve the food and drink, pin up torn flounces and fallen hems, and—

'Where's it being held?' Tony asked.

'Cumberland House, on Pall Mall. Eleanor, why are you smirking like that?'

Eleanor quickly smoothed her face over, and reminded herself to be more discreet. 'I was thinking that a number of the people attending must be bringing servants, milady. I could slip in easily enough, and while I may not be able to impersonate a lady of quality, I've been a maid all my life – well, most of it. If Lady Suzanne were to turn up as if she *intended* to attend and then developed a sudden headache and went home, I could gain entry as her maid and investigate!' She realized that she'd shown too much enthusiasm again, but really, why not? This might *work*.

'An excellent idea! And I can accompany my wife,' Andrew said. His face had clouded over when she mentioned Lady Suzanne, but cleared again as soon as it became evident she wouldn't need to do more than step inside before leaving. 'Eleanor, I congratulate you! Who'll notice one more maid there?'

'Wait,' Lady Marguerite said abruptly. 'Eleanor, please tell me that you know about the *other* aspect of these balls?'

Eleanor had the sensation of one foot hovering above a hitherto unsuspected abyss. 'Ah, what other aspect, milady?'

'Vampires attend most society parties, but *these* balls have

97

a higher number of vampire guests than usual. I've been told that the custom is indeed for guests to bring a servant with them, a maid or footman, but those are ones used to giving blood with a lancet or knife, for . . .' Her mouth curled into a tight little moue of disapproval. 'Refreshments.'

Oh. She should have thought of it before, but she'd been months away from Lady Sophie's household, and had grown used to a diurnal schedule, rather than alternating day and night service and living on the whims of someone who depended on her household for blood. A ball full of vampires. Naturally they'd want refreshment.

Eleanor looked down at the faded scars on her forearms, left behind by knife and lancet from where she'd bled for her previous mistress. Once she'd considered it merely part of what she had to do for her wages, but even then she'd never actually been enthusiastic about it, unlike some very young maids. Anima hated all vampires, and had been revolted at the very idea that Eleanor could do such a thing . . . but Anima was still quiet at the moment, asleep or lost in thought, and besides, this was Eleanor's choice.

She could do this one more time. She had to be able to, because certainly none of the League would know how to open a vein and fill a glass in service . . .

'They might not ask me,' she said, her voice firm. 'And even if they do – it's only a little blood. I can do it, milady.'

'This is—' Charles began.

Eleanor raised her hand to cut him off, as haughty as she'd been taught to be when counterfeiting Marie Antoinette. *What had he been about to say? Impossible? Unthinkable? Not going to happen?* 'Charles, I'm not taking this risk lightly, but I beg you to consider, what if there's some critical information to be gained there which could help us track down Talleyrand and aid Sir Percy? How would we feel, if we didn't try our utmost? I'm one of the League. I have the right to take risks too.'

'It's still a risk you shouldn't have to take,' he said firmly. 'You're throwing yourself recklessly into danger, just as you did last night.'

She desperately sought the words to convince him – to convince all of them. 'I admit that may have been a foolish risk. But this isn't. It's a *necessary* risk.'

Lady Marguerite frowned, toying with the lace at her wrist. 'My friends, I have no wish to put *any* of you in danger. But in my husband's absence, we must come to a decision. Eleanor is a full member of the League. We have trusted her with our secrets – can we not also trust her judgement?'

'After last night?' Andrew muttered.

'Be reasonable, old chap,' Tony said abruptly. 'Eleanor was in an impossible situation last night, with milady directing one thing and Charles another. I'm not saying that lingering to have a nice little chat with Chauvelin's secretary was the best idea possible, but it gained us information we wouldn't otherwise have.'

'And gave information to him too,' Andrew said. Then he sighed. 'You're right, Tony, and I'm being unfair to Eleanor. The whole thing's a blasted mess, and I wish we had the Chief with us to cut through all this folderol. When's the ball, milady?'

'Two nights away,' Lady Marguerite answered.

'This *is* an unnecessary risk,' Charles broke in. He removed his eye-glasses, the gesture aggressive, and the sunlight glinted off them as though off a drawn sword. 'You wouldn't send any other woman in there alone to investigate. You wouldn't send your wife, Andrew. It's not fair or just to abandon Eleanor in there to . . . to open her veins for any vampire who's thirsty.'

'Do you have a better idea?' Andrew demanded.

'Yes! One of us can go in disguised as a footman. If something should go wrong . . .'

He broke off, the words hanging in mid-air, the rest of the sentence filling itself in for the listeners. *We could defend ourselves. We could claim that we're nobles and the whole thing is some sort of joke. We could fight our way out.*

Eleanor knew that with Anima's help, she might have a far better chance of escape than any of the men, but she couldn't say that. She rose to her feet. 'Milady, sirs, may I talk to Charles for a moment? In private? While the rest of you keep on planning?'

'What an excellent thought,' Lady Marguerite said quickly. 'You may use my dressing-room next door while the rest of us discuss the details.'

Charles sulked after Eleanor, his shoulders hunched and his head bowed. Once the door was closed behind them and the two of them were alone, he dropped his composure enough to glare at her. 'This is arrant folly!'

'Yes, I know it is,' Eleanor agreed. 'But we don't have any better ideas. Or do you?'

He ran his hand through his hair, spoiling its careful arrangement. 'If you had a younger sister who was going to put herself into this sort of danger, what would you say to her? Consider that carefully, because by God and Heaven above, I'd like to say it to you and make you understand how little I want you to risk yourself this way. Having you alongside us is one thing, but you'll be *alone* in there.'

A shaft of light filtered in through the door to Lady Marguerite's bedroom, standing open on the other side of the room. It glittered on the cosmetic cases and hairbrushes which lay on the dressing-table. Otherwise the two of them were in shadow, hidden from the world and even from the rest of the League.

'You've had me – well, the Chief's had me – sneak into a household or a shop before now while posing as a servant,' Eleanor argued, attempting to ignore the growing sinking feeling in her stomach. If Charles kept on reminding her how dangerous this was, she'd lose her nerve. 'This is the middle of London. They can't just kill me and bury my body in the garden.'

'I understand that Cumberland House has excellent rose gardens,' Charles said darkly. 'And how could we come looking for you? Even if Andrew or Suzanne should ask what happened to their maid, they could say you'd left the house and they'd no idea where you'd gone. *London* isn't safe these days. There are more disappearances than ever before, and with dozens dead after the riot last night . . .'

'Dozens?' Eleanor gasped. It had been frightening and shocking, and she'd heard glass and timber breaking, but she hadn't expected that level of mortality.

Charles nodded soberly, and with just a hint of *I told you so*. 'They're blaming French spies for inciting it. Parliament may have to take steps. Now do you understand why we were so concerned about you?'

Eleanor folded her arms and looked him in the eye. '*You* were on your own in the mob as well. Shouldn't I have been worried about you?'

'That's different,' he said dismissively. 'A woman on her own is in far more danger.'

Eleanor could feel the words pricking her tongue like pins, struggling to get out, to make him understand how *little* he understood, to drive him to feel as guilty as she did . . . yet instead she took a deep breath. Danger lay ahead for both of them. They were *friends*, and both of them were to go into mortal peril – her to this ball, and no doubt him to France soon enough if the Chief needed him, where the smallest slip could mean his execution. How could they be arguing like this?

'I beg you to accept this,' she said, her voice softer. 'I'm not doing it because I want to put myself at undue risk, and

I don't *want* to give my blood to vampires. You once told me that you respected my choices. Please, Charles . . . let us not quarrel. Let us remain friends and support one another. Don't argue with me now when I need all the courage I can muster. If milady could go to this ball, then I'd *let* her go. But apparently she can't,' she ended, a little sourly.

She saw his feelings pass across his face like sunset through a window – the flush of challenged pride, and then the deeper emotion of shame.

'I'm sorry, m'dear,' he said. He turned away to lean against one of the wardrobes which crowded the room, the muscles in his shoulders tensing, then relaxing. 'I fear we are all overstrained by our concerns at the present moment. I have enough friends who are in danger: I would rather not see you added to their number. I accept your choice, but pray do not ask me to like it.' He looked back at her, locking her in his gaze.

Eleanor felt a lump come to her throat, and couldn't meet his eyes. 'I trust you to take good care of yourself as well. Be careful how you go walking by night.' She knew from past experience that while his short sight made his day vision poor, his night vision was even worse.

Charles snorted, a fraction of a chuckle. 'Any other requests, m'dear? More feasible ones?'

'Actually . . . yes.' Anima might be silent, but Eleanor was sure she'd be very vocal when she spoke again, once she knew what Eleanor had agreed to do. This seemed a good moment to find something to mollify her. 'This is going to sound ridiculous, I fear, but do you know anything about vampires doing . . . something significant . . . around the reign of King John?'

Charles turned to blink at her in confusion. 'What a curious question!'

Eleanor had *known* it'd be difficult to explain why she was asking. She fell back on, 'There were some old stories back in the village where I was born, about some sort of war. I know it was before vampires took oath in England not to hold public office or military rank.'

Charles nodded. 'Magna Carta, yes. Now that was signed in 1215, over five centuries ago. All sorts of fighting going on then. It was when England held a number of continental possessions but didn't manage to hold *onto* them, if you take my meaning. Lost Normandy, lost Aquitaine – that was where your namesake came from, Eleanor of Aquitaine – all muddled up by the Crusades, too. Britain lost Brittany and the Auvergne as well, and there was the Albigensian Crusade against the Cathars.' He saw her look of confusion. 'I'll tell you about that one later. Poor chaps, probably not their fault. Anyhow, it ends up with the French against the English and Flemish and German, and the French win at Bouvines and conquer Flanders, and then John signs Magna Carta in England the next year. His barons were all against him after his losses in France. The year after that France invades England and . . .' He shrugged. 'There's a deuce of a lot of things going on then, Eleanor, and from what I've heard, vampires were fighting on all the sides, and it went on for a good hundred years. Though if there's some manner of folk tale back in the village you come from, I have a few old friends who'd probably like to hear the rest of it. Maybe when this is over?'

'Perhaps,' Eleanor agreed. It didn't sound promising, though. She hadn't expected there to be so *much* history to sift through. 'And nothing about . . . magic?'

'Ah, the witch hunts!' Charles frowned. 'I fear those stories would only give you nightmares.'

'Worse than the Revolutionary courts and the guillotine?'

'Mm,' Charles said. 'Well, perhaps not. Even so, I'm not sure how it would apply. I could write to some of my friends at Oxford?'

'It's nothing significant,' Eleanor said hastily. Anima had drummed the need for secrecy into her. 'Just a thought. Thank you for answering my idle curiosity.'

Though, it struck her, perhaps it would be quite simple to hide one war under cover of another. Who would notice more deaths in a conflict that lasted a hundred years? She'd never really considered it before, but any wars must be so *convenient* for vampires who didn't obey the laws of man and society . . .

CHAPTER EIGHT

Outside the coach, Eleanor could hear the sounds of London by night in the fashionable quarter of Pall Mall. There were no shouts from rioters this time, or yells and breaking glass. Instead there was the ripple of hoofbeats, the calls of coachmen to each other, and a gentle throb of conversation and footsteps. One couldn't escape the smells of London, though, even here; a waft of horse dung mingled with the stink of lamp oil and burning torches, and the perfumes of those who could afford them drifted through the streets like passing ghosts.

Opposite her in the back of the carriage, Suzanne fussed with her hair in the light from the lamps mounted on the coach walls. Sir Andrew was up at the front, not willing to let any groom drive his horses if he had a choice in the matter, but Suzanne was delicate enough – in his opinion, at least – that he'd chosen to bring her in a closed carriage rather than an open curricle. Eleanor wasn't objecting. The end-of-April air had turned cold and she was grateful for the shelter from the wind.

'Do I look as I should?' Suzanne asked, not for the first time. 'I won't disgrace my Andrew?'

'You look lovely, milady,' Eleanor reassured her. It was

entirely true. Normally Suzanne was a very pretty young woman, with tumbling dark brown curls and a rosy complexion, as dainty as a porcelain shepherdess but far more alive and vivid. As she was now, with her hair powdered and styled elegantly high, and in the heavy embroidered satins of ten years ago, she looked as if she could have stepped out of a painting, or come straight from the court of the King of France. The deep green gown had been made over from Lady Blakeney's own clothing, and Eleanor herself had spent a while sewing it. While the de Tournays had managed to retain a few valuables during their headlong escape from France, they hadn't been able to bring their wardrobe with them.

Of course, the King of France was dead now, and most of his court with him, and all their clothing remade or gone to rags . . .

Eleanor had dyed her own hair to a moderate brown and applied a few touches of disguising paint and powder to her face. This was possibly the one part of London which would be full of people who'd know what Marie Antoinette looked like and might question why a maid bore too close a resemblance to her. There was no need to attract unnecessary attention.

The carriage came to a stop, and a few heartbeats later Andrew flung the door open, offering his hand to Suzanne to step down. Conveniently for him, the style for men had changed less. While there might be a difference of an inch or two here or there, his elegant coat and breeches were still entirely appropriate. He didn't wear a red ribbon around his throat as Suzanne did, even though, to Eleanor's knowledge, he'd probably earned the right to wear it several times over, given how often he'd escaped capture and the guillotine.

Eleanor scrambled down out of the carriage as tidily as she could, and stood a couple of demure paces behind Suzanne, taking the opportunity to look around. Cumberland

House was *big* – it stretched for dozens of yards down the street, bay windows protruding at regular intervals like fortifications. The entrance they stood in front of was gleaming marble, and the pavement they stood on was actually *clean*. She waited as Andrew nodded to his groom, a signal to return with the carriage in an hour, then followed the aristocratic couple inside.

'Sir Andrew and Lady Ffoulkes,' Sir Andrew said, presenting the invitation to the major-domo who'd stepped forward to meet him. He patted Suzanne's hand where it lay on his arm.

The major-domo didn't need to do more than glance at the writing on the card. Naturally someone in his position would know all the relevant names, and relationships, of the invited guests, and wouldn't require a formal statement that Lady Ffoulkes was originally Suzanne de Tournay. 'The party is directly ahead, milord,' he intoned, 'up the main staircase.' His gaze flicked to Eleanor, where she stood in her plain muslin gown and shawl. 'And this is . . .'

'My wife understood that under the circumstances, it was required to bring a servant,' Sir Andrew said. He didn't trouble himself to look at Eleanor, which was exactly as it should be.

'Of course,' the major-domo said. Did he sound . . . pleased? Satisfied? Eleanor wasn't entirely sure of the undertones to his voice, but they left her feeling uncomfortable. 'To the right and the second door, girl, and someone will tell you what to do.'

Eleanor bobbed a curtsey and obeyed. She cast a look back and saw Suzanne sparkling with enthusiasm as she ascended the stairs, a smile touching her lips at the bright sound of music. The young woman was a very good actress – or perhaps she was just enjoying this taste of 'proper' clothing and a chance to dance. And while she might not have admitted it to her parents or husband, the illicit and forbidden was always intriguing . . .

The room that Eleanor walked into was as well appointed as the others she'd seen so far, with plush carpets and dark crimson wallpaper, but instead of being full of expensively dressed guests, it was crowded with people dressed like *her*. A row of a dozen men and women sat around a long table, but it was cheap wood, out of place with the rest of the fixtures, and the benches they sat on were similar basic stuff. They all had ribbons with different colours looped around their necks, and lancets and scalpels were set out in front of them on varnished trays. All of them had their sleeves rolled back or pushed up, and some of them already had bandages marking fresh cuts. There was a harsh tang of cheap gin to the air. The seated servants had been murmuring quietly to each other, but they fell silent as Eleanor entered, their eyes on her.

A tall, thin woman with the authoritative air of a housekeeper caught Eleanor by the shoulder. 'Are you here to provide blood, girl?'

'Yes, ma'am,' Eleanor replied, dropping an automatic curtsey. She knew how to deal with housekeepers. 'I was told to come along here.'

'Good, good.' The harsh grasp on Eleanor's shoulder turned into a semi-approving pat. 'Who is your master or mistress? And what's your name?'

'Lord and Lady Ffoulkes, ma'am, and my name's Nellie.'

The housekeeper turned back the muslin drapes of Eleanor's sleeves to examine her inner forearms, and her thin lips curved into a relieved smile. 'Ah good, you know your business. We won't need to show you what to do. Now tell me, are you married?'

'No, ma'am,' Eleanor replied, wondering why that question had been asked.

Elusive

The housekeeper rolled her eyes and glanced over her shoulder to the footman who'd been assembling a tray of implements. 'I *told* her ladyship that we'd never be able to find out by asking that question – the good girls won't discuss it and the sluts won't admit to it. But oh no, she wants to offer proper virgin blood to the guests. Thank goodness this is the last ball here for a while.'

The footman shrugged. 'You can mark her as a possible, Mrs Davis. They won't care by the end of the evening.'

The housekeeper nodded, then turned back to Eleanor. 'Now listen carefully, Nellie. We're going to give you several ribbons to mark what type of blood you are and how much you've given. When one of the footmen comes to you, fill the jug he'll give you and take off one of your red ribbons. That's to stop you from giving too much.' Her words had the air of repetition, doled out without conscious thought. 'Once you've finished, you can go along to the kitchen and lend a hand there while you're waiting for your master and mistress to finish upstairs. Do you understand?'

'Yes, ma'am,' Eleanor replied. It all sounded very civilized and reasonable. When she'd been in Lady Sophie's service, it had been perfectly simple – giving blood was part of her service. Perhaps it was her trips to France and her experience of the Revolution which made her feel differently now, and made this whole room appear like some butcher's table at the market with chickens waiting for slaughter.

'Good girl,' the housekeeper praised her, and pinched her upper arm. 'Nice and healthy, good muscle. You're up from the country recently, I think? I can still see the roses in your cheeks. Go and sit down, put on these ribbons . . .' She handed Eleanor five red ones and a single pink one. 'And wait your turn.'

Like a housewife checking stock before sending it to market, Eleanor thought sourly, but she did as she was told. She

109

didn't expect to glean any gossip from Mrs Davis, but her fellow servants might be more informative.

'Are you here all night?' the girl on her left whispered as Eleanor took a place on the bench. She was younger than Eleanor, looking barely eighteen, but the scars on her arms betokened experience. Her chestnut hair was curled in a style that was a little too old for her, and her gown was of nicer fabric than Eleanor's, nice enough that it must have been a gift from a mistress that had been made over.

'I'm here till milord and milady have finished,' Eleanor answered softly. 'Milady said she wasn't sure how long she'd stay tonight, but . . .' Her shrug indicated a shared understanding of just how unreliable masters and mistresses could be. She looped the ribbons round her neck and took stock of the lancet and bandages in front of her. There was a small bowl of neat gin too – that was where the smell had been coming from – and gauze, to clean the wounds and blade. All very usual. 'Who brought you?'

'Lady Janet,' the girl answered. 'Marchioness of Somerset, or she was until her great-grandson married, but don't tell her that!' She giggled. 'I'm Louise. It's rather dull down here, but at least we're sitting down, and they say that after midnight . . .'

'Yes, what happens after midnight?'

'Extra pay,' the man on Louise's other side said, smirking with satisfaction. '*If* you're up for it by then. You look like you've got the health for it.' He himself was bursting with ripe vigour, cheeks ruddy and dark hair sleek, his bulging arms and shoulders stretching his footman's jacket as tight as a sausage skin. He could have served as an advertisement for the health benefits of beef tea or pork pies.

Eleanor would have asked for more details, but they were interrupted by a footman with a silver tray and jug, and the entire table fell silent. A man at the far end was selected. He used his lancet to nick a vein and quickly filled the jug before wiping and binding the new wound. The most noise he made was a hiss between his teeth as he cleaned the cut and the lancet with some gin.

It wasn't a large jug. It would have filled a couple of the cups which Lady Sophie used to drink, back when Eleanor had been in service to her, and *she* had got by on two or three cups a day. The vampires upstairs must not be drinking heavily, which was a distinct relief to Eleanor. Of course they couldn't go round draining people dry the way that aristo-crats had been accused of doing in France, but, well, it was hard not to worry . . .

It was at that moment that Anima woke up, looking through Eleanor's eyes at the scene and recoiling in horror. If she'd been a cat, her hair would have stood on end and she'd have been spitting. Even as an elderly woman – albeit one living inside Eleanor's soul – there was a strong impres-sion of bristling fury and unsheathed claws. *What are you doing?*

Spying on a high-society ball in order to find out more about the disappearance of Talleyrand, and a conspiracy which may involve vampires, French aristocrats, or both, Eleanor informed her. 'Extra pay, you say?' she asked the man next to Louise.

He tapped the side of his nose. Three bandages wrapped his left forearm, but he showed no trace of weariness yet. 'Between you and me—'

'And the rest of this table,' a sour-looking woman opposite said.

He shot her an unfriendly look. 'Some of the ladies and gentlemen upstairs like to *see* it being taken, if you know what I mean. Of course, that's not going to happen till most of the people who don't partake of the red stuff have left. But when it does, it'll be enough to buy you a few new ribbons.' He leered in what he probably thought was a

111

friendly manner. 'Haven't seen you round at these events before.'

'Milord – well, milady was the one with the invitation, but milord wasn't interested in attending before,' Eleanor explained. She knew the virtues of sharing a bit of information in order to open, as Sir Percy would have put it, channels of communication. 'She's Lady Ffoulkes, as was Suzanne de Tournay.'

There were various nods and sounds of comprehension along the table. Eleanor mentally noted the people who clearly recognized Suzanne's name. They'd be the ones who knew more about matters above stairs, and might have useful information. 'Who brought all of you?' she asked, and listened to the responses.

You're not spying on aristocrats, you're gossiping with servants, Anima snapped.

If you think that the second doesn't lead to the first, then you haven't been paying much attention for the last few months – or for most of your life. When you were alive. Eleanor realized, a little late, that the final comment might be hurtful, but Anima had just vanished for the last few days without a word of explanation. Did she expect Eleanor to simply sit around and wait for her attention, like a . . . well, a servant?

Then it was Eleanor's turn to fill a silver jug with blood. She went about the business of opening a vein with the ease of practice, receiving an approving nod from the housekeeper who'd come over to supervise. When the conversation restarted, it was clear that she'd been accepted by the group.

The night spun on, occasional drifts of music filtering down from upstairs, with new servants arriving and leaving as the hours passed. Anima had retreated to sulk, which allowed Eleanor to pay more attention to the conversation. And she found herself accepted in a way that she *hadn't* been yet in the Blakeney house. There she was still an outsider, even if she'd been serving in the household for nearly a year. Her closeness to Sir Percy and Lady Marguerite – and certain of their visiting guests – set her apart from the other servants, yet she certainly wasn't going to suddenly become one of the upper class either. But here, among other maids and footmen opening their veins for their superiors, she was just one of a group of people who knew their place and were appreciated by their masters and mistresses, who did an arguably unpleasant job in return for a good wage. It all made sense. It was *practical*. She didn't have to think about awkward facts which didn't fit into the quiet rhythms of service.

She didn't have to *think*.

Weariness finally washed over her. She'd just given her fifth jug of blood and disposed of her fifth red ribbon. Thought was unnecessary. It was easier to obey, to fall back into the habits of a lifetime and accept the realities of life. She'd tried to slip away from the table twice now, using the standard excuse, but had been escorted back each time. They were taking more precautions than she'd expected. The gossip she'd picked up from the other servants had given her a few names which might be useful, but otherwise this evening had been wasted. She could only hope that Lord Andrew had gathered more information in the ballroom than she had in the servants' hall, however short a time they'd stayed.

Someone pressed a mug of soup into her hands, and she drank from it gratefully. Louise had left a while ago. The ruddy man was still there. Over to one side Mrs Davis was talking to a stranger in footman's livery, her hand outstretched for coins. Something about her posture and the proprietary air with which she gestured at the group of servants with their bandaged arms jabbed at Eleanor more viciously than any needle. *As if she owns us.*

She remembered last summer, and a conversation with

Fleurette, who had then believed Eleanor was just a girl from the country who needed to be converted to the ideals of the Revolution. Of course, Fleurette's words had been naive and innocent, mere repetition of popular opinions from the broadsheets, so *obviously*, blatantly simple that they couldn't possibly be true. And yet they still rang in her ears . . .

Nobody should have to choose between selling their blood or starving. You've spent too much of your life being lied to. It was unfair and you have a right to be angry . . .

Mrs Davis deposited her pay – her bribe? – into an inner pocket. She turned to the table of exhausted servants and clapped her hands together. 'Now who would like to earn an extra shilling?'

'I oughtta be getting back to milord's,' a wan-looking young man said, supporting his weight on his elbows as he leaned forward. 'Promised I'd be leaving when I'd done my bit.'

'Aren't you the one who came with Lord Swansedge? My dear boy, he's still upstairs.' Mrs Davis drifted forward and took his chin in a professional grasp, turning his face to inspect the colour of his cheeks. 'But you've given enough for one night, I think. Perish the thought that we'd risk the health of any of you! England needs more men and women with your stamina and determination to give proper service.' Her smile appeared, for a moment, to show sharper teeth than a cat's, or a vampire's. 'I should have made myself clear beforehand. This *special opportunity* to earn an extra shilling, or even two, is only for the people here who are really *healthy*, and who want to prove their loyalty and willingness to serve.' Her voice dripped with an enthusiasm which Eleanor had heard in France, where men and women in tricolour sashes and rosettes spoke lovingly of the joys and virtues of informing on one's neighbours and watching executions.

This was her chance. Eleanor sat up straight, squared her shoulders – she'd have pinched her cheeks as well to add a little more colour if she'd had the chance – and did her utmost to look sincere. 'I'm ready and willing, ma'am!'

Some of the others at the table chimed in a few moments later, a couple of them giving Eleanor looks of unabashed dislike for having managed to speak first. But the remainder kept their heads lowered and their eyes on the table, their mouths very firmly shut. Eleanor recognized the posture; she'd used it often enough herself when trying to avoid being chosen for an unpleasant duty. *Those who know what's involved either very definitely want it, or very definitely want to avoid it and stay well away.*

'Good. Very good.' Mrs Davis looked down the line of servants at the half-dozen who'd volunteered. 'Now step aside for *just* a moment, and go next door – John, see to it,' she instructed the footman. 'And then you'll be going upstairs.'

'The shilling, ma'am?' a young maidservant, barely sixteen by her looks, said timidly. She was another one whose dress was too good for her station; it must have been originally a larger woman's, cut down for her use. All the marks on her arms were comparatively fresh. Eleanor wouldn't have thought her up to providing any more blood. There was a telltale pallor to her cheeks and she was practically swaying on her feet.

'You'll get that afterwards,' Mrs Davis answered, her tone shifting from sweet encouragement to suggest harsher measures, such as the switch or even dismissal. 'Behave yourself and act properly, and you won't have any complaints.'

So tell me, is she bewitched by vampires? Controlled into obedience? Forced to do their will? Eleanor asked drily.

No, Anima admitted, back again. Her mental tone was sullen. *And I never claimed that everyone who obeyed vampires was compelled into their service. A great many people simply want full pockets and a quiet life, and someone else to be providing the blood.*

115

Why do you sound so annoyed about it?

I can forgive forced obedience where their victims have no choice. But that woman – she has a choice, and has chosen what she is doing, and if one of you bleeds to death she will not care in the slightest. She'll probably cover the matter up and see to it that you're deposited in a side street for the constables to find. I can preach you a sermon on free will later, if you wish, but I would have thought that by now you would have had enough of people selling their fellow men.

That was true. Eleanor had seen it in France: people betraying each other to escape the guillotine. But that hadn't been for money – it had been from fear. Was Mrs Davis simply encouraging other people to open their veins so she wouldn't have to do it herself?

Eleanor managed to manoeuvre herself close to the girl who'd just spoken as they followed the footman to the room next door, where they were offered mugs of hot beef tea, still steaming and fragrant. 'Are you certain that you're up to this?' she asked her softly.

The girl visibly pulled herself together, doing her best to manage a smile. 'Oh, of course, I was just feeling a little faint for a moment.'

'You're looking a trifle pale—'

'Shut your mouth,' the girl hissed, her accent abruptly dropping gutterwards. 'Have you seen what some of them up there tip for a bit of private bleeding? My parents *need* that money. You stay out of it!'

'Is there something going on over there?' Mrs Davis asked from the doorway.

'Nothing, ma'am,' Eleanor and the girl quickly assured her in unison, then glared at each other.

The ruddy fellow, still red-cheeked despite his bloodletting, patted them both on the shoulders. 'There, there, girls. There's enough for all of us. No need to argue.'

Am I correct in understanding that since you still have some blood left in your body, you intend to go and donate it to vampires personally rather than via a jug and glasses? Anima enquired coldly.

I need information, Eleanor snapped back at her. *If you have any better ideas about how to get it, then I'd be only too pleased to hear them!*

'Now remember,' Mrs Davis lectured them, as the footman handed round fresh lancets, 'be careful how much blood you let! I don't want to have to apologize to your masters and mistresses tomorrow if you pass out and have to sleep it off in an attic. Though I'm sure none of you would do anything so wicked.' She stifled a giggle daintily with the tips of her fingers. 'Now don't give me any reason to be ashamed of you.'

'Is she always like that?' Eleanor asked the ruddy footman – Leo, his name was – as they were led up the back stairs.

He rolled his eyes. 'Them as can't do, teach, and them as won't open a vein think they can tell those of us who do how it should be done. You can tell no lord nor lady's ever asked *her* for a drop of the red stuff.'

While Eleanor agreed on all points, she couldn't help thinking that Mrs Davis still came out of the situation with more money and more power than Eleanor and Leo. A house-keeper couldn't be turned off as easily as a common servant, and if Eleanor and Leo were getting tips for the evening, then Mrs Davis was probably collecting at least twice as much for facilitating the whole business. It wasn't fear that prodded the housekeeper onwards: it was greed.

There will always be those who are prepared to sell out their brothers and sisters for wealth or favours, Anima noted. Without changing tone, she added, *If you turn left here at the top of the stairs then you can run down the corridor to the matching stairs at the other side of the house, and make it outside before you're stopped.*

Could. Won't. I'm not leaving, Eleanor answered.

Mrs Davis marshalled the group towards the narrow stairs, which wound upwards, the servants filtering round them like sand reversing up an hourglass. *We can come up with some excuse to justify your actions to your friends in the League,* Anima suggested. *They won't be surprised that you fled.*

It was like one of those moments when one was splashed with boiling water while cooking or doing the laundry; at first it was only an instant's pain, but then it grew hotter and deeper, aching all the way down to the bone. The words echoed in Eleanor's head. *They won't be surprised that you fled.* Was that all she really was to the League? Someone who'd run away from danger?

Anima must have sensed her fury, for she quickly tried to justify herself. *Merely sensible caution, such as they have constantly urged on you. Didn't they tell you just a few days ago that you should have stayed out of danger?*

Andrew had. Charles had, and that had *really* hurt. But Lady Marguerite had said that Eleanor was one of them. Eleanor wasn't a coward, she wasn't even a *sensible* coward, and she wasn't going to turn tail and scurry away like a rat when so much was at stake.

If you're not going to be helpful, then stay out of my way, she thought coldly.

Anima faded like mist, her presence dissipating till only the faintest echo remained at the back of Eleanor's mind. *Call on me when you need my help. We both know you will.*

The music had been growing louder as they filed upstairs, but it was relatively dark. Downstairs had been well lit, bright enough to count every hair on Leo's muscular forearms or every turned seam on Louise's gown. Up here, in the 'polite' area of the house, while they might have the new Argand lamps along the walls just as the Blakeneys did, the lamps were turned down to burn with the bare minimum of light.

The thick walls closed them off from the noise of London outside; they might have been walking into a tomb.

Silent now, the footman led them into a side room – a repurposed powder-closet, Eleanor thought, still thick with the odours of violets, civet and musk. They were waved over to take their seats on chairs against the wall, and then the footman crossed to the door on the far side and opened it to murmur to someone, through a blast of music, 'They're ready now, milord.'

And the vampires came drifting in.

They moved with more urgency than Eleanor was accustomed to, quick darting lunges hastily restrained, but their eyes glittered with hunger. Some of them were in black silk grave-clothes, as though already wrapped for their coffins, while others were in the full panoply of ten or twenty years ago, with the women in skirts so wide they had to enter the room one at a time. Where living men or women would have been breathing hard and flushed with the exercise of vigorous dancing, the vampires were as pale as bone. The paint on their cheeks and lips stood out starkly red. And all of them, without exception, carried small liquor glasses, the sort that would only hold a swallow or two of spirits. They hadn't been drinking alcohol, though: the glasses were stained from previous draughts of blood.

Leo was the first to react, unbinding one of his bandages to reveal a fresh cut in his arm. Without a word to him, a couple of female vampires pushed forward, nearly jostling with eagerness, and held their glasses to be filled from the dribbling wound. They threw them back in the same way that Eleanor had seen some of the League drink brandy, gulping them down in a single swallow, eyes wide for a moment before closing in satiation. When they licked their lips, their tongues were briefly as red as though they'd been alive.

A moment later, others were pushing forward to have their glasses filled. Their attention was on the living flesh which bled rather than on the servants. Eleanor and the others might as well have been items of furniture. A few of the male vampires dropped coins into the laps of the servants, mostly shillings, though out of the corner of her eye Eleanor noticed the faint-looking girl collecting a couple of half-crowns. She tucked them away in an inner pocket with what looked like a conspiratorial nod to the gentleman who'd tipped her. Eleanor herself kept her head down and didn't meet anyone's eyes, but she did listen.

And oh, how they talked.

Some of the vampires who'd already taken their refreshment directly from a chosen servant lingered, perhaps in hopes of another glass, perhaps simply to watch. Others edged in until the whole room was full of silk and chatter and what Eleanor could only define as the smell of vampires. It wasn't like the smell of corpses, it had no stink of decay, but it reminded her of rooms which had been empty so long that the dust had become as hard as stone, or aristocratic tombs where the corpses might have been dragged out to be burned by Revolutionaries. But a presence – a presence of *absence* – still remained. There was a hunger to the room, an emptiness; it was a vast and gaping ravenous maw that yearned to inhale and swallow up everything that lived within the house's walls, and then spread wider still.

Words whirled by above Eleanor's head as the vampires prattled briskly to each other, mingled with the sound of music and the clatter of heels on a well-polished dancing floor. 'And you won't believe this, my dear, but . . .' 'He *said* so, but with the number of mistresses he keeps . . .' 'This talk of banning slavery must be stopped before it gets any further. If we can deal with Wilberforce . . .' 'The Dauphin is in Austria, of course, but there's no clear candidate for

Regent with his mother dead, and indeed no obvious leader left unless we allow Austria or Italy to claim authority . . .'
'Well, if you ask *me* about what happened to Talleyrand, I can only say that he shouldn't have annoyed certain people . . .'
The man standing beside the speaker cut him off with a surreptitious prod to the ribs and a murmur in his ear.

Eleanor pricked up her ears at that last statement, and stole a glance across at the speakers as she filled another glass. They were both young, or appeared young. One of them was in funerary black silk, the natural dark colour of his hair showing underneath the powder, managing to look mildly drunk and debauched in spite of the fact that alcohol had no effect on vampires. The other, who'd cut him off, was in classical white satin, still perfect despite the ravages of the ball and dancing, and had the air of a sympathetic uncle, belied by the sharpness of his green eyes.

Eleanor strained every nerve to focus on their conversation. They seemed to be the loitering sort, rather than wanting to continue dancing. With the demand for blood slackening off now, perhaps she could get their names from one of the other servants while their services weren't required.

Her plans were cut short by a cold gloved hand which caught her chin and tipped her face upwards, and she found herself looking directly at her previous mistress, carrying a glass like all the other vampires.

'Why, Nellie!' Lady Sophie exclaimed. 'What a delightful surprise!'

CHAPTER NINE

Eleanor knew by heart the proper etiquette of how to behave towards her mistress. It was etched into her muscles from years of training. She knew when to curtsey, when to make excuses, when to bow her head and accept a scolding, and when to flee the area and allow some other servant to take the blame. Unfortunately, none of her experience had prepared her for a situation such as this: confronting a *former* mistress while providing blood for vampires and surreptitiously spying on them.

She tried to duck her head, but Lady Sophie's firm grip on her chin wouldn't allow it. 'Aren't you pleased to see me, Nellie?'

'I just didn't expect to see you here, milady,' Eleanor stammered. Other vampires were looking curiously at them, and she knew the other servants in the row would be paying attention as well. 'I'm very sorry, I hadn't thought you'd come to an occasion like this . . .'

'Silly Nellie!' Lady Sophie laughed, her voice sweet and silvery and polished. 'Why on earth shouldn't I be here?'

Eleanor hastily calculated the odds, and decided that a show of blank ignorance was the most likely to be believed. 'I thought only people who'd escaped France were invited, milady.'

'Very true.' Lady Sophie shifted her hand, patting Eleanor's cheek and then twisting one of Eleanor's curls around her fingers. 'I came as someone's guest, you see, my dear. But what a charming colour your hair is! How very sensible of you.' Without letting Eleanor explain the current dark brown shade of it, she went on, 'Who brought you here? I thought you were with the Blakeneys, and everyone knows that little Marguerite wouldn't be invited to an event like this.'

'Marguerite Blakeney?' one of the vampires in black grave-clothes asked. He had an indefinable air of age about him, which went far beyond the powdered white hair of his wig or the drawn lines of his face. 'I've heard that name some-where before.'

'Marguerite Saint-Just as was,' another vampire put in, fanning herself needlessly. 'You know. The Saint-Cyr business.'

'Oh, her.' The questioner's mouth curled in an unpleasant manner. 'Has nobody dealt with her yet?'

'Her husband is a leader of fashion,' Lady Sophie explained, 'and she's found a place here in England. For the moment, at least. But you haven't answered my question, Nellie.'

Eleanor had been hoping the digression would go on for longer. 'Please, milady,' she said, drawing out her words hesitantly, 'not *in public*.'

Lady Sophie looked around at the other vampires in the room, all of whom were visibly taking an interest by now. 'Mmm. Perhaps you have a point, Nellie. Come, walk with me.' The yank on Eleanor's hair would have brought her upright if she hadn't already been rising to her feet.

'Taking the girl for private refreshment?' the dark-haired vampire who'd mentioned Talleyrand earlier commented. 'I thought that wasn't till later?'

'Oh come now, it's nearly one in the morning,' his white-haired friend chided him. 'Hardly anyone breathing's left next door.'

'Fie, gentlemen,' Lady Sophie said, with a sparkle to her eye and a tone to her voice which suggested she'd be rapping knuckles next. 'Little Nellie here used to serve on my estate. I claim prior acquaintance.'

She steered a path through the crowd and Eleanor followed, like flotsam in the wake of an incoming tide. For a few seconds Eleanor had the luxury of actually seeing the dancing, and it was both beautiful and somehow unnerving. Red ribbons lay against white throats in a constant reminder of the guillotine. Steps began and ended with a jerk of the head, like some nod of final farewell. They passed near the musicians, and Eleanor saw that they – all living humans, none vampires – were playing with a frantic abandon which flushed their cheeks and made them sweat with effort, a constant ripple of notes which never stopped. A chill ran down her back as she let Lady Sophie lead her into a side room. This didn't feel like a celebration of life and freedom: it felt more like a memory and repetition of hatred, a pledge to never forget, and a promise of oncoming vengeance. Beneath the tapping of feet she seemed to hear the clattering of bones.

Lady Sophie closed the door, shutting them into the small side room together, and turned to inspect her more closely. Her dark hair was powdered so skilfully that it gleamed as white as marble, or as white as her skin, and Eleanor recognized the deep violet dress she was wearing as one that she'd embroidered herself, setting careful stitches into every silver lily. While she appeared as soft and smooth as a summer camellia blossom, her eyes were as hard as gemstones. 'So tell me, Nellie,' she asked sweetly, 'what *have* you been up to?'

'I was working for the Blakeneys, milady,' Eleanor said, carefully feeling her way. Lady Sophie had hinted, when first she donated Eleanor to the Blakeneys – like a fan or a pair of gloves, Eleanor couldn't help feeling – that she knew Sir

124

Percy was involved with the League of the Scarlet Pimpernel. But that didn't mean Eleanor should *confirm* this was the case, still less admit that Sir Percy himself was the Pimpernel. 'For tonight Lady Marguerite loaned me to Sir Andrew and Lady Suzanne, because none of the other servants knew how to . . . well.' She gestured at the bandages encasing her arms.

'Yes, yes. But what happened in France?'

'France, milady?' Eleanor asked, doing her best imitation of innocent stupidity.

It didn't work. Lady Sophie gave her a look which could have been used to clean tarnish off silver. 'I'll allow you that little bit of obfuscation because I respect your loyalty to your new mistress, Nellie,' she said coldly. 'But remember that first and foremost you belong to *me*.'

Eleanor lowered her eyes. Less than a year ago, she'd have listened to a statement like that and thought nothing of it, because *of course* aristocrats talked like that about their servants. Yet . . . the Blakeneys didn't. Other members of the League might drop casual phrases such as 'my man' or 'my cook' or 'my valet', but they'd never claim they owned their servants either. And as for France . . . well, that country had drawn a very bloody line under such statements and put an end to them in the most final of ways.

But all of this didn't change the fact that Eleanor was on her own here, and if Lady Sophie chose to accuse her of something – stealing a piece of jewellery, for instance – then Eleanor would find herself straight in front of a magistrate. Assuming she made it out of the building alive. She'd found it easy to scorn Anima's warnings earlier, but this very personal interest from Lady Sophie raised the stakes frighteningly high. For a moment she cursed the luck that had brought her former mistress to this ball tonight of all nights.

What a good thing she now had so much experience in lying.

'Yes, milady,' she said, slurring her voice a little, the way that some of the other servants downstairs had been doing when on the point of collapse from giving too much blood. 'I'm sorry, milady.'

'So?' Lady Sophie didn't sound particularly mollified, but not too suspicious either. 'What happened in France?'

'Sir Percy and some of his men took me across, milady. They didn't mention any names, and I couldn't ask. They had me doing all the cooking and cleaning while they planned.' The only truthful bit of that was the fact she'd gone across with the League, but she wasn't going to tell Lady Sophie any names if she didn't have to. 'They had a scheme to rescue the Dauphin.'

'I know all that, you—' Lady Sophie bit back what Eleanor suspected would have been *you stupid girl* and visibly composed herself into smiling kindness. One could barely see her fangs. 'So what did they *do*?'

Fear gave Eleanor's invention wings. 'They substituted me for Marie Antoinette in her cell, milady, and then they went and rescued her son from the Temple prison, and lots of other people too, they told me. They might have left me there, but she was a very noble lady. She said that she wouldn't leave someone else to die in her place. She went back to the cell and then some vampires came and took her away. I later heard as how they made her one of them.'

Eleanor bowed her head in feigned respect, and hoped that Lady Sophie would accept the story. After all, it cast Eleanor in the role of convenient body double and game piece rather than an actor in her own right. Eleanor could see that Lady Sophie preferred her that way. The lower classes should know their place, after all. What was more, it provided a good explanation for why Eleanor didn't know any of the League's private plans and couldn't pass them on.

Lady Sophie frowned. 'And you *let* her do that?'

'I couldn't stop her, milady,' Eleanor invented, 'nor the rest of the League.' She was about to go into detail on how the rest of them had said very heroic and noble things about choice and sacrifice and so on, but then she remembered previous advice from Sir Percy: *The more you talk, the more chance there is that somebody will notice a flaw in your story.*

'Hm.' Lady Sophie sounded aggrieved but convinced. 'In that case, why are you still with the Blakeneys? Why haven't you come back to my service? You haven't even visited your mother.'

'I didn't think they wanted me to leave, milady,' Eleanor said, trying to think of an excuse. She was mildly surprised that Lady Sophie even *remembered* that Eleanor had a living mother. 'Maybe they thought they'd want me to impersonate the ghost of the poor dead Queen?'

'That wouldn't be beyond what I've heard of the League,' Lady Sophie muttered. 'So. We both know you're telling me a great many lies, don't we? I'm sure that's what they told you to tell anyone who asked. You're a good girl. But what *did* happen?'

Eleanor's heart clenched tight. She'd actually dared hope that Lady Sophie believed her. But behind that mask of powder and paint was a mind just as sharp as Lady Marguerite's, or Citizen Chauvelin in France.

She hesitated, and Lady Sophie prompted her with a crook of her finger. 'Speak, Nellie. You weren't always this silent. We used to be quite talkative, didn't we?' Her tone invited confidences.

Oh no we weren't, Eleanor thought. She was discovering just how much she hated being called *Nellie* once more. She'd grown used to being *Eleanor* – a grown woman, a League operative, someone who deserved respect. *Nellie* was a maid who'd never looked beyond the household walls, a menial, someone worth so little that Lady Sophie could call her whatever she wanted without caring about her reaction.

Anger gave her the wits she needed, and a story that Lady Sophie might believe, as well as a chance to follow the trail which she'd come here for in the first place. 'Milady . . . I promised not to tell. I swore on the Bible! There were things going on over there. The Prince of Paris . . .'

Lady Sophie's dark eyes turned to black ice, like the heart of a millpond in winter. 'Him. I see. It appears I must ask questions elsewhere.'

Eleanor let herself sway, as though weakness was taking hold. 'Milady . . .'

'Yes?' Lady Sophie leaned closer.

'What did they mean earlier when they were talking about Lady Marguerite Blakeney and the Saint-Cyr business?'

'I suppose it's not much talked about in the Blakeney household. You know she has a brother? Well . . . apparently he was paying court to the daughter of the Marquis de Saint-Cyr. The Marquis ordered him beaten for his presumption, which may or may not have been justified. I don't know what the boy said to the girl. But then pretty Marguerite dropped a word or two in the ear of some of her Revolutionary friends, such as Citizen Chauvelin – yes, they were friends back then. And within a few days, the Marquis and his sons were sent to the guillotine.' It was a narrative as casual as a dinner table conversation, but Eleanor could feel Lady Sophie's attention on her, as sharp as needles. 'I'm polite to the woman in public, of course, but *that's* the person whom Sir Percy married. He grew a trifle cooler to her after he discovered the truth, I'm told.'

'I . . .' Eleanor's hand went to her mouth as she remembered fragments of conversations she'd overheard. 'I never thought . . .'

'But I'm sure you see now, my dear Nellie, why she's unwelcome at these balls.' Lady Sophie sighed, a little too dramatically. 'We must all make sacrifices at the altar of Society. I wouldn't come myself, except that sometimes one really needs to hear all the latest gossip. Now, did you hear anything more about the Prince of Paris—'

The door swung open, and two vampires entered. It was the ones she'd seen earlier, the friends with dark hair and white hair. 'Lady Sophie,' the dark-haired one said with a bow. 'Might we request your presence?'

Lady Sophie drew herself up to her full height. Her head might be lower than the two men, but her styled and powdered hair easily overtopped them. 'Gentlemen. I am *busy.*'

'Not too busy for us, surely?' The dark-haired man had the smirk of someone who'd cajoled countless ladies into indiscretion and gentlemen into gambling dens. 'If you'd like us to carry the girl away for you and dispose of her, then we can certainly do that and save you the trouble.'

Eleanor had been among Revolutionary soldiers and in sordid drinking establishments in France, but she'd never felt quite as *alone* as she now did. If she cried out, if she screamed for help, would any of the aristocrats dancing next door notice? Would any of them *care*?

'Fie, you're frightening the poor girl!' Lady Sophie's tone was playful, her eyes less so. 'Little Nellie here will wait for us while we speak in private, won't you? A spare room . . .' She looked around at the doors.

'The place is a sad crush tonight,' the white-haired man said. 'Unless we wish to dangle her out of the window while we talk . . .'

'She can wait in the main room. Here, my favour.' Lady Sophie plucked a ribbon from the bows which ornamented her bodice, and tucked it into Eleanor's hair, her fingers cold where they brushed against Eleanor's skin. 'Now, you don't need to be carried, do you?'

'I can walk, milady,' Eleanor protested. 'Truly I can.'

Lady Sophie's attitude abruptly shifted and she leaned in close to Eleanor, her wide skirts rustling and the scent of blood on her breath mingling with her lilac perfume. 'When this is all over, you can come back to my household, Nellie. After all, with the Queen of France now a vampire, they won't have any further use for you . . . and I always look after my own.'

Eleanor looked into Lady Sophie's eyes – wide, carefree, ageless eyes – and for a moment she thought she was about to vomit. *You loaned me to the Blakeneys on a mission you knew might kill me. You sent me to them by public stagecoach on my own because you couldn't be bothered to pay for someone to escort me, and I was nearly kidnapped the moment I stepped off the coach. You said earlier that we used to be 'quite talkative', but you never once troubled to exchange a word with me, unless it was about my duties or my blood. You consider me your property. Your blood stock. Your investment.*

It was as though the final piece of some intricate clockwork had locked into place, or as though she'd managed to adjust a telescope so that she could see some distant location with absolute clarity. She *didn't* want to go back with Lady Sophie. The possibility had always been there in the background, an option which she could take if everything else failed and all other chances were lost. But it was no longer a place where she could return and be happy. She'd seen too much. She'd *learned* too much. Basing Manor wasn't a place for a woman who knew something about revolutions.

But if she said so right now, then she'd either be a prisoner or dead, with (as Sir Percy would put it) a sporting chance of one followed closely by the other.

'Of course, milady,' she lied with absolute sincerity. 'I'm sorry, milady, I'm so tired . . . but it's so good to know you're there again, looking after me. I don't think they ever trusted me in the Blakeney household. It's such a relief to be back doing what I should be doing and not having to worry about . . . things.'

'Good little Nellie,' Lady Sophie said. And was that just a note of relief to her voice? 'Soon all of this will be over for you.'

Little Nellie? I'd be taller than you if you weren't wearing heeled shoes nearly as high as your hairstyle, Eleanor thought with a tart burst of spite as she nodded. Lady Sophie's words didn't reassure her. They could be interpreted in two different ways, and the second one wasn't at all comforting.

Lady Sophie waved Eleanor to the door before turning back to the men. 'And what is so important that you need to disturb my private business?'

The edge to her voice made Eleanor scurry away, though by now her head was aching and her limbs felt leaden. She'd never given this much blood before.

She entered the main room, where the vampires were still dancing and the orchestra still playing as though they would never stop. Would this go on till dawn? Probably, if the musicians were paid well enough. Nobody bothered to look twice at her. She stepped to the side of the door, as though waiting for a command, but hesitating inwardly. If she stayed here then she might be able to overhear something of interest, but she ran the risk of Lady Sophie finishing her discussion and coming out to find her. She couldn't rely on a second stroke of luck such as the two other vampires interrupting again. Yet the noise of the music and dancing made it impossible to hear a quiet conversation on the other side of the door. She'd need a miracle to have such keen ears.

Perhaps magic could help.

Anima? she queried.

There was a pause, one clearly intended to make a point. *Yes?* Anima finally said. *I told you this was folly, and now you've proved it . . . oh.* The downturn of disappointment in her voice as she realized that Eleanor didn't require a rescue was almost risible, and her tone in Eleanor's mind was harsh with annoyance. *Well? What do you want?*

You can command winds. Can you coax a breeze to bring me the conversation from next door? Then we'll leave, I promise. Eleanor would be more than grateful to be out of the house as soon as possible.

Apparently Anima was also in a hurry to leave, for she didn't argue or try to set conditions. *Give me control – trust me, I won't do anything rash – and I'll demonstrate. You simply hook the wind around your fingers like this . . .*

Eleanor felt the world grow distant as Anima took control and summoned her powers, using Eleanor's body and mind as Eleanor might use a pair of tongs to manipulate hot coals. The old mage made no such attempt to push any further, however, merely working her spell. The air glittered in front of Eleanor's eyes as though it was full of swirling currents, and her dress fluttered in a sudden twist of air which might have been mistaken for a draught, but which was far from that.

'. . . necessary to meet you for further instructions in a public place, rather than a private visit to your home.' That was the dark-haired man, his voice carrying on the breeze to Eleanor's ears. 'I regret that it wasn't sooner, but we're only just back from France, and on a different ship from *The Watchful Maid*, which couldn't match her speed.'

The Watchful Maid. Something pricked at the back of Eleanor's mind. She'd heard something like that recently . . . Dear God, *La Surveillante*! It was a direct translation! They were talking about the very ship which the League had been tracking. She strained her ears still further, unwilling to miss a single word.

'I have no doubt you took your time,' Lady Sophie answered tartly. 'You are the world's laziest man, de Courcis!

Poor Castleton here will be led into bad habits at your side. He'd do well to make his own way in future.'

'We're inseparable,' the dark-haired man – de Courcis – said cheerfully. 'Always at your service, of course, but apart from that we cleave together like Achilles and Patroclus, or Damon and Pythias, or Hamlet and Laertes, or—'

'What my friend is saying is that we are *always at your service*.' The other voice must be the white-haired man, Castleton. 'We wouldn't wish you to have any doubt of that. And we carry out our duties with all possible speed, as circumstances allow.'

'It's good to know that *someone* is reliable,' Lady Sophie replied. 'So did you have any difficulty in reaching Paris with your consignment?'

'None at all. We kept him drugged, of course, he's too wily to risk otherwise. It seems entirely the wrong direction to be carrying him, however.'

'The Prince of Paris has his pawns set out for the endgame,' Lady Sophie said. 'I must thank him when next I write for sending you to act as my servants.'

'While I would be delighted to be of assistance,' de Courcis said swiftly, 'I fear that—'

'Do *not* contradict me.' There was a small noise – Eleanor wasn't sure what it was, but it might have been a man's pained intake of breath, a suppressed gasp of agony – and then silence. 'I have not endured for over a thousand years by suffering contradiction from children like you. I believe in making matters plain from the very beginning. Do we understand each other?'

'We do.' De Courcis struggled for control and effortless civility, but Eleanor could hear the pain behind his voice. 'I apologize for any lack of courtesy on my part, milady.'

'Good. Castleton?'

'At your service, milady.'

'Excellent. Then I believe we're almost done. Wait here while I fetch . . .'

Eleanor could complete that sentence. *While I fetch Nellie.* She let the breeze vanish, and walked briskly through the room, collecting a tray of discarded glasses on her way to pass for one of the mansion's own servants. A couple of the vampires cast glances at her, but then looked away – perhaps disregarding her, or perhaps because of Lady Sophie's ribbon in her hair. She felt a cold thrill run down her spine with every step, imagining Lady Sophie entering the ballroom and calling for her to come back. But no voice shouted her name, nobody tried to grab her, and nobody moved so much as a finger to prevent her exit.

It was almost insulting how easy it was to retrace her steps through the house and find her way to the servants' entrance. Though perhaps it was because there were already so many men and women here who'd opened their veins for the vampires: there was no need to take an interest in just one of them.

Charles and Tony were waiting behind the mansion, dressed as middle-class young men out for a night on the town, loitering with a group of coachmen and footmen over an endless game of dice. She saw the relief on their faces as she approached, and she felt her heart leap in response.

They *saw* her. She wasn't *Nellie* to them, she was *Eleanor*, a friend and a colleague rather than a pawn and a farm animal – and that was something which had changed her world.

CHAPTER TEN

'Out of the question,' Andrew said firmly. Too firmly, in fact, to Eleanor's ears. Unlike Sir Percy's orders, which always came from a place of casual certainty, Andrew knew that he *could* be disobeyed, and that right now it was staring him in the face.

Unfortunately, everyone else in the room knew it too.

Lady Marguerite adjusted a fold of her gown, which Eleanor recognized as the equivalent of setting her jaw and squaring her shoulders, and gave him the iciest of smiles. 'My dear Andrew, what else do you expect me to do?'

'The moment you leave England – no, the moment you leave London – Chauvelin will know it. Haring off to Paris won't help your brother any more than what we're already doing.'

'It isn't *just* Armand,' Lady Marguerite said. 'It's Percy as well. He is in dire need of this new information, and could be walking into even graver danger than we thought. How do you expect me to sit here when I could be assisting my husband?'

Eleanor was watching the argument from a comfortable chair in the corner. Not a stool, for once; her bedraggled condition, blood loss and the cuts to her arms had so appalled

Lady Marguerite that she'd been given no choice in the matter. She felt little urge to object. The whole dispute seemed to be taking place at a distance, like a theatrical performance, and she was struggling not to drift into sleep. Charles had been giving her looks mingled with equal amounts of *I told you so* and *Have you no regard for my feelings, coming so close to death?* to the point that half her battle to stay awake was to spite him by proving how healthy and unaffected she was.

She also felt a twinge of guilt. She'd lied about how she'd managed to overhear Lady Sophie and the two men, leaving out any mention of magic. So far the League had accepted her account of events, but she was unpleasantly aware that she was having to lie more and more in order to explain her special abilities. What would happen when she finally had to tell the truth – and was she making it worse for herself every time she misled them? Even leaving aside questions of religion and virtue and being a good girl, common sense said that when someone staked their life on being able to trust you, they expected an equal trust and honesty in return.

Don't be a fool, Anima whispered. *You're doing the sensible thing. They'd never believe you anyway. Now pay attention, I want to know what they're going to do.*

'Let us consider the known facts again,' Andrew said, changing tack. 'A conspiracy of vampires in France, which has allies in England, apparently including Lady Sophie, holds Talleyrand as a prisoner, having smuggled him over from England and into Paris. They're connected to this business of the "Prince of Paris", and I'd lay odds he's a vampire as well. And they have some sort of plan on a large scale in which he's a mere pawn.'

'Chauvelin was apparently on the right trail after all,' Charles said. 'Astonishing!'

'Don't underrate Monsieur Chauvelin,' Lady Marguerite warned him. 'I'd lay high odds that he knows more than he told me. He doesn't trust me, after all, any more than I do him.' A vicious little smile touched her lips.

'More than that I can't say for certain, as yet,' Andrew said. 'But at least now we know where to focus our search. Paris.'

'And what do you propose to do while you're there?' Lady Marguerite demanded. 'If this is a conspiracy of vampires – and let us be fair and just here, they may have living supporters as well, and we can all guess why – then how do you intend to infiltrate it? We can't have poor Eleanor here open her veins in order to listen at every door in the city!'

'We do have a trail to follow now, though,' Charles put in, but he was frowning. 'That of de Courcis and Castleton.'

'De Courcis I barely know,' Andrew said. 'He has a bad reputation. I wouldn't indulge in his company, however much a refugee from the guillotine he might be, and I would have thought twice about taking Suzanne to the Victims' Ball if I'd known he'd be there.'

'Bad in the sense of being a rakehell drunkard, gambler and lecher, sir?' Eleanor asked. 'Or . . . well, *really* bad?'

Andrew hesitated, possibly moved by the thought that some members of the League could also be described as inhabiting one or more of those three categories. Reluctantly he said, 'I'll admit I've not known anything worse of him than that. Yet from what you say, he's part of this league of vampires, and kidnapped a man.'

Eleanor bit her lip before she could comment on the number of times she'd known members of the League do such a thing. Instead she changed the subject. 'What should I do about Lady Sophie? She's certain to come looking for me now . . .'

Lady Marguerite reached across to pat her hand soothingly. 'We'll spin some tale about you arriving home in a sorry state and having to be sent to Percy's Scotland estates to recover. Our people will keep their mouths shut. We certainly won't hand you back to her, Eleanor. You're safe here.'

'As if we'd even consider it!' Charles exclaimed hotly.

'Thank you,' Eleanor murmured, hot tears pricking at her eyes. She'd never been afraid of returning to Lady Sophie before. But now . . . she'd rather go and live in France.

'What about Castleton?' Andrew asked Charles, courteously looking away from Eleanor as she rubbed her eyes with the back of her hand.

'I never could understand why de Courcis and Castleton dealt together so well,' Charles said, staring at his own cup. 'Castleton was the kindest of men, the most reasonable and understanding, a true scholar . . .'

'You knew him at Oxford?' Lady Marguerite asked.

'Yes,' Charles said briefly. He clearly wanted to leave the matter there, but the silence of the rest of the room compelled him to expand on it. 'He's a few years older than I am – or was, before he turned vampire. He was a genius in the physical sciences and mathematics. We both left our studies there at much the same time. I because my father called me home, he due to his increasing illness. He contracted consumption as a child, and it grew worse as he became older.'

Eleanor knew Charles well enough to hear the undertone of loss beneath his words, the note of betrayal. Whatever Castleton might be now, he'd been a friend to Charles then. 'I'm sorry,' she said softly.

Charles twitched a bony shoulder in a shrug, as though to ward off her sympathy. 'Whatever choices he's made are his own. I suppose he thought turning vampire was a remedy to his disease, as it is to all human weaknesses. But this talk of conspiracies between vampires disturbs me deeply.'

'I fancy it disturbs us all,' Andrew said. 'I'd always thought the intentions of our bloodless kin to be aligned with our own. I have a great-great-great aunt who's the mildest of women, and her sole interest is cataloguing species of butterfly. I've never seen her as the sort of person to be involved in dire conspiracies and the fates of nations.'

'People will be people,' Lady Marguerite said. 'We can't put the blame for this on all vampires, any more than we'd accuse all the living of being like the Committee of Public Safety in France. Honestly, my dear Andrew, I'd be surprised if there *weren't* a few ladies and gentlemen who'd existed for centuries and planned on that basis.' Yet her eyes were troubled, as though considering problems beyond the scope of the discussion.

Sir Andrew nodded. 'Returning to particulars, what I suggest we do is follow our two known targets across to the *other* side of the Channel, to Paris, and then track them within that city. We can link up with Sir Percy there as well, updating him on the latest information we've uncovered, and join forces in our search for Talleyrand. And who knows, he may be close on the man's heels already.'

'But how will those two enter Paris, given that they're vampires?' Eleanor asked. 'It's hard enough for us to smuggle ourselves in and out of the city, with all the guards and regulations. They'd be arrested the moment they were seen.'

'That is a very good question,' Lady Marguerite said, 'and I wish I knew the answer. But I do have a couple of thoughts which may help us. Unfortunately, one of them involves my staying here.'

Andrew's face brightened. Clearly he already approved of this plan. 'Do go on, milady,' he said.

'We agreed earlier that Citizen Chauvelin's not telling us everything he knows, and unlikely to. Though I'll admit I hate the man, he's incorruptible. But others in the Committee for Public Safety are glad to take bribes, and have open pockets and ready tongues. Assuming Percy hasn't already laid siege to them,' she added as an afterthought.

'But we'll never get near them if Chauvelin's in Paris . . .' Charles said.

'Quite. Which is why I must somehow ensure that he stays here for at least a few days longer. I'll plead for more time to investigate, assure him that I'm on the trail of this conspiracy . . . whatever it takes.' Lady Marguerite's face was set like iron, as rigid as those of the women Eleanor had seen going to the guillotine. 'That should buy you some time in the city without his insufferable scrutiny. And a window for Armand to escape if he needs it.'

An idea slowly unfurled in Eleanor's mind, whole and complete and beautiful. This, surely, would work, and allow her to truly prove herself to the rest of the League, to genuinely be one of them. 'What if there was a way to slow him down even further?' she asked. 'To slow everyone down?'

'Explain,' Lady Marguerite ordered. Then she smiled. 'Please?'

'If there was some sort of activity elsewhere in France that appeared to be caused by the Pimpernel, even if it might look like a failure, then wouldn't it draw attention there, and away from Paris? That would let the Chief and Andrew and the others investigate more freely.'

Lady Marguerite pursed her lips thoughtfully. 'That's actually a rather clever thought, Eleanor. France is being wound up to a fever pitch of suspicion. It would be extremely helpful to have the Committee chasing hares all across the country. Did you have somewhere in mind?'

Mont-Saint-Michel, Anima whispered at the back of Eleanor's mind, giving it its proper name rather than the Republican renaming of Mont-Michel. *It's just the sort of place your Pimpernel would like to liberate.*

'Mont-Saint-Michel?' Eleanor suggested, somewhat less certainly than Anima. But she was right, there were all sorts of innocent prisoners there, including Fleurette. 'It sounds as if it's a very significant prison.'

'We'd never make it inside,' Charles argued, but his face was thoughtful, and just a touch hopeful. Was he thinking of their friend Fleurette too?

'You wouldn't need to,' Andrew said. 'Leaving a false trail in the nearby town might be enough. Look . . .' He pulled a map of France from the tangle of maps, newspapers, notes and four-volume novels which covered the table, then spread it out, pointing at a dot in the curve of a bay in the northwest corner. 'Mont-Saint-Michel itself is on this island, several hundred yards out from land, but when the tides go down you can walk to it across the estuary flats. When the tides are up, however . . . well, it's a difficult place to besiege.'

That it was, Anima murmured.

What do you mean?

Memories, memories, though I never reached there in time. Now listen to what they're saying.

Lady Marguerite drew closer to examine the map. 'If we can use Percy's contacts among the smugglers . . .'

Andrew rubbed his chin. 'I'm going to need Charles in Paris afterwards, but . . .' His gaze flicked from Eleanor to Charles and back again. 'If Tony goes with the two of you, then you can base yourselves at the town of Pontorson and mount a diversion. Under normal circumstances I'd think twice before sending you, Eleanor, but—'

'Do you doubt my courage?' Eleanor demanded indignantly.

'I doubt our ability to keep you safe,' Andrew replied, deadly serious. 'This won't be some stroll with the Chief in charge and half a dozen of us around you. And even if you weren't the mirror image of the late Queen, your arms mark you out to any Frenchman as someone who's provided blood to vampires. Under the Law of Suspects, one accusation against you could see you in gaol, and even on the steps of the guillotine. We're almost in June – how long can you keep yourself muffled up and hidden away?'

'The Chief's recognizable at a hundred yards' distance, and he gets away with it,' Eleanor said sourly.

'The Chief's a genius at disguise. Don't bristle so; I'm sending you. Assuming that milady agrees.' He dipped his head to Lady Marguerite. 'But I'll be honest, if we weren't so short of men, and with the Chief missing, then I'd think twice about it, and perhaps order you to stay here with milady and keep Chauvelin distracted instead.'

Frankly, Eleanor would rather be in France. Even if he was in England and not able to operate with his full range of authority, she had a healthy fear of Citizen Chauvelin. Yet she'd gain nothing by arguing further with Andrew, and he *was* letting her go. 'I understand,' she said.

'Well, I'm not sure *I* do,' Charles put in. 'Look here, Andrew, you're right when you say France isn't a safe place for Eleanor—'

'No, but nor is England,' Lady Marguerite interrupted. 'Has it occurred to you that my house may be watched? That Sophie, whom we now know is a partner in this conspiracy, knows her face, as now do de Courcis and Castleton as well? It may not merely be a matter of refusing to hand her back to Sophie . . . this house may no longer be safe for Eleanor at all.'

A cold chill wound its way up Eleanor's spine, and her fears of Lady Sophie pursuing her to this place of safety returned. She'd tried to cling to the assumption that once she was out of their sight, they'd consider her below their notice and forget about her. 'Oh,' she said.

Charles nodded slowly. 'I beg your pardon, milady. I hadn't thought of that. And we can't even send Eleanor back home to the Basing estate, either.'

Eleanor's heart clenched. She might not *want* to return there any time soon, but it was where her mother lived. 'My mother—' she started.

Charles patted her shoulder comfortingly. 'She'll be safe. After all, you've had no contact with her these last few months, have you? They'll know she's not involved in any of this.'

Eleanor could only hope he was right. She felt every proper affection a daughter *should* feel for her mother, of course, but equally, she'd been only too pleased to move out and find gainful employment elsewhere. 'Then it'll be safest if I don't draw their attention to her by going near her?' It was reasonable, but she couldn't help feel a sudden pang of loneliness at this enforced and possibly final separation from her mother.

'Exactly,' Andrew said. 'So, Tony will go with you two, and between the three of you I'm hoping for something dramatic. No doubt Charles can forge some documents suggesting you have a plan to rescue the most important prisoners. Only be sure you get out of town before the Revolutionary Guard arrives and starts making arrests.'

'And then we sail up the river to Paris?' Eleanor asked eagerly, jabbing a finger at the map.

'Sadly that river you're pointing at is the Couesnon and not the Seine,' Sir Andrew said gently, 'and it goes nowhere near Paris. In any event you'd have to travel upstream, which wouldn't be fast. It's a trip of more than two hundred miles, and even ten miles these days in France is dangerous.'

Eleanor tried not to pout. Maps had a sprawling lack of logic compared to embroidery designs; they were higgledy-piggledy and all over the place, rather than being sensibly laid out to make a coherent and elegant whole. 'Then we ride to Paris disguised as soldiers?' she said.

'Then *Tony and Charles* ride to Paris disguised as soldiers,' Andrew said firmly. 'You, Eleanor, will be passed back to the smugglers, and they'll either return you to England or hide you in the Channel Islands until further notice. Don't look at me like that, Eleanor; this order is not subject to discussion.'

Eleanor chewed her lower lip, not bothering to try to hide her mutinous feelings. 'What if you need me in Paris?'

'We're unlikely to need a lookalike for the late Queen this time. And no, before you try the argument, I don't expect we'll need someone to imitate her ghost either.'

As this was one of the ideas which had crossed Eleanor's mind, she looked hurt but forgiving. 'I can play the servant better than *any* of you,' she tried. 'Or what if you should try to parley with some vampires in hiding, and you wanted someone with you who'd obviously be one of their servants?'

Andrew sighed. 'I don't *enjoy* arguing like this,' he said plaintively. 'I'd far rather the Chief were here and could weigh the risks against the potential rewards, or "catch the single hair of bald-headed Fortune", as he's so fond of saying. But I do have a conscience. We've already put you in far too much danger. I will *not* have you going to Paris, and that's final. I trust milady agrees with me?'

'I do,' Lady Marguerite said firmly. For a moment she looked as though she was about to provide her own catalogue of reasons, but then she simply shrugged. 'Sometimes one must accept one's leader's decisions, Eleanor.'

A very rude word came into Eleanor's mind.

Language! Anima said, shocked.

Charles was about the only one in the room who looked genuinely pleased. 'I confess that takes a weight off my conscience,' he said. 'The Chief would never forgive us for putting your life at risk to rescue Talleyrand. He'd call it bad arithmetic, and dishonourable to boot.'

'Then since we're all agreed, that ends the current discussion,' Lady Marguerite said, ignoring Eleanor's silent fuming.

'Come into my bedroom and let me take another look at your arms, Eleanor. Gentlemen, I'll leave the logistics to you, and you can explain the plan to Tony when he arrives.'

Eleanor followed, biting her lip again to prevent herself from giving way to her thoughts. She was surprised when, instead of inspecting her bandaged arms, Lady Marguerite waved her to sit down instead.

Lady Marguerite then pulled her own chair up close enough that she could take Eleanor's hands in her own. 'So, my dear, do you want to tell me the truth?'

'The truth?' Eleanor quavered, conscious of Anima's spirit bristling in chilly caution.

'Oh, you put it over quite well, but I couldn't help noticing a few holes in your story about the ball. Would these vampires truly allow you to listen to their private talk? How could you overhear a whispered conversation when you were in such a noisy room?'

Eleanor stammered, caught between the urge to confess to a sympathetic listener and the knowledge that it would be utter folly and probably see her consigned to Bedlam. 'I have very good hearing, milady, and they weren't trying to whisper as such . . .'

'There's more to you than just your wits and your courage, Eleanor.' Lady Marguerite lowered her voice. 'Percy told me about how *something* happened during the rescue of the Dauphin, in the sewers. How some sort of light erupted from you which drove the vampires away. He's too much of a gentleman to press you on the subject, of course. But I? I'm a woman who loves her husband and her brother beyond all reason. They're all I truly have in this world. If there is something, *anything* you can do to help them, then . . .'

'Then what?'

'Then I will do my utmost to persuade you to do so,' Lady Marguerite said. Her eyes were as cold as ice, and for a moment she reminded Eleanor of Chauvelin at his most merciless. 'Whatever it takes. Is there something that you want? Is there anything I can offer you?'

Eleanor flinched away, unwilling to see such a pitiless expression on the face of the woman she admired and served. 'Milady, *please*! It's not like that.'

'Then what is it? Why can't you say? Are you being blackmailed? Are people holding someone prisoner that you care for?'

'No, no!' Eleanor protested. Her stomach turned at the idea that Lady Marguerite might think she was some sort of traitor. 'You know that's not it, milady. I don't *have* anyone apart from the League here or my mother at home.' *Anima, let me tell her . . .*

She's unreliable, Anima answered coldly. *She'd do anything to save her husband and brother.*

And you'd do anything to get revenge on the vampires. You two deserve each other!

'We know something's been troubling you. You sleepwalk. Or did you not know that?'

Eleanor froze. 'No,' she whispered. 'When?' *Anima? Do you have anything to do with that?*

Anima didn't answer.

'Percy once saw you in our library, at two in the morning. You were turning the pages of one of his books in German – and we both know you don't understand that. Then you closed it and walked upstairs back to your bed, and you didn't remember in the morning when he asked you about it. Alice told me you've left your bed on other nights as well.' Lady Marguerite paused, and her tone shifted from interrogatory to sympathetic. 'Eleanor, my dear, I want to *help* you. It's obvious that you're keeping some sort of secret, and that you're not best pleased about it. You've always trusted us before. Can't you trust me now?'

Eleanor's throat squeezed tight and her eyes burned with the urge to cry. She wanted to trust the other woman. She wanted to *desperately*. Not to be alone with this secret any longer, not to have to lie to her friends, not to have to keep on juggling the stories she told like a showman at a fair. She wanted to get *away* from this constant burden. Helping aristocrats escape the French was easy by comparison. Living with Anima's thirst for vengeance and unrevealed plans for the future was a constant drip of pressure that pushed her further and further away from the people she should trust.

She opened her mouth to speak.

Don't tell her! Anima demanded.

And stay your host for the rest of my life? Lying a little more every day?

I may have been unfair to you. It's possible that I shouldn't have placed you under so much pressure, or borrowed your body to read in Blakeney's library at night. But don't you see that I have no other choice? And don't you remember everything I've done for you? You swore to keep my secret!

The words flew by in the space of a moment, all while Eleanor was still drawing in her breath. She felt pinned like a butterfly between the two women's wishes, as ready to break as cheap crockery. *You've been lying to me. You 'borrowed' my body. You'd do it again if you thought it was 'necessary'. How can I trust you?*

She had the impression of Anima steeling herself for something she didn't want to do. *Very well. Listen to me. I swear by Almighty God, by Christ and all the saints, that once you've resolved this current plot, I'll leave you, whatever the cost to myself. I just need a little longer. Come up with some excuse that she'll believe. I know you can do it.*

You swear? Eleanor demanded, unable to quite believe it but desperate for it to be true.

I swear.

147

Eleanor suppressed the thought that perhaps they might not succeed. They would. They *had* to. *Very well.*

But now she had to come up with an excuse that Lady Marguerite would believe.

Or, perhaps . . . admit that there was no excuse the other woman would ever accept.

'I can't tell you,' she said. 'I'm sorry, milady, I swore an oath to someone else and I can't break it. I promise that it's nothing against you or Sir Percy, and it's nothing to do with the Revolution. I'll do whatever I can to help him and you, you know that. I went to that ball and I opened my veins because I thought I might find something out, and I *did*, and I've told you what I know. I can't do more than that.'

'Won't or can't?' Lady Marguerite asked.

'Can't. Would you really trust me if I broke my word to someone else just because you asked me?'

'I don't necessarily need to trust you,' Lady Marguerite said coldly. 'I merely require the truth. You do realize that if I open the door and tell Andrew and Charles that I don't think you should go with them, then you won't be going to Mont-Saint-Michel, or anywhere else? I have a duty to keep them safe.'

'By sending them to France to help Sir Percy, and rescue your brother?' Eleanor asked before her brain could overrule her mouth. 'How is that keeping them safe?'

Lady Marguerite flushed with anger. 'They'd all choose the risk to help Percy!'

'Well, I'm choosing that risk too!' Eleanor retorted. 'Can't you believe me?'

'After you've told me so many lies?'

Eleanor was about to snap back that she'd had no choice, when a little fragment of perspective made her hold her tongue and think. 'You're the one saying that I've told you lies,' she said slowly. 'If I've . . . *kept silent* . . . about matters

148

which weren't the League's concern, then I had the right to do so. The League claims my loyalty, not my soul.'

'It's easy to make such decisions from the perspective of safety.' Lady Marguerite sounded weary now, rather than angry. 'It's simplicity itself to think that you can start a fire and be able to control the results. I've done that, and I've been burned. I simply cannot take the risk, Eleanor. I'm *ordering* you, as your direct superior in the League, to tell me the truth. If your loyalty to us truly matters, if you're genuinely faithful, then you should recognize that you have no choice. Sometimes one can't keep one's word. Sometimes . . . one has to accept the lesser evil. Tell me now, be honest with me, and we can draw a line under this. But if you hold your tongue, then I will have to tell Charles and Andrew that you can't be trusted.'

Eleanor's eyes burned with unshed tears. She took a ragged breath, knowing that she was destroying her future.

Sometimes there are no good choices. She didn't know whether the thought came from her or Anima.

'I can't tell you,' she said, and her voice shook. 'I'm sorry, milady. I *can't.*'

Very gently, Lady Marguerite took Eleanor's hands in her own and squeezed them. 'I knew you'd say that. And if you had told me, then I would never have been able to trust you in the same way again. A woman who'd break her word once will break it a second time. But I had to know. I'm sorry, Eleanor, but I had to be sure.'

Dimly, through the sudden shrieking anger that filled her heart, Eleanor remembered how Sir Percy had tested her once before too, letting her assume she'd be killed if she didn't betray the League. She wondered if all the men in the League had been put through the same trial. Was their 'word of honour' considered enough, as *gentlemen*? How many times would her employers feel the need to push her to this point for their own satisfaction?

She choked back something between a laugh and a sob. 'You and your husband are going to drive me too far someday, milady.'

Lady Marguerite pressed a handkerchief into her hand. 'Come now, Eleanor. You'd feel the same way if it was your own family. Dry your eyes. And remember . . . Andrew can say what he likes now, but when it's you and Tony and Charles in France, things may take an entirely different course. Who knows? It might be that the sensible thing will be for you to accompany them to Paris after all. You being there could be the crucial element in whatever happens.'

Eleanor scrubbed her eyes with the handkerchief and looked at Lady Marguerite – bright, vivid, vital, bewitching, beautiful. 'And you trust me to do that, milady?'

'Haven't I just said so?'

Yet Eleanor could sense unspoken words beneath Lady Marguerite's lovely smile, under the porcelain and rose of her beautiful face. She remembered what Lady Sophie had said about the Marquis de Saint-Cyr. How he and his sons had been sent to the guillotine because Lady Marguerite had wanted to protect her brother. She remembered being sent to run through the streets of London with an armful of books, to protect Lady Marguerite's secret letters.

'*I have a duty to keep them safe,*' milady had said.

But could Eleanor trust her to keep *Eleanor* safe?

CHAPTER ELEVEN

A dozen trips across the Channel, and Eleanor still suffered from seasickness. Here they were *again*, sneaking into France by night in a smuggler's boat, and once more her stomach roiled as she stared at the horizon. (Sir Percy bribed so many of the smugglers that he must be practically funding their entire industry. No doubt the brandy and wine which filled his cellars were a by-product of this generosity.) They'd been tiptoeing down the French coast for the last couple of days, and she'd slept for most of it, recovering from her loss of blood at the ball. Seldom had she been so grateful to be lying in a narrow wooden bunk with a blanket over her head. She'd slept so deeply that she hadn't even heard Anima talking to her, and she *certainly* hadn't been walking in her sleep.

Still, all good things came to an end, and now she was on her feet again, as they were within a few hours' distance of the bay where she, Tony and Charles were to be put ashore. She turned at the sound of footsteps to see Charles approaching her, and steeled herself for what would doubtless be a new set of dire warnings about the dangers they were about to face.

Instead, he leaned on the ship's rail next to her, and said quietly, 'I don't know how to thank you.'

'Thank me?' Eleanor stammered, taken aback. 'Whatever for?'

'For the suggestion of Mont-Saint-Michel.' He stared towards the horizon, but his gaze was clearly on some distant object, or person, of his imagination. 'And for the chance to rescue Fleurette from there.'

The gears of Eleanor's thoughts seized up as though someone had thrown a whole sackful of wooden shoes into them. She stood there, slack-jawed, uncertain of what to say. While she naturally felt sorry for Fleurette, and she'd like to see the woman at liberty, Chauvelin's daughter was safer in there than in a lot of other places in France. Eleanor hadn't actually been planning to rescue her. It would be a gamble for the Pimpernel himself – and the group of them, while they might be competent, didn't add up to a single Sir Percy Blakeney.

Don't be a fool, Anima advised. *Smile nicely and take the credit. It's not undeserved. The woman's been on your mind too. Do you think it's pure coincidence that you suggested the place where she was a prisoner? And not just for her own sake – wouldn't it be convenient if Chauvelin owed you a favour?*

This was almost more discomfiting than Charles's thanks. *Are you telling me that I've been wanting to get her out of there but wouldn't confess it to myself?*

That's between you and your conscience, Anima replied smugly. *But if you truly want to convince the Committee for Public Safety that the Pimpernel is here, then a genuine rescue would be a great deal more effective than merely scattering a few scraps of paper decorated with five-petalled red flowers. They may be paranoid, but they're not stupid.*

'But what will we do afterwards, even if we can manage it?' she asked, abandoning the proper speech which Lady Marguerite had drilled into her. 'She'll be in twice as much trouble if we rescue her. They'll be certain then that she's a traitor.'

'England,' Charles said, as though this resolved all problems. 'Lady Blakeney can give her shelter.' He smiled at Eleanor. 'I know what you're thinking. You're convinced this is some foolish gallantry of mine. That I'm overly grateful for her help in Paris and have decided purely on the basis of one meeting that she's a kind and gentle woman who doesn't deserve her fate. That I don't know my own mind. Perhaps that I should be gently shaken until I come to more sensible conclusions?'

'Well, not exactly,' Eleanor lied, having been thinking all that and more.

Charles shrugged. 'That may all be so. But, Eleanor, pray consider that the poor girl is truly innocent of the Republic's misdoings. Before I met her, I'd have been willing to blame any Frenchman, or Frenchwoman, for complicity in France's crimes. She showed me that anyone, even Chauvelin's own daughter, can deserve rescue. For that . . . I feel I owe her something. I can't just leave her there in danger of execution.'

Eleanor remembered the way that Charles and Fleurette had looked at each other when first they met. Although she knew the bond between herself and Charles was far more than this single fraction of acquaintance between him and Fleurette, a pang of jealousy twisted uncomfortably in her belly. But the thought made her ashamed of herself, and she dropped her eyes. 'What if she doesn't want to come?' she said. 'What if she should feel it'd be too traitorous to flee France for England with us?'

'An interesting point, but I'd rather discuss it with her when she's safely out of prison,' Charles said, unexpectedly firm. 'I understand, Eleanor. You believe I'm taking this all far too fast, that I have no way of knowing how she'll react. Well, if she calls me a spy and a fiend, I will endeavour to take it like a gentleman and . . .' he vaguely waved a bony hand. '. . . find some other way of handling matters. But I have hope. Even if it's for the daughter of our worst enemy. Surely she deserves rescue just as much as the Dauphin did?'

Now Eleanor felt truly ashamed of herself. 'I'm not denying you have a point,' she said. 'I'm just saying that it's not going to be easy. Have you ever rescued someone who didn't want to go?'

'We'll find a way,' Charles said, avoiding the question. 'You can reason with her, one woman to another. If we had Lady Blakeney with us I'd turn her loose on Fleurette, but as she's not here—'

'Who's not here?' Tony said, appearing from behind them.

'Lady Blakeney,' Eleanor said, thanking the heavens that he hadn't heard the rest of the conversation. At least, she hoped he hadn't. She was certain he'd have reacted far more strongly if he had.

'A good thing she isn't,' Tony said firmly. 'She's far more effective back home, keeping Chauvelin confused and gathering information. Besides, she'd be wasted on a mission like this, where we're just causing a diversion. Have you sighted Mont-Saint-Michel yet?'

'Which way is it?' Eleanor demanded, conscious of Anima's own urgency to reach there. The other woman wanted something – but what?

'Port,' Tony said, then caught Eleanor by the shoulder and turned her in the correct direction as she stood there confused. 'That is, to the west, this way. Just give it a few more minutes and you'll see the, ahem, scale of the problem.'

As Eleanor stared hopefully across the dark waves, Charles said, 'Tony, old friend—'

'Out of the question,' Tony interrupted. 'I know what you're going to say, and the answer is no.'

'The place is full of political prisoners,' Charles pointed out. 'Ladies and gentlemen who haven't even been charged with anything more than suspicion, held there solely in order to put pressure on their families. We could strike a real blow to the whole system in France by setting them free.'

Tony sighed, his mobile face drooping like that of a well-bred dog. 'Milady and Andrew both warned me you'd suggest this, and they also explained why it wouldn't work. These people can't go back to their families. They'd be arrested then and there. Furthermore, my friends, these are people from all over France – we couldn't escort them all back home, and they'd be easy for the Guard to track if we were simply to turn them loose.'

'Wouldn't the Chief have tried it?' Charles asked.

'Now you're being unfair,' Tony said. 'We all know very well that what the Chief might think or try is a cut above our level.'

'Whatever he might *think*, it'd be helpful if he'd share it with the rest of us a bit more,' Eleanor muttered. 'Even the rest of you. I'm accustomed to having these conversations go above my head, and I don't expect to be let in on everything, but he could at least have told milady what he was up to before he left. She's his *wife*.'

'You shouldn't say that sort of thing,' Tony rebuked her, in tones which suggested he entirely agreed. 'The Chief knows what he's doing. We must operate under conditions of absolute secrecy, which is why only the Chief knows the full details of any operation or his future plans. With Chauvelin constantly at our shoulder, or other minions of the Committee of Public Safety, we can trust nobody.'

'Except each other,' Charles added.

'Well, obviously, old chap. There's no need to point that out.' Tony's sidelong glance at him was sharper than Eleanor had expected from the generally well-meaning and vague aristocrat. 'I haven't even told my beloved wife the full details of what we get up to. Women talk, you know. Oh, not you,

Eleanor, don't take it the wrong way, but it's a sad fact that once a woman hears something then it's all around her circle the next morning. Look at my mother and sisters. They even read my mail.'

'They read your mail?' Eleanor said, shocked.

'Not any more. Long story. Percy was involved.' Tony took a deep breath, visibly pulling himself back to the original subject. 'So in *any* case, I think we can agree there are all sorts of perfectly logical reasons why we could never expect to succeed in any attempt to actually rescue the prisoners from Mont-Saint-Michel. And if you look over there, you'll see the largest reason . . .'

The sky was finally beginning to pale with the coming of dawn, and now Eleanor could clearly make out the distant form of Mont-Saint-Michel. It really *did* look like a mountain. The islet was crowned by harsh, high walls and topped by the angular shapes of church towers, with a spire reaching heavenwards like an unsheathed sword. Below that, she could discern the shapes of normal buildings, clustered round the abbey walls like children round their mother's skirts, and cascading down the slopes, with a final wall at the bottom to stand against the encroaching sea.

Yet . . . she frowned. There was some sort of untidiness around the elegant lines of the spire and towers, like lichen on a statue. 'Is the abbey crumbling?' she asked. 'The stone-work looks misshapen.'

'It's the other way round.' Tony levelled a spyglass and peered through it at the spire. 'Yes, I'd heard rumours of this, though Charles will know more than I do about the whole business. They're setting up an optical telegraph.'

'They've progressed that far?' Charles snatched the spyglass from Tony with more haste than carefulness and stared through it himself. 'Dash it all! This could be a significant inconvenience.'

'What's an optical telegraph?' Eleanor asked.

'It's not finished yet,' Tony said reassuringly. 'With a bit of luck, we can be in and out before they've completed it or linked it up to the rest of the line.'

'It might actually be an asset,' Charles said slowly. 'After all, if we can start a panic about the League down here, and the news reaches Paris within hours . . .'

'But it's days from here to Paris!' Eleanor said in shock.

'That's the issue.' Charles passed her the spyglass and helped her hold it properly to her eye. Suddenly the view of the distant spire came into focus. The ancient stonework was enwrapped by a confusing mess of scaffolding and timbers, like ivy on a garden statue. 'You see, Eleanor, it's not complete yet – they haven't set up the signalling arms.'

Eleanor took a last look at the distant islet, then returned the spyglass to Tony. 'So what *is* an optical telegraph? Apart from something which has arms and can get news to Paris inconveniently fast?'

Tony waved a hand at Charles, who lit up with that special happiness he always had when someone called on him for an explanation. 'Our resident scholar can explain it better than I can.'

'You've heard of beacons?' Charles began. 'Or smoke signals?'

Eleanor had certainly *heard* of them, but she couldn't see how they were applicable here. 'They set fire to the wood scaffolding up there to send a message?'

'That's an idea we shouldn't rule out,' Tony noted.

Charles went on in some detail, but he managed to convey the basic idea that the arms on the contraption atop the spire could be seen from a distance and could signal basic codes. The messages it conveyed could then be passed along a line of similar such buildings all the way to Paris or beyond.

157

Eleanor frowned as she took in the concept. 'This sounds dreadfully straightforward. Why haven't *we* built something like this in England?'

'It's been suggested,' Tony said. 'The Admiralty's looking into it, I'm told. It's not as if any of the League can bring them in-person witness accounts, m'dear, given how hard we work to be considered the most frivolous of fribbles.'

'The man in charge of the prison – I think his rank is Warden – is a collaborator of the Chappe brothers, the men behind this contraption,' Charles explained. He took another look at it through the spyglass, his face wistful. 'Guillaume Duquesne. Studied at the Sorbonne. That's the university in Paris, splendid place—'

'Or it was until the National Convention closed it down last year in order to reorganize things,' Tony sighed. 'Many a fine glass of wine have I had with some of those students . . .'

'They may have closed it, but they can't take ideas out of people's heads,' Charles said. 'Duquesne's a very bright fellow, but he's one of those who's overly loyal to the Revolution because his old family name and prior education put him in danger if he's suspected.'

'A bit like Talleyrand, then?' Eleanor said. 'Or like Talleyrand was?'

Charles nodded. 'I haven't met him in person, but he's supposed to be an expert in the physical sciences. Even has his own balloon. That would be why they've assigned him here, no doubt – to ensure that the optical telegraph's completed on schedule.'

'So it might be a good thing if he's focused on science rather than current politics,' Eleanor said thoughtfully. 'That could make him easier to manipulate.'

'We're only here to make a diversion,' Tony said firmly. 'And 'pon my soul, Eleanor, you're growing positively devious! Sometimes I wonder if we should have brought an innocent flower like you into this sort of business. Wouldn't want to corrupt you, after all.' He laughed.

Eleanor didn't laugh with him. She knew what Sir Percy would have said: *Good thinking, Eleanor. Always wise to take a careful look at your hand of cards before you start to gamble.*

And they might be about to take a very large gamble indeed.

They entered Pontorson just as dusk was falling, trailing in dusty and weary, like any travellers on the roads these days. Tony had a bandage knotted round his head, more of a rag than the clean linen it had once been, while Charles had hidden his eye-glasses and peered around vaguely at the busy town. Eleanor followed behind them, bags slung over her shoulders, keeping her step obedient and her head low. For the moment she was just the sister of two men who'd made their way across France in search of better employment and greater safety from the ravening beast that the Revolution had become. A woman like that would let her brothers do the talking – in public, at least.

It didn't take long to find a convenient inn. Within a couple of hours Tony and Charles were downstairs, drinking the local cider and picking up any local gossip. They'd probably be doing it for the next few hours. Eleanor, meanwhile, was sitting in their shared bedroom and staring out bitterly through the narrow window at the stars above and the street below.

She knew no single woman of good character would sit drinking in a public inn as the men were doing. Oh, she might have got away with it if she'd been posing as a wife, or if she'd actually been working as one of the maids, but on her own, or even with her 'brothers'? Unthinkable. It would have drawn far too much attention to her, and they couldn't risk that. Yet this didn't make it any easier to accept being left up here, on her own, in a room that stank of old tallow candles, where the sheets were mended and the straw mattresses probably had fleas, and the boards underfoot creaked with every step she took and—

You're fretting yourself into a temper, Anima said. *Stop it.*

Eleanor's mood eased a little. At least Anima was someone else to talk to. *Where have you been?*

Where could I be except here in your mind? Anima said sourly. *If I've had little to say, it's because you're all managing matters quite well so far, and because it's growing harder to speak with you. I save my strength for when I need it. So, what are your plans to slip into the abbey?*

Eleanor felt a moment's unease, as she might have done when checking yarn and finding an unexpected thorn or bristle caught up in the wool. *It's going to be difficult. Tony's against the idea in any case, but Charles still wants to get Fleurette out of there . . .*

As do you, Anima reminded her.

True enough, but Charles seems . . . She didn't want to confess her brief flare of jealousy to Anima, even if the old mage was probably already aware of it. Surely Eleanor's own friendships with the men in the League proved that men and women *could* be friends without it meaning any more than that. *I'm worried he'll try something reckless. It won't be too hard to get onto the isle itself, we can just cross the causeway at low tide. But even if we can steal uniforms from somewhere and infiltrate the prison, which is all the abbey is at the moment, then what if we can't persuade Fleurette to come with us?* A thought seized her. *Do you have any sort of magic which could convince her to join us – at least until we're safely out of there?*

Alas, no. Bernard – a healer I once knew – could have used his powers to sicken her, and perhaps you could have escorted her out while claiming to be taking her for medical attention. But I lack such abilities. Still, there's a great deal that can be done with

160

drugs, which would have the benefit of quieting her objections too . . .

Eleanor paused, absorbing this. *Could your friend Bernard have sickened vampires too?* she asked idly.

No. How can one sicken what is already dead?

Anima's response was harsh enough that Eleanor turned her attention away from the conversation to the street outside. The noise from the public rooms below had died down, and she could hear the distant sounds of horses' hooves, slow and dragging, and the jingle of harnesses. Curious about who'd be riding at this time of night, she craned to see better.

There were two riders on weary horses, wrapped in cloaks against the sea breezes. As they came to a stop beneath the inn's torches, one of the men's cloaks slipped open and she caught a momentary glimpse of a tricolour sash before he pulled it closed again. He murmured something to the other rider.

Fear seized Eleanor, as cold as seawater. What were representatives of the Committee for Public Safety doing here? And travelling so late at night? She *had* to hear what they were saying. Without even thinking about it, she made the gesture with her hands, and focused her mind, in the way Anima had shown her previously, bringing forth the breezes which would bear their words to her ears.

'Far too public,' the second rider said. 'And the risk of loose lips – no. Unacceptable. Which other inns did you suggest?'

'The Black Cat, citizen, or the Golden Chicken.' He paused. 'The Black Cat has a poor reputation, but they'll take care of our horses well enough and we'll run less risk of being observed.'

Eleanor racked her brains. Yes, Tony had mentioned it earlier, and had absolutely refused to consider spending the night there while Eleanor was with them, although it bought

161

supplies from the smugglers who'd brought them in. It was clearly one of *those* places, even if both the men were too straitlaced to call it that in front of her.

While she was thinking, she snatched up her shawl and slipped on her shoes.

'Better make it the Black Cat, then,' the first rider said. 'You're sure it will be safe?'

'For an unknown traveller, perhaps not, but for two armed men travelling together?' The second man shrugged. 'They may be thieves, but they know when not to test their luck.'

'Very well, then.' The horses began to move again, trudging along with the slow pace of utter weariness.

Common sense dictated that Eleanor should let the others know before running off on her own to follow strangers into the night. But if she waited any longer, and delayed to ask for permission, then she might not be in time to see where the two riders went. Even if they'd said they were going to the Black Cat, they could still change their minds. The situation was too dangerous *not* to know why they were in Pontorson.

Eleanor slipped out of her room and hurried down the narrow stairs, making her way out through the stables and onto the street without anyone noticing. She drew her shawl tight around her head and shoulders to hide her face, and followed the ambling horses, staying in the shadows.

The Black Cat was in a less salubrious part of Pontorson. The buildings overhung the alleyways as though they disapproved of the muddy paths and garbage below. Eleanor had managed to follow unobserved – at least, she hoped she was – by staying at a safe distance and relying on her sense of hearing as much as her sight. There were few other noises. In fact, the whole area was unhealthily silent. There were no open windows with light blazing out, or sounds of music coming from the neighbouring houses. A couple of other people had been out on the streets, but like Eleanor they had

162

their collars turned up or shawls drawn close to hide their faces, and they'd also stayed in the shadows.

She'd had plenty of time during her stealthy pursuit to consider what a stupid and risky idea this was. The only thing which had kept her at her task was the awareness of how dangerous the Committee's representatives might be to what she and the others were planning. It was comparatively easy to plan a diversion with rumours of the Scarlet Pimpernel when nobody was expecting such a thing. To do it directly under the enemy's nose was another thing entirely – even the Chief would baulk at such a thing.

Well, perhaps not the Chief. But he managed to get away with every sort of escapade.

Eleanor watched from a distance as the men entered the Black Cat; a few moments later their horses were led round to the stables. Another minute, and light suddenly gleamed through the shutters in one of the upstairs rooms.

She skulked across to crouch in a nook beneath it, huddling under her shawl like a beggar, and crooked her fingers to summon the breezes again. *Anima must approve of what I'm doing to be helping me like this, despite her silence,* she thought.

'This place has fleas,' the second man said, suddenly audible. 'I apologize, citizen—'

'I have little need for sleep,' the first man said. 'Besides, we will be leaving before dawn.'

'But the local authorities . . .' the second man began, with a whine to his voice which suggested it wasn't the first time he'd raised the subject.

'Manton, your sincere nature does you no favours. They *cannot be trusted.* Look at the current state of Paris. Why, they say the Widow Capet has turned vampire and stalks the streets at night, slaughtering any victims she can find. That may be exaggeration, but it shows the public mood. There are counter-revolutionaries everywhere, spreading rumours and doubt. If the capital of France harbours traitors, then how much more the outskirts? And consider the news we carry, and our followers.'

There was a noise of liquid being poured – water? Wine? And then the second man, Manton, spoke again. 'At least we should be free of the sanguinocrats here. Any traitors will be purely human. It almost seems a pity.'

'Why so?' his superior enquired.

A frustrated snort. 'Because it means the people of France still haven't learned! Even though we're giving them a better future and have thrown off the yoke of the King and the aristocracy. The National Convention's in power now, the people rule France, but *still* there are fools or villains who want to restore the old ways, to enrich themselves, or to put the boot back on their own necks. It makes no sense. Why does a freed animal want to crawl back into its cage?'

'If I could answer that question, Manton, then perhaps we could change France here and now, rather than doing it year by year.' A creak of wood; someone had sat down, probably the speaker. He sighed. 'Curse these boots . . . Manton, I sympathize with your frustration, but we must be patient. Let us borrow from the Church's doctrine and say that instead of Original Sin, we have Original Stupidity. France must be educated. But in the meantime, for the country's own sake, we must protect her from herself.'

'As with the Drownings?' Manton's voice was colourless, as though he was trying to avoid showing any feeling. He stressed the word *Drownings*, as though it was some event that both men knew about.

'If necessary, yes.' His superior's voice was merciless. 'What would you have done if you'd been there? Something . . . rash?'

There was a pause, then Manton said hoarsely, 'I would have followed orders.'

'Quite. Remember that following orders is generally the safest thing to do.' There was another gurgle as more liquid was poured. 'In this case, the Committee's being positively merciful. Anyone at Mont-Michel who's genuinely innocent is going to be released. No Drownings here, simply justice and the law. And the rest, well . . . it'll be quick.'

Eleanor went very still. They were going to execute prisoners at Mont-Saint-Michel? And how few would be classed as 'innocent'? Fleurette . . .

'Thorough efficiency is the best way to serve the greater good,' the speaker went on. Did he sound as though he was trying to convince himself? 'We can no longer afford to have long queues of prisoners clogging up the penal system while they wait for trials. It's not just to the prisoners, any more than it is to the rest of the population. The sooner we clear out the prisons under the law, the sooner France can return to a more natural state. This sort of firm action will *prevent* more wholesale executions such as the Drownings. Jean-Baptiste Carrier was a fool to drown innocents along with the guilty. If the people are to trust the new laws, they must see that they're properly applied and justly carried out. The soldiers following us will help with that.'

Eleanor pressed her knuckles against her mouth, forcing herself to stay silent. Soldiers on the way here? That was supposed to happen *after* the League's action took place, not before!

'At least it shouldn't take long.' Manton sounded as if he was trying to reassure himself as well. 'With a bit of luck, we'll be back in Paris in plenty of time for the new Festival of the Supreme Being.'

His superior snorted, and there was the sound of him refilling his glass. How much was he drinking, Eleanor wondered? 'I wouldn't want to miss something which was so dear to Citizen Robespierre's heart. I can only hope our soldiers don't have any more "little incidents" that slow them down further. The longer they delay, the more chance that word might reach Mont-Michel beforehand and . . . disturb the prisoners there. It'll be easier for everyone if they aren't pre-warned. For the prisoners, too,' he added as an after-thought which he clearly didn't believe.

'The weather's no man's friend at the moment,' Manton said, 'and the rain's a day or two behind us, which means it's probably making the troops' lives miserable.'

'All the more reason for them to hurry up and reach us here,' his superior said heartlessly. 'Go and ask the innkeeper if that food he promised us is ready yet, Manton, and fetch some more wine while you're at it.'

'And check he hasn't sold off our horses too while we were up here talking?' Manton joked.

'He might be the sort of man to do that, but he's also the sort to have more sense than to cheat us when we're on official business. We might find some counter-revolutionary activity right under our noses.'

Both men laughed, then Manton left the room, the door creaking shut behind him. Eleanor stared at the wall of the hovel opposite, letting her thoughts spin like a whirligig.

Charles and Tony would no doubt be angry with her for stealing out on her own, but . . . well, if she hadn't, then they wouldn't have had any warning of what was coming. The three of them would have been caught between Mont-Saint-Michel in front and a troop of armed soldiers behind, and while Eleanor might not be a military tactician like some in the League, she had every sympathy with cornered rats.

And in any case, their Chief, Sir Percy, wasn't here to give orders, which meant she wasn't technically disobeying. Her conscience was clear, and would be even clearer if she managed to return to their room in the inn before the men found she was missing and started worrying about her.

I may have taught you too much about logic, Anima said wryly.

Logic only works if the other people are prepared to listen to you, Eleanor answered. *I've yet to see it be a satisfactory tool when someone on the scaffold of the guillotine is explaining why they shouldn't be executed. So, what do you think of the situation?*

I think you've been lucky, Anima answered, *but you can't rely on luck, no matter what your Pimpernel likes to say. Yet . . . there has to be a way we can use this in our favour.*

It was good to have Anima thoroughly on her side for once. It was probably because the prisoners in Mont-Saint-Michel were all living humans, rather than vampires: it meant that Anima's hatred for vampires was no longer a weight on the scales. Nobody could object to rescuing *innocent* people from certain death, or even counter-revolutionary people, whatever their degree of innocence. The question was how to do it. These men were an unwanted complication, a knot in the thread that spoiled the design.

Eleanor's thoughts suddenly came to a stop as a new idea unfolded itself in her mind, like a pattern all stretched and pinned and ready for cutting.

Or perhaps . . . this might be an *opportunity.*

CHAPTER TWELVE

The morning breezes carried a chill with them from the distant sea, cutting through Eleanor's clothing as she walked behind the horses. Her hands had been lightly tied together, and a rope ran from them to the saddle of the man ahead, stiff-backed and arrogant in his black clothing and tricolour sash.

The stones of the long causeway were still wet from the retreating tide. There was no escaping the smell of the sea. Remnant strands of seaweed had been left behind like discarded threads of yarn across the pale canvas of sand and saltpans, as if to remind the humans riding across this empty landscape that the tide would reclaim it soon enough, locking Mont-Saint-Michel away behind the impassable barrier of the angry waters.

Eleanor felt uncomfortably exposed. The wide reaches of open land and shore left her nowhere to hide. There wasn't even a comforting tree trunk or two, pointless as it might have been to cower behind them. Anyone could see her. Anyone could shoot at her. The phrase *a moving target*, over-heard from some random conversation between members of the League, bobbed up and down in her mind like a flailing swimmer desperate for attention.

Though of course nobody was going to shoot at a prisoner on her way to gaol in Mont-Saint-Michel, in the company of two representatives of the Committee of Public Safety. There were plenty of other things for her to worry about besides being shot, such as being discovered in the act of counter-revolutionary activity and infiltrating the abbey-turned-gaol.

With a pang of guilt, Eleanor wondered if this was how Andrew felt *all the time* while the rest of the League were cheerfully dashing into peril. Perhaps she should apologize to him, once this was all over. And she did have Tony and Charles with her. If only Sir Percy himself had been here. No doubt he'd have had a far better plan than the one they'd hastily hammered together.

A guard post stood at the end of the causeway. The two men manning it were standing to attention, models of Revolutionary alertness – probably assisted by the fact that they could see Eleanor and her escorts coming from a good distance, and would have every reason to want to look sharp for the benefit of Committee representatives. This location offered no excuses for being taken by surprise. Though perhaps if there had been heavy fog or mists . . .

Unlikely, with the wind from the sea, Anima said unprompted. *Even if I could raise a fog at low tide thick enough to hide a mass escape – and you have yet to tell me how you propose to manage that – the fugitives themselves would be lost in it. They might wander towards the incoming waters rather than the shore, and be caught by the tide before they could reach safe land.*

Eleanor shuddered at the thought, imagining herself wandering in blinding mists until she was dragged down by treacherous whirlpools. She then hastily converted the movement into a cowering huddle as one of the guards glanced at her.

'Another one for the prison, citizen?' he asked.

Tony snorted, in an excellent imitation of Chauvelin, and

nodded. He held out a hand to receive his papers back from the other guard. 'Straight up the road from here to the gates, then?'

'As you say, citizen,' the guard agreed. He paused. 'Is there any news from Paris?'

'There are reports the Widow Capet stalks the streets as a vampire,' Tony said ominously, 'and that she's aided by the Scarlet Pimpernel. I'll welcome the day when both of them meet the Republic's justice.'

The two guards nodded vigorously, clearly grateful for their positions far from such danger. 'Pass on, citizen,' the first guard said, saluting.

Tony returned a nod, and led the way onwards into the . . . well, Eleanor wasn't quite sure what to call it. A sprawl of houses and buildings lined the road which zigzagged upwards towards the abbey at the highest point of the island. Not quite a town, but larger than a village, and very definitely a place where people lived, rather than just some sort of barracks for the guards who operated the gaol. Shop signs hung above doorways, and more than one tavern had its doors open, even at this time of the morning, inviting custom. Chickens squawked in backyards as they passed, and children played in the street, running pointless races or kicking around pieces of garbage until some adult drove them away or set them to work. And of course the omnipresent garlic hung in garlands over the doors of houses, next to tricolour flags still sodden from the morning rain.

The people showed less interest in visitors from the Committee than in other places Eleanor had visited. No doubt they were used to prisoners being delivered for incarceration. She glimpsed a pitying glance or two thrown in her direction, but nobody was foolish enough to express open sympathy for a prisoner.

If she really *had* been a prisoner, Eleanor would have been panicking by this point. Fortunately, things were going according to plan – at least, so far.

The road wound steadily upwards, past terraced gardens and even small orchards. Eleanor was panting as she tried to keep up with the horses, her feet aching on the unforgiving stones, calves throbbing from the height they'd already climbed. As she looked off to the side, she could see the island unfolding below her, close enough that she could have thrown a pebble and watched it bounce off the roofs of the houses further down.

The abbey itself waited ahead of them, its high buildings arranged in a circle around the central church and spire – the Merveille, Charles had called it, and it truly looked a marvel. The half-finished construction of the optical telegraph was clearer now, and Eleanor could understand *why* they had decided to put it there. It would be visible for miles and miles, a single point on an empty horizon.

As she looked upwards, goggling at her surroundings like a lady of leisure rather than a prisoner, she saw something begin to slowly *rise* above the surrounding walls – something curved, no, globular, with a contraption dangling below it. 'What is *that*?' she gasped, forgetting herself for a moment.

Tony and Charles looked up, and Tony's eyes widened. 'That'll be Duquesne's balloon,' he said, his voice low. They were still a few dozen yards from the gatehouse and wouldn't be overheard yet. 'It's tethered to the ground below – you can see the rope linking it, attached to the basket. Lucky devil.'

Eleanor's first instinct was to utterly deny that anyone fooling around with such a thing could have anything resembling luck, but then she remembered she was supposed to be a prisoner, and kept her mouth shut. Though, thinking about it . . . there was a certain allure to the idea of being so high above the ground, looking down on the crawling humans below like God himself, or at the very least an important angel. Wouldn't it be a fantastic thing to do, in every sense of the word?

Could you fly when you were alive? she asked Anima.

No. Anima paused. *But how does it stay up? What . . . witchcraft is this?*

It's something to do with heating the air that goes into the balloon, Eleanor answered, vaguely recalling Tony and Charles discussing the subject on their journey here. Tony was an enthusiast, and greatly regretted that rescuing prisoners by balloon would be impractical. *I don't think they can direct it once it's in the air, though.*

Anima didn't respond, but Eleanor had the sense that the old mage was considering something, and that she didn't wish to share her thoughts with Eleanor. To be fair, Eleanor was somewhat preoccupied herself with the knowledge that their pretence was about to reach the next level of danger.

Charles shot Eleanor a quick, surreptitious glance of mute apology and sympathy for her position. There would be no further chances for private words, or even sympathetic looks. Then the men both straightened in their saddles and approached the gatehouse at a brisk pace, forcing Eleanor to stagger along behind in order to keep up. The guards presented arms, and one of them demanded, 'Who goes there?'

'Citizen Legrange and Citizen Manton, to see Governor Duquesne, and a prisoner for your gaol.'

'Well then, let's see your documents, citizen.'

Eleanor's spine crawled with nervousness as the guard looked over the papers which they'd removed from the real representatives of the Committee. Those gentlemen were currently reposing in the Black Cat's cellar, tied up with sacks over their heads, and would be shipped out the next time the inn's proprietors took a delivery from smugglers, to be dumped further down the coast. It had cost most of Tony's money to arrange it, and all three of them knew that it was only a stop-gap measure to buy them the couple of days they needed. In the meantime, Charles had forged some additions to the documents and letters they carried, which would hopefully be enough to get them into the abbey . . .

Admittedly the *next* step in their plan was somewhat undefined, but Sir Percy always said that the important thing was to catch the single hair on Fortune's head as she flew past. Or in other words, to take opportunities when you saw them.

'And who's the woman?' the guard asked, returning the papers.

'Anne Dupont, of Lyon,' Tony answered. 'Accused of—'

'Wait, let me guess!' The man who strode into the gatehouse was stocky and square-built, his mud-brown hair ruffled and untidy, and the skirts of his coat had streaks of dirt and oil where he must have wiped his fingers. He looked far more bright and cheerful than Eleanor was accustomed to seeing in Republican officials. They normally affected a sober, depressed look, and any little glints of sadism and satisfaction at the thought of executions were hastily explained as mere enthusiasm for the cleansing of France. 'Counter-revolutionary sympathies?'

Eleanor bit down on her tongue to suppress a sigh of relief. They'd avoided the biggest potential flaw in their plan; the Governor *didn't* already know the two Committee representatives, and they weren't going to be unmasked on the very doorstep.

'You're absolutely correct, Citizen . . . Warden Duquesne?' Tony hazarded.

The new arrival clapped Tony on the shoulder. 'We get them all the time here, citizen. One might almost say they're positively squeezed within the walls here. Many more and we'll be making counter-revolutionary jam, ha ha!' His laugh wasn't the inane bray of amusement which Sir Percy took such pains to cultivate, but had a genuine note of mirth, inviting the other person to share in the joke.

Of course, it was a very *bad* joke.

Tony managed an appreciative chuckle, while Charles stared at the horizon with a face of stone. 'As long as you can fit one more in – for the moment, at least – then we won't have any problems, citizen. Though I'm afraid she's not the only reason we're here.' His accent was faintly Parisian, supporting the name and origin on his stolen identity papers.

Duquesne frowned and ran a hand through his hair, demonstrating why it was so messy. 'The telegraph? Well, I don't want to cast aspersions, but I would point out that it won't actually be needed or useful until the entire set of mechanisms is complete. We're right at the end of the line out here, you know. No point me rushing matters and putting the men at risk when there's no actual need for it.'

Eleanor's opinion of him shifted in his favour. Perhaps he was a Revolutionary gaoler and a man of dubious character – the two often went together, after all – but at least he appeared to care for the wellbeing of his men. He even sounded like one of the League, if any of the League had been French.

'Considered putting the prisoners on the job,' he added, 'but you just can't trust these *ci-devant* aristos or their counter-revolutionary friends. Far too much risk of sabotage. Not to mention the fact that they just don't have the strength or skill that a good Republican workman does. Soft white fingers and manicured fingernails aren't suited to a proper job of hammering. No, it's a good thing I can rely on the workers the Republic's assigned here. And with any luck we'll have it ready for tests by the end of the week. Will you be wanting to inspect it up close to?'

'Not so much a question of desire, citizen, as a question of duty,' Tony said blandly. 'You know how it is back in Paris. If you don't sign every line and initial every page, they're convinced you must have skimped on your duty somewhere. Better to make sure I complete my tasks here in proper order. Then I can go back to them with indisputable proof that any problems with the line can't be blamed on you.'

Duquesne's eyebrows rose. 'You're an understanding fellow,' he said, with a slight undertone of suspicion to his voice.

Tony shrugged. 'Citizen, I have the sense to recognize a major new development when it's in front of me. Everyone who's had a hand in this optical telegraph business is going to benefit, even those of us who've just been sent to check on its progress. Just imagine hundreds of them, all across France, carrying information from one side of the country to the other in mere hours! If I were a priest, I'd call it a miracle.'

'You're in the right place for that,' Duquesne commented, glancing up at the spire. His gaze lingered fondly on the balloon near it. 'Well, I'll be happy to show you how it's all going. You can stay the night, I hope?'

'We'll be glad to,' Tony answered, and Eleanor breathed an inward sigh of relief. They needed the time to come up with a workable plan, but it was easier if they were actually invited to stay rather than having to force the issue.

'I'll have a guard take Citizen Dupont here to join the other women at their work.'

'One thing before she goes,' Tony said quickly. 'While Citizen Dupont here was a collaborator rather than an aristocrat, it's possible that she knows a few things – a few names – which she hasn't shared with us.' His smirk was as near as his amiable face could come to Chauvelin's sneer. 'We'll have a word with her later, or tomorrow morning. Once she comes to terms with the prospect of spending the rest of her life here, she might change her mind about being cooperative.'

Eleanor played her part by doing her best to look subdued yet defiant, visibly biting her lip.

Duquesne nodded wisely. His gaze flicked over Eleanor, judging and dismissing her as just another prisoner. 'Best be sensible, girl. You don't want to end up like the last couple of prisoners who made a run for it, do you?'

'What happened to them?' Charles asked.

'Oh, the man on duty in my balloon spotted them crossing the sands during low tide, towards the mainland, and, well, you have to make an example in these cases, don't you?' He spread his hands, carelessly amiable, once more sharing a joke with people who he thought would understand. 'Haven't had any more attempts at *that* lately.'

'Good job,' Tony congratulated him, and managed to make it sound as though he believed it. 'Now, about the optical telegraph . . .'

A firm hand grasped Eleanor's shoulder, and she was marched away, leaving the men talking.

The guards talked over her head as they marched her to join the other women prisoners, ignoring her just as they would have a sheep being led to market. At least they'd untied her wrists. Eleanor listened, but heard little of any use. Though nature had already set firm boundaries on this place to make it a convenient prison, the guards weren't slack. They complained to each other about patrols, night duty, and the perils of going up in the Warden's balloon. It didn't bode well for possible rescues.

Relax, Anima said, sounding unusually cheerful. For once she was the one at ease while Eleanor was fretting. *Your plan so far has worked. Don't drive yourself into a panic until it's actually necessary.*

Are you sure you feel all right? Eleanor asked, rather worried.

Pfft. I'm probably inspired by your own good mood. There's only one thing which could really go wrong at this point . . .

The leading guard unlocked a heavy door. 'Get yourself settled in,' he told Eleanor, 'and when you come down for lunch with the rest, you'll be allotted work. Don't make any trouble and you won't get any.' He gave her a firm shove, and she stumbled forward: the door was heaved closed and locked again behind her as she caught her balance.

The murmured conversations in the room had been interrupted by her arrival. Twenty or so women turned to stare at Eleanor.

The long room was the same heavy grey stone as the rest of the abbey – or at least, all that Eleanor had seen so far. The stone bricks marched round the walls in a perfectly even pattern, as neat as Eleanor's best embroidery, split at the east by three tall narrow windows which let both sun and wind into the room. Columns ran the length of it, spreading outwards as they reached upwards and turning the ceiling into a regular network of arches. It felt almost inappropriate for women to be sitting in this place and sewing army uniforms.

And yet that was what they were doing. Instead of monks vowed to holy service, a mixture of women, clearly from different levels of society, were sitting together, coarsening their fingers on harsh fabric and rough thread. Their dresses ranged from ones which might have been in the windows of Paris modistes, or adorned women of the highest ranks, to cheap cottons and wool, and muslins designed to display the wearer's charms to the audience. A specifically male audience. There was no hair powder here, no cosmetics, no elegant slippers; these women wore clogs and wrapped themselves against the cold in shawls made from sacks and blankets.

But it was very clear who was in charge. A woman at the far end of the room, whose white hair was a result of age rather than powder, and who carried herself as though she was still wearing Court dress with panniers, cleared her throat. 'Young woman,' she said, 'who are you?'

Eleanor was about to reply when a squeal from one of the groups of women cut her off. Fleurette leapt to her feet, casting away her makeshift shawl, and ran to throw her arms around Eleanor. 'You came!' she exclaimed, her blue eyes still as absolutely trusting as before.

Eleanor returned the embrace for a moment, grateful beyond words for the warmth and support, for the presence of a friend here in the middle of their enemies. She'd expected Fleurette to recoil from her, to need to be cajoled into trusting her – at least, enough so they could get her out of the place. She hadn't expected Fleurette to actually be glad to see her. To *hug* her.

What do you think you're playing at? Anima demanded sharply. *Let go of her and get on with your plan.*

Eleanor bit her lip to stop herself forming the words in her mind which she'd very much like to think. Anima was right, damn her eyes, as the men of the League would say.

Reluctantly she separated herself from Fleurette, holding her at arm's length and taking a moment to inspect her. The girl – really the same age as Eleanor herself, but she couldn't help thinking of Fleurette as a girl rather than a woman – didn't look ill exactly, but equally didn't look as if she'd been getting enough to eat. Her golden hair was pinned back in a neat braid rather than falling in its usual cascade of curls, and her pretty pale blue muslin dress was frayed at the cuffs and stained at the hem. 'It wasn't exactly my idea,' she said ruefully. 'Are you well?'

'Oh, I'm perfectly well,' Fleurette said, 'though it is so cold here! But when all these other brave women – and men –

endure such temperatures without a word of complaint, how can I possibly object? Everyone is so very *interesting* here, Anne. I've learned so much.'

'You have?' Eleanor had been concerned about how this meeting would go. She now realized that she hadn't been concerned *enough*. She hadn't taken into account that Fleurette was genuinely sincere about almost everything, and that exposing her to a whole gaol full of independent thinkers might have . . . unwanted results.

'Kindly introduce me to your friend, Fleurette,' the dignified woman demanded.

'Of course, Madame Thiers,' Fleurette said quickly. 'I'm sorry, I was just so pleased to see her. This is Anne Dupont, and she's a member of the League of the Scarlet Pimpernel!'

CHAPTER THIRTEEN

Eleanor felt her mouth open and shut like a landed fish and the colour drain from her cheeks. The world seemed very far away all of a sudden. She had to be imagining things. Fleurette couldn't have just said . . . what she'd just said, in front of a room full of other people, who might *believe* her. What if someone in the room was untrustworthy and reported her words to the Warden that evening? What if they were *all* untrustworthy, and dragged her in front of the Warden by main force this very minute, and the next thing she knew she'd be facing the guillotine . . . ?

'Don't be ridiculous, Fleurette dear,' Madame Thiers said firmly. She cast her eye across the room, and gazes dropped abruptly to needlework. 'I'm certain that under *no conditions whatsoever* would anyone walking in here be affiliated with such a desperate, dangerous, *English* set of spies. It's quite out of the question.' She rose to her feet, putting aside her own partly sewn shirt. 'Let us continue this conversation somewhere else, where we won't be spreading such unthinkable rumours.'

Fleurette didn't look particularly crushed. 'Of course, madame.' She tugged Eleanor to follow, and Eleanor, still somewhat stunned by the last few minutes, did so meekly.

The small side room they went into might once have been for prayer or private confession, but now was stacked full of fabric on one side and completed clothing and sacks on the other. Light leaked through the slats of the shutter which covered the narrow window. There was barely enough room for the three women to stand comfortably, though Eleanor was even less happy about the way Madame Thiers occupied the space by the single door, blocking off any hope of escape.

While Eleanor might have eventually approached the other prisoners and informed them of her true identity, she hadn't planned to do so the moment she walked through the door. She tried to think of some way to neutralize Fleurette's incriminating words. Hopefully her silence so far could be explained as shock at the accusation. 'Fleurette, you shouldn't say things like that—' she tried.

Madame Thiers took no notice of her. 'Fleurette, my dear, I thought that we'd discussed the whole question of sharing too much information and when not to do it.'

Fleurette pouted, twirling a loose golden curl round her finger. 'But surely if Anne's here then she's part of a plan to rescue us! Isn't that something we should share with our fellow prisoners?'

'Only when we're certain of how it will work,' Madame Thiers said firmly. 'Committees and discussions are all very well, but they aren't suited to prison escapes. That, my dear, is the difference between theory and practice.'

Eleanor rapidly reorganized her thoughts. Madame Thiers was clearly the key to the women's side of the prison, and she was apparently willing to cooperate with Eleanor in organizing an escape. This wasn't just snatching a single hair from Fortune's head as she sped past; this was gratefully accepting Fortune's generosity as she dropped opportunity in your lap.

Though was this just a little too convenient? Eleanor had

seen betrayals before. She knew how easily people might turn their friends over to the authorities to save themselves. She'd like to think that she could trust Fleurette's judgement – as Fleurette clearly trusted Madame Thiers – but then again, Fleurette believed her father, Chauvelin, was a sincerely good man.

It would have been far better if Eleanor could have spent some days observing Madame Thiers and the other women, assessing their trustworthiness and judging how best to deal with them. Unfortunately, time was among the many things which Eleanor didn't have – along with her liberty, her freedom of movement, and any sort of support, other than two members of the League who had to keep playing their own roles, and an ancient mage's ghost in her head.

'Forgive me,' she said, addressing Madame Thiers, 'but might you, speaking hypothetically, already have a plan for escape?' She'd picked up the term *hypothetically* from Charles, who was fond of using it.

'That would depend on whether you actually were a member of the League of the Scarlet Pimpernel,' Madame Thiers replied. She peered more closely at Eleanor. 'Young woman, has anyone ever told you that you look extremely like our late Queen?'

Well, that answered a couple of questions for Eleanor. Only a royalist would refer to the late Marie Antoinette as 'our Queen' rather than 'the Widow Capet' or worse. And only someone who'd actually *known* Marie Antoinette in person would recognize Eleanor's resemblance to that lady. She decided that Madame Thiers probably wouldn't betray her. 'We need to urgently organize an escape within the next couple of days,' she said. 'Unfortunately, we have very little time, so if you already have a plan, madame, I would be very grateful to hear it.'

'Why is it so urgent?' Madame Thiers demanded.

Eleanor glanced sideways to Fleurette. 'This has to stay within the walls of this room,' she said. 'I'm serious, Fleurette. It could cause a panic if you tell anyone else.'

Fleurette nodded. 'Of course, Anne. I'm not going to teach you your business.'

And when did it become my business? Eleanor pondered gloomily. All she'd ever wanted was to become a modiste and embroiderer, not a spy or organizer of escapes from gaol.

Eleanor turned back to Madame Thiers. 'The problem, madame, is that there is a troop on the way here with orders to end this place's function as a prison. Prisoners are either to be released as innocent, or . . .' She didn't finish the sentence. 'We must therefore think of a way to extricate you before the troop arrives.'

'And how do you know about this?' Madame Thiers asked.

'We intercepted their forerunners,' Eleanor said vaguely. She might be trusting Madame Thiers to a degree, but she wasn't going to reveal Charles and Tony to her yet. 'None of us wish to gamble on how many of you might be judged guilty of counter-revolutionary activity.'

Madame Thiers brooded for a moment. Then she said, 'Fleurette, leave us. I must ask Anne some questions in private.'

Fleurette hesitated. 'You do trust Anne, don't you? It's not going to be like it was with Marie?'

Madame Thiers rolled her eyes heavenwards. 'Of course not, child. Out with you, and don't say a word for the moment.'

Fleurette hugged Eleanor again. 'I'm so glad you're here,' she said, every word absolutely sincere. 'I feel so much better now.'

The door closed behind her, and Madame Thiers appeared to relax a shade. Some of her effortless authority dropped away like a discarded veil, revealing lines of worry and eyes that had seen too much. 'Fleurette's a dear child,' she said, 'and quite unlike her father, so I'd rather not disturb her with talk of unfortunate necessities.'

'Was what happened to Marie an unfortunate necessity?' Eleanor guessed.

'Marie fell down the stairs and broke her arm.' Madame Thiers might as well have been discussing the shirt she'd been sewing. 'That's what happens when you're overheard talking to the guards. She really should have known better.'

Eleanor wasn't surprised that Madame Thiers was capable of such ruthlessness. She herself had done worse in defence of other maids, and that had been before she'd even heard of the League of the Scarlet Pimpernel. Still, a frisson of fear trickled down her back at the thought she was alone with this woman, with neither of them entirely trusting the other yet. Sir Percy might enjoy dangerous situations for their own sake; Eleanor did not. 'As I see it, madame,' she said, 'we have three problems: firstly we need to get out of the abbey, secondly we need to reach the mainland, and thirdly we need to get you and the other prisoners away from the general area.'

Your ability to reason convincingly is improving, Anima said approvingly. *Evidently I'm a good influence on you.*

This would be an excellent time for you to reveal that you can hold back the tides to assist in our escape, Eleanor answered, though without much hope. *Or anything else of that nature.*

There may be something . . . Anima said. *Let me think.*

Madame Thiers nodded briskly. 'You can forget the third point, Mademoiselle Dupont. We have a plan for that.'

Eleanor raised an eyebrow.

Madame Thiers sniffed. 'My dear young woman, if you're not going to share any of your secrets then I'm certainly not going to share mine. I have yet to see any definite proof that you're here to help us, whatever Fleurette may have said. In fact, I find myself wondering exactly how *she* knew that you belong to the League of the Pimpernel. Her father is hardly the sort to prosecute his enquiries within earshot of his tender daughter.'

Eleanor weighed the need to convince Madame Thiers of her sincerity against the fear of revealing too much information. How she wished Sir Percy was here! His mixture of charm and command would have Madame Thiers agreeing with whatever he said. Finally she said, 'I'm sorry, madame. Some secrets aren't mine to tell. I would be grateful for your help and your trust, but I don't know how to convince you, and I'm not going to start telling you secrets when I've barely known you for ten minutes.'

Madame Thiers nodded, thin-lipped. A further weight seemed to settle on her shoulders. 'Then it seems we're at an impasse.'

Eleanor came to a decision. She *wasn't* required to come up with an escape plan on the spur of the moment. Her current task was to gather as much information as possible, and then share it with Tony and Charles later. Hopefully they would also have noted some weak points in the abbey's security while Duquesne was making them welcome. 'Let's consider practical matters,' she suggested. 'If I can present you with a workable plan, then would the men who are prisoners here be willing to comply?'

'They would,' Madame Thiers said firmly. 'If not on my word alone, then my husband – he's incarcerated with them – would persuade them.'

'You see each other frequently?'

'At some of the meals,' Madame Thiers explained, 'though we're made to sleep apart in separate dormitories. It's worse than a workhouse! However, some of the guards are willing to permit clandestine meetings, and a few of us still have jewellery saved to bribe them, or we offer some other form of payment. We are not all of us from the upper classes, Mademoiselle Dupont.'

'So, your daily schedule . . .'

'We are woken at dawn, much as the monks who once lived here would have been. We are allowed breakfast, then we work till noon; lunch, then work till sunset, and supper; then to our dormitories, and we are expected to sleep. As you've seen, we women are set to sewing. The men are more confined, as only those prisoners who are actually *trusted* are allowed to work on the scaffolding for that new telegraph device. Alas, the Warden is a careful and suspicious man. Still, I understand that in some gaols it is worse. Many of us have influential connections or relatives in the government, so we must be kept alive and relatively healthy . . . for the moment. The Committee of Public Safety wants us kept safe – until it has no further use for those who care for us.' Her mouth twisted as though she had tasted vinegar.

Eleanor continued to question her about her work schedule and patrols, and everything that she could think of. But time and again she came up against the fact that Madame Thiers simply didn't know enough about the security arrangements beyond the prison quarters. The other woman answered willingly enough, but Eleanor could still see the distrust in her eyes. She was prepared to give Eleanor the benefit of the doubt, to a degree – but she was still holding something back.

Fleurette was waiting for them outside, her assigned needlework idle in her lap. She seized on Eleanor as the two of them came out. 'Forgive me, madame,' she said to Madame Thiers, 'but Anne and I haven't seen each other for months! I have so much to ask her.'

'As long as you talk quietly and don't disturb the others,' Madame Thiers said indulgently. She turned to address the other women. 'Let us welcome Anne here. She is one more victim of charges of counter-revolutionary activity, and no more guilty than any of the rest of us. I trust you can sew, Anne?'

'Madame,' Eleanor said, quite sincerely, 'if nothing else, I can certainly sew.'

She settled down with Fleurette in a far corner of the room. The previous chatter resumed, but she knew that the other women would be watching and listening to her. This was not a moment to jump up and proclaim loudly, *Yes! I am a member of the League of the Scarlet Pimpernel!* or to mention Tony, Charles, or anything else sensitive. 'So how were you brought here?' she asked, as she began to hem an otherwise complete shirt.

Fleurette's eyes went dark at the memory. 'It was tremendously distressing,' she said. 'They all treated me politely, not like a prisoner or anything, even though Bibi wasn't there, but they said that there had been reports of questionable activity in the house, and that I should be grateful I wasn't up on trial that very minute. I think . . .' Her eyes flicked from side to side, and she leaned closer. '. . . Adele must have told them something about that night. You know, the night you and Charles were there, and Bibi let you go free. They are no doubt using me to remind him where his loyalties must lie.'

'I thought you'd wedged a chair under her door handle so she couldn't get out and snoop,' Eleanor murmured.

'Well, true, but she must have been suspicious. And these days, suspicion is enough. It's not how it was meant to be. It's not how it *should* be.' There was a new note of firmness to her voice which Eleanor hadn't heard before.

'Supposing you could escape this place,' Eleanor said carefully, 'what would you do? Where would you go?'

'I'd find good honest work in a village somewhere,' Fleurette answered. She'd clearly thought this through. 'Then

187

I'd find a way to send a letter to Bibi in Paris so he wouldn't worry about me. And then I'd find a way to influence the local Committees and whoever was in authority to make things . . . well, *better*.' Her smile was radiant. 'I know it sounds awfully small and petty, Anne, but isn't that ultimately what all good teachers tell us to do? Start with little things and build great ones?'

Eleanor found herself mute. She had no response to such a basic, ordinary, straightforward declaration of intent . . . or at least, not a *good* response. The one that came bubbling to her tongue, and which she choked back, was a flat denial. *It can't work. It won't work. You'll only get hurt.*

She chose not to say it because she recognized it was, in the most literal sense of the term, *thoughtless*. Eleanor had met people in France – and now in England, too – who were taking steps to change their countries. Granted, there were a few problems in their way, such as vampires and politicians and Bow Street Runners, as well as the entire Committee of Public Safety, but that didn't make Fleurette *wrong*, it just made her reckless and naive.

Previously, Fleurette had preached the virtues of the Revolution, considering it only a matter of time until minor details – particularly details involving guillotines – were remedied. Now she apparently wanted to resolve these issues herself. Eleanor was torn somewhere between pride and terror for her friend – and, just a little bit, for herself. After all, France was currently proof that the common people *could* change the world.

But change it for the better? That was another question.

Anima was laughing at the back of her mind. *No wonder the Committee wants to clear the gaols! If they're all like this, then they're providing a fine education for innocents like this girl. Behind all the locks and bars, they're breeding their own counterrevolutionary activity.*

'Anne?' Fleurette prompted her. 'What do you think?'

'I think you're very brave,' Eleanor replied. 'But I'm also concerned what the authorities may do if we leave without, ah, their permission.'

Fleurette pursed her lips thoughtfully. 'Well, I certainly can't go back to Paris and ask Bibi for help. That would be so unfair to him. It would place him in a conflict between his duty and his paternal affection for me. I do worry about him, Anne. Nobody will be looking after him without me there. Oh, Louise and Adele may mind the house, but it's not as if either of them *care* about him.'

Her voice had a lost, forlorn note as she spoke of her father, and Eleanor felt a need to comfort her. 'I saw him less than a month ago. He was . . . in good health. Hard at work.'

'What sort of work?' Fleurette demanded.

'Pursuing a conspiracy of vampires,' Eleanor answered. It wasn't a lie, after all. 'I don't suppose you know anything about that?'

'Oh, Bibi never mentioned his work to me,' Fleurette said. 'And he kept all his private documents in the *locked* drawers of his desk.'

One of the women sitting near them, close enough to overhear, murmured something unpleasant-sounding in which Chauvelin's name was briefly audible.

Fleurette looked down at her sewing. 'Everyone here has a very unfair and inappropriate opinion of my father,' she whispered, in the nearest that Eleanor had ever heard her come to bitterness. 'He's not a bad man.'

They were interrupted, rather to Eleanor's relief, by one of the other women in the room bursting into tears. Her neighbours comforted her, with murmurings that it was all her cousin's fault she'd been imprisoned.

'It seems rather unfair if she's being blamed for her cousin's actions,' Eleanor said to Fleurette.

'I think she was sent here to put pressure on him,' Fleurette murmured. 'Just as I was on Bibi. I think it's the people putting pressure on people who *really* need to be investigated.'

The words stirred something at the back of Eleanor's mind, some half-remembered words or thought, imperfectly recalled, but somehow feeling *correct*. It was like the first knot in a tangle of yarn finally coming unravelled. What Fleurette had just said didn't explain everything, but it did explain *something*. If only Eleanor could think what it was.

As the minutes ticked by, Eleanor found herself sympathizing more and more with Sir Percy's firm control of the League and the way he had demanded an oath of total loyalty from all the other men who worked with him. She'd never realized before how nerve-racking it was to be at the mercy of a whole room of people who knew who she was, and who could turn her in to the authorities at any moment. Every second glance, every murmured conversation made her want to twitch. Why did Fleurette have to be so foolish and expose her? What if they were considering how best to hand her over to the guards? Where could she run?

You can't, Anima said, *so stop panicking.*

You're hardly being a great deal of help, Eleanor snapped back. *You said earlier that you might be able to do something. Well? You're at risk here just as much as I am.*

Anima heaved a weary sigh. *We are at risk, as you put it, because of* your *choices, so control your tongue and mend your manners. I was here once before, long ago, and I remember some secret passages, but it will do us no good to go searching for them by day. You must be patient and stop fretting about your personal danger.*

It isn't just me, Eleanor argued, trying to prod the old mage into something resembling urgency. *Tony, Charles and I all agreed we must do something before the troops get here and start*

carrying out executions. Even if some of the prisoners are released –
Fleurette, Madame Thiers – others are sure to be found guilty.
These are deaths we can prevent, people we can save.

Did you think you could just walk in and produce a plan like
some brilliant general?

The Pimpernel would, Eleanor persisted.

You're not the Pimpernel, and I suggest you think very seriously
about that fact, Anima said flatly. *You're in the right place at the*
right time, but there is nothing you can do until nightfall. Attend
to your sewing, and to your friend.

She refused to say anything more.

The weary hours ground by until sunset. This was apparently
not one of the days when they were allowed to meet the men
at meals; food and water were brought to the set of rooms
where the women lived and worked. They were allowed
cheap tallow candles for light, but it wasn't enough to sew
by after dark, and they retired to their dormitory early.

There had been no word or signal from Charles or Tony.
Eleanor suppressed her nervousness. They couldn't rush
things, after all. No doubt the men were reviewing the situation on the other side of the locked doors, assessing the
number of guards, plotting a way to deal with them. Not for
the first time this day, she questioned the wisdom of their
plan; rushing in like this without information or backup had
been reckless in the highest degree.

But if we hadn't done anything, then the Committee men would
have arrived, and the troop after that, and then . . .

Sitting on her cot, she daydreamed about how easy things
might have been if mages like Anima still walked the earth.
Anima was occasionally free with stories about the glories
of her day and the powers that she and her fellows had
controlled. They could have flooded the soldiers out with
rainstorms, sent them all to sleep, or given them bellyaches

which would have kept them in their beds. Or bemused them with mists, or shaken the earth under their feet until the causeway to Mont-Saint-Michel fell to pieces . . .

Loud footsteps sounded down the passageway outside, and rough hands fumbled with the lock. The dormitory became abruptly tense, with women glancing at each other in fear.

This wasn't a regular visit by the guards. Something was wrong, and Eleanor had a sinking feeling it involved her. For a moment she was tempted to hide under her cot, but common sense reminded her that would be an overt confession of guilt. Guilt of *something*, whether or not the guards were here for her personally.

She waited, resigned, as the door was flung open with a crash and two guards stalked in. 'Anne Dupont!' one demanded. 'Where is she?'

'Here, citizen,' she said, rising to her feet and grateful that she hadn't yet stripped down to her shift for the night.

'You're to come along with us. The Warden has questions for you to answer.' He signalled her to join them.

Eleanor could feel everyone's eyes on her. She walked across with as much dignity as she could manage, the image of an aristocrat going to the guillotine looming unhappily large in her head.

'Anne!' Fleurette exclaimed desperately. The woman next to her tried to hush her, but others were murmuring in tones of fear mingled with pure panic. 'Will you be all right—'

The lead guard looked around the dormitory, and sighed. 'Calm yourselves, women,' he ordered. 'The girl herself is innocent, as far as we know – or no more guilty than any of the rest of you. It's the men she was with that the Warden wants to ask her about.'

Eleanor's stomach clenched as though she was in a storm at sea and trying not to vomit. *Dear God, no. Charles and Tony are in trouble. They may already have been arrested . . .*

192

She barely managed to control her face and show no more than the usual amount of terror that might be expected from a prisoner being dragged off for questioning. 'I'll answer any questions you want, citizen,' she quavered, cold with fear, 'but I never met them before they brought me here.'

'Then you'll have nothing to worry about,' the guard said in brusque comfort. 'Come along, don't keep the Warden waiting.'

The dormitory door slammed shut behind her, and the second guard paused to turn the key in the lock again. Eleanor was engaged in a desperate weighing of odds. Should she try to escape now, or pretend innocence and go with them? If Charles and Tony were prisoners, then she could do more to free them if she was at liberty herself. Being questioned and then locked away again – the best possible outcome of this night-time inquisition – was little or no use. She had to act.

Anima, she demanded, *I need your help.*

I'm glad to see you've kept your nerve. Anima's voice had a strange undertone of satisfaction to it. *Breathe deeply. Summon your anger.*

This was the third time Eleanor had used the old mage's power in this way, and the first time she had truly appreciated the magic. She felt a change in perception; the air around her, down to the very breath in her lungs, was possessed of different degrees of solidity. Some was as fine and light as silk, other parts as raw and heavy as canvas or felted wool. Her surroundings became contoured like an unmade bed, all bumps and wrinkles, flowing into each other in elegant slowness as though they were dancing.

Now, like this, Anima said, and Eleanor reached out to lay her hands on the two men. Anger and fear kindled a flame in her, and it *sparked*. Lightning jumped from her to them, bright enough to dazzle, hot enough to scorch her fingers.

She flinched back, but the contact had been enough. The two men went down as though someone had knocked them over the head with the nearest convenient blunt object, thudding to the ground and lying there without even a moan.

A wave of weariness swept through Eleanor, and she leaned against the wall to hold herself upright. *This* was why it wasn't a good idea to let Anima play tricks with magic. She was the one who paid the price for it afterwards.

Don't delay, Anima urged her. *Down here and to the left—*

A moment, please, Eleanor interrupted. She hastily unlocked the door and reopened it, pulling the key from the lock.

The women inside looked at her in blank incomprehension, then at the unconscious men visible at her feet. Madame Thiers was the first to recover her speech. 'What is going on?'

Eleanor tossed her the heavy key. 'Here. Hide this in case you need it later, but stay here for the moment. Let the guards assume I ran off with it.' She saw Madame Thiers open her mouth again. 'I don't have time to answer questions for the moment. I'll be back as soon as I can.'

She quickly shut the door before any of the women – especially Fleurette – *could* ask questions, and hurried to follow Anima's instructions.

At least, whatever happened to her and Tony and Charles, she'd given Fleurette and the other women a fighting chance . . .

CHAPTER FOURTEEN

The grey stone walls were unpainted, unmarked, all alike. They surrounded Eleanor, looming in towards her. Now that she was on her own in this maze of passages and small rooms, panic reached out to clasp her tightly. Sir Percy would have scouted the place first, had maps, known how many men guarded it, and a dozen other things which she, Tony and Charles hadn't been able to accomplish. How could she possibly find her way to where the men were being kept, let alone rescue them?

No. Blind fear was *not permissible*. She imagined all the housekeepers she'd ever known standing behind her and glaring at her, and the thought made her want to giggle. She bit her lip to stay calm. She could manage this. The abbey had boundaries, outer walls, with the sea beyond. She simply had to circle the place – very, very carefully – until she found Tony and Charles, and then . . .

You need to find shelter first, Anima insisted. *They won't do anything to your friends tonight. Hide yourself, then emerge later while they're asleep and only the night patrols walk these corridors.*

But Anima couldn't *know* that. *If Tony and Charles are prisoners and they're questioning them, then* . . . Eleanor didn't want to think about it. Perhaps they'd simply been locked in a cell and left there till the morning, as Anima said. Or perhaps . . . not. Eleanor refused to take the risk. *Can you help me? You said you knew the geography of this place. It looks as if it hasn't changed in the last five hundred years or so.*

Indeed, the abbey looked as if it hadn't changed in over a thousand years. The stones in the walls might have stood there since the birth of Christ. The place itself had no softness to it, no feeling of kindness or shelter. There was only the cold grey granite and the sea and wind beyond. Human beings like the prisoners – or the guards, she supposed – might make temporary homes for themselves by filling up their rooms with normal human things, but once they were gone, then only the stone and sea would remain.

For a moment Anima was silent, then she said, *Perhaps. Turn right at the end of this corridor. That should bring us into the monks' ambulatory. Their cloister. Where they used to take walks for exercise,* she added, clearly realizing that Eleanor didn't know the term. *I suspect these godless ruffians will be using it for storage. There are staircases in the inner wall.*

Eleanor obeyed the old mage's directions. Nobody seemed to have come after her yet, but every muffled footfall, every echoing whisper, made her throat tighten with fear.

As Anima suspected, the room had been used to store supplies. Small loss, as it was an unattractive place. Eleanor couldn't help thinking that the monks would surely have preferred a few glimpses of the world outside their walls while taking exercise. But no, the walls were bare and only a few windows let in light at the near end of the room. Worse still, the supplies hadn't been stored in good order. They were stacked in confusing piles, with sacks overspilling other sacks, making the place more dangerous than a forest floor overburdened with roots. It was fortunate that Eleanor was accustomed to working with little light to help her, from years of serving by night in a vampire's household. The faint moonlight that came in through the meagre windows only made the darkness seem more threatening.

Over there by the pile of bales, Anima prompted. *You see the staircase? Look closely at the stonework a foot or so to its right.*

Is this your hiding place? Eleanor asked suspiciously. She wasn't going to just huddle in some secret closet for hours while Tony and Charles were being questioned.

No, no, Anima reassured her quickly. *It is a secret staircase, if I remember correctly. It will let us reach the floor below, and from there you can decide how best to proceed.*

Eleanor squinted at the large stones in the near darkness, running her hands over them in the hope of finding some secret catch or lever. *I can't find anything,* she reported.

If it's remained hidden for over five hundred years, then it will hardly be obvious, Anima replied tartly. *Give me control of your hands and body so that I may open it. Do I have your permission?*

For a moment Eleanor thought she heard something strange in Anima's voice, a tone which made her hesitate. It was like wading into a stream and feeling a stone begin to turn under her foot – not yet falling, but suddenly being aware that the riverbed was false and unreliable and far from safe. But that was folly. Anima *depended* on Eleanor for her own existence; she had no reason to betray her living host. Anima had supported Eleanor every step of the way to get to Mont-Saint-Michel. Why should she doubt her now?

Just as she'd done when she allowed Anima to cast spells, Eleanor relaxed. Briefly her vision was doubled, and everything around her took on a strange, tilted perspective. Then it was normal again. She found her hands rising to probe the walls with a more definite knowledge, and beneath her fingers something shifted. Anger – Anima's anger – rose sourly in her throat, and she pushed at it more strongly. This time it clicked, loudly.

Someone will hear! Eleanor protested. Was that approaching footsteps coming down the corridor towards the ambulatory?

You had better hope they don't. Anima's shove, with Eleanor's hand, was hard enough to make Eleanor bite back a gasp of pain, but the level of force was apparently necessary. With a grating shudder, a crack showed in the stones, and opened further as Anima threw Eleanor's weight against it. Even with all Eleanor's strength the gap was barely a foot and a half wide – just enough to squeeze through.

Pitch darkness yawned within. The smell of dust that had not been disturbed for centuries assaulted Eleanor, and a cold breeze embraced her like a ghost. *We'll have to go back and fetch one of the lamps,* she thought, beginning to turn . . .

And then stiffened where she stood. She was no longer in control of her own body.

Anima raised Eleanor's hand, and a faint white-blue light flickered around it, the colour of distant lightning. *This will suffice.*

The riverbed of uncertainty had become a downhill slope of awareness that something was definitely wrong and that Eleanor herself was unable to stop her own descent towards whatever was about to happen. *Anima, what are you doing?*

Nothing for you to worry about, Anima answered, and this time her disdain was clear, though tempered by a distant pity. *I told you once that I would have objectives and requirements of my own, aims that had nothing to do with the League of your Pimpernel. That time has come. I've assisted you in the past, and now I'm calling in my debt.*

Eleanor felt panic seize her – she didn't know what Anima had in mind, but this blatant dictatorship suggested the worst. She had no control over her body, though. She squeezed through the crack between the door and the wall, the stones scraping painfully against her hips and shoulders. Before them, a stairway led downwards in a narrow spiral, somehow crammed by a cunning architectural design into the thickness of the interior wall. The dust on the steps was as thick as snow, tinted blue-white by the flame of lightning which still burned on Eleanor's hand.

You said you wouldn't ask for my obedience! Eleanor protested, struggling . . . but there was nowhere for her to brace herself against the force which controlled her body. Her rage was like a child's tantrum pitted against an adult's strength. She could scream inside her head as much as she wanted, but it didn't break Anima's hold on her body. All that her anger did was suppress her own cold sickness at how Anima had stolen her will. This control went all the way down to her bones. *You said you'd respect my opinions and consideration, not whatever this is! I thought I could trust you!*

Anima sighed. She reached across to an interior lever, hesitating, then let it be. *No, better not to close this entrance yet – I don't wish to make enough noise to rouse the whole abbey. Child, there are times in our lives – and after them, I suppose – when the situation is simply so desperate that no allowance can be made for morality, or friendship, or any such . . . happy things. I regret what I am doing to you, but I have no choice.*

Eleanor continued struggling as Anima began to walk down the stairs. Rather belatedly, she was putting the pieces of the puzzle together. *You wanted to come here. You gave me the idea of Mont-Saint-Michel as the diversion in the first place, and then didn't try to persuade me otherwise when I suggested the rescue plan to Charles and Tony. Why?*

If I tell you, will you stop fighting?

No! The staircase curved round and round in a ferociously tight descending spiral. Eleanor realized that by now they must be below the level that held the church and the area where the men worked. They were descending into the bowels of Mont-Saint-Michel.

I suppose I would do the same myself. But you willingly gave me permission to take control of your body, Eleanor, which removes your strongest shield and your greatest weapon against me.

I thought I could trust you, Eleanor repeated, her anger solidifying in her belly like a lump of coal. *Where are you taking me?*

Down, Anima answered. *To speak with someone.*

Who could live down here, deep below the deepest cellars of Mont-Saint-Michel? Eleanor could feel Anima's own discomfort at their current surroundings – the old mage didn't like to be underground – but it was drowned out by Eleanor's own rage.

The stairs finally came to a stop, and a short corridor led to a heavy door. It was unlocked, but its weight and age, and the damp air, meant it had stiffened in its frame. Anima was forced to throw Eleanor's body against it to shove it open.

. . . and as she did so, Eleanor heard what might have been a very distant whisper of footsteps high above.

At this precise moment, she'd welcome even the arrival of a dozen guards armed with pistols. She hastily fanned the flame of anger in her heart, trying to distract Anima lest she notice, and resumed her spiritual struggles. *You've spent all this time telling me that vampires were evil because they controlled people. How is that different from what you're doing to me now?*

This thought actually seemed to shake Anima's control. Eleanor seized the opportunity, struggling against the displacement which had left her as a helpless burden inside her own body. Briefly she could taste her own blood as she bit her lip, feel the growing bruise on her shoulder from where she'd thrown herself at the door, and then it snapped again, leaving her distant from her own perceptions.

It's exactly the same, and you know it, she tried once more. *You realize that. Don't do it. Let me go, and . . .*

And there can be trust between us again? Don't be ridiculous.

Anima paced forward, raising her fire-wreathed hand. Light jumped up to reveal a large circular room with a vaulted ceiling. It appeared grand and luxurious at first, but as Anima turned her head and Eleanor could see it more clearly, she realized it had been stripped of all but the sparsest furnishings. The heavy bookshelves against the walls stood empty. The table at the centre was bare save for a candelabrum, and piled with dust. Chairs – heavy wooden ones, the sort which needed to be dragged across the floor rather than the elegant gilt chairs with silk cushions that adorned Lady Marguerite's salon – lay fallen to one side, or pushed back towards the wall. Various mottled areas of dust on the wall showed where pictures or tapestries had once hung and had then been removed.

Anima snapped her fingers, and sparks jumped from her hand to the candelabrum, lighting the candles which it held. As their flames leapt up, she let the lightning fade from her hand and continued to look around, her thoughts a seething pot of growing desperation. Finally her gaze fixed on something – a low mass on a pallet towards the back of the room, covered with a blanket. The whole of it was covered by the omnipresent dust. She gave a small grunt of satisfaction, breaking the silence. 'There,' she said, using Eleanor's mouth to speak, and strode across the room towards it.

Is this some sort of ancient magical weapon? Eleanor asked dubiously. *When I asked you about enchanting swords or guns I thought you said such things couldn't exist.*

'Of a sort,' Anima answered, speaking aloud. She reached down and pulled back the blanket.

Eleanor flinched, or would have, if her body had been her own to command. A dead man lay on the pallet, hands folded on his breast, dressed in a black robe which looked like the ones the monks here must have worn. His grey hair and beard were thin and his jowls sagged with age, but otherwise

201

he looked healthy enough. If he hadn't been dead she would have thought he was simply asleep.

Then the thought ran across her mind like ice on a window-pane – if nothing's been touched down here for years, how could a dead body look as though it had only died yesterday? There was only one way she knew for a body to be so incorruptible. Well, two, perhaps, but she doubted that he was a saint. *Is he a vampire?* she asked.

Anima's response was a wash of stinging fury. She grabbed the corpse by the shoulder and shook him, lightning coiling around her fingers to flicker across his body like St Elmo's fire racing across the rigging of a ship at sea. Eleanor could feel the stir of magical power – and more than that, she felt a *response* of the same power in the body which her hand was touching. 'Bernard! Bernard, wake up!'

And to Eleanor's utter shock, the apparently dead body opened his eyes.

He tried to speak, then coughed, struggling for air. With a rasping noise which made Eleanor's own throat feel painful, he rolled over to one side and spat out an unpleasantly dark wad of saliva. As his breathing became more even, he looked up at Eleanor, his eyes focusing on her. 'Who are you?' he asked in French.

'Name me as Anima,' Anima answered. 'Previously you knew me as . . .' Eleanor couldn't hear the word she spoke next, though the man, Bernard, clearly did. She was unsurprised that Anima wanted to keep her true name secret from Eleanor. It was just one more lie on top of a pile of them.

'What . . . year is it?' Bernard stammered.

'The year of our Lord seventeen hundred and ninety-four.'

Bernard paused for a moment, then laughed. 'That would explain why my body tells me I have grown old. When I lay down to sleep, I had little thought of doing it for so long. How fares the world?'

'Badly and getting worse. Here, take my hand.' She offered him Eleanor's hand. 'You will feel better if you stand up and walk around.'

'I see you have not changed in the slightest,' Bernard said as he rose to his feet. 'You are still quick to offer opinions, advice and teaching in all disciplines save your own.'

He clearly knows you well, Eleanor said drily.

Be silent, Anima snapped. 'In that case, as we're being honest with each other, I'll get the worst over with first: the vampires won. Our brothers and sisters are either dead or hiding so thoroughly that I cannot find any trace of them.'

Bernard took a deep breath as though punched in the belly, but his face remained impassive. 'I suspected as much from your late arrival.'

'I will go into more detail when we have time for it, but I have an urgent question for you now, and a request. With your permission?'

Bernard waved a hand in invitation for her to continue. He paced across the floor, each step coming more smoothly than the last, as though he had merely been stiff from over-sleeping instead of having been in some sort of magical trance for . . . over five hundred years? The very thought was somehow blasphemous to Eleanor. She'd come to terms with Anima's control of the wind and lightning, but this?

'What exactly happened?' Anima asked. 'I was intercepted on my way across France, before I could meet with the others. Drugged, chained and imprisoned, and left to starve. The histories have been cleansed of all mention of our kind. This girl, my apprentice . . .' She gestured at herself, tapping Eleanor's breastbone. 'She knew nothing of us. What do *you* know about what happened?'

Bernard didn't look at her. Instead he kept his eyes on his feet as he paced across the floor, marring the smooth dust with his sandalled prints. 'You must understand,' he said, 'that I know very little myself. I was the one who stayed behind.'

'Yes, I know that. I was told this place would be maintained as an outpost, and that someone with the skill to place himself in a sleep-trance would remain to guard it. I hadn't expected it to be you, but – well, I admit I am glad to see you again.'

Bernard glanced sideways at her from under his thinning eyebrows. 'Sentiment? From you?'

'I thought myself alone. Now there are two of us. Even the meanest scholar of mathematics would say that doubles our strength, and a philosopher could no doubt argue that two wills working together are a multiplier of force rather than simple addition. At least, that's what Gilbert would no doubt have told us.'

Bernard looked back at his feet. 'God have mercy on his soul,' he said, his voice flat.

Eleanor felt Anima's sudden grief – this Gilbert must have been a friend, rather than simply an acquaintance. 'Do you know what happened to him?' she asked quietly. 'Or is it simply that five hundred years must have swept away all traces of his life by now?'

'We had word that he died in Copenhagen,' Bernard said gently. 'Like you, he was travelling to Paris, but he had further to go. You were coming from Vienna, I think?'

For a long breath Anima was silent. 'I have little memory of what happened,' she finally confessed, 'or where I was travelling to, or what our plans were. I managed to preserve my essential soul, but my memories are . ... damaged.'

Eleanor had paused her struggles while they spoke. She was far too interested in what they had to say. Anima was speaking more freely than she'd ever done during the months she'd spent within her. Eleanor felt instinctively that if there was any way to persuade Anima to relinquish her clasp on Eleanor's will, then it would come from Anima's own history, and the truth about what happened between the wizards and the vampires.

'You know nothing? Nothing at all?' Bernard's face tightened into lines of fury. 'Then why in God's name did you wake me from my sleep? Do you have any idea what that means for me?'

'You can restore your sleep once we're done here,' Anima said coldly, 'or come with me, whichever best pleases you. But you must understand that I had no other choice! Those refuges which I can remember have all been destroyed, or overrun and broken. If there are still others of our kind out there, they are hidden so well I have no hope of finding them. What do you expect me to do, Bernard? Stand on a high place and call the lightning in the hopes that someone else will notice me? The vampires would find me first – and what do you think they'd do to me?'

'Probably much what they'll do to me, now you've led them here!'

'That at least you're spared.' Eleanor could feel her mouth curling in a dry, mirthless smile. 'The people of France have risen in revolution against their kings, their nobles and their vampires. Now they hunt the vampires just as the vampires once hunted us. They drag them out in daylight and place a stake through their hearts, before cutting their heads off. Truly, if it were not for my apprentice's weak stomach, I'd stay to watch as often as I could.'

'Your apprentice. There's a story there, I fancy.' Bernard pulled at his beard thoughtfully. 'How did you obtain her?'

'You remember I said that I was imprisoned and left to starve? I bound my spirit into a book before I died. When this girl found the book, she awoke me.'

While Anima was clearly trying to make it sound like some Sunday's light amusement, Eleanor could tell from the way Bernard's eyes widened that what she'd said must be somewhere between blasphemy and heresy, and possibly both. 'That practice is forbidden!'

'Only because everyone who tried it died,' Anima said, 'and I was going to die anyhow. I am a persistent woman, Bernard, and I was in a vengeful mood.'

'You still are.' He turned and began to pace again. 'The other reason it was forbidden is that the few successes were all mad ghosts who had to be exorcized.'

So exorcism *did* work. Eleanor added it to the store of things that she intended to discuss with Anima later, at some point when she was back in control of her own body and could have an extremely full and frank discussion with the older woman about her actions tonight.

Anima folded Eleanor's arms. 'I will gladly discuss philosophy and logic with you to prove that I have not lost my reason, but not now. I need your help, Bernard.'

'To what end? I can tell you all I know about our brothers and sisters, but . . .' He spread his hands, and his frustration showed clearly on his face. 'That was five hundred years ago. What was the point of my staying behind and placing myself in sleep? It seems I have only wasted my time and slept my life away.'

'No,' Anima said quickly. 'No, quite the contrary. You may be the only chance we have to strike back. Listen. My apprentice has promised me the use of her body—'

I did not! Eleanor shrieked, forgetting her resolution to stay quiet and listen to the conversation.

Anima ignored her. 'But though her spirit is willing, its bond to the flesh is too strong for me. I am constantly struggling to maintain my link to her body. Can you help us?'

Bernard's frown deepened. 'Anima, you are my sister and I have no reason to insult you by doubting your word, but it is hard to believe that a young woman would willingly sacrifice herself in this way.'

'She knows the stakes at play,' Anima argued, as Eleanor continued to scream and struggle. 'She's seen the vampires gathering power in England – that's her country of birth – and forcing more oppressive laws on the people. She understands that sacrifices must be made. I give you my word that she freely and knowingly gave me her permission.'

But not for this!

I'll give you your body back when we're done. We'll merely be . . . exchanging positions as to who's in command and who's providing advice. Don't you understand, Eleanor? I can't risk dissolution. I'm finding it more and more difficult to maintain my link to you. This is as painful to me as it is for you, and I wish things could be otherwise, but I have no choice. For the higher purpose—

Eleanor projected a very crude thought about what Anima could do with her higher purposes.

There, you see? Ultimately you're nothing more than a maid who's spent most of her life washing the dishes and preparing vegetables. And opening your veins for vampires, of course. Anima's tone had developed an unpleasant note of self-justification. *You may have gathered a certain amount of trivial polish in the last few months, but your judgement is still . . . limited. I have the right to make this decision for you.*

The words *Declaration of the Rights of Man and the Citizen* briefly flickered through Eleanor's memory, from the time Charles had made her read it so as better to play the part of a revolutionary. *I have the right not to be turned into your slave!*

Child, Anima said wearily, *this is for the greater good, and thus for your own too.*

Bernard was unaware of the inner argument going on, or of Eleanor's resistance, of course. He pulled at his beard again. 'It would be a matter of aligning her body and brain with your spirit,' he mused, 'and while I haven't done it before myself, I've heard of it being done in at least two cases, where a spirit from a dying man or woman was transferred into a living body that was empty of soul, due to accident or illness. It's not impossible.'

Eleanor's heart sank.

'But does she understand the full implications of this?' he went on. 'If you place her in danger—'

Anima laughed. 'I could hardly place her in more danger than she already does herself! The girl's in league with a conspiracy and regularly risks the guillotine.'

Bernard frowned. 'What's a guillotine?'

'Oh, one of those modern things they've invented to kill each other with. Quicker than hanging, at least. Believe me, I'll keep her safer than she keeps herself. And at least I won't let her open her veins for vampires.' Anima pulled back her sleeve to bare the cuts on Eleanor's arms.

'Well, I can hardly leave her in that sort of situation,' Bernard said. With a sick feeling, Eleanor realized that he *wanted* to be persuaded. Just as the Committee fed the nation of France with stories of terror and cruelty, Anima was providing him with a tale of self-sacrifice and noble heroism, but it was merely two sides of the same coin. People yearned to believe, and so others would tell them what they wanted to hear. 'And as she's given her permission . . . Sit down in one of these chairs, and let me assess the humours of her body. Or your body, if you like.'

What about Charles? And Tony?

I'll have the full use of my powers once I'm more securely seated in your body. I'll set them free as I leave. Eleanor, I'm not a monster. I'm just trying to do what's best for all of us.

Eleanor didn't have to formulate the thought, *Which means discarding me like a worn-out shift.* She knew that Anima would understand it, would feel her helpless anger seething like a boiling pot. But the seething water could do nothing against the iron of Anima's control. *Perhaps I should try to understand.*

208

Perhaps Sir Percy himself would choose to sacrifice a pawn for greater gains . . .

Far away, months ago, she remembered standing beside the Chief and Tony in a grassy lane, desultory rain damp on her face, the smell of growing things all around her, as distant from this cold dead underground cellar as possible. *The League doesn't leave anyone behind,* he'd said.

No. Sir Percy wouldn't have accepted this. But all the logic, all the rational thought, all the argument in the world wasn't affecting Anima in the slightest, and none of it gave Eleanor the strength to force her back. The chair was cold from years of disuse. Eleanor's body shivered as she seated herself.

'What are you doing?'

The voice came from the doorway. Fleurette stood there, one shadow among many others, but the mass of her tumbled golden hair glowed in the candlelight. 'Anne? Are you all right?'

'Is she another of your apprentices?' Bernard asked Anima.

'No,' Anima said, and the sparks of light began to trace their way over Eleanor's hand again. 'Allow me—'

Eleanor knew what would happen. Just as she'd felled the guards earlier, Anima would now strike Fleurette down. And oh, it might not be painful, she might not *hurt* the other woman, but she would certainly walk away and leave her behind. Fleurette would remain a prisoner here with yet another memory of 'Anne' betraying her, just as she'd once had to face the fact that Eleanor was an English spy.

Logic and reason had been useless, and thoughts of her own peril hadn't been enough, but sheer and utter fury for Fleurette's sake made the breath catch in Eleanor's throat. Fleurette had come down here to help Eleanor; she deserved *none of this.* For the first time since Eleanor had entered the stairwell she took a conscious gulp of air. Anima was about to hurt her friend, and she quite simply couldn't endure it. *Wouldn't* endure it.

'No,' Eleanor said, and slapped her hand down on the arm of the chair hard enough to hurt. The air appeared to fizz and shudder around her, as tense as a storm before breaking, and Anima screamed inside her head. Eleanor bit her lip till the blood flowed, tasting it in her mouth, salty and vile. She thought of the times when she'd let her blood for her mistress to drink, for loyalty, for obedience, for a fair day's wage. She couldn't do that any more. She had choices now. And she wanted other people to have those choices too.

I might have been your collaborator, but I refuse to be your tool, she said, and breathed again, feeling at home in her body once more. Anima had . . . receded, like a tide going out, leaving Eleanor feeling stained by her presence. The old mage was still there, lurking, but her withdrawal felt like shame as much as defeat.

It was wrong, and she knows it. Knew it.

'Anima was wrong,' she said to Bernard, rising to her feet and looking up at him. He was tall, several inches taller than her, though he lacked bulk, and now he looked even older than he had just ten minutes ago. 'She is *not* my mistress. And she *doesn't* have my permission to take my body.'

CHAPTER FIFTEEN

'So please correct me if I have this wrong,' Fleurette said, her brow furrowed in thought, 'but you are telling me that Anne here—'

'Eleanor,' Eleanor reminded her. She'd grown tired of being addressed by her alias, and given how much Fleurette knew already, she'd decided she might as well reveal her proper name. It would be one fewer lie on the pile of falsehoods which lay between them, and that made Eleanor feel a little better.

'Forgive me,' Fleurette said. 'I'm so used to thinking of you as Anne. So anyhow, *Eleanor* is haunted by the ghost of a sorceress, and this gentleman here is a sorcerer, and there used to be sorcerers hundreds of years ago but they were all utterly slain by vampires?' She gave a little shrug. 'I suppose that makes sense. Vampires would commit that sort of crime. Are the League of the Scarlet Pimpernel all sorcerers, or is it just you, Eleanor?'

Eleanor was a little taken aback by this easy acceptance. She'd assumed that Fleurette would probably be horrified, or call for a priest to exorcize Eleanor, or disbelieve it all, or decide Eleanor had gone mad, and quite possibly all at the same time. Instead, the other woman seemed to be taking

Genevieve Cogman

the whole affair as a glorious display of wonders, rather than a gross insult to her understanding of the natural order of things. 'I'm the only one. As far as I know,' she added hastily, suddenly struck by the thought that the other members of the League might have secrets just as drastic as her own. 'And I am not precisely a sorcerer myself; Anima was casting spells through me.'

'I fear that is not entirely accurate.' Bernard had sat down while Eleanor tried vainly to summarize recent events for Fleurette, and was resting his chin on his fist. The angle of the candle-flames made him appear even older again than a quarter of an hour ago. 'Anima does have a shred of magic left, because she is not entirely dead in, if you like, a spiritual sense: it is what she's used to bind herself to you, and to sustain herself as a ghost. But that is the sole part of her which remains . . . alive, if you like. She no longer has the power to exert herself beyond those boundaries – only that which you have given her. Once a person has truly passed beyond the veil of death, they can no longer use magic, which is a thing of life and the living world. That is why vampires cannot call on our powers themselves, thanks be to God.'

'Anima once told me that,' Eleanor agreed, 'but she said . . .' Her voice trailed off. Anima had also said that Eleanor lacked any sorcerous power or magic, or whatever one chose to call it. Yet if Anima herself was no more than a ghost, then . . .

You lied to me, she said in her mind.

She could barely feel Anima's presence now. The old mage had withdrawn like a viper into its nest, and was probably just as dangerous. Yet Eleanor had no sense of anger any more, only of shame.

Bernard coughed. 'Possibly there was some misunderstanding, eh? I'm certain that if she was helping you cast spells and telling you about magic, she was merely planning to ease you into the realization later that you are a mage yourself. Perhaps for when you had time to spare from this heroic conspiracy of yours. Such things always require a person's full attention. Mind you, I'm not quite sure that I understand current goings-on yet myself . . .'

She, Eleanor, a mage, with her own powers? He was right, she needed time to fully comprehend this, to actually accept it. Instead she compelled herself to face the reality of the moment. Grief and betrayal would have to wait till later. 'At the moment, sir . . .' She wasn't sure how to address him, but she didn't want to offend him by accidental rudeness. Not when she was about to call on his help and power. 'My friends and I learned that there will be representatives from the government arriving here shortly to put all the prisoners on trial, and it's almost certain many of them will be sent to the guillotine. Executed,' she quickly added in explanation. 'I believe my friends have been discovered and arrested, and certainly my own escape will have placed me under suspicion. We must do *something*.'

'Bring in the forces of the League by sea and stage a grand escape,' Fleurette suggested happily.

Bernard spoke before Eleanor could point out the problems with this approach, a note of authority in his voice. 'The sea here is not deep enough for ships, child. You will have to make any escape on foot. At the moment the tide is high, but it will be low enough for the causeway to be passable just before dawn.'

'How do you know that, sir?' Fleurette asked.

'My affinity is for the waters of the earth.' He pointed a finger at Eleanor. 'Just as hers is for the airs and the winds. And since I know what you are going to ask me next, I can use my mastery of bodily humours to set sleep upon people – if they are close to me or I can see them – which may be of some use in your escape.'

213

'You can read minds!' Fleurette gasped.

'No,' Bernard said, rather sourly, then looked over at Eleanor, 'but I can read the expression of a young woman who wishes to know how she can make use of me. Don't be too hard on Anima, child. She and you have some striking similarities. In her place, you would have been tempted as well.'

Eleanor would have replied *extremely scathingly* were she not in the throes of panic. They were both looking to *her* for directions, for a plan, for some way to salvage this situation. Perhaps this had all been her idea in the beginning, but Charles and Tony had supported her. They'd agreed that this was the only possible thing to do. Without them, without their advice . . .

She closed her eyes for a moment and took a deep breath. There was no point thinking, *What would the Chief do?* The Chief wouldn't have got himself into this position in the first place. Better to consider what Eleanor would and *could* do.

'When you cause people to sleep, how deeply do they slumber?' she asked.

'As if they'd been drugged, though a loud enough noise might wake them. Other mages would be more resistant, but from what you're saying, there won't be any here. Our usual policy was to bind them and lock them up before they could wake.' His lips quirked into the first smile she'd seen from him since they met. 'What, you think I've never done this sort of thing before?'

'And how many can you affect at a time?'

'Perhaps half a dozen.' For a moment he looked as though he was about to add some further explanation, then decided against it.

Eleanor nodded. 'And you know the current plan of the monastery, Fleurette?'

'Most of it,' Fleurette said, brightening at the chance to

contribute something. 'I'm sure some parts have been changed since Citizen Bernard has been asleep down here. The Merveille was only built in the thirteenth century, after all!'

'Citizen Bernard?' Bernard asked. He raised a bony finger before Fleurette could commence an explanation. 'On second thoughts, you can tell me . . . later. Perhaps after I've seen this Merveille, whatever it is.'

'In that case . . .' Eleanor began, leaning forward.

The plan was simplicity itself. Eleanor and Fleurette would sneak forward through the corridors until they saw a couple of guards, then flee from them like innocent prisoners (as much as any prisoner was innocent), until Bernard could place a spell of sleep upon them. The unconscious guards would then be hauled into the nearest storeroom, gagged and bound with their own clothing, and left to sleep till morning. They would then repeat this with as many other guards as they needed to. Thankfully, Fleurette had confirmed that the guards generally patrolled or stood position in pairs.

They'd overheard enough to be certain that Tony and Charles were prisoners. Eleanor couldn't be sure yet where the plan had gone wrong, but apparently Guillaume Duquesne had noticed something that he shouldn't, or failed to observe something which he should have done, and the two men of the League had been ridiculously outnumbered when he'd called for the guards. Heroic determination and noble valour only went so far when faced with pistols and superior numbers, as any aristocrat who'd fled or fallen before the Revolution could testify.

The problem came as they approached the area that Fleurette had identified as being of greatest danger, and where Charles and Tony had probably been locked up, if they were indeed prisoners. Bernard had muttered that it would have been the abbot's lodgings, in the days when this was truly a monastery. Now Guillaume Duquesne used the connected suite of rooms as bedroom, office, dining room, and private set of cells for dangerous prisoners. He didn't clean them himself, of course – that was a job for trusted female prisoners. Such as Madame Thiers, who'd described them to Fleurette.

'The lower level is just round the corner and down the corridor from here,' Fleurette whispered, as the three of them hid in a larder. 'I don't know how many guards will be there, though. There seem to be more than usual for this time of night. They're probably hunting you, Eleanor,' she added cheerfully.

'And you, if they've realized you're missing,' Eleanor said reluctantly. 'I should have sent you back to the dormitory—'

Fleurette snorted. 'Bah! As if I'd have gone! Do you really think I'd let you risk your life for our sakes without helping?'

'But you do support the Revolution.'

'Yes, but the *true* Revolution! Not what some people have made of it.' Fleurette's eyes shone with sincerity in the candle-light. 'A revolution which arrests me and forces my father to do wrong because of threats to my safety isn't the one I believe in. It's been stolen and infiltrated by evil men who aren't following its true principles. I believe that people like my friends who were detained here can help restore the true spirit of the Revolution.'

'Can we leave the philosophy till later?' Bernard wheezed. His voice was harsher than it had been before. 'I am finding this more difficult than I had expected.'

Eleanor frowned. She raised the candle she was holding so that she could see him better. His hair – what was left of it – had more white in it than previously, and wrinkles creased his face as though he had aged ten years since they'd left his sleeping place. 'Master Bernard, is something the matter?'

'Nothing of importance,' he said dismissively. 'Tell me, as

Anima's apprentice, have you been trained in the art of feeding her power?'

'I don't think she ever called it that,' Eleanor said, 'though she did ask me to concentrate on my anger, or clear my mind, when she was casting spells.'

'Not even the standard lectures on submission of will and focusing emotion?'

'No. And she isn't speaking to me now, either.' *Are you?* she asked, in case Anima felt like contributing, but the old mage was still silent.

Bernard looked between her and Fleurette. 'Are the two of you willing to help me by lending me your strength? It should enable me to lay a working of sleep on the whole area ahead of us.'

Fleurette turned to Eleanor. 'I'd like to help, if you say it's all right.'

Eleanor swallowed. She didn't want to lead Fleurette along any paths that might endanger or hurt her, should the vampires realize that someone else knew about sorcery. She didn't even want to estrange Fleurette still further from her father, Chauvelin. Whatever else (and there was a good deal else) she might think of the man, she knew he sincerely loved his daughter. But at the same time, if she could help them, and if Bernard could make everyone fall asleep, then they might be able to complete their rescue with a minimum of danger . . .

She nodded. 'Please tell us what to do, Master Bernard.'

'Give me your hands.' His fingers closed around hers, thin and frail. Surely they hadn't felt this old when Anima woke him? 'Relax. Incline your hearts towards me. That is, feel goodwill towards me, believe that we are striving towards the same ends. Close your eyes if you must, and—'

Fleurette squeaked and jerked her hand away. 'I'm sorry,' she gasped. 'It just felt so strange.'

'Perhaps it had better just be Eleanor, until you've had more training,' Bernard said gently. 'Do you feel anything, Eleanor?'

It had felt as though her blood *hummed* in her veins. It was strange, as Fleurette had said, but not as strange as it would have been before her own experiences with Anima. It was tolerable. 'I do, yes.'

It didn't hurt. It didn't even feel particularly tiring. It was like a tide washing through her. In at first, forming a connection, and then out again, streaming from her and into Bernard. Eleanor calmed herself, as she had when Anima cast spells, and placed her trust in him, as she had with Sir Percy.

Bernard released her hand and took a step sideways to lean against the wall. He started to cough, and it took him a moment before he could stop. 'Go,' he whispered, 'but be careful. They should all be deep in sleep, but I cannot be certain. I shall wait here.'

The abbot's lodgings – no, the Warden's lodgings – were unnaturally quiet. A faint breeze stirred the air from some open window, but otherwise there was no movement, no speech, no distant humming of the Carmagnole or some other song, no stamp or creak from a guard shifting position, and no casual chatter or crisp orders. Nothing. It was all as it *should* be, if everyone was fast asleep. The sheer unnaturalness of such silence in an inhabited place stirred the hair on the back of Eleanor's neck.

At least there was no shortage of light. Lanterns hung at the intersections, and candles burned in the lesser corners. She set down her own candle and let Fleurette lead the way, both of them moving with careful stealth, unwilling to disturb the hush with their footsteps.

The rooms themselves were more elegant than the basic architecture Eleanor had seen elsewhere in Mont-Saint-Michel. They tiptoed through Duquesne's parlour, past cushioned chairs and engravings hanging on the walls, book-shelves full of heavy volumes, schematic diagrams unrolled on the table and held down at the corners. And they passed sleeping guard after sleeping guard. With every step Eleanor's confidence grew, fanning a flame of hope in her heart. Just a little more luck, that was all they needed, and hadn't they had enough bad luck already? Surely they *deserved* a little good luck by way of recompense?

More stairs – this place was a warren of narrow curling stairways – and downwards again. Past two guards sagging back against the wall, snoring like drunkards. And there, ahead of them, were two heavy wooden doors – one standing open, the other closed – with bolts on the *outside*. Those must be the cells. Why would anyone put a bolt on the outside of the door unless it was intended as a prison cell? And why else would there be guards dozing just outside them? Fleurette gave a little squeak of enthusiasm and hurried ahead to the closest door, the one whose bolt was shut.

Guillaume Duquesne suddenly stepped out from the shadowy corner which had hidden him and scooped her close with one arm, clamping her against his body. A kerchief was knotted around his lower face, making him look like a theatrical highwayman. But more importantly, far more urgently, he had a pistol in his other hand, and he placed it against Fleurette's head, the barrel nestling into her golden curls. 'Come out from there,' he said, 'and don't try anything. I assure you I will shoot.'

Fleurette gasped in horror, struggling in his grasp and trying to kick his ankle, but he handled her with casual competence. 'No!' she whispered, keeping her voice down. 'Don't . . .'

Eleanor knew what the other woman was saying. It wasn't *Don't shoot.* It was *Don't come out.* Fleurette's first thought, her only thought, was for Eleanor's safety, not her own.

It shamed Eleanor. She didn't deserve that sort of gener-osity. She took a deep breath and stepped forward a pace, fully into view. 'Please let her go,' she said.

'Aha!' Duquesne said. 'A pair of young ladies. Coming to find your friends, are you? Well, you can go in the cell next to them. A very clever plot. Haven't had that sort of escape attempt before. I'd like to say I'm impressed, but as it didn't work we'll have to admit there were a few flaws in it, won't we? I daresay we'll find out what you used when we can have a look at the containers.'

Eleanor's thoughts stuttered as the conversation slipped out of the path she'd been expecting. 'What?'

'Oh, bags, pots, whatever . . .' He lowered his pistol from Fleurette's head, though he kept a firm grip on her. 'Poisonous herbs, am I correct? With timed fuses so that they'd burn when you were a safe distance away, and release their noxious vapours into the surrounding air? A very cunning way to put the guards to sleep. Much more effective than trying to drop laudanum into the stew, which *has* been tried. If I hadn't real-ized what was going on when I saw the other men collapsing and thought to cover my face, I daresay I'd be taking a nap myself. Unfortunately for you, I'm still awake. Now be a sensible girl and walk into the cell with the open door, Anne Dupont, or whatever your real name is, and I'll lock the two of you in for the night. You played a good game, but you lost.'

Eleanor wished she could read more of his expression, but the kerchief did a good job of hiding his face. She couldn't be sure whether he was bluffing or deadly serious. A member of the League wouldn't even threaten a woman, let alone put a pistol to her head – but if Duquesne was the sort of believer in the Revolution who felt that anything was justified, then he might indeed shoot Fleurette. She also wondered how he'd managed to resist the spell of sleep when all the other guards were snoring. Bernard had said *Other mages would be more resistant* . . . If he was a mage like Anima or Bernard, could she persuade him to help them?

'It wasn't herbs,' she said experimentally. 'I cast a spell on everyone here. I advise you to release my friend, or I'll do the same to you.'

Duquesne's eyes widened in what looked like genuine surprise and disbelief. Then he actually laughed, a belly-laugh which echoed between the cold walls of the abbey. 'Magic? Spells? Oh come, my dear, let's not have any of that nonsense. Such things are tales for children, or romances of the past. I'm a man of science, not some superstitious fool. I can tell you're an intelligent woman. Do me the courtesy of returning the favour.'

It could all have been lies, an overly vigorous protestation from someone who was well aware of what vampires might do if they found a hidden mage, but it sounded sincere to Eleanor. Duquesne had no hidden powers . . .

. . . or at least none that he was aware of. What if he was like Eleanor, and might have power if only someone taught him how to awaken it?

The thought came to her like the wind before a thunderstorm, and made her shiver in what Duquesne doubtless assumed was fear. *Just how many people have power but don't realize it? How many of them could be mages if only they knew?*

No wonder the vampires would kill to keep such a thing secret.

'Come now,' Duquesne said reassuringly. 'I'm not going to hurt a pair of young women who were probably forced into wrongdoing by the counter-revolutionaries in the cell next door. In fact, you might even want to spend your time thinking about everything you can tell me about them, mm? It would make life easier for you, and for this young lady.' He changed his grip to Fleurette's shoulder, then gave her a quick shove forward. 'Into the cell with you now, and don't make me hurt you.'

Fleurette nearly stumbled over the outstretched leg of one of the sleeping guards, and Eleanor suddenly remembered that the guards had *pistols* . . .

She just needed a distraction, something to make Duquesne look in the wrong direction for a moment. If she'd been hiding, she could have thrown a pebble, but unfortunately she was completely within his line of sight. She couldn't expect help from Bernard; there was no sign that he was close enough to overhear events or take action. There had to be something she could try . . .

Like this, Anima said, suddenly audible in Eleanor's head. The image which followed was like an embroidery design, a set of threads to pull, close to the tug of breezes which brought her distant conversations, but reversed in form – a push rather than a pull. Anima wasn't trying to drag Eleanor's mind through the pattern, she simply offered it. *Decide on your chosen direction and will it so.*

Eleanor focused on the far end of the corridor, just where it curved, and let her mind work through the set of mental threads, tugging on them as though she was straightening a piece of knitting. A thrill of pain ran through her head, as though someone had stabbed her temples with a needle from side to side. But in the shadows of the corridor a sudden breeze tugged at the air, and dirt or gravel scratched on the floor.

'What's that?' Duquesne snapped, looking away from the two women as he raised his pistol towards the noise. Eleanor ducked to one side and grabbed the pistol from the belt of an unconscious guard, rising to level it at him. Meanwhile Fleurette, bless all the saints, had the sense to take a couple of steps away from him, out of his reach, while his attention was distracted.

The sound of Eleanor cocking her pistol was painfully loud in the quiet corridor.

Duquesne turned back to her, and she had the impression that for a moment, behind the kerchief covering his lower face, his mouth had gaped in shock. But he recovered quickly. 'Come now, my dear, we both know you have no idea how to use one of those things.'

'I know enough to cock it before firing,' Eleanor snapped. The fact that he *hadn't* cocked his pistol while threatening the two of them was part of what had given her the courage to try this. He'd assumed they'd both be terrified by the mere waving around of a lethal weapon.

It wasn't as if it took time or effort to cock a pistol before firing. But when two pistols were concerned, if one was cocked and the other wasn't . . . How much difference might a single second make?

'I know what I'm doing,' Eleanor went on, her confidence increasing as he failed to attack. Blatant lies, of course. Her knowledge of pistols, and of firearms in general, was pitiful in the extreme. As Sir Percy said, if they reached a point in a plan where *Eleanor* had to fire a gun at someone, then the plan had probably failed beyond all redemption. But she'd seen the men practising. 'Now I want *you* to walk into that open cell, citizen.'

'Or you'll kill me? I think we both know you haven't the nerve for that.' Was he trying to smirk insolently under his kerchief? He glanced sideways at Fleurette, probably estimating his distance from her and his chance of grabbing her again.

Eleanor realized that she didn't need Sir Percy's planning abilities or physical prowess at this moment. What the situation called for was Lady Marguerite's ability to act, to convince anyone of anything. And in this case, to convince Guillaume Duquesne that if he didn't walk into that cell then she was going to blow his brains out.

'You have the man I love a prisoner,' she lied blatantly,

ignoring Fleurette's gasp of shock. 'He's locked in that other cell. I know what will happen if you arrest me, *citizen*. He'll be found guilty and sent to the guillotine. I will do anything not to let that happen.' A hot blush stained her cheeks. It was true she cared about Charles, she liked Charles . . . she wished that it might be possible for her to be in love with Charles . . . but the world in which they lived made such a thing impossible, and so she didn't really *love* Charles. She couldn't. It was impossible.

But she could lie for him.

'Perhaps you don't believe that a woman's prepared to kill you, citizen,' Eleanor went on. 'I'm not like Charlotte Corday. I couldn't kill a man for *political* reasons.' She'd heard stories of how the woman had murdered Marat in his bath, and gone to the guillotine for it. 'But if it's a choice between you and the man I love . . .'

She heard her voice shake as though she was listening from a distance, but her hands remained steady. 'Then I swear to you by God and all his saints that rather than let him die, I'll pull this trigger and shoot you, and face whatever judgement God may send me. I don't want to kill you. I don't want to kill anyone.' She felt the fury of an inner thunderstorm trembling behind her voice, aching in her head, humming in her ears like the wind in high branches. She was speaking the truth now. 'But if you don't step back into the cell and let me lock you in, Citizen Duquesne, then *I will shoot*.'

Something in her words, her pistol, or simply her eyes, made Duquesne step back, and then back again, framed by the open doorway. He hesitated there, no doubt weighing the obvious choice: face Eleanor's gun now, or face the Committee's inevitable judgement when someone had to take the blame for whatever had gone wrong.

It's not enough, Eleanor thought, starting to panic. *He's going to try to rush me . . .*

Then Fleurette threw herself against the open door from the other side. She'd sidled round there while Eleanor was speaking, and the door blocked her from Duquesne's view. The impact, with her full weight behind it, sent him staggering back into the cell as the door hit him in the face. Both Eleanor and Fleurette jumped for the bolt, their hands meeting on it as they slammed it shut together.

'Let me out!' Duquesne shouted from behind the heavy wooden door. 'Don't be a fool, woman! There's no way you can get away with this! You'll never be able to leave Mont-Michel!'

Eleanor ignored him. The most important thing right now was to reach Charles and Tony. Hope, so long suppressed because it would have been a painful distraction from the task at hand, abruptly bloomed and grew to full flower. They'd *done* it.

There was just one thing she had to make absolutely certain of first. 'You do realize that I was lying, don't you?' she said quickly to Fleurette as she fumbled with the second cell's bolt. 'I had to convince the Warden that I was prepared to shoot him. Charles and I are merely friends, the very best of friends, for he's an excellent man, a true comrade, but—'

'Of course you are,' Fleurette said, a little dimple at the corner of her mouth. 'It's been quite obvious to me since I first saw you together.'

'Excuse me?'

'Oh, that you're friends!' Fleurette said hastily. 'I'm sure I'd never think anything else. It was very heartening to see how much you and he trusted one another, when first we met. You must tell me more about him later.'

Eleanor wasn't entirely sure Fleurette was convinced. Still, for the moment she could only pray that the cell door had muffled her words from Charles. With an effort she thrust the bolt back and opened the door.

Two slumped figures snored quietly in the cell. One of them was in full view. The other, when Eleanor checked, was dozing to one side of the door, no doubt with aspirations of assaulting the next guard who entered. Bernard's spell had been unspecific. *Everyone* in the area was asleep.

A sigh of relief lifted her spirits, tinged with a note of pain that matters couldn't and never would be that way. Saying it out loud had forced her to recognize it. If she truly loved – that is, if she truly *cared* about him, she had to find a way to take a step back, before either of them took some foolish action which would damn him in the eyes of the world . . .

'Fetch that water-bucket,' she directed Fleurette. 'We need to wake our friends up. We have a great deal to do.'

CHAPTER SIXTEEN

Tony and Charles were occupied with planning their grand escape. Eleanor was glad – no, *delighted* – to have people more experienced than herself negotiating the situation, especially as the gentlemen prisoners, now released, had strong views on the subject. Besides, she had something more immediately pressing to concern herself with.

Bernard was dying.

He lay on a couch in the corner of Duquesne's office. His hair was completely white now, a wispy fringe around his head like an ancient monk's tonsure, and his flesh had fallen away to leave him wrinkled and gaunt. His hands had trembled when he tried to write something, and while his voice was faint but steady, it was only because he took the utmost care to control his breathing. Each complete sentence was a planned endeavour, and Eleanor could tell that he found it more and more difficult each time.

The remaining guards had been dealt with. Once released, the prisoners had taken them by surprise and outnumbered them. Now the various cells and smaller rooms were crowded with shackled or tied guards, and all the lights burned brighter as previously imprisoned husbands were reunited with their wives, or parents with their children. However, all this didn't change the fact that they were still inside the abbey, with the rest of the town outside and liable to react fiercely to a mass escape of prisoners. And beyond that lay the greater all-encompassing barrier of the sea. The only way out of here would be at low tide, and it had to be done before the troops arrived.

It was better for the men of the League to be handling the matter, Eleanor had decided. This whole operation – one that she'd suggested, influenced and *urged* the men to attempt – had nearly ended in catastrophe. If it hadn't been for Bernard, and a few lucky moments that even Sir Percy would have considered improbable, they would have failed and all still be prisoners. Or worse. Far better that Eleanor retire and assume a more proper role, not making suggestions in areas about which she was ignorant, and that she listen to what she was told when informed that something was impossible . . .

Though they *had* succeeded so far, hadn't they?

Eleanor ruthlessly stamped down that flicker of gratification. There was nothing to be proud about when it had been pure *luck* which brought them out of this alive and safe. And they still weren't out of it yet.

She held a cup of tea to Bernard's lips, one arm behind his shoulders to support him. 'You should rest,' she said.

'There is very little point in resting when I am going to be dead shortly, and facing the Lord for his final judgement on my deeds,' he croaked. 'If I must go to Him unshriven and unabsolved, then at least let me not appear before him with my tasks incomplete. There's more you need to know.'

Eleanor would have waved off his talk of death as the babble of an old man, except for the fact that he *hadn't* been this old a few hours ago. It was as though the years through which he had slept were now accumulating like some giant wave, about to drag him down and sweep him away in the undertow. 'Then tell me,' she said, trying to ignore the argument going on in the background about how best to flee the island.

She looked up in surprise as Charles took a seat next to her, flopping down in an ungainly manner which didn't suit the propriety of his stolen uniform, or his usual decorum as a gentleman. 'Forgive me for joining you, I pray you,' he said. 'Tony can repeat *No* and *No again* until those ladies and gentlemen are ready to hear it. In the meantime, I'd far rather have an intelligent conversation with my saviour, and with a person who I understand shouldn't be on this island at all.'

'It was my fault you were in such danger in the first place,' Eleanor protested, turning to get a better look at him. He didn't have any obviously serious injuries – a black eye, which he'd claimed was a mere bagatelle – yet she could see he was weary to the bone, and at the same time strung so tightly that the most discriminating fiddle-player would have ordered him to relax. Sir Percy would have known what to say. Yet he wasn't here. It was only Eleanor and Tony, and while on the one hand Tony showed no sign of such tension, on the other hand she suspected he didn't know how to relieve it either. 'I never meant to risk your life—'

Bernard coughed in an admonitory fashion, pushing her wobbling teacup away from his face. 'Child, if you are going to cast sheep's eyes at this gentleman, perhaps you should do it at some point later, when I am not dying in your arms.'

Eleanor stiffened with such rigidity that she nearly spilled the tea all down his robe – which would have served him right. 'I have committed an error and I'm apologizing for it,' she said coldly. 'Which is more than certain other people have done.'

'Really? Whom?' Charles asked. 'And you need not apologize, Eleanor, we took the risk in full knowledge of the danger.

We could do no less, as . . .' His eyes flicked sideways to the arguing group, which had apparently designated itself Committee for Public Rescues, and she guessed his remaining words would have been *English gentlemen*. The thought didn't really make her any more comfortable; it only drew the dividing line more clearly between the two of them.

'I need to pass on certain information,' Bernard said as firmly as he could. 'If this young man should not be listening . . .'

'He may as well,' Eleanor sighed. She'd lied to Charles for long enough. It would be a comfort finally to tell him the truth. Besides, he knew far more about historical matters than she did – he might well be able to contribute to the discussion. And of the two of them, he was far more trustworthy than she was. 'I have the utmost faith in him. Please tell me what you need to, Bernard – I am sure he will not abuse our trust.'

Charles's throat jerked as he swallowed, and for a moment he couldn't look her in the eye, but he set his hand on hers and squeezed it in a silent declaration of thanks.

Bernard looked between the two of them, rolled his eyes, and sighed. 'Very well. To begin with, I need to tell you that vampires were first known to have existed during the time of the Roman wars in Britain, under the Emperor Nero.'

'Wait, that can't be right,' Charles interrupted. 'It's on the record that they were in Rome before that, for the whole of the Julio–Claudian dynasty. And prior to that we have records and first-hand evidence of their existence in Phoenicia, Greece, even Mesopotamia—'

'This is not an academic debate!' Bernard croaked, in a voice that tried to thunder and only managed to wheeze. 'Where did you get this information?'

'Oxford, Cambridge—'

'Oxford may have some claim to learning, though I know nothing of Cambridge. But you're in error, boy. Take it from one who was a great deal closer to that end of history than you are. I last opened my eyes under John Lackland, and what is old today was, well, less old then. Oh, there may be creatures of folklore with a more distinguished history – the lamia, the vryolakas, the alukah. But the vampire as we know it today, the rich leech who preys on humanity while placing himself or herself high in society, pulling strings behind the scenes, first occurs during Boadicea's wars. Read your Tacitus. Or do you doubt me?'

'I don't doubt that you're a man of learning,' Charles said, with more respect than he had done earlier. 'I could close my eyes while listening to you and be back at my college, being lectured by any of a dozen professors of my acquaintance. But is it possible, sir, that further evidence has been discovered since . . . Wait, did you say that you remember the reign of King John?' His brow furrowed. 'Does this have anything to do with Eleanor asking me to look for records of ancient mages?'

Eleanor felt a fierce pride in Charles. He wasn't *stupid*.

Bernard hesitated, clearly drawn by the appeal of a thoroughgoing discussion, but then shook his head regretfully. 'Clearly you'll have a great deal to talk about once I'm no longer here. Eleanor, the other thing which I should have told Anima, and must tell you in her absence, is that the clue to the whole matter is in London. Hidden there. Hidden deep.'

'What is it?' Eleanor asked eagerly. Even if she wasn't going to run off on some crusade against all vampires as Anima and Bernard might wish . . . well, she still wanted to know.

'We could not find out,' Bernard sighed. His voice was fainter now, every word forced out with desperate urgency. 'We trapped the vampires' agents, living humans, and cleansed them of their hold. Once they could speak freely,

231

one of them told us that something of great importance lay beneath London, something which could not be moved. It had been there since the time Boadicea herself torched the city, and their masters and mistresses thought it vital enough to guard fiercely against any harm, but dared not approach it for fear of discovery. I wonder, was it that which drove them to stamp us out so thoroughly, because they thought *we* knew? Did we brew our own destruction? *Fons et origo . . .* Our original sin, the man said, before he died . . . Were we responsible?'

'Bernard!' Eleanor said urgently. He had the look of an ailing grandfather now, wandering in his memories. 'Bernard, listen to me! Can I lend you strength again? Will that help you? If you show me how, or if Anima can show me . . .'

'Too late.' Bernard's hand closed on hers in a failing grip. 'Once I woke from my sleep, I had very little time to return to it, and I made my choice. I know the world has changed. Perhaps the vampires have changed as well. Or perhaps not. My friend Matthew – they trapped him at Oxford, but he wrote to me from there. He knew more. He was a friend to the Dominican Order, who had intended to build a priory there. He tried to send word to me, but he was lost. So many of us were lost.' His eyes fluttered shut for a moment, then reopened. 'Forgive Anima. I knew her when she was alive. She was not an evil woman.'

She would have stolen my body, Eleanor thought, but she had the tact to keep her mouth shut. She'd ask Charles about Oxford and the Dominicans, whoever they were, later.

Bernard must have seen the refusal in her eyes. 'There is little enough time for any of us until we must answer for our sins before God. Don't add to the weight on your own conscience. I wish a priest were here . . .'

'I'm sorry,' Eleanor said quietly. She had actually thought to ask whether any of the prisoners here were ordained, but none had been. While confession before dying wasn't something which troubled her own conscience, she felt sorry for this old mage. He'd waited so long, and in the end had been able to achieve so little. She wished she could have helped him in some way. As little as she wanted to speak to her own passenger, her conscience prodded her to ask Anima, *Is there anything you want to say to him?*

There was a moment of shocked surprise that Eleanor was willing to communicate, then Anima said, *Let me speak. Give me your mouth, your voice. I swear I'll do no harm to you or anyone else with it, but I beg you, let me bid him farewell.*

Eleanor hesitated. She still remembered the horror of being trapped inside her own body, a helpless prisoner. Could she honestly trust Anima not to do the same thing again?

Would I be any more convincing if I wept and pleaded with you? Anima demanded. Her tone was one of demand rather than supplication, but there was a desperate need behind it. *This once, in hundreds of years, I can speak to a man who knew me and recognized me, and I'll go into the dark myself soon enough. If some day you want anyone to have pity on you, then take pity on me now and let me say goodbye.*

I didn't know you cared for him . . .

I don't. Not in that way, at least. But he's the only thing left behind of the world I knew.

Eleanor thought about her own feelings of loss and loneliness, of how she was no longer one of the servants, but would certainly never be one of the aristocrats. She deliberately forced her anger and caution aside. *Very well.*

'Bernard,' Anima said through her mouth, and there must have been some difference to her voice which other people could hear, because Charles looked at her askance and Bernard's hand tightened its grasp. 'Bernard, you haven't wasted your time. You've told me about London, about the vampires' secret. You waited, and I'm grateful. Go in peace.'

'You won't . . .' Bernard's voice was barely a whisper, scarcely audible over the argument still taking place on the other side of the office.

'I won't,' Anima reassured him.

He smiled, a faint twitch of his lips, and closed his eyes.

A few breaths later, he was gone. Eleanor gently settled him back against the couch. She could feel that Anima had withdrawn again without requiring any struggle or argument, and she was grateful for that.

'Are you going to explain all that to me as well?' Charles asked. 'Starting with who he is?'

'I will,' Eleanor said quickly, 'and I do have the utmost faith in you. That wasn't a lie. But for the moment, please, let us arrange our escape first; our explanations can come second.' She paused. 'How did you come to be found out by Duquesne?'

'An unfortunate roll of the dice.' Charles patted his black eye tenderly. 'That is, one of the men on guard here happened to know the officials whom we were impersonating, and even more unfortunately he had the sense to wait till we were out of earshot before breathing a word in Duquesne's ear on the subject. We might have been able to brazen out a flat accusation of imposture, but instead Duquesne set a few traps for Tony in his conversation. By the time we realized we were in too deep for our liking, we were trapped by the rising tide, to borrow a metaphor from our current location. We did our best to lie, and I was in the depths of fear that the next thing we'd see would be you in the prison cell along with us,' he added quietly.

'You kept me safe,' Eleanor reassured him. 'The guards who came to fetch me clearly believed I was only your ignorant pawn. They'd have been far more careful had they thought me a true counter-revolutionary.'

Charles breathed a sigh of relief. 'I'm glad of that, at least.

234

But for the moment, as you say, let us consider our escape. Faith, I think they've scarcely noticed our absence from the discussion over there. Come, Eleanor, let us quietly rejoin it—'

'Ah, Charles!' Tony could apparently detect their coming from behind and while in the middle of a noisy conversation. Possibly it was due to desperation on his part for some other member of the League to solve the difficult situation they still faced. 'I believe our friends have some questions for you.'

'For me?' If Charles had been a young stallion, he would have rolled his eyes and put back his ears. 'Unless it concerns forging documents, I fear I can be of little use.'

'You're far too hard on yourself, young man,' Monsieur Thiers said. He was as definite and uncompromising as his wife, who was standing by his side supportively. Eleanor could hardly blame Charles for flinching before the united pair, or Tony for wanting to back away from them. 'But we would like to know how it is that you dealt with all those guards, especially as you and your friend here had apparently already been arrested.'

'Ah,' Charles said thoughtfully. 'That is—'

'We'd brought in some bags of poisonous herbs, monsieur, to put them to sleep,' Eleanor said quickly. Duquesne's suggestion was so plausible that she'd decided to steal it. What better compliment to pay him? 'The gentlemen here had placed them with timed fuses at various points in the abbey, as we arranged beforehand. I set fire to the fuses and then came down here to release them, with Fleurette's help.' She shot a glance, a silent plea for support, at Fleurette, who'd somehow clung to the fringes of the conversation despite not being a person of any particular authority.

Fleurette nodded enthusiastically. 'It's as she says, Madame Thiers. Citizen Duquesne was still awake, having covered his face, but we managed to trick him into the spare cell.'

235

Monsieur Thiers didn't look entirely convinced, but no other explanation really made sense. He nodded. 'Now, to more urgent matters. We have our own plans for what to do once we're on the mainland, but first we need to leave Mont-Saint-Michel. The next low tide will be at around four hours after midnight, which would make it the perfect time to leave, but the town below the abbey will notice if we simply walk through the streets. There are enough men there, even if they aren't soldiers, to raise the alarm and hold the causeway, or simply to free the guards here in the abbey and take us prisoner again.'

'If you were to go very, very quietly . . .' Charles suggested.

Madame Thiers shook her head. 'The gates of the abbey . . . well, I won't say there are gossips out there who spend every waking hour watching them in order to spread news of prisoners going in and out, but if we open them then someone *will* hear, and someone will look, and . . .' She spread her hands in a manner suggesting inevitable capture.

Tony chewed his lower lip. 'A word with my compatriots in private, I think. Excuse me.' He grasped Charles and Eleanor, and towed them towards the most distant corner of the room. 'It seems ridiculous to have reached thus far and not be able to pull off the rest of the trick,' he muttered, slumping. 'Come, Charles, share your thoughts. I've already been thoroughly quashed because I suggested they might need help blending into the villages beyond this confounded islet. Apparently their need for assistance from the League of the Scarlet Pimpernel is near to non-existent.'

Charles patted him on the shoulder. 'Brace up, old fellow. It's a good thing they have their own ideas. How on earth could we shepherd them through France and onto a ship bound for England if they didn't? Be grateful for it, and let's direct our minds to more positive approaches. What would the Chief do?'

Tony frowned. Then he smiled. 'He'd have the rest of the League masquerade as soldiers and lead them out of here under "armed guard" to the mainland. Simple enough, if we had the men, the costumes, and the authority.' His face fell. 'Dash it all, I wish he were here. I can't help thinking that perhaps we shouldn't have attempted this . . .'

Charles looked between the two of them. 'And what would we have said to our own consciences if the troops had turned up tomorrow, and half the people here had been executed? Where would Monsieur and Madame Thiers be then? I know the Chief likes to say that all this is for sport, for the love of the game, but we know that's not true! It's for the people who'd suffer otherwise, at the hands of this malignant government and Revolution—'

Eleanor bit her lip, and forcibly dragged herself out of the morass of despair which had been tempting her. An idea crossed her mind, and she interrupted Charles to voice it. 'They've had the women prisoners sewing,' she said. 'Among other things, they've been making uniforms.'

'Ah!' Tony didn't need her to draw him a map. 'Yes, I see. We can have all the men pose as soldiers, marching the women out of here . . .'

'But if there'll be locals watching the gates, we can't simply leave them standing open, or close them behind us and leave the fortification apparently unguarded and empty,' Charles pointed out. 'It'll all need to be done according to standard procedure. The longer we can avoid suspicion, the greater our advantage.'

A spark lit up behind Tony's eyes. 'I have the perfect solution to that.'

'You do?'

'The balloon.'

'Tony, not all problems can be solved by ascending in a balloon!'

237

'This one can,' Tony answered cheerfully. 'We shall wave the prisoners out through the door, disguised as guards, close the doors behind them and shut ourselves in as per normal procedure, and then float merrily off into the dawn high above their heads. Nobody ever looks up. And even if they did, why would they assume it was anyone other than Duquesne?'

'But Eleanor—' Charles began.

'Will crouch down and hide herself under a blanket. But I tell you, nobody *ever* looks up. Trust me on this one.'

'Yes, but how do you direct the damned thing? We'll be at the mercy of the wind, driven to any which quarter. We might be lost at sea and vanish into the waves without a soul to mark our passing!'

Eleanor closed her eyes. She knew the answer to this. It lay, just this once, directly between her hands, if she had the courage to take it up. *Anima?* she asked.

Yes, Anima answered. She'd clearly been listening. *I can show you what to do.*

'Tony, Charles, I can only ask you to trust me on this,' she said out loud, 'but supposing we could be certain of a wind in the right direction, then would this work?'

'Undoubtedly,' Tony said. His eyes narrowed, the expression ill-assorted with his friendly face. 'Is this something to do with the way all the guards were put to sleep? Or that mysterious fellow who showed up out of nowhere and whom none of the other prisoners recognize? Or the time we were in the sewers under Paris and you did something deuced inexplicable to frighten off the vampires?'

'Possibly,' Eleanor admitted.

'Well, I've always liked the deuced inexplicable. Not like Charles here – the poor fellow prefers his mysteries properly explained . . .'

'I have faith that science will resolve these questions,' Charles said solemnly, 'but in the meantime I trust that

Eleanor can arrange matters as she says. I worry, though, that it means she will not return to England as we'd planned.'

'I can't see that Eleanor herself is particularly worried about that. So in that case, no more questions.' Tony clapped them both on the shoulder unhesitatingly, and Eleanor did her best to conceal a smirk of victory at the thought of staying in France. 'Let's be about it!'

'Excuse me?' Fleurette said, approaching with a winning smile. 'Charles I know, and Eleanor I know, but you are . . . ?'

'Merely a humble servant of the Scarlet Pimpernel,' Tony said austerely.

'You told Monsieur and Madame Thiers to call you Anthony,' Fleurette pointed out.

Tony coughed. 'Yes, well, one can't necessarily have everyone calling people "you" all the time, it'd get so beastly confused. What can we do for you, young lady?'

Fleurette settled a smile on her face like armour, and folded her hands as though in prayer. 'If you're going to Paris, I'd like to come with you.'

Tony looked as though he'd have liked to call for another private conversation and retreat even further into the corner, except there was nowhere further to go. 'And what gives you that idea?'

'Rumour amongst the prisoners says that the Pimpernel himself is in Paris, so you might be going to join him there?' Fleurette guessed. 'Or are you going back to England?'

'We might be going to Marseille, or Lyon, or anywhere,' Tony countered. 'There are people in need of the League's help across France.'

'You can't expect us to tell you everything we're up to, Fleurette,' Eleanor said soothingly. 'You were telling me earlier how you planned to find work in a village, weren't you? That you intended to try to better the world around you one step at a time?'

'I *was*,' Fleurette said. Her smile wavered on the edge of a pout. 'But I've come to see that my duty lies elsewhere.'

'A woman's duty is with her husband,' Tony said sententiously.

'But I'm not married yet.'

'Oh well then, it's with your . . .' Tony came to a grinding halt as he realized exactly where his words led. *With your father.*

Eleanor would have applauded Fleurette's argument if it hadn't just cornered them in an awkward position. She decided to approach the matter with brutal practicality, given that neither of the men were likely to. 'Fleurette, you've already been arrested *once*, and you believe, and I agree, that it was to put pressure on your father. If you go back to Paris to join him there, the same thing is likely to happen again. You were worried yourself about this when we talked earlier. Is that really fair to Citizen Chauvelin?'

'I can't believe you just said that,' Charles muttered.

Eleanor had trouble believing it herself, but she was aware that Chauvelin's one weak spot was a genuine love for his daughter. Allowing Fleurette to throw herself directly into the lion's mouth would be cruel, and Eleanor didn't want to be cruel.

Well, not to Fleurette, at least.

Fleurette chewed her lower lip for a moment, then gave the three of them a flashing smile. 'Don't you understand that if I simply disappear from here, it will only cause him more concern? Once I rejoin Bibi in Paris, he can make arrangements for me to stay elsewhere, until . . . this is all resolved.'

'And if we don't take you, then you're going to threaten us?' Charles said. He had the same look Eleanor had seen on him once before, when he'd believed that she'd betrayed the League to Chauvelin in order to save him and herself from immediate arrest. The weary understanding of a man of the world who knew such things could happen, but had hoped they wouldn't happen to him.

'I? No! Never! What do you take me for?' Fleurette's cheeks blazed a furious red and angry tears glowed in her eyes. 'Do you think, after all that you've done, that I'd place you in danger? Are you suggesting I'd inform on you?'

Eleanor made hasty quieting motions, aware that the Thierses were looking in their direction. 'I'm sure that wasn't what Charles meant at all!' she lied.

'Well, actually, I did,' Charles said apologetically, 'but I'm willing to admit I could have been wrong. A gentleman admits when he's made a mistake. Forgive me, mademoiselle. The stress of the last couple of days, you understand.'

Fleurette sniffed. 'I wouldn't threaten you. I wouldn't *do* that sort of thing. If you say no, then I'll just have to make my way to Paris by myself. On my own,' she added, in case the point was insufficiently clear.

'I . . . see. Well, we'll consider the matter.' Tony might have an eternally optimistic outlook on life, but Eleanor knew he'd be aware of what could happen to a pretty young woman travelling across France on her own. 'Why don't you go and wait with Monsieur and Madame Thiers while we consider how best to arrange this.'

'We can't take her with us,' Charles hissed, as soon as Fleurette was out of earshot. 'The idea's absurd.'

Eleanor nodded in agreement. 'Charles is absolutely right. She's not used to travelling in disguise or avoiding attention. She has to stay with the Thierses – they'll take care of her. We still have to persuade them to go along with the plan, too . . .'

Tony patted Eleanor in an avuncular way. 'Don't get yourself into a pother,' he advised her. 'The Thierses themselves will be on our side; we'll have no difficulty in enlisting them to take care of her. As for the plan, the tide will argue in our favour. There's no time to waste – they and the other prisoners will have to act with haste or be trapped here when it rises again.' He grinned. 'Besides, a charming young lady like herself will have no desire to go up in a balloon. All we need to do is tell her no, firmly, strongly, and definitively.'

Eleanor opened her mouth for a moment, willing to point out the possible flaws in this approach. Then she considered the words *charming young lady* and the fact that while Tony, and others in the League, might consider her a surrogate younger sister or cousin of sorts, they would certainly never rate her as a *young lady*. She shut her mouth again.

'You're certain about this, old chap?' Charles asked, casting Eleanor a worried look.

'Not the slightest fragment of a doubt,' Tony affirmed cheerfully.

'It looks so pretty,' Fleurette said with a sigh, peering out over the edge of the basket from where she'd been crouching with Eleanor – out of view, just in case anyone did spot them. 'Who would have thought it would burn so well?'

The light of the burning optical telegraph scaffolding rippled out across the wet causeway and flat terrain, still drenched from the retreating tide. There was no way they could have left this weapon of communication intact, ready for final completion. Charles and Tony had delayed lighting the fuses – which the freed prisoners had been glad to set – until the column of prisoners was safely on the causeway and away from the islet. It had also allowed time for Tony to prepare Duquesne's balloon for ascension, and to explain the various ropes and other equipment.

But it was true, what Tony had said. Nobody looked up at the empty sky. Nobody ever looked up. People gathered in the night streets of Mont-Saint-Michel to point at the flaming scaffolding, but nobody thought to look in the opposite direction, to where the balloon was floating across the wet sands and towards the land. Their attention was all on the locked building and the roaring flames of the timbers which sheathed the Merveille; the balloon had drifted silently away, gone before anyone even thought to look for it.

Beneath the balloon, the landscape was spread out like a map, the lines of roads and fields cutting it into pieces like a dissected puzzle. Occasional lights burned in the windows of houses, or flared on street corners, but otherwise the moonlight held the land in a grip of stillness. A charcoal brazier, cunningly forged to direct the heat, kept the air in the balloon hot and them aloft. It was the most fantastic, most terrifying, most wonderful thing that Eleanor had ever done.

They floated through the air – flying! – eastwards, towards Paris, under the comforting veil of night. Eleanor had been able to call a wind in the proper direction, at the cost of a nosebleed and a splitting headache, but that didn't matter. It was her power, not Anima's, something she would have to learn. And nothing else could possibly matter, compared to *this*.

'You're cold,' Charles scolded her, wrapping a blanket round her shoulders. 'There's a bitter chill up at these heights.'

'Yes, come and sit down here in the corner of the basket, next to me,' Fleurette said. She pulled Eleanor down to huddle against her. 'Or you'll catch a cold and will need hot baths and all that manner of thing. Do they give people calves'-foot jelly in England when they have pneumonia and inflammations?'

'I've known it done,' Eleanor said, 'though my mother could never have afforded it. She always favoured mustard plasters, and onion syrup for a lasting cough . . .'

She trailed off. Now that she was distracted from the glory of the flight, her conscience was persecuting her. She'd

243

promised Charles she would explain. When would she have a better opportunity, or more discreet circumstances?

Are you going to try to stop me? she asked inwardly.

Anima was silent. Then, after a pause, came the faint whisper, *Do as you will.*

'Charles,' she began. 'Tony. Fleurette. There is something I need to tell you all. But before I begin, I would be grateful for your promise to keep it secret. I can't demand it, but—'

'Of course we will!' Tony said cheerfully. 'Can't betray a lady's secrets, what? Deuce take it, I'd be shunned by all right-thinking men and thrown out of every club I belong to.'

'Not even to Bibi,' Fleurette vowed. 'You're my *friend*, Eleanor.'

Charles touched his fist against his heart. 'I'm embarrassed that you need to ask me. Aren't we long past such things?'

Eleanor swallowed. For a moment she wanted to cry, but only for a moment. This sort of trust deserved joy, not tears.

'It happened last year,' she began, and the story went on into the night.

CHAPTER SEVENTEEN

Sir Andrew Ffoulkes held out a wordless hand for the mug of tea which Eleanor had just poured, and downed it in a single gulp.

'You're taking this all rather poorly, Andrew,' Tony argued, having apparently decided to pursue a lost cause all the way to its inevitable end. 'I mean . . . it worked.'

'Worked,' Andrew snorted. He was dressed as a common labourer. His coat and shirt were shabby, his tricolour rosette battered from daily wear, and his hands were clearly those of a man who laboured for a living. His broad shoulders and muscles looked far more appropriate in clothing like this than his usual well-cut silks and velvets. 'Tony, correct me if I am wrong, but I was under the impression that the three of you were supposed to be mounting a *diversionary* operation! To be followed by the return of Eleanor to England. No offence, m'dear, we all know your quality and eagerness to help, but Paris at the moment is dangerous in the extreme. To be frank, much as I value Charles and Tony's assistance, I'd prefer you to be safely back on the other side of the Channel. If it weren't for the fact that the Chief's hot on his current trail, *I'd* prefer to be on the other side of the Channel.'

'We were thoroughly diversionary,' Tony said. 'Left a little five-petalled red flower scrawled on some paper in Duquesne's office and all that. Not to mention burning down the optical telegraph scaffolding, stealing a balloon—'

'We're currently at war with France, Tony, in case you haven't noticed, and flagrant acts of aggression on that scale are only going to muddle the Pimpernel's position vis-à-vis the situation,' Andrew said through gritted teeth.

'And freeing several dozen prisoners,' Charles said quietly. He'd been reserving his ammunition and allowing Tony to draw Andrew's fire. 'Some of whom, perhaps all of whom, would have faced the guillotine if we hadn't acted. Isn't that the League's original purpose, Andrew?'

Andrew smacked a hand on the table. 'Dash it all, Charles, we know you couldn't have walked away and left them! Don't try to play the martyr! But at the same time, let's not pretend there's anything in the current situation which could make me happy.' He cast an obvious glance at the ceiling. Fleurette was in the upper room of this small apartment, and had been politely requested to pay as little attention as possible to the discussion going on downstairs, while they resolved the best way to return her to her father. Eleanor hoped she wasn't listening but wouldn't have gambled good money on it.

They'd travelled perhaps fifty or sixty miles in the balloon, all in one night. The thought still gave her shivers of delighted achievement. She now fully understood Tony's obsession with the things, even though Charles had been less enthusiastic, constantly muttering about the height of their travel and the difficulties in landing safely. (Eleanor had to acknowledge he had a point there: their descent had been rather precipitate and involved a great deal of screaming.) After that they'd taken to the roads, just another group of travellers making their way to Paris, and had arrived only this morning, joining the long queues at the city gates. The forged papers which Charles had provided served their turn, and they'd entered the city with barely a second glance from the weary guards.

The four of them were now encamped in one of the cheap sets of rooms which the League maintained across Paris as emergency hideaways. Fleurette's first impulse had been to fly to her Bibi to reassure him of her safety, and it had taken all Eleanor's eloquence to persuade her to wait until they could be sure he wasn't watched. Until then, they were having to keep her as isolated as possible, not seeing any of the rest of the League, nor overhearing their conversations . . .

Eleanor could understand why Fleurette was fretting. But really, the other woman had forced her presence on them in the most entitled fashion, demanding their assistance and placing them at risk, positively blackmailing them with her own safety. She sympathized with Andrew's annoyance.

'If we'd let her run off on her own,' she said, hoping to mollify Andrew, 'then she would certainly have found herself in difficulty.' And wasn't that an understatement! Even after days of travel and dingy from wayside dust, Fleurette had caught the eye of passers-by. She wouldn't have been able to survive in domestic service, as Eleanor did: some young man of the house, or visiting guest, would have pressed his attentions on her, and that never ended well. For the servant, at least.

The world wasn't safe for young women, nor was it fair when it came to assigning the blame for things that might happen to them. Eleanor was ready and willing to stage her own revolution about *that*, if it would ever be possible.

'Don't think you've avoided my notice, Eleanor,' Andrew growled. 'I'd send you back to England this minute if I had the men to spare. The Chief doesn't approve of us playing a lone hand the way you tried to do. I would have thought Tony and Charles could keep you under control, but apparently I was mistaken. If you hadn't crept off and listened under windows, and inspired Charles and Tony to this folly . . .'

'Then we'd never have known about the prisoners being executed?' Eleanor asked sweetly.

Andrew wordlessly held out his mug for more of the overstewed tea, his frown settled firmly on his face.

'We honestly regret causing you worry,' Eleanor said, trying to sweeten his mood. If he were to brood further on the matter, he might decide to send her back to England after all. 'But truly, it was one of those situations like the Chief's favourite proverb, the one about seizing Fortune as she flies past. And what would Chauvelin have said if we'd taken Fleurette to England?'

'For all I know, he might have been relieved.' Andrew sighed. 'You've missed the news, so allow me to share it with you. Some patriots – heaven send their friends better aim next time – recently attempted to assassinate Jean-Marie Collot d'Herbois from the Committee of Public Safety, and then Robespierre himself a few days later. Paris is in a ferment.'

'Paris is always in a ferment,' Tony objected. 'It was in a ferment even before the Revolution, and a lot more fun in those days too.'

Andrew waved a hand at him, too weary to do more. 'They're talking about new laws, old fellow. Using phrases like "the existence of free society is threatened" and "clemency is parricide". I don't know about you, but that sort of talk worries me. We operate on a narrow enough margin of safety as matters stand. If any of the League were to be captured and forced to speak . . .'

'Chauvelin already knows who a fair number of us are,' Tony said, his good mood slipping away, 'and now we have his daughter sitting upstairs, reading a Bible and darning our socks. Is he even in Paris yet, or still in England? How long did Lady Marguerite manage to delay him?'

'Here in Paris, and kept busy on errands for the Committee. She bought us a few days before he abandoned hopes of immediate success and returned here.'

'I have great difficulty believing that Fleurette would send even a rat to the guillotine,' Charles interjected. 'She and her father have one thing in common: they keep their word. If she promises to say nothing about us, then I believe her.'

Andrew shrugged. 'An innocent word here, an accidental comment there, and who knows what she might say? Even the best of women are vulnerable to lapses of that sort. Is there no more tea, Eleanor? I'm parched. The streets are thick with dust.'

It is better to keep my mouth shut and continue listening to this conversation, Eleanor told herself firmly, *than to open it and remind them that there are some things they shouldn't say in front of me.* She shared out what was left in the teapot. *Though if only Lady Marguerite had been here in the room when he said that . . .*

'Is Chauvelin likely to think we're trying to blackmail him when we return his daughter?' Charles asked. 'This all seemed a great deal simpler at Mont-Saint-Michel.'

'Oh, almost certainly,' Andrew agreed. 'It's what he'd do, after all. Fortunately he'll remind himself of our "foolish English honour" and decide that we lack the wits and determination to do what he'd do in our place, and he'll snatch her out of our arms with the greatest speed. I'll ask the Chief, but probably what we'll do is send him a letter to arrange a clandestine meeting, and hand the girl over by cover of night. He'll likely smuggle her out of Paris as soon as possible while publicly denying all knowledge of her whereabouts. We'll all be happy, and Eleanor can go home to England without needing to play chaperone for her any longer.'

'What's the Chief up to at the moment?' Eleanor asked.

'He has some further leads on the Talleyrand kidnapping,'

Andrew said. 'After a meeting with Saint-Just a few days ago, he said that he'd found a new trail worth pursuing. That's Lady Marguerite's brother Armand, Eleanor, in case you were wondering. Saint-Just has promised to keep a low profile and tell us if Chauvelin attempts to blackmail him, so that's one weight off my mind. We have an escape route prepared for him too, should the need arise. I haven't seen the Chief for a couple of days – nor Jerry and George, who were with him – but he's due to check in this afternoon. I'll break the news to him then. Better still, you can come with me, Tony, and explain it all to him yourself.'

Eleanor vaguely recognized *Jerry* and *George* as two other members of the League – Sir Jeremiah Wallescourt and Lord George Fanshawe – but knew little of them beside their names and titles. Many of the League's members blurred together for her into a fashionable and languid haze of bored English aristocracy, eager for the direction which Sir Percy gave them. But she nodded, relieved to have the responsibility for Fleurette off her shoulders. Perhaps she was just as grateful for leadership as all those young men were.

'What's the current news of the war?' Charles asked, while Tony drooped at the prospect of explanations. 'We've been keeping to the back roads for the last few days and even then, Paris should have better reports than the towns on our way.'

'According to the papers, the French are taking the offensive on the Spanish border. The Austrians have made advances in Flanders. Morale's been good on their side since the Dauphin was safely bestowed with them. Oh, his aunt Madame Élisabeth may still be his guardian, but everyone knows it's his cousin Francis, the Archduke of Austria, who's giving the orders. The fact that little Louis is alive and well is reminding quite a few Frenchmen that he's the true heir to their throne. It's a strong argument for peace. Well, to everyone except France's current leaders.'

'Which no doubt inflames further local talk of counter-revolutionaries,' Charles said cynically.

'Quite. England's more active on the seas, of course. Word is that America's trying to get grain convoys through, but our fleets are in the way.'

'And in the meantime, Paris starves,' Eleanor said quietly. She'd seen that much in the streets on the way to their hiding-place. Hunger was as present a spectre as it had been last year, winding the noose of terror ever tighter, and driving every right-thinking Parisian to watch for traitors and counter-revolutionaries.

'The nature of war, m'dear.' Andrew shrugged. 'It's not as if any of us like it either.'

Eleanor didn't answer. She couldn't think of anything to say that wouldn't be a scream at *someone* – the aristocrats who'd oppressed the people, the revolutionaries who'd started all this, the ones who'd failed to carry it through properly, or even the soldiers from England, Austria and everywhere else who were just obeying orders. More and more, Fleurette's dream of making a *better* Revolution seemed unfeasible. Yet it was so very sweet, so tempting, to imagine that all these problems could be resolved. That aristocrats of all nations would no longer enjoy their riches while others starved, that men would no longer fight wars because of their rulers, that a woman could walk through France without being assaulted or worse . . .

Andrew set down his empty mug. 'Have courage, m'dear, you won't have to endure it here for much longer. We'll have you back in England in a snap of the fingers. Now I should be on my way, and you with me, Tony. Unless there's anything else I should know?'

Eleanor, Charles and Tony looked at each other, and shook their heads or shrugged. Once again, Eleanor felt a pang of gratitude that the men were keeping their silence about everything she'd told them. Oh, she knew they'd given their word of honour, and that they were men who believed in honour, but . . . there was always a niggling little worm of fear and distrust.

She should know better by now, though.

Andrew hesitated for a moment, as though suspecting they were holding something back, but in the end he shrugged and beckoned Tony to follow him. 'We'll be back later,' he said. 'Stay indoors, however tempted you may be to listen under windows. The streets aren't safe.'

The rickety door closed behind them both, and Eleanor sank back onto her battered stool with a poorly controlled sigh of relief.

'You should have known he wouldn't be too annoyed with you,' Charles reassured her, misapprehending the cause of her concern. 'He admires your courage, as do we all. Andrew couldn't truly blame us for something he'd have been the first to do in our place.'

'Charles . . .' It was the first time they'd been properly alone in the last few days, and there was a question Eleanor desperately wanted to ask him. 'What do you think of all this business of magic and spells?'

Charles tilted his head to inspect her, adjusting the eye-glasses which he'd donned now that they were in private. 'I have some thoughts on the matter, it's true – but does it worry you?'

'What you think about it worries me,' Eleanor confessed. 'I'm not sure that I can rid myself of it, even if I might want to. Yet there's no explanation for it, no way to understand it, and the Bible condemns witches and necromancy . . .'

'I believe you're looking at this from the wrong direction. This isn't an art, it's a craft. You say there's no explanation for it, but what you should rather be saying is that there's no explanation *yet*.' He spoke with unusual fervour. 'Consider how the body of human knowledge has advanced in the past five hundred years. This departed soul, this Anima, may have viewed her abilities from the limited perspective of her century as magic, but there's no reason for you to do so.' He paused, searching for words. 'Look at the wonders which men are achieving now! The balloon which carried us from Mont-Saint-Michel, the optical telegraph. Men of science like Volta and Galvani have developed ways to generate electricity – tamed lightning – from chemical compounds. There are whole fields of study about how such things react with human bodies – galvanism, mesmerism and magnetic force . . .'

Eleanor's heart warmed at the idea this might not be a phenomenon totally outside the sphere of nature, and something inside her which had been wound tightly for months slowly began to relax. 'Do you mean that? Truly?'

'I wouldn't say it if I didn't,' Charles vowed, earnest sincerity in every line of his face. 'I would never lie about something which mattered so greatly to you. Truly, I believe this is not some sort of inexplicable curse. It is a discovery whose time has come and which has returned at a moment in history when it can be examined and understood.'

The image of herself as a pet rabbit or dove in some scientist's laboratory made Eleanor hesitate. 'I don't want to be the object of study,' she said quietly. 'I've heard stories of what happens to freaks of nature and oddities, made to perform tricks, with professors of all kinds poking and prodding at them . . .'

'Oh, Eleanor . . .' Charles rose and dragged his own stool over to beside hers, putting one arm around her shoulders as he sat down again. 'I'd never let anyone abuse you in such a way. My word on it.'

Eleanor knew it was folly to relax into the shelter of his arm, that it could only lead to future difficulties, and they had no future, but oh, it was sweet to be sheltered there. It wasn't just the casual brotherly care which other members of the League would give. Charles knew her. He knew her secrets, now. And still he said he'd protect her, that she was worth protecting, and that he cared about her . . . about *Eleanor*. Not Eleanor the housemaid, or Eleanor the brave heroine, or Eleanor the cunning listener under windows, but simply Eleanor herself.

'Charles,' she said, trying to think how to phrase her question.

'Yes?'

'What happens . . . when all this is over?' She didn't try to elaborate on the *all this*. The war? The Revolution? The League? Any or all of it?

Charles sighed. 'I try not to think about it, m'dear,' he replied, demonstrating that he had quite obviously thought about it. 'For the moment, my father makes little objection to me spending time at Court or in society. In fact, I believe he approves. He considers it appropriate behaviour for a young man of breeding. Quite unlike my years at Oxford.' For a moment his voice was wistful, clearly remembering happier times. 'But sooner or later he'll expect me to take up my duties as heir to the family lands, small as they are. There will be little time for indulgences like this.'

And one of those duties, Eleanor knew, would be a proper marriage and producing an heir of his own. She was quite emphatically not a proper marriage prospect. However much she already knew all this, the thought still made her close her eyes and blink back tears.

'Then again,' Charles went on, very tentatively, as though putting the idea into words might cause it to fall to pieces, 'he might accept me coming home with a French lady of rank. One whose life had been destroyed by the Revolution, where she'd lost everything. With witnesses who could vouch for her blood and position, anything might be possible.'

His words hung in the air.

Eleanor was the one who broke the silence. 'It wouldn't work,' she said, her voice raw. It felt as if every word came out bloody and painful. For a moment his suggestion had allowed her to see what life with him might be like, had given her a glimpse of happiness – and then thrown her down yet deeper into hopelessness. 'Impersonation only goes so far. My hands would betray me, my voice, my every reflex and habit . . .'

'We could try,' Charles argued. 'The others would help us, coach you, vouch for you. I beg you, my Eleanor, don't give up so quickly!'

My Eleanor. She cradled those words, let them warm her, and then folded them away in her memory like pressed flowers. 'I can't spend the rest of my life as a fraud,' she said. 'I may be good at lying, but I don't want to be nothing but a . . . a *fake* . . . until my deathbed. Even if nobody ever found us out, even if they never even suspected . . . I couldn't do it. I'm sorry.' She was gulping back tears now, swallowing them so she could speak, knowing how much her response was hurting him as much as herself. 'I'd live in fear. You would too. I'm sorry, I'm so sorry . . .'

His other arm came round her and he held her, letting her rest her head on his shoulder and sniffle into his jacket. 'I can't think of any other chance we have,' he murmured.

'I don't think we have any chance,' Eleanor answered, her voice barely a whisper. 'Only what we have now.'

'I refuse to accept that,' Charles vowed. 'We'll find a way.' His arms tightened around her. 'Consider how far we've come, how much you've already achieved. *Anything* is possible. Who knows where the world will be in a year's time.'

'I'd like to believe, but . . .' The cold cynicism of a lifetime in service bridled Eleanor's tongue. She might want to believe, but she couldn't.

'Then for pity's sake don't give up yet. Will you promise me that?' Charles tilted her head so he could look her in the eyes. 'Let us . . . believe in miracles, perhaps?'

'Yes, miracles,' Eleanor said softly, conscious of how very close he was, of his arms around her, his support, his . . . yes, she could admit it, his love . . .

'Oh!' Fleurette's voice broke through. The two of them jumped hastily apart and turned to see her standing in the doorway, her hand to her lips. 'I'm sorry, it was so quiet I thought I could come downstairs, but I didn't mean to interrupt, I . . .'

'It's nothing,' Charles lied hastily. 'Eleanor was upset.'

'I was,' Eleanor corroborated, hoping against hope that Fleurette would believe them.

Fleurette looked between the two of them, her sparkling blue eyes not the least bit deceived. 'I think we could all do with some more tea,' she suggested. 'And then you can tell me about how you're going to return me to Bibi.'

'Well, the others have gone to discuss matters with, ah, people,' Charles said vaguely. 'We hope that we'll be able to arrange something very soon. They should be back later with news.'

Fleurette positively glowed. 'Thank you! It's not that I don't like you both, but he'll be so worried.'

But as the hours passed, Tony and Andrew didn't return.

CHAPTER EIGHTEEN

'Let us consider this in an orderly manner,' Charles said firmly, despite the fact neither Eleanor nor Fleurette had attempted hysterics, drama, or anything more than a firm statement that *something* should be done. He moved the remains of their breakfast from the table – bread from the day before yesterday and ham from the day before that. None of them had any appetite in any case. He then laid out pen, ink, and paper. 'What do we know?'

Barely anything, because the Chief told Andrew very little and Andrew told us even less, Eleanor thought. But that wouldn't help the current situation, nor would it give Fleurette any confidence in the League. In fact, there was little to stop Fleurette simply walking out of the door at this very minute and into the streets of Paris, which could be disastrous for all of them. She racked her brains for some useful item to contribute.

'If they've been arrested, then it's not public. That is, nobody is aware of their true identities,' she finally said. 'It would be in all the newspapers and discussed on every street corner if so. I suppose they might have been arrested for some other crime, and held for questioning? Trespass, or something of the sort?'

Charles frowned. 'True enough, but it might also have been some serious crime, such as criticizing the government in public. In which case, they're still in almost as much danger as if they'd been taken brandishing tokens of the League and with full confessions.'

Fleurette looked as if she wanted to object, then fell silent, chewing her lower lip. Clearly her recent experiences had forced her to recognize *some* of France's current inequities. She knew better than to suggest that once they were found innocent all would be well. 'I know you can't say anything *important* in front of me,' she finally said, 'but could you be vague, perhaps? I'd like to help. If there is something wrong . . . well, Tony was kind to me and helped save my life, and I know both of you are upright, virtuous people. Even if you are a little misguided.'

'Thank you,' Eleanor said. She could sympathize with Fleurette's feeling of being caught between loyalties. 'Yet I fear we only know a few vague generalities ourselves. We know that the Chief was looking for . . . a person who'd gone missing. Do we actually know any *more* than that, Charles?'

'Well, we know one person he spoke to about it, and that's . . . er, let's call the fellow A,' Charles said. He clearly meant Armand Saint-Just. 'Someone who gave him a lead on the matter, Andrew said. That's our logical next port of call.'

An unpleasant thought wormed its way into Eleanor's mind. 'Yet what if A is being spied on, and that's why the Chief and the others have vanished?'

Charles shook his head. 'Unlikely, m'dear. For that you'd have to hypothesize watchers and spies who were effective enough to then capture the Chief, Jerry, George, Andrew, Tony – the whole merry crew. And do it without any major public disturbances. I'm not saying it's impossible, but . . .'

'They might all have been conscripted into the army, and

have gone along with the soldiers in order not to attract attention. They could then be planning to sneak away and return to Paris once they have the opportunity.' Fleurette offered. 'After all, they *are* all strong young men, or at least Tony is.'

Charles made a note on his paper. 'That's actually a very good thought,' he said. 'It'd take a bit of effort and fore-thought to slip away from the middle of an army patrol.'

Fleurette glowed with pleasure at his praise. 'So it might not be anything serious at all?'

'It might not be,' Eleanor agreed. Yet she didn't believe it. 'And it's possible Andrew and Tony went to help the others escape from conscription . . . Would they have left a message behind for you if they did, Charles?'

'They would,' Charles agreed, making another note. 'We'd fixed on a location to leave letters – er, pay no attention to that part, Fleurette, though I suppose it doesn't matter if I don't tell you where it is. So, the first order of the day is for me to see if there are any letters which explain the current situation. After that, I'll call on our friend A, to find out exactly what he told the Chief earlier which set him on his trail.'

Of course, Eleanor thought, all this was the happier solu-tion. The one which held a convenient answer to where the rest of the League had gone, and which didn't involve immi-nent peril and the Revolutionary Guard breaking down the door. She didn't want to be the spectre at the feast, but someone had to raise other possibilities. 'Do you think this disappearance has something to do with, ah, T?' she asked. 'That somehow our friends have walked into deeper waters than they expected?'

'Is the T for Talleyrand?' Fleurette asked.

Charles pointed his pen at her angrily. 'You were listening to our conversation yesterday?'

'Well, of course she was,' Eleanor said wearily, 'and any of us would have done the same under the circumstances, even a lady of quality. Be reasonable, Charles. Poor Fleurette wishes to rejoin her father.' *And we want her off our hands too,* she thought, *however nice a person and good a friend she is. Why do we have to be on opposite sides like this?*

Charles looked from Eleanor to Fleurette and back again, and Eleanor tried to guess at his thoughts. She wondered if he felt himself alone, outnumbered by the two women. 'Your suggestion about what you should do sounds entirely practical,' she said, wanting to reassure him that she was entirely on his side. 'But what should Fleurette and I do in the meantime? We might attract too much attention if we come with you.'

He relaxed a little. 'Dear heavens, no! I fear that, ahem, the place I'm intending to visit certainly isn't a location where I could take two gently bred young ladies. A's lodgings are in a better part of Paris, but even then I don't think the Chief went there directly. He'd meet him at the Twelve Apostles down the street. No, you'll both have to stay here for the moment. I apologize yet again, Fleurette, but it's too dangerous for you to return home until we have the matter arranged with your father.'

Fleurette lowered her eyes demurely. 'Of course, monsieur. I don't want to place Bibi in danger by suddenly appearing on his doorstep. People might connect him with the Mont-Saint-Michel incident.'

Having it put like that made Eleanor's heart sink. *The Mont-Saint-Michel incident.* Due to her eagerness to take action – and to prove herself? – what had been intended as a minor diversion had become something which might result in her and Charles being hunted throughout France. This wasn't just the issue of being a member of the League of the Scarlet Pimpernel; this was *personal.* She felt a greater sympathy for Andrew's gripes, and yet again mentally flag-ellated herself for her impulsiveness.

'We'll do as you say,' she vowed. Charles, after all, had been doing this for years. She was the newcomer, lacking his experience. While sitting here within the confines of these walls nagged at her, she refused to run the risk of endangering her friends again. She'd let him take the lead. 'Only, please, for pity's sake, don't abandon us here all day without any news or messages. We'll have nothing to do but worry ourselves about you and the others, and fret at every footstep on the stair. I understand that you can hardly speculate on how long all this may take, but . . .'

Charles put down his pen and reached over to pat her hand. 'I understand entirely, m'dear. It's not long past eight o'clock. We heard the church bells as we were finishing break-fast, didn't we? I'll be back here by noon, and if not, then I'll send a boy with a note for you. That way you can be reassured I haven't vanished into some oubliette.'

Eleanor truly wanted to leave the matter there, but . . . she couldn't. There were only the three of them, here in the middle of Paris, surrounded by enemies who'd see them all sent to the guillotine as spies or counter-revolutionaries if they were discovered. The Chief might manage gay opti-mism, but it was beyond her powers. She bit her lip, and finally forced the words out. 'And what if something goes wrong?'

The humour and cheerfulness drained out of Charles's face. 'It won't,' he vowed.

Repeated church bells sounded noon across Paris. In rich houses, all the little clocks tinkled twelve o'clock. In the streets, people shouted to each other that it was midday and that various items were for sale. The sun glared in through the window and threw shadows on the floor, long and black.

Eleanor stared at the doorway as though, even now, at the last second, some message might arrive. She'd *known* this might happen but had desperately hoped to be proven wrong. It had given her time to prepare, though.

'Perhaps he's just late,' Fleurette said, not for the first time. 'Why, a thousand things might have interfered with his mission. We shouldn't be too quick to judge . . .'

Eleanor took a deep breath, trying to settle her stomach. 'We can wait another hour if you like, but I fear that will only make it harder for us to escape Paris.'

'We?' Fleurette's voice rose in pitch. 'Escape Paris?'

'I'll do my best to help you reach a village outside the city,' Eleanor reassured her. 'You can write a letter to your father from there, and he can come to you without risking your safety, or his own.'

'And what about you?'

Eleanor couldn't bring herself to look Fleurette in the face. 'I'll try to make my own way back to England and let the other members of the League know what's taken place.' She would have to tell them that she'd failed. Again.

'You're just going to . . . run away?' Mockery or sarcasm would have hurt less than the honest disbelief in Fleurette's voice.

Eleanor twisted the fabric of her dress between her fingers helplessly. 'There's nothing else I can do. I don't know where they've all gone, or what happened to them . . .'

'Surely you've been told *some* of the League's secrets,' Fleurette objected. 'No doubt they have hiding places and contacts?'

'No.' It was painful to admit it. 'All that I know, I know from overhearing conversations or from having gone there myself. The Chief's the only one in the League who knows everything. And I'm the newest, rawest, most inexperienced recruit on their lists. The rule has always been need to know, and for the most part, I *don't*. I trail along behind them and do as I'm told.'

'Surely you're exaggerating,' Fleurette said, but there was a thread of doubt behind her voice. 'Charles and Tony have treated you as an equal throughout, and Andrew scolded you just as he did them—'

'He didn't,' Eleanor contradicted her. 'Had he truly thought of me as their equal, he'd have been far harsher in his reprimands . . .' She heard her own voice shaking. 'And I'd have welcomed it, Fleurette, I truly would, because it would have meant he respected me and considered me as something more than just an . . . an auxiliary, an adjunct, a tag-along permitted to assist when the presence of a woman makes things easier! *Look* at the way the men act towards me! I'm their little sister when they're in a good mood, but the moment I contradict them or show a lack of respect, I assure you that they remember their position – and mine.'

'Even Charles?' Fleurette asked softly.

'Charles is different.' And even then, there was still a gap a dozen leagues wide between them in any way that might lead to a shared future.

'I think you're being unfair,' Fleurette finally said. 'I'm not denying they have their little ways, but they can learn better. Tony listened to you, after all, and took your advice about how to escape, and he's kept your secret. Perhaps all the other men need is simply time and experience. A revolution in a man's habits is rarely a matter of a single day. Does your Chief himself treat you like that?'

'I suppose he's different as well,' Eleanor admitted. 'He has his own quality. I respect him for that without it being a question of birth or breeding. But . . . anyway, we don't have time for this. I've already made too many mistakes. I wanted to prove I could be of use, but look where it led us all. It would have been my fault if Charles or Tony had been killed in Mont-Saint-Michel!'

'But they weren't.'

'But they could have been. Luck is no excuse for folly.' Eleanor forced herself to relax her grip on her dress. 'I should have recognized my own limitations earlier. I can only apologize to milady—'

'Stop that right now and listen to me!' Fleurette jumped to her feet, her hair bouncing out in an aureole of golden curls around her head. 'You are making me *ashamed* of you! When the market women marched on Versailles, forcing the King and all his family to come back to Paris because of bread prices, do you think they said please and thank you? When the National Assembly swore not to disperse until they'd agreed a new constitution, did they say that perhaps they weren't up to the job? When the people of Paris stormed the Bastille and tore it down, did they decide halfway through that they weren't capable of such a deed, because nobody had done such a thing before? No! And are you telling me you're worth less than any of these people?' She grabbed Eleanor by the shoulders, her eyes burning with conviction. 'I know if you'd been there, you would have been right alongside them, marching with them towards the revolution. No, you'd have been in the *vanguard*. How can you believe so little of yourself?'

'But I failed . . .' Eleanor protested, half-mesmerized by Fleurette's force of will.

'Everyone fails. My father told me so himself. But this has never stopped him from gathering his strength and trying again!' She actually shook Eleanor. 'Be the woman I know you are, and tell me what we're going to do next!'

'I . . .'

'Well?'

'Have you considered leading a revolution yourself?'

Eleanor muttered. 'I think you'd be a great deal better at the job than most of the people currently on the Committee of Public Safety.'

'That comes later,' Fleurette said serenely. 'For now, we need a plan, and you have more experience than I.'

It wasn't what she could or couldn't do, Eleanor realized. It was a matter of what needed to be done.

Which meant she was going to have to use all her resources, however little she wanted to, and however distasteful some of them were.

She nodded. *Anima?* she called. *Are you still there?*

Where else would I be? Anima replied, but she bridled the sourness in her tone to a mere aftertaste.

'Very well,' Eleanor said to Fleurette. 'I'm thinking. But don't blame me if you don't like the first stage of my plan.'

'Of course not,' Fleurette said sunnily. 'I won't say a word.'

It was impossible to approach Chauvelin's house unnoticed. The dwelling was on a street in the Marais district of Paris, a *nice* part of town. Clean pavements, no broken windows, barely any beggars, and no hustling mob of street merchants, drunks, speakers lauding the Revolution or keen-eyed vigilantes hunting counter-revolutionaries.

There was one man loitering on the corner of the street who'd taken care to dress in casual clothing but still wore army boots. Instead of shying away from him or avoiding his gaze, Eleanor marched directly towards him, Fleurette a few nervous steps behind. 'Good afternoon, citizen!' she said cheerfully. She held out a small pouch. 'Can we ask you to donate for the poor and wretched of the city of Paris? Support the children of the Revolution!'

The two of them both wore cheerful tricolour shawls over their heads and shoulders, like many other women in Paris, and bright tricolour rosettes on their bosoms. Eleanor had combed some brown dye from her meagre stocks through Fleurette's hair before leaving their lodgings, and painted her friend's face in a manner far too gaudy for a girl of good upbringing. She could only hope it worked.

The man looked her over, stared at her rosette – or rather, at her bosom – then grunted and waved her away. 'Be off with you. Haven't got a sou to spare.'

Eleanor sighed, muttered something barely under her breath about some people who just didn't have proper revolutionary principles, and trudged down the street, making her way to the doorway of the first house.

Fleurette caught up with her, eyes sparkling. 'I can't believe that worked!' she whispered.

'The Chief calls it refuge in audacity,' Eleanor murmured back, 'and besides, nobody really wants to look closely at someone who's asking them for money.' She raised a hand roughened from work, and from recent balloon-handling, and knocked on the door.

Several houses later, they hadn't received a single sou. The servants who answered the doors had no money to spare, and the housekeepers, if called to the door, had no money they *wanted* to spare. But the man on guard wasn't even bothering to watch them now, turning his attention to other passers-by.

Halfway along the street stood Chauvelin's house. Eleanor and Fleurette trailed round to the servants' entrance, as they had done with all the other dwellings. But instead of knocking on the door, Fleurette shuffled round to the garden side, where several flowerpots stood, and fished out a key from under one of them. She gave a quick triumphant grin to Eleanor, who returned it.

Eleanor listened with her ear to the door for a moment. The kitchen sounded empty, as far as she could tell: good. The longer they could avoid a confrontation with Chauvelin's servants, the better. Old Louise, the housekeeper, would probably go along with whatever Chauvelin wanted, but the maid, Adele, was a more dangerous quantity. She was spying on Chauvelin for the Committee, and Chauvelin knew it. The sort of tangle which people like Chauvelin and Sir Percy understood, but Eleanor didn't want to. However, the longer they could keep her ignorant of Fleurette's return, the better.

Possibly better for Adele too, given what Chauvelin might do to ensure his daughter's safety . . .

Fleurette turned the key in the lock and let them in. The kitchen stood empty, and the fire had been banked. Eleanor suppressed a sigh of relief. Louise must be out shopping.

From elsewhere in the house came a faint echo of voices.

Eleanor grabbed Fleurette's arm before she could hasten to find her Bibi, and impressed upon her with the most emphatic gestures she was capable of that Fleurette should stay here in the kitchen, or retreat into the storeroom if absolutely necessary. She herself would investigate the voices first and find out who else was in the house.

Fleurette pouted, but obeyed, and Eleanor slipped off her pattens – the wooden soles would be too noisy on the floor – then tiptoed in the direction of the voices.

The first thing she could actively make out was a name. '. . . my dear Saint-Just . . .'

Panic and horrified realization clutched at her. Chauvelin and Armand Saint-Just? Meeting at Chauvelin's house in private conversation? Could this be the reason why every member of the League in Paris had gone missing?

Common sense stopped her before she could flee back to the kitchen and escape the house. There was a perfectly good reason why Chauvelin might be speaking with Armand in private. If he really had some form of compromising material, as he'd implied to Lady Marguerite, then he certainly wouldn't want to threaten Armand in *public*. This might even be a chance to gather valuable information of the sort that Armand wouldn't tell her in person.

Fortunately she knew the layout of Chauvelin's house from the period she'd spent last year working in it as a housemaid. She edged along the corridor towards the stairs. The voices were coming from upstairs, probably from Chauvelin's study. They grew clearer as she approached.

'. . . this final cleansing of the Dantonists, now safely gone to the guillotine, will hopefully mean the end of the National Convention's internal disagreements. That should mean fewer difficulties for you, I trust. It's difficult for a man to have too many masters.'

'I assure you I have always known which orders to obey,' a second voice replied drily.

'Oh, I know you have. You're a clever man, my friend Chauvelin. I've no reason to interfere with your work. Just as you, I trust, have none to interfere with mine.'

The second voice was unmistakably that of Chauvelin, but the first didn't *sound* like Armand Saint-Just, from the times she'd heard him speak before. The speaker had a power and fluency which Armand lacked. Eleanor could imagine whole parliaments listening to that voice.

'My only interest is the safety of the Republic. If you've come here to discuss something else, Saint-Just, then I am either deaf or uninterested.'

'I'm solely here to provide you with a warning.' Eleanor tiptoed closer, to the bottom of the stairs. 'You may have heard that Robespierre's sending me back to Belgium soon, to take oversight of the Army of the North.'

'I'm aware of that, yes. I wish you the best of fortune.'

'In a few days, the twenty-second I believe, there's to be a new law passed. You will want to be sure you are absolutely above suspicion, my dear Chauvelin.'

'You consider that I'm not?' Chauvelin's voice was mild, but Eleanor could hear an undertone of confrontation.

'Certainly not! I have the utmost faith in you. However, there will doubtless be accusations thrown around, given the law's provisions, and . . . well, it behoves us all to ensure we are safe. Would you agree?'

'So long as it serves the Republic,' Chauvelin agreed silkily.

'And you, of course, will be well out of all this in a few days, in Belgium.'

'Engaged in battle,' the other man pointed out, 'or at the very least, directing it. Nowhere in France is precisely safe.'

Eager to hear more, Eleanor crept to the bottom of the stairs and, as though luck had determined to turn against her, her shoulder nudged a tall vase standing on one of the newel-posts. It rocked in place, its base grating against the niche which held it . . . and began to topple.

Eleanor's imagination didn't even need a heartbeat to draw a picture of what would come next. The shattered vase, the men upstairs rushing down to investigate, capture, ignominy, ruin, disaster, prison, the guillotine, in any and all possible sequences. She clutched at the falling vase, clasping it against her body with both arms, one desperate hand grabbing for its overly ornate lid. Her sweaty fingers slipped against it . . . and then held. She stood there, gasping in controlled panic, her arms locked around the heavy piece of porcelain in a death grip.

Then she heard the footsteps.

Eleanor looked up to see two men standing at the top of the stairs, looking down at her. One was Chauvelin, but the other was a total stranger, a handsome young man in his twenties in stark black and white.

Utter despair threatened to wash over her. For a moment she considered dropping the vase and simply running out of the house, then down the street, leaving Fleurette to take care of herself. If she was fast enough . . .

Chauvelin sighed. 'Anne, I thought you knew better than to try dusting those yourself. They're too heavy for a girl to lift.'

Eleanor's head spun in astonishment and disbelief, but the habits trained into her made her push the vase back up into position and drop a curtsey. 'I'm very sorry, citizen,' she murmured to the floor, her head bowed.

'I must be on my way,' the stranger said, ignoring her. 'I trust you'll consider what I've said.'

'Of course,' Chauvelin replied. 'I wish you the best of fortune in Belgium.'

They walked down the stairs together, past Eleanor, and Chauvelin saw the stranger to the door – the front door, not the side kitchen one that Eleanor and Fleurette had entered through. He was polite about it, but brisk, and Eleanor had the sense he was keeping half an eye on her. Enough to know if she should try to run, or even slink away in a more subtle fashion.

He didn't give me away, though, she told herself. *That means he wants to talk to me. And I think I need to talk to him, because if anyone knows what's going on in Paris at the moment, he does . . .*

Finally the strange Saint-Just was safely out on the street, and Chauvelin closed the door, locking it behind him. He turned to fix her with a cold stare. 'I assume you have a good reason for being here,' he said. 'I would not wish to hand you over to the authorities, after going to the trouble of lying to Louis-Antoine de Saint-Just about you.'

'I'm afraid I don't know who that gentleman is,' Eleanor apologized.

'You should,' Chauvelin mused. 'You really, really should. Yet we are wasting time, and time is a currency in high demand these days. What do you have for me?'

With a squeal Fleurette burst through the door from behind Eleanor, and flung herself towards her father, grasping his hands in hers. 'Oh, Bibi, I'm so happy to see you again!'

Eleanor was tempted to reply, *Your daughter, for a start,* but she deliberately held her tongue and looked away. This reunion had no need of her interference.

Yet it still made her feel so very alone.

CHAPTER NINETEEN

'I am not being sent up to my bedroom to brush my hair and do my sewing while you and Eleanor talk in private without me,' Fleurette declared. 'I'm not a child any more, Bibi.'

'I wouldn't think of having you leave,' Chauvelin said. He turned the key in the door of his office. 'There, that should prevent any unfortunate arrivals. Explaining your presence here will be . . . difficult.'

In a small voice, Fleurette said, 'I wanted you to know that I was safe and well.'

'I am more relieved than I can say to know this is the case. But even so, my daughter, I fear you will need to leave Paris for the moment. There are those who would still try to use you against me, however innocent you may be.' He turned to Eleanor, who was standing by the window and trying not to eye the locked door too nervously. 'I take it you expect some sort of reward?'

'Fleurette is my friend, and I'm glad to have helped her,' Eleanor said, 'but I don't know how much interest you had in the welfare of all the other prisoners at Mont-Saint-Michel.'

'Very little,' Chauvelin admitted, without a trace of shame. 'I will not pretend otherwise. I confess I have no liking for

Citizen Duquesne, and I can and will view his embarrassment with great pleasure, but otherwise . . . well, you've done your Pimpernel proud, young woman. Even he is not usually quite so overt in his actions.'

'One wouldn't think so to read the newspapers or hear the gossip.' According to word of mouth, the Pimpernel had once snatched up a dozen aristocrats from across France overnight. One, even, from the very steps of the guillotine.

'I am rather surprised to see you here alone, under these circumstances. If the League wished to ransom my daughter back to me, I would expect something more, well . . . efficient.'

Eleanor's pride was stung. She opened her mouth to protest that she'd in fact done extremely well for a single-handed piece of work like this, then shut it again. Finally she said, 'You will have to assume the other members of the League are working on more *important* matters, Citizen Chauvelin.'

He's not speaking like a man who already has the rest of the League under lock and key, she thought. *Surely if he had them imprisoned, if he knew where they were, then he'd already be gloating rather than fishing for information. So who else could be behind their disappearance? Someone none of us have thought to suspect?*

Chauvelin shrugged. He took a seat at his desk and opened his snuffbox, leaving her standing as though she was just some servant reporting to her master. 'So. What do you want?'

Eleanor had spent hours thinking about how she might reply to such a question, and most of her answers would reveal far too much to Chauvelin. But she needed to move forward somehow. 'What can you tell me about Talleyrand?' she asked.

'Ah.' Chauvelin took a pinch of snuff, and sneezed. 'So you're running errands for Marguerite Saint-Just now, mm?'

'Our interests coincide,' Eleanor replied, rather pleased with how suggestive and unrevealing an answer that was.

Chauvelin gave her a look which implied she should not think herself as clever as she clearly did. He had lost weight, since she last saw him in London. His face was even thinner than before, and while he might be neatly groomed and impeccably dressed in black and a tricolour sash, his greenish eyes were bloodshot and deep-set from a lack of sleep. 'Desgas mentioned that you'd been trailing behind her. So what do you know?' he asked. 'Or what have you found out?'

'I'd be grateful if you could tell me what you know first,' Eleanor said, with as pleasant a smile as she could manage for a man who was no doubt considering how best to send her to the guillotine. 'I can tell you that the trail we've followed leads to Paris.'

'How interesting. That is where my own trail began.'

'Bibi . . .' Fleurette pleaded.

'Oh, very well.' Chauvelin leaned forward. 'Word came to me through the usual channels – some willing, some less so – that apparently Talleyrand would be returning from England to lead some form of assault on the National Committee. Such rumours are normal enough, and I usually discount them. But then I received word from England that there were irregularities about his departure.'

'You received word from England?'

'My dear young woman, do you assume your League are the only spies in existence?' Chauvelin's smile was almost pitying. 'England has many agents beside them, from here in France, and elsewhere, in Austria, Italy, Prussia . . . Every country sends their own agents across the world for information. Be very careful next time you are sharing news in an English inn. Who knows whether the person next to you is listening?'

Eleanor swallowed. She'd heard Sir Percy and the others refer to 'Chauvelin's agents' before now, but the idea they might infiltrate England, like worms riddling an apple, was extremely unsettling. England was supposed to be *safe*. 'And Talleyrand is still an important figure to the Republic?'

'Charles-Maurice de Talleyrand-Périgord,' Chauvelin said, rolling out the words, 'is a viper who has betrayed every cause he ever served, while claiming the very best of reasons for his actions. Yet people continue to welcome him to their bosoms. Why should that be, do you think?'

He seemed to genuinely want an answer. 'Because he's rich?' Eleanor offered. 'Or because he's of noble birth?'

'You have a better grasp of the realities of life than I'd thought.' Chauvelin took another pinch of snuff, and sneezed. 'I'll grant you that those are two reasons which would normally purchase forgiveness for any number of crimes, but in this case his property has been confiscated and his birth – well, here, at least – is meaningless. No, Talleyrand's saving graces are his intelligence and his ambition. He is *useful*. When I hear reports that he is preparing some sort of devastating move against the Committee for Public Safety, or even the National Convention, then I grow concerned, and I make it my business to share my worry with all those around me. Would you say that you are sufficiently worried yet, Anne Dupont or whatever your real name is?'

'I'm extremely worried.' *Not least because he's somehow caused all the League here in Paris to vanish, including the Chief.* 'And I do have a possible source of information . . .'

'Oh?' Chauvelin leaned forward. 'Do share this with me.' There was an unspoken *if you want to leave this room as a free woman.*

'I think I'd rather not, citizen.'

'I might be able to provide you with . . . some motivation to do so.'

'Bibi,' Fleurette murmured. She'd been quiet up till now, though Eleanor hadn't forgotten she was in the room. 'She did help us . . .'

'Oh, not *that* sort of motivation,' Chauvelin said with a casual wave of his thin hand. Eleanor didn't believe him for a second. 'Marguerite Saint-Just wants certain letters connected to her brother, does she not? To prevent his almost certain conviction if presented as evidence? I'm sure she's made you aware of the fact . . . Yes, I thought so.' Apparently Eleanor's face was not as impassive as she'd like. 'No doubt she would be pleased if you obtained them for her.'

'I think she'd be far less pleased if I spoke out of turn, citizen,' Eleanor replied.

'Oh? She *must* have changed.' Chauvelin left that dangling in the air like a hook, and appeared vaguely disappointed by Eleanor's refusal to ask about it. 'Still, the offer remains. Find me something useful about Talleyrand – names, addresses, connections – and you may have those letters. Armand Saint-Just is in enough trouble in any case. I hardly need to add to it.'

'Has he been arrested?' Eleanor asked, afraid her last source of information might have slipped between her fingers.

'Not yet. The fool keeps spouting counter-revolutionary sentiments – though not enough to have him arrested, at least for a few days more – and entertains actresses with royalist sympathies. The two together are a fatal combination. I'm far from the only person who watches his movements and contacts. If you must speak with him, I would ask you to be discreet.'

Eleanor felt like a child, trying to match her wits against Chauvelin's – a man who'd been playing this game for years while she'd been scrubbing floors in Lady Sophie's household, and who knew all the ins and outs of Paris. Yet she knew if she showed any weakness, he'd seize his opportunity and press her for advantage. 'I'll keep that in mind,' she said, as coolly as she could. 'Who was the other man called Saint-Just with you just now, then?'

'A distant cousin of theirs. He has the ear and confidence of Robespierre. I would tell you to avoid him, but if you should come in contact with him again then it will be far too late for you in any case. Do you have any more relevant questions? I have a great deal to do and little time to do it in.'

'Who is the Prince of Paris, and how is he relevant to Talleyrand?' Eleanor asked.

Chauvelin sighed. 'If I knew that, then I might be able to place my hand on the truth behind these rumours. One theory is that the Prince is some vampire who claims a royal title, French or otherwise. This is unlikely, as those of royal blood are seldom, if ever, turned vampire. It complicates the family tree. Another guess is that it refers to little Louis Capet somehow, the boy you'd call the Dauphin, but my sources tell me he's firmly in Austria.'

Anima? Eleanor asked inside her head. *Can you think of anything I've forgotten? Or anything he might be persuaded to tell us?* She still felt a bitter resentment towards the old mage, but she was willing to respect her cunning.

No, Anima answered. *It'd be pointless to ask if your friends have been arrested – it would merely inform him that you don't know where they are. Say your farewells and leave while you can.*

One last thought seized Eleanor. 'If you were hiding in Paris,' she asked Chauvelin, 'where would *you* hide?' She knew the League's perspective on the matter, but she wondered if their enemy's view might prove useful. If he'd provide it, that is.

'Under a false identity,' Chauvelin said without hesitation, 'and either above or below suspicion. Or do you mean in a physical sense? Paris is full of hiding places. The old mansions, the warrens where the poor crowd together, the old limestone mines under the West Bank districts. The Catacombs are there, where they moved the dead from the Holy Innocents and the other cemeteries . . . Paris is worm-eaten with tunnels, and many of them are hidden from public records by the aristocrats who ordered them dug, or the minions who kept their secrets. Many establishments place a guard on their cellars for fear that vampires may crawl out of some forgotten entrance.' He shrugged.

'Thank you,' Eleanor said. She was still painfully afraid of him, but she wasn't going to take any risks until she was safely out of his reach. And he *had* answered her question in more detail than she was expecting.

Chauvelin looked at her thoughtfully. 'You do realize that once you've left this house, it will be pointless to make any accusations against me? Your previous gambit will be useless. My word will be the one that is believed.'

'I realize that, yes,' Eleanor said, trying to quell a growing sense of panic. Was he going to permit her to leave and then have her arrested as she was walking down the street?

'Good. Because I am about to give you possibly the best piece of advice you will ever be offered. Leave Paris now. If possible, child, leave France. In a few days . . . certain events will be taking place. Show some sense and return to England, bid farewell to Marguerite Saint-Just and find yourself a proper occupation. You've demonstrated that you have intelligence and determination. Use that wisely.' He took another pinch of snuff. 'I will not give you any further warnings. Be on your way.'

Was that it? Eleanor hesitated, looking towards Fleurette.

The other woman rose to her feet and came across to embrace Eleanor. 'Thank you for saving me,' she murmured in Eleanor's ear. 'I don't know when I'll see you next, but . . .'

Elusive

I don't know if I'll ever see you again, Eleanor thought. The idea was surprisingly painful. 'Be more careful in future,' she replied, returning the hug. 'And . . . do what you said you were going to do. Make a better revolution.'

Chauvelin snorted. No doubt he'd managed to overhear their words. However, he made no further comment, and merely sat and watched as Eleanor left the room.

She imagined his gaze on her back as she sidled out of the house and walked down the street. From now on, she was on her own in Paris, and with only one trail to follow.

One thing Charles *had* told Eleanor before he left was where Armand Saint-Just's lodgings were, a fact for which she was profoundly grateful. Yet she didn't try to approach them openly. After all, Chauvelin had indicated the man was being watched. Instead she made her way down the street, soliciting passers-by for donations and being turned down. It gave her the opportunity to look for watchers, though she had to shy away from a couple of men who assumed she was offering more personal services and tried to coax her into alleys.

What she hadn't expected was for another woman to grab her arm and drag her over to the side of the street. 'What d'ye think you're doing?' the woman demanded, in a tone which owed more to Paris argot than Eleanor had ever encountered before.

'Just trying to make a living,' Eleanor snapped back, rubbing her arm where the woman had grabbed it. 'What's your game?'

'Same as yours, but this ain't your street, it's ours. You think we're going to let some come-down aristo make money off our territory?' The other woman was as vigorously decked out in Republican colours as Eleanor – more so, if anything – but she was a dozen years older, somewhere in her late

279

thirties, and she had the muscles of a washerwoman or vegetable-hauler.

Eleanor's heart sank. This was one obstacle she hadn't anticipated. 'Anyone has the right to make a living wherever they can find it,' she riposted, uncomfortably aware she'd been trained to speak polite, *proper* French rather than the casual slang of the streets.

'Oh? Well, strikes me you'd find it harder to do it with a couple of black eyes, or half your hair pulled out.' The threat was delivered as casually as Chauvelin's earlier warnings. 'Not so likely to get a few sous from generous men that way.'

Eleanor backed against the wall. 'Don't get me wrong,' she quickly protested, 'I'm not wanting to make trouble. I didn't know this was your area.'

'A lot of people say that.' The woman advanced on her. 'Most of them know when to go somewhere else, too.'

Eleanor could fight back, but a brawl in the street would attract the Guard. 'Perhaps we could make a deal?' she suggested hopefully.

'There's no more room for anyone else begging round here,' the other woman said firmly.

'No, see, I'm supposed to be carrying a message, but the woman it's from told me to not let any of the man's friends see me,' Eleanor lied quickly. 'If I go back without handing it over, my mistress'll beat me or turn me off without a character. If I give you all the donations I've picked up so far, can you get me round the back to hand over my message? Then I'll leave you be. You know these streets, I don't. You'll know where the back way is to his lodgings so that nobody'll see me.'

The woman hesitated. 'How much have you got?'

'Five sous,' Eleanor lied.

'Give me ten and it's a deal.'

'Five now, five when you get me there.'

The woman nodded and extended a calloused hand. Her arms were marked with old burns, and Eleanor recognized the relics of hot irons and scalding water from her own days in service. *Laundress. I thought so.* She reluctantly dropped the coins into the woman's hand and followed her down a side alley. 'Who's the man?'

'Armand Saint-Just.'

'Oh, him.' The careless scorn in the woman's voice made her opinion clear. 'The fool's got no money. Your mistress is wasting her time.'

Eleanor shrugged. 'So who does have any money, these days?'

The woman chuckled as she led the way down a side alley. 'You once did, from how you talk, or your mistress did.'

A thread of fear walked its way up Eleanor's spine. One little cry of *Aristo!* or *Counter-revolutionary!* and there'd be nobody to get her out of trouble. 'I scrubbed floors then and I scrub floors now,' she answered as though it was nothing more than a shared joke. 'The people at the top may change, but as for us . . .'

'It's still better than it was,' the woman said firmly. They turned down another side street, and she led the way to one of the battered doors which lined it, paint flaking and hinges rusty, and knocked on it. 'Eh, Etienne! You awake in there?'

A pause, and then an old man as decayed and weather-beaten as the door itself opened it, spitting some tobacco into the gutter. 'What is it?'

'Girl here with a private message for one of your tenants.'

The old man extended his hand wordlessly.

Eleanor suppressed a sigh and counted a few sous into his palm till his eyes narrowed in satisfaction, then another five into her guide's. 'Thank you,' she told the woman.

'Who is your mistress, anyhow?' the woman asked casually.

Was her tone a little *too* casual?

Eleanor tapped the side of her nose and winked. 'Can't say, won't say, but you might see her on the stage one of these nights.' She turned back to Etienne. 'I have a note for Armand Saint-Just, citizen.'

'Follow me,' he grunted.

Armand was in his rooms, and Eleanor was profoundly grateful for that little drop of divine mercy. If she'd had to wait in Etienne's cubbyhole downstairs for his return, she feared she would have run screaming down the street from an excess of accumulated tension. Also, Etienne stank of chewing tobacco and decaying socks.

Armand had tipped Etienne another sou and beckoned Eleanor into his rooms, hastily pulling his cravat straight. While he had dark hair rather than Lady Marguerite's red-gold, they both had the same blue eyes. 'Well?' he demanded. 'You have a message for me from Jeanne?'

'No, monsieur.'

'No? Then why are you here?'

'Monsieur, do you not recognize me?' Eleanor stepped forward so the light from the open window could fall on her more clearly. 'I'm Eleanor, the maid from Blakeney Manor. Sir Percy pointed me out to you once and told you that I work with the League.'

Armand looked stunned past words, but he eventually found a few. 'Yes . . . yes, I recognize you now. But what are you doing here in Paris, girl?'

'I told you, monsieur,' Eleanor said, rather irritated by his slow comprehension. Lady Marguerite was far quicker-witted than her brother, it appeared. 'I work with . . . well, for the League, and I came to Paris with Charles and Tony. I know Charles came to see you this morning, but he didn't return at the agreed time.'

'Charles was with you? The . . . Forgive me my language, mademoiselle, but the fool should have said as much! When I passed on Percy's message to him, he said that he'd see to it at once. He never mentioned you, or any other dependants . . . Are there others too? Should I expect more of the League at my door?'

Eleanor felt a prick of shame. 'I did my best to come secretly, monsieur,' she apologized. 'But you should be careful. Chauvelin and others have men watching you.'

'I fear that is hardly news.' He wandered over to the window, staring out at the street below thoughtfully. 'Forgive me, mademoiselle. I believe I can trust you, yet that does not mean I can tell you everything. A moment to think, please.'

'Of course,' Eleanor agreed. She was so taut with tension that she felt she must be vibrating like a violin's string. Yet in an odd contradiction, the fact that he was hesitating and *not* telling her everything reassured her. It spoke well of the man's discretion, and explained why Sir Percy trusted him. She sent up several belated prayers of thanks that she'd been able to find this back way in and that Armand had recognized her. While he was preoccupied, she glanced around the room. It was a typical young man's combined receiving room and study, with writing materials spread across the table and yesterday's waistcoat draped over a chair to restore its shape. The furniture was old and good quality, but not well polished. Eleanor spent a moment imagining a day doing nothing but polishing furniture, with no dangers or threats to distract her from honest cleaning and hard work.

Armand turned back to her. 'Very good. I'll tell you what I can, though I can't name any names. I'm sorry that Charles did not return to you as he should have done. I imagine Percy wanted his immediate help. Take a seat, and let me pour you some wine.'

'Monsieur . . .' Eleanor began, unwilling to lounge around

283

drinking wine, and barely willing to sit down in the presence of a near-stranger.

Armand rolled his eyes. 'Pretend you are an ardent revolutionary, mademoiselle. They would not hesitate to sit and drink. It will take a few minutes to bring you up to date on all that has passed, and you are clearly footsore and tired. This may be a time of revolution, but I consider myself a gentleman.'

Eleanor could hardly object any longer. She sat down on the least cushioned of the chairs and waited while Armand fetched two glasses of wine from another room. He offered her one and then sat down opposite her. 'To the League, and to Percy!' he said, raising his glass. 'And to my beloved sister Marguerite.'

Eleanor took a polite swallow, reassured by his clear sincerity. 'So what *is* going on, monsieur?' she asked impatiently.

'You know about Talleyrand?'

'I know he's missing and that the Chief's looking for him. I also know that Chauvelin's looking for him too.'

'Excellent. Well, the fact of the matter is that Percy's discovered a secret organization based here in Paris. The men behind it have been engaged in kidnappings in France, and elsewhere.'

'But why?' Eleanor asked.

'Their own selfish advancement.' Armand drank again, and Eleanor felt bound by courtesy to do the same. 'They've been seeking out known counter-revolutionaries and royalists, so the prisoners can be presented en masse to the public in a show trial. It'll be a bloody affair with a predetermined conclusion. Poor Talleyrand is but one of their victims. They intend to gain public support and seize power from the Committee of Public Safety. A sad business.'

Eleanor could only nod agreement.

'Now,' Armand went on, leaning forward, his blue eyes

burning with intensity, 'you may ask, why should we care if the Committee takes a well-earned fall from its current heights? Well, the League doesn't care a whit about them, but the prisoners deserve better. Percy's been working to discover where in Paris these prisoners are concealed. After all, if this conspiracy finds out that we're on their trail, they'll only go to ground and it'll be that much harder to find them again. I believe he has most of the League out tracking their movements.'

It did all sound plausible, now that Armand was explaining it to her. The day's tension started to recede, leaving Eleanor profoundly exhausted. Perhaps things weren't as bad as she'd feared. 'But why didn't Charles return, or at least send word as he'd promised?' she asked.

Armand frowned, as though thinking the matter over. 'Well, I sent him to Percy directly, so possibly Percy had an urgent errand for him. That might even be a good omen, mademoiselle! It could mean the chase is nearly at an end. No doubt Charles knew you'd come to me, and I would be able to reassure you.'

It made sense, and explained the current situation. Yet Eleanor couldn't help but feel that she was missing some vastly important point, something of great urgency. If only she wasn't so desperately tired. 'They're all safe, then?' she asked.

'As safe as any man can be in this time and place,' Armand reassured her. 'Or any woman, either. And I'll see to it that you're kept out of trouble here until you can be collected.' He gave her a charming smile which she recognized from Lady Marguerite. 'Have no fear, mademoiselle. Sit back and relax. For you, this is the safest place in Paris.'

Eleanor's head was spinning. She put down the half-full glass of wine, and saw as she did so that her hand was shaking. She was as dizzy as though she'd been out working in the August sun for too long, and the light was playing tricks with her perspective. 'But what about . . .' she mumbled, about to say *Fleurette*.

Charles should have told him about Fleurette.

But in that case, why hadn't he asked about her?

Eleanor! Anima was calling her, from far away, from a distance that felt like miles, far too far away to be heard, or even to care about.

It was too much effort to think. Eleanor closed her eyes and fell into sleep.

CHAPTER TWENTY

When Eleanor woke again, she could hear distant music playing and a faint murmur of conversation. *There's a party going on,* she thought dizzily, *and I should be waiting on the guests. I must have overslept, I need to wake up . . .*

She opened her eyes and stared at a whitewashed ceiling she didn't recognize. She was lying on a pallet on the floor, covered by a blanket, in a makeshift cell about eight feet square. To one side of her was a curtain of plain sackcloth, and on all the other sides were iron bars, running from floor to ceiling, too close to squeeze between.

She sat up in a burst of panic, looking around. Her cell was part of a whole row, laid out like table settings along the side of a large room full of candlelight and shadows. The other walls of the room were white, ornamented with gold, and paintings stared down at the prisoners in their cells. The ceiling of the room was a huge painted fresco showing some Arcadian landscape of green fields and gay shepherds and shepherdesses, but the flickering lighting made the merry figures appear to stalk through the bushes as though hunting prey. A large keyring, heavy with weighty iron keys, hung mockingly from a hook beside the door.

'Eleanor!' Charles was in the next cell. He pressed himself

against the bars which separated them, hands knotting help-lessly around the cold iron. 'You're awake!'

Eleanor's head was spinning and there was a foul taste in her mouth. *You know what happens to women who accept drinks from strange men?* Well, now she did. 'Charles,' she said. 'I . . . that is, I'm delighted to see you, but I really wish that you weren't here . . .'

'A feeling shared by all of us, m'dear.' Sir Percy! He was two cells further along from Charles. Tony and Andrew were sharing the cell between them. Further down, she thought she could make out other men between the bars – Jerry and George? The perspective made it difficult to be certain. 'How do you come to be here?'

Someone had helpfully left a mug of water next to her pallet. She took a drink to clear her throat before replying, and glanced behind the sackcloth curtain. Unfortunately, all it concealed was a closet-sized space and a chamberpot. 'I went to ask Armand Saint-Just for help, Chief. He offered me a drink, and . . .'

'He sent us right into an ambush,' Andrew said, squatting on his heels in his own cell. 'It makes no sense.'

'If someone was threatening the woman he's in love with,' Tony started, his tone suggesting that he'd made this sugges-tion more than once now.

'A man – or a woman – might act unwisely to protect a lover,' Sir Percy said judiciously, 'or a child, or a brother . . . but for Armand to direct us *all* into this captivity is truly beyond my capacity to understand. I wish my Marguerite were here. She might be able to explain his actions.' He considered this statement. 'Then again, I find myself greatly comforted that she isn't here. My beloved wife would prob-ably rescue us all, and it's hard for a man to live with himself when his wife so easily outdoes him, what?'

'Who are our gaolers?' Eleanor asked. 'And where are we?'

She reached through the bars to take Charles's hand and he returned her clasp, his fingers warm against hers. She was cold, she realized. This place had the same underground feel as the vaults below Mont-Saint-Michel and there was a chill to the air. 'To answer your second question first, we're somewhere under Paris. I believe this location is connected to the old limestone mines, but it's a great deal better decorated.'

'I think that's a Greuze,' Tony added, pointing at one of the paintings which showed a woman in a ridiculous hat exposing far too much bosom. 'They're not cheap.'

Money – no, *wealth*. Hidden properties. Tunnels deep below Paris. The distant music – dance music, the graceful elegance of a minuet – mocked Eleanor as she sat there in squalor. 'It's vampires, isn't it? Aristocrats who've been hiding down here. And now they've gone and kidnapped us all.' Her temper boiled over. 'They're supposed to be on our side, surely? We've been helping them!'

Sir Percy sighed, and for once he sounded truly weary, rather than merely pausing for a breath before returning to the forefront of the action. 'It appears, m'dear, that I have made a truly catastrophic mistake in where I placed my trust. I can only apologize to you all.'

The resulting storm of disagreement from the assembled members of the League drowned out the distant music. Jerry and George wished to make it clear that a few rotten apples didn't spoil the whole barrel. Eleanor suppressed her own thoughts on how in fact they *did*, while Charles pointed out how many living aristocrats and other innocents they'd saved. Andrew and Tony also reminded Sir Percy of their own wives, met, rescued and married through the agency of the League.

'And Eleanor surely agrees!' Charles added. 'Don't you, Eleanor?'

'To be honest,' Eleanor said, somewhat morosely, 'I'm

wondering why I'm still alive. All you gentlemen are of noble blood and have, well, value. I'm not sure I'm quite on the same level . . . to any French aristocrats, that is.'

'Could it be—' Charles started, then remembered he had promised to keep silent about certain matters. He glared at Tony through the bars as the other man opened his mouth too, then shut it again.

'I won't lie to you, Eleanor,' Sir Percy said. His tone was calm, in command once more. 'I fear they mean to use you as a tool to force our hands.'

Threaten to kill me and see how the men react. 'Well . . . that's a pleasanter alternative than some I'd considered, Chief,' Eleanor replied.

'For pity's sake, they're supposed to be gentlemen!' George expostulated from the far end of the cages.

'They lured us into traps, attacked us with superior odds, and now have us locked up in cages like chimpanzees in the menagerie at the Tower of London,' Andrew snarled. 'Odds are they propose to hand us over to Chauvelin with a bow on top.'

'I don't think so,' Eleanor said thoughtfully.

'Why the definite opinion?' Sir Percy asked. 'I agree with you, but I'm wondering what triggers it on your part.'

'I . . . encountered him this morning, or the morning of whatever day it was before I was drugged,' Eleanor confessed. 'I was returning some property of his. He was still looking for Monsieur Talleyrand, too. His attitude towards vampires is even more definite than his attitude towards the League. I can believe he'd make a bargain with us to arrest some vampires. I can't believe he'd make a bargain with vampires to capture *us*.' Curiosity impelled her to add, 'Where is Talleyrand, in any case? Is he here too?'

'He is.' Darkness entered the chamber together with the voice. It was centuries removed from life and daylight, propelled through dead lungs and an icy throat only by an effort of will. Although the candles still burned, the vampire in the doorway appeared to stand in his own shadow, his eyes like chips of ruby and his hands and face as white as the lace ruff at his throat. His clothing was decades – maybe even centuries – out of fashion, heavy with metal embroidery and gems, but he wore it with the air of a man who set the mode and permitted others to follow it. Other shadowy figures crowded behind him, but for the moment allowed him to take the forefront.

'I fear we have not been introduced,' Sir Percy said politely. The others had fallen silent, willing to allow the Chief to speak for them.

'You may address me as Charles de Valois,' the vampire said coldly.

'Lud, that doesn't mean a thing to me.' Sir Percy laughed in his most stupid manner. 'All those Charleses in France. Were you the fellow who needed Joan of Arc to prop him up on the throne?'

The vampire's lips drew together tightly in anger and his fists clenched. 'I am the brother of Louis the Eleventh, commonly known as the Spider King. Perhaps that will aid your memory, though I find the English are pitiful in their self-interest. No doubt you could tell me more about your cravats than about the countries surrounding your own.'

A prince, Eleanor thought, and then her mind jumped to fit two pieces of information together. *The Prince of Paris?*

'Well, my cravats are a matter of deep fascination and high art,' Sir Percy said apologetically, 'while you're merely another self-important *nouveau riche* who expects me to recognize his name.'

Charles de Valois took a step forward, his lips drawing back in a snarl. 'I am the brother of the King! And I should have taken the throne myself!'

A masked woman in deep purple and lavender came forward and laid a hand on his wrist. 'Forgive me, sire,' she murmured, 'but after all the trouble we've gone to in order to obtain these fools, it would be a waste to allow them to provoke you. It is the English manner to sneer when they lose.'

Eleanor's heart seized up in her chest. She knew that voice. She knew that dress – she'd helped sew it. This wasn't just any vampire; it was her previous mistress, Lady Sophie, Baroness of Basing. But what in heaven's name was she doing *here*? However involved in the conspiracy she may be, what would make her risk coming to Paris, with all the dangers to a vampire of a sea voyage and the Revolution?

Sir Percy yawned. 'Sink me. I'd thought there were some rules of honour here in France about royalty not giving their blood to vampires, still less becoming them. Demned if I can remember, though, and the situation clearly proves other-wise.'

Charles de Valois took a deep hissing breath between his teeth. 'As the lady here says, you can only jeer at me from behind the bars of your cage. I wonder why I bothered to speak with you.'

'Boredom?' Andrew offered helpfully.

'Nonsense, the fellow can't be bored. He has so much good company down here, after all.' Tony looked ostentatiously from left to right of Charles de Valois. 'Though I confess I can't see it at the moment.'

Eleanor had no intention of joining in the mockery. She was far too occupied with pressing herself back against the side of her cell and hoping she wouldn't be noticed. Of course, Lady Sophie might not point any fingers at her for fear of being recognized by the League herself. Why would she wear a mask unless she didn't want them to know it was her? And every instinct of Eleanor's being revolted against the idea of taunting her superiors, however tempting it might be, even when they had you locked in a cage. Especially when they had you locked in a cage. It was hard to imagine a situation where the people who locked you in a cage did so with the best of intentions. The protagonist in the sort of novel Lady Marguerite read would probably have fainted at this point, and Eleanor honestly couldn't fault them for doing so.

Charles de Valois drew out a gold-and-enamel pocket-watch and inspected it. 'I do not have time to waste with you,' he said, 'so I will be brief. I require answers on a particular subject. If you can provide them, it may bode well for your future. If not, well, we do not need *all* of you.' It was a blatantly obvious line of threat, and Eleanor saw all the men draw themselves up in varying postures of defiance.

'That sounds reasonable enough,' Sir Percy agreed imperturbably. 'After all, we require a few answers ourselves.'

Lady Sophie murmured something inaudible in Charles de Valois's ear, and he nodded. 'Very well,' he said. 'I suppose it can do no harm to listen to your appeals. However, I shall go first. This relates to the business last year, when you supervised the rescue of the Dauphin from the Temple prison and escorted him out of France with his aunt.'

Eleanor's attention sharpened. After all, she'd *been* there, impersonating Marie Antoinette to help carry off the exploit.

'In the sewers,' Charles de Valois continued, 'you were met by a group of my people, who asked you to surrender the Dauphin so they could take him to safety.'

'Not quite how I remember the affair,' Sir Percy murmured.

'Your memory is human and thus imperfect.' Charles de Valois stalked a few paces closer to the cells, though still, Eleanor noted regretfully, a good arm's length beyond any

293

attempts by Sir Percy to reach him from between the bars. 'During this meeting, a very curious flaming light was produced by someone present. Can any of you tell me more about this?' His tone was casual, but the candlelight caught on his eyes as he stared at them, unblinking.

Keep your mouth shut! Anima ordered, abruptly present in Eleanor's head and choosing to speak.

You don't need to tell me that! Eleanor was the one who'd been there and done it, creating a light which had driven the vampires back. Anima had described it at the time as *burning your own life*. The vampires were dead things and couldn't endure the flame which she'd produced. They must have realized they might have a mage on their hands, and naturally they wanted to stamp out this last flicker of opposition before it could grow any larger. Or possibly worse, they wanted to investigate how far it went.

If they discovered Eleanor was responsible, and that she was simply sitting here under lock and key . . . well, perhaps she could call that light again and drive them back for a while, but she wouldn't be able to sustain it for long. And the rest of the League were here as well, hostages for her compliance . . .

'A pocket of sewer gas?' Sir Percy offered helpfully. 'I've never liked those places, myself. One's boots are never the same after a stroll down there.'

Charles de Valois turned to Lady Sophie. 'Which one?' he asked.

She shrugged. 'All the men hold some position in society, sire. The girl is the least important—'

'Flash powder,' Charles said. He released Eleanor's hand and stepped forward to the bars. Without his eye-glasses, his face was strangely naked and innocent. 'The stuff they use in theatres. Lycopodium powder. You get it from clubmoss plants, don't you know. Throw it on an open fire and it produces the deuce of an explosion. Burn it under more controlled conditions, and, well . . .' He shrugged.

Eleanor looked at him in shock. Then she bit her tongue very hard to ensure her face didn't show the slightest trace of disbelief or argument. Her stomach was busy tying itself into knots.

'Lycopodium powder?' Charles de Valois drew out the word, tasting it as though it was strange to him. 'I've never heard of the stuff. De Courcis, you're the one who frequents theatres. Can it be true?'

De Courcis emerged from the shadows behind Charles de Valois, with Castleton a step behind him, and a heavily veiled woman in black behind them both. He was in the modern clothing of a London man of rank, and he paused to settle his cravat. 'They do have a substance which they use in theatres to brighten the lamps or cause explosions, sire, but I couldn't tell you any more than that. Castleton here was the one who went up to Oxford.'

'It's true that the dried spores of certain mosses and ferns will explode on contact with flame,' Castleton said quietly. His tones sounded more human than those of the other vampires, more normal, less distanced by years or centuries of death. He looked across the room at Charles, and their eyes met before he looked away again. 'It's not impossible.'

'What was the use of recruiting you if you aren't aware of this manner of weapon?' Charles de Valois demanded. He lashed out in an open-handed slap, which left the marks of his long nails across Castleton's face in thin red slashes.

Castleton swayed from the blow, then bowed in apology. 'Sire, it is the endeavour of our representatives at the universities to avoid creating, testing, or even suggesting such weapons. These are the province of the amateur researcher, or amateur hero.'

'Castleton, *why?*' Charles demanded suddenly, glaring at his former friend.

The question hung in the air. Finally Castleton shrugged. 'I wanted to live. Someone who wasn't suffering under a death sentence from the weakness of their constitution probably wouldn't understand such a thing. I had very little time, and still so much I wanted to do. Now I shall have the rest of eternity to do it.'

Charles de Valois appeared bored by the subject. 'To say a thing is not impossible doesn't prove that it is true.' He turned to the woman still standing behind him, draped in heavy black silk and veiled so thickly that Eleanor couldn't even make out the colour of her hair. 'Madame, it seems that we must rely on you for a final judgement.'

The woman lifted her veil, and if Eleanor could have shrunk even further back into her cell, she would have done. It was the woman, the vampire, who'd previously been Queen of France, and was now the terror of the streets of Paris, the nightmare of gossip, the legend which the inhabitants of the city had made for themselves.

Marie Antoinette was still recognizable – yet she wasn't like the pictures that hung in stately houses in England or Austria, or other places where paintings of aristocrats could still be openly displayed. Her face was stiff with powder and paint, but even that couldn't hide the erosive scars which marred it. It was as though someone had smeared a beautiful portrait with raw alcohol or grease, and then tried to cover it up by painting over it. The marks of Eleanor's fire and the fresh water of the Seine would never, could never, be removed. Her hands were covered with silk gloves, but the silk couldn't hide that the fingers were twisted into claws. Her hair was powdered and styled, but too thin. She was a ruined work of art.

And she knew it. One could see it in her eyes.

Yet Marie Antoinette still walked like a queen. She ignored the condescension in Charles de Valois's voice, the way he beckoned her forward as though she were a papillon dog, and moved with the calm poise that Eleanor had tried to imitate but never quite succeeded in doing. Her gaze swept over the prisoners, pausing for a moment on Eleanor, then moved back to Charles in his own cell. Something stirred in the darkness of her eyes.

'Yes,' she finally said. 'I recognize the man, your highness. My memories are . . . somewhat confused, I admit, but I am certain he was the one responsible. His story is likely true.'

Charles looked as stunned as Eleanor felt. However, he had enough training ground into him to sweep an unsteady bow. 'I regret having caused you—' He bit off the word halfway through, and Eleanor wondered what he'd been about to say. *Your Majesty? Your Highness?* If becoming a vampire removed one from the royal line of succession, then was Charles so proper that he refused to give her an improper title? 'I am sorry for the events which took place, madame. The situation was . . . unavoidable.'

Meanwhile, to the side, away from the confrontation which had drawn all eyes, Eleanor's brain was spinning. *She* was the one who'd caused the light, and Marie Antoinette, newly a vampire and beyond all self-control, had been trying to kill *her*. She had attempted to rip her throat out, had dragged her down to the bottom of the Seine, and would certainly have succeeded in finishing her off (and Charles as an after-thought) if it hadn't been for the convenient arrival of a group of the Guard armed with guns loaded with wooden bullets. (One of the only times Eleanor had ever been glad to see the Guard.)

Why would Marie Antoinette lie, and lie to protect *her*?

Charles de Valois looked a trifle discontented, much like

a child who'd been informed that he should be happy to settle for turnips rather than demand strawberries. But finally he shrugged, resigned. 'It seems the situation is not as dire as you thought,' he remarked to the masked woman.

'Believe me, sire, I am more than happy to have been mistaken,' Lady Sophie said.

Within, Eleanor could feel Anima relaxing her alarm, though only by a fraction. Her spiritual windows were still barred, and she was tentatively peering through the cracks in the shutters. *I take back a few of the things I've said about that young man of yours,* she remarked.

Only a few? Eleanor asked, trying to ignore the *of yours*.

Well, he didn't manage to warn us about this, or stop us being imprisoned, did he? None of them did.

'Thank you for your assistance, madame,' Charles de Valois said to Marie Antoinette. 'You may leave us now.'

'My son?' she asked, and the raw edge to her voice was palpable enough to bring tears to Eleanor's eyes. The former Queen of France might have become a vampire, but she hadn't lost her deep love for her son.

'Will be back in Paris soon enough, and you can have him then. Haven't I promised you that?' Again, Charles de Valois treated her as though she was a pet spaniel, ready to fawn at his ankles at the least shadow of kindness. 'It will simply be a matter of . . . the incident, and then you'll be reunited. Now please excuse us while we see to business. Feel free to entertain yourself in the city above.'

For a moment Marie Antoinette's eyes lingered on Eleanor again, but then she dipped a polite inclination of her head towards Charles de Valois and donned her veil once more, departing the room like a shadow.

'I take it that you were responsible for . . . that,' Sir Percy said.

'For her elevation to her current status? Indeed.' Charles

de Valois appeared to be in a positively good mood now, ready to trade barbs as though he were at Court.

'I'm not sure I'd term that an elevation.' Sir Percy's tone was his most pleasant and light-minded, but Eleanor could sense the anger behind it. 'Here the lady is crawling in the wormholes below Paris, scarred for the rest of her life—'

'Her *eternity*, if you would,' Charles de Valois interrupted. 'That is how we prefer to think of it.'

'Sink me, I'm not sure that dubbing her as scarred for eternity makes the matter any better!'

Charles de Valois removed a quizzing-glass from an inner pocket and inspected Sir Percy with it. 'And yet before me I see the man who stole her son and prevented the two from being together. For shame, sir! I almost regret the benefits which I'm going to confer upon you.'

'Such as freedom?' Andrew suggested.

'Freedom is an arguable benefit. You need only consider the mob above to see how widely it is misused. Knowing one's proper place is preferable for both master and servant.'

Eleanor could almost feel the shock and disgust rising from the members of the League, like smoke from wet wood and damp leaves. She wasn't sure whether they were more infuriated by being compared to the Paris mob, or by the suggestion that they were somehow to become the servants. It would almost have been funny, if she hadn't been sharing the cells with them.

'Do continue,' Sir Percy said pleasantly.

'Within a month or two you will regard us with the same proper respect and awe as your friend Armand Saint-Just.' Charles de Valois slid his quizzing-glass away smugly. 'We may need to explain your absence, but then, you are all known for frivolous trips and absences, aren't you? You will return to England and help to support the *proper* order of things there. Eventually you will all join our ranks. Your reputation, *Sir Percy Blakeney*, will help do a great deal to make it fashionable.'

'Demn it,' Sir Percy choked. 'My greatest strength used against me!'

Charles de Valois snorted. 'I assure you that in time you will come to prefer our eternity to your little mortal length of days. Simple, no?'

'No,' Sir Percy said. 'Not at all. And while we're at it, what is the "incident" which will be taking place soon?'

Lady Sophie laid delicate fingers on Charles de Valois's arm again. 'Sire, I urge you to be careful. There is a time to speak, and a time to be silent, and these mortals have been unduly lucky before now.'

'Bah. Why would they object to seeing the National Convention destroyed?' He shrugged. 'But you may have a point, madame. I will give them time to think while we wait for the news from Armand.'

Eleanor had been doing a great deal of thinking already. Charles de Valois had just confirmed her suspicions. What the vampires did to Armand, and what they proposed to do to the League, was exactly what Anima and Bernard said they'd done to human servants back in Anima's time. They'd probably still been doing it ever since too, despite their claims that they neither could nor would do any such thing. She scrambled forward to grab the bars. 'Wait! Please!'

Charles de Valois pinned her with his gaze, and she could feel Lady Sophie's eyes on her as well, though more subtly. To him, visibly, she was nothing more than a crawling worm, or a woodlouse unearthed from beneath a paving stone. 'Silence, slut, while your betters speak. We have no need to keep *you* alive.'

'It's about Monsieur Saint-Just!' Eleanor gasped, getting the words out as quickly as she could.

He hesitated for a moment. 'Well?'

'Citizen Chauvelin knows about him,' Eleanor prevaricated. 'I was spying on the citizen earlier. He has men watching Monsieur Saint-Just, and he said that he was going to have him arrested today or tomorrow. I don't know what's going on, I don't understand any of this, but Lady Marguerite ordered me to be sure nobody harmed her brother . . .'

There was silence from the other cells, and Eleanor realized in a surge of relief that the rest of the League *trusted* her. They really did. They were prepared to back whatever she was doing without question and assume that she had a good plan in mind.

'Is this so?' Charles de Valois demanded of Sir Percy.

Sir Percy shrugged his broad shoulders. 'It could well be. Of course, I've been a prisoner here the last couple of days, but I know that Monsieur Chauvelin's suspected my wife's brother for months now. If matters have progressed to the stage where he intends to arrest poor Armand, it wouldn't surprise me in the least.'

Eleanor let a few tears trickle down her cheeks. 'I didn't even get the chance to warn him before . . . before . . .' *Before he drugged me and brought me here,* she thought viciously.

'He is too valuable to waste, sire,' Lady Sophie murmured.

Charles de Valois shrugged in turn. He did it far less impressively than Sir Percy, being less well built and less elegant, even when he was in silk and velvet and Sir Percy was in workman's clothing. 'Oh, very well. Have him recalled to this safer area. Let him . . . bring food down for our guests.' The thought made him smile, a curve of skeletal lips and a glint of teeth. 'Let him change their candles. We wouldn't want them to have to sit in the dark, would we?'

The thought made Eleanor shudder. She wriggled back from the bars again, her head low so as to conceal her expression. She didn't want to risk showing even the hint of a satisfied smile. This was better than she'd dared hope.

301

As the vampires swept out of the room, she wriggled over next to Charles so she could whisper to him through the bars.

I believe we have the same idea in mind here, Anima said, more a statement than a question. *Now pay attention. This is what you'll need to do . . .*

CHAPTER TWENTY-ONE

Their conversation was restricted by the knowledge that sound carried underground, and the vampires might be listening to anything they said. Not Charles de Valois, of course – such things were what a nobleman had servants for. But those servants, like Castleton and de Courcis, or even Lady Sophie, might be lurking around corners with their ears pinned back for the slightest whisper of words such as *magic* or *escape plan*.

Eleanor doubted that Lady Sophie was actually a servant, however frequently she might call Charles de Valois *sire*. She was pulling his strings, Eleanor had no doubt about it. But then who *was* ultimately in control of whatever was going on down here?

Of course, that led to the question of *What exactly is going on here anyhow?* A question which none of the League could fully answer. Information was being passed by whispers down the chain of cells, and Eleanor was aware that she'd have a great many questions to answer once they were all out of here and in a place where it was no longer necessary for Sir Percy to transmit his requests for information via Andrew and then Tony, and receive responses in the same way.

(Had Sir Percy recognized Lady Sophie? Of course, the message had come back. Why hadn't he said anything? *M'dear, I'm not sure what would happen if I did, and I don't like to multiply risks in unknown territory. Isn't that what the William of Ockham chap said, Charles?*)

The whispered conversation had been temporarily redirected into matters of philosophy and strategy, leaving Eleanor sitting at the far end of the line of cells while the men argued. She huddled under her blanket to keep warm and went over the steps of the plan with Anima instead of trying to find out who William of Ockham was. *He probably couldn't sew, anyway.*

By the time that Armand arrived, the candles had begun to burn low, and the discussion had died away. His footsteps were audible from a distance: good solid heels resounding on the parquet and stone floors, rather than the silk and leather shoes and near-silent steps of the vampires. Mysterious creaking noises resolved into a small wheeled trolley which another man behind him, balding and less well dressed, was pushing along. It was loaded with plates, bowls, a tureen of stew and jugs of water, as well as fresh candles. The smell of the stew swept through the room, coarse and humble when compared to the elegant surroundings, speaking of pork, onions, turnips, bay leaves, perhaps even the rich goodness of dumplings . . .

Eleanor's stomach rumbled.

You can't, Anima warned her. *We believe they put their blood in the food to pass on their influence.*

I know, I know, you've told me, Eleanor replied, irritated. *I'm more concerned about the other man with him. What do we do if he's sensible rather than stupid?*

We hope that your Chief's having one of his lucky days, Anima said sourly.

Eleanor wished she had a good counter to that. She was

already greatly disturbed by the way that the cells were laid out along the wall of the room . . . like a stable or a dairy, an arrangement for feeding animals. If the French people had revolted against this, no sane person could blame them for it.

'Now I'm certain you all have strong feelings about the current situation,' Armand began, head held high like a young aristo facing the guillotine, overlooking the mob with an attempt at dignified pride. 'But I hope that in time you will come to appreciate my position.'

'Sink me, Armand,' Sir Percy said cheerfully, 'I'll admit to more than a few strong feelings. After all, by the look of things, you've sold us all out to a nest of lunatic royalist vampires who intend to see us dead or worse. Time isn't a thing which we have in great supply. I'd question how long before they begin opening our veins for their nourishment, to save themselves from having to roam the streets of Paris. If you *have* a position, you might want to explain it to us now. Think of it as practice for when you try to do so to your sister later.'

'Marguerite will understand,' Armand said with perfect confidence. 'She has always been the most intelligent of women. Once the true order of things is explained to her, how could she fail to grasp it?'

'Time was she believed in the Republic,' Sir Percy said. 'That was in the days when she spoke of a better world, when she was as quick to judge the noblemen who abused their position as you've always been. Yet you've changed your opinions and turned your coat, it appears. What was the cause? Gold? Power?'

For a moment Armand blinked uncertainly, as though he wasn't sure how to reply to this question and had missed a step on some mental stair to an answer. Then he lifted his chin defiantly. 'I may reject the aristocracy, but I can support a meritocracy. There are some of us who are simply more fitted to own land, to command others, to rule, and I *know* that my sister will agree with me.'

'Really? Have I always been that deceived in her?' Sir Percy's voice shifted to deadly serious. 'I gave her the benefit of the doubt once before, when I trusted her. Should I have followed my first instincts and kept her at arm's length?'

Armand's brow furrowed. He was a handsome young man, Eleanor would give him that, but again she observed that he didn't have his sister's quickness of comprehension. 'What are you saying?'

'I'm saying that if your sister shares your opinions on this subject, and that she'd willingly have us all locked up and forced to take orders, then, faith, she's not the woman I thought I knew.' Sir Percy folded his arms, lounging like a proper gentleman of high society. 'Then again, she's always been willing to use others for her own ends. Remember the time when you were beaten like a dog by the Marquis de Saint-Cyr's men, just for addressing a few words to his daughter, and what my Marguerite did in return? She reported the Marquis and all his family for counter-revolutionary activity, and he and his sons died for it. One little word to Citizen Chauvelin, and . . .' He snapped his fingers. 'I should have recognized years ago that the two of you were struck from the same mould. What need for honour when you can betray any trust?'

'You don't understand!' Armand stalked towards the cells, almost at the bars now. 'She didn't realize what would happen. She did it to save me! You said that you'd forgiven her—'

'My error,' Sir Percy drawled. 'I can see better now. She married me for my money, nothing more. The woman has no more virtue than you do, and if I weren't a gentleman I'd call her by a more appropriate term—'

Armand lunged at Sir Percy through the bars, and really, he had no right to look so utterly surprised when Sir Percy caught his wrist and dragged the other man close up, before planting his fist in Armand's belly. As Armand slumped floorwards, gasping for air, the balding man grabbed a jug of water and emptied the contents in the League's direction. 'Back!' he snapped, as though dealing with mad dogs. 'Get back!'

Eleanor took a deep breath, feeling the movement of air through the chamber and out of it, and flung her hands open. Wind slammed against the room's two doors, knocking them shut.

That's right, Anima said approvingly. *Now the next part.*

She held her hand through the bars and concentrated. When she'd done something like this once before, she'd been focusing through the flame of a lamp. Now she had nothing except the fire of her own will, her memories of the sun high above these cold tunnels, and the knowledge that her friends were with her and believed she could do this.

Lightning kindled around her extended hand, burning blue-white and radiant, then pure white, as clear and perfect as the diamonds which Eleanor had once seen on Lady Sophie's neck. Forcing it to burn was like lifting a dozen baskets of wet laundry, scrubbing a hundred rooms. And yet it could be done, Eleanor understood, if she was willing to do it. Fuelling this flame was a matter of effort, but more than effort, *choice*. She appreciated more clearly what Anima had meant when they'd done this in the sewers of Paris. *The fire of life unleashed by those who are willing to spend it.* Something which vampires couldn't endure – nor could their influence on humans, whom they'd forcibly enslaved, withstand it. Because they couldn't and wouldn't make that sacrifice. They'd chosen exactly the opposite.

The rest of the League were turning their heads away from

the light, but Sir Percy grabbed Armand by the hair and forced him to look towards it. 'Time to wake up, my lad,' he murmured.

'Here! You put that out!' Another jugful of water hit Eleanor, and she turned her head aside to gasp for breath. 'Stop doing whatever it is you're doing, you slut!'

Yes, please keep doing that, she thought with whatever part of her mind she could spare from sustaining the flame. *Continue to be stupid, you idiot, you brainless sweeping of the Paris street, shout at me, throw water at me, do whatever you want, only for pity's sake don't run for help.*

Armand went rigid, convulsing, his heels drumming on the floor. His whole body jerked as a thin ooze of dark liquid dribbled from his mouth, staining his cravat and dripping to the floor.

That's done it, Anima whispered, very distant at the back of Eleanor's mind. It felt as though she'd deliberately withdrawn herself – to see if Eleanor could handle things on her own, perhaps? *The influence has left him. You can stop now.*

Eleanor let the flame die away. Sparks still danced in front of her eyes, but they were the beginnings of a headache rather than any form of natural, or unnatural, fire. She slid down to her knees, pressing her forehead against the cold metal of the bars in the vain hope it might stop the hammering pain.

Armand's eyes fluttered open. 'Oh, Percy . . .' he groaned, his face a mask of mingled shock and self-disgust.

'You get away from him or I'll shoot,' the balding man declared, finally remembering that he had a pistol tucked into his sash. He drew it, cocked it and pointed it at Sir Percy. 'Now.'

'I don't think your lords and ladies will be too pleased with you if you shoot a valuable prisoner,' Sir Percy said casually, his blue eyes mocking.

'That's true enough, mate, but the joke's on you. They told

me who I could shoot if you and your boys started playing up.' His wave of the pistol in Eleanor's direction was eloquent enough. 'So you back off and let him be. You all right, boss?'

Sir Percy released his grip on Armand and backed away from the bars. 'Let us not be overly hasty,' he said. 'I don't suppose you feel any strange sensations yourself? An urge to examine your way of life, perhaps, or reconsider your current employment?'

'Ha! They told me you'd try to bribe me too. No luck, mate. I get a good wage for an honest day's work. So no more grabbing, no more lighting matches or whatever that was, and no more talking clever. Or you don't get no food or water for another twelve hours, and I don't change the candles, so you'll be sitting in the dark on empty stomachs. You hear me?'

'We hear and obey,' Andrew said.

'And none of your lip neither! If it were up to me, I'd—'

'Thank you, Balogne,' Armand groaned, pushing himself to his feet. He swayed visibly, barely managing to maintain an upright position. 'Good man. You saved me, and I'll be sure to say as much to the lords and ladies when we get back to them.'

'Just doing my job,' Balogne grunted.

'Now be so good as to keep them covered with your pistol while I fetch their food. We clearly can't trust them not to try anything.'

Balogne nodded, all fierce attention and cocked pistol. Thus he was taken completely by surprise when Armand broke the empty jug over his head. He went down in an ungainly sprawl. Armand then hurried over to where the keys were hanging on the wall, and a moment later the League were being released from their cells.

'First things first,' Sir Percy said, cutting through Armand's repeated attempts to apologize to everyone. 'Andrew, throw that fellow in the cells. Pick whichever one you like. George, Jeremiah, watch the doors. Armand, what is this incident that de Valois mentioned?'

Armand lost what little colour he had. 'They're going to assassinate the Committee for Public Safety, Percy, and a fair number of the National Convention while they're at it.'

'They're mad,' Tony said, breaking the sudden shocked silence. 'How do they believe they'll be accepted back into power afterwards? Everyone will blame them for the assassination. And surely they don't have the military strength to seize power – or do they?' he added, uncertain.

Armand shook his head. 'No. That's why they wanted Talleyrand.'

'As a spokesman?' Charles asked, brow furrowed.

Sir Percy shook his head. 'No, quite the opposite. I see it now. He's the *scapegoat*, isn't he? With all he's done, they can easily accuse him of any crime and have the mob believe it. Eleanor told us that Chauvelin had already heard rumours he was planning some sort of coup. And with no government worthy of the name, and utter chaos at the top, and the urgent need for a solution . . .'

'The restoration of the Dauphin as king,' Armand completed his sentence. 'They have friends in Austria who'll support them. And . . .' He shrugged.

'Well then!' Sir Percy struck his hands together briskly. 'Sink me, this wasn't what I expected to be doing when I woke up this morning, but it seems, my friends, that we must rescue the Committee of Public Safety.'

The pause hung in the air as the men exchanged glances. It was Andrew who spoke. 'Chief, you *know* we're at war with France.'

'The fact has not escaped me,' Sir Percy said. 'However, as we're neither qualified nor authorized to offer terms for a truce, I fear that lies outside our scope.'

Andrew drew a deep breath, clearly unwilling to be arguing with Sir Percy and unenthusiastic about his topic, yet unhappily resolved. 'If the Committee dies and the Dauphin takes power, the odds are that the current wars will cease. Austria's already sheltering the Dauphin. Once he's in power as he should be, they'll come to terms. In fact, the Dauphin—'

'I'd say rather those behind him,' Sir Percy broke in.

'It'd be the same if they were living humans, and it was his aunt and uncle whom we were arguing about,' Andrew said stubbornly. 'What I'm saying, Chief, is that it's to our advantage, and to England's advantage, if we shut our eyes and simply walk out of here.'

The words hung in the air, impossible to retract.

Sir Percy looked around the group of men. 'Faith, Andrew, you're more serious than you were on your wedding day! But you've made some good points, and I'll answer them.' He raised a finger. 'Firstly, I'd point out that we've all made the acquaintance of de Valois now, and his friends who are cooperating with him to stage this coup. Frankly, I do not consider them . . . trustworthy. If we follow your suggested course of action, we're placing *them* in charge of France. Now, I'm not saying that all vampires are like the ladies and gentlemen who paid us a visit earlier. Heaven forfend! I've known a great many whom I'm proud to call friend, and whom I'd trust with my lands or my life. But these ones . . . not so much, I fear, especially given their stated intentions towards England. I put it to you, all of you. Do you wish to effectively place Charles de Valois on the throne of France?'

Heads were shaken, some more reluctantly than others.

Sir Percy raised a second finger. 'And my second point is that there have been times over the last few years when we have had it within our power to commit murder. I'm not just referring to Monsieur Chauvelin; I'm thinking of members

311

of the Committee for Public Safety, or other highly placed members of the current administration. Sink me, I could probably have removed Robespierre himself if I'd put my mind to it! And yet . . . we refrained. That poor girl Charlotte Corday may have stabbed Marat, but it wasn't, and I pray to God it will never be, a course of action which we would accept. Because, my friends, we are men of honour, and we are not assassins.'

Perhaps under other circumstances they might have argued with him, but standing together in the candlelit, unknown depths beneath Paris, his words held them like a spell. They could not dispute the simple statement of his belief in them – a belief which perhaps held them to a higher standard than each man might have aspired to on his own – and they didn't *want* to.

Eleanor was a half-step outside that charmed circle. She wasn't a *man of honour*. She'd never even dreamed of being one. But when Sir Percy called on their better selves, and said *we are not assassins*, it spoke to the part of her which would like to believe such things could be possible, even for maidservants. It was the part of her which agreed with Fleurette that revolutions could, and should, happen. And that the world could be made into a better place. *For that to happen, perhaps we need to draw the lines between what we will and will not do before we even start, or else we find ourselves with the guillotines chewing up innocent and guilty alike . . .*

'So how is this assassination to take place?' Sir Percy asked, turning to Armand as though the entire discussion had not been necessary.

'Gunpowder,' Armand said. 'Beneath the Tuileries Palace, where the National Convention meet. They intend to detonate it during the session on the twenty-second . . . that's today,' he added somewhat belatedly.

'Then we've no time to waste,' Sir Percy said.

'There's one thing I don't understand,' Charles said. 'We know now that it's true what the Committee has said, that vampires can control a person's will. Forgive me for reminding you, Armand, but we've just seen the evidence of it. Why don't de Valois and his people do as much to the Committee, rather than trying to kill them? Are the Committee simply taking better precautions?'

I probably shouldn't say that I told you so, Anima commented, *but I really did tell you so.*

What good would it have done to convince me? Eleanor replied. *They're the ones who believe it now.*

Armand swallowed. 'It's not that, Charles. It's because other vampires are controlling the Committee already. Younger ones, who weren't aristocrats or in positions of high power when the Revolution started. They saw their chance and took it. They'd never have had true power otherwise, they'd always have been subservient to their elders. It infuriates the Prince – that is, de Valois and the rest of them. Living humans may be the ones who started the Revolution and carried it through, but now that the Committee has settled in at the top . . . well, these other vampires saw it as an opportunity to get their fingers on power.'

'But don't they know all their previous lords and masters are hiding down here?' Tony demanded.

'They know, but they can't send soldiers down into these depths without revealing all their own secrets. It's . . . not pretty.' Armand's face was haggard. 'God help me, I've been hearing them talk about this for days now and never thought to question it.'

There was a dreadful stillness from the part of Eleanor's mind where Anima was usually prone to offer comments. Somehow this stillness was worse than outright hysterics or mad laughter.

Anima? Eleanor said nervously. *Are you all right?* As much as a disembodied spirit in the last throes of existence could be *all right*, she supposed . . .

All this time, all my thoughts, all utterly pointless, Anima snarled, civility peeled back from her voice to leave the raging fury of a wolf. *I've thought that there must be some great secret to the vampires being defeated here in France, to the way that they were driven out and hounded from the country. I hoped that maybe some fortunate soul had found a way to save the living from their hunger. But no, Eleanor, no! Far from it! It's merely a vampire civil war, fought with humans as proxy soldiers! Factions contending against each other, and now they're using far more dangerous weapons to do it than ever before. I'm damned, Eleanor, and for nothing. I've come all this way, survived over five hundred years, to find out that there is no salvation, no hope, no rescue. What kills vampires? Only other vampires. God have pity on us all.*

Yet Sir Percy didn't bat an eyelash. 'It would seem we have quite a laundry list of problems to deal with,' he remarked. 'Still, first things first. We have an urgent appointment at the Tuileries Palace. Armand, I'm counting on you to lead us to the nearest exit to that location. You know these cursed underground passages, I presume? The rest of us would stumble around in the dark till Doomsday. Can we depend upon you?'

With a visible effort, Armand pulled himself together and smoothed his hair back into place. 'Of course, Percy,' he said. 'It's not far. We're somewhere under the Île de la Cité at the moment, so maybe half an hour if we hurry.'

'Then let's be about it.'

I don't believe it, Anima muttered as Sir Percy chivvied the group into motion, handing out candles, and marshalled them into a quick march, following Armand down a barely lit corridor. *How can he be so . . . so unthinking, now that he knows the truth? How can he simply shrug and carry on with his little self-appointed mission, when the threat is so much greater?*

Eleanor thought she understood Sir Percy's attitude better than Anima did. *He's dealing with the matter at hand, and leaving larger issues until he has the time to plan properly,* she replied. *What good would it do if he were to react the way you'd like, and tear his hair and vow vengeance? How would it actually help us in our current state of danger?*

It'd make me feel better, Anima answered, barely audible. Half her mind still seemed distracted, as though taking in the full extent of the latest piece of bad news. Eleanor herself wasn't sure that she could fully believe it. At least her headache had eased.

'Are you all right?' Charles murmured in her ear. He was at her side, a shoulder to lean on should she need it, though she hadn't. Not yet.

'I'm well enough,' Eleanor began, and then put her finger on the point which was truly worrying her. 'Armand hasn't spoken to me. Did I do something wrong? What if I couldn't cleanse him enough . . . ?'

Charles chewed on his lower lip before answering. 'I believe he's ashamed, m'dear,' he answered. 'And like any man, he doesn't want to admit it. He should thank you, but how can he do such a thing when he'd have to admit his own weakness?'

'But he wasn't weak,' Eleanor argued, keeping her voice to a whisper. Sound carried in these underground passages. 'Anima said it could happen to anyone. It could have been done to us too . . .'

The ornaments and gilding caught the light of their candles as they passed, like fleeting glimpses of watchful eyes. The air smelled of dust, mould and damp. She wondered how many human servants had to live down here, to keep the vampires served in the fashion which they no doubt required. And what happened if any of them tried to flee?

Charles wouldn't meet her eyes. 'And yet he's probably

at this very moment thinking of what he might have done to avoid it,' he said. 'He drugged you and brought you down here, Eleanor. How can I forgive such a thing?'

'And yet if he hadn't, we might all still be sitting in those cells.' Sir Percy had somehow drifted up alongside them, despite being six feet tall, equivalently broad across the shoulders, and having been *in front* of them not five minutes ago. 'Good work, m'dear. We'll have a great deal to discuss once the current situation is resolved. But here and now, I wanted to tell you that you still have my trust.' He clapped her shoulder, much as he might have done to one of the men. 'I told you once before that I know how one can become caught between two promises. You did a man's work today, Eleanor. I won't forget.'

Eleanor ducked her head in embarrassment, her throat and eyes suddenly burning with repressed tears. 'Thank you, Chief,' she whispered.

Wasn't this what she'd wanted? Full recognition, credit, thanks and acknowledgement? Why, then, did she wish so ardently that she was sitting and sewing somewhere out of danger, where she could focus on the craft she loved rather than facing the constant risk of the guillotine?

'Don't blame poor Armand,' Sir Percy went on. 'The poor fellow's having to face what he did, and it boils down to two choices, neither palatable. Either he was a weak-willed traitor, or he was a helpless victim. I'll ask my beloved Marguerite to speak with him later, when this is all over. But for now, do you think what he says is true about the Committee? That some of the fellows up there who're crying death to all sanguinocrats and counter-revolutionaries are in fact dancing on their puppet strings?'

'I think it's possible, Chief,' Eleanor said cautiously. 'That is, it's not impossible.'

'I assure you that it *is* possible.' The voice came from the other side of Eleanor, close enough to make her heart jump into her throat, and a pair of black-gloved hands wrapped round her upper arms, the fingers cold as a corpse's through the silk. 'Now restrain yourself. I am supposed to kill you – but I'd rather not.'

CHAPTER TWENTY-TWO

Eleanor tried to twist her head to look behind her, but Marie Antoinette literally shook her, as a mother might shake a naughty child. 'Hush,' she cautioned Eleanor, and the rest of the League. 'I am not the only one abroad in these corridors hunting you down.' Her voice was strangely like Eleanor's own. Amid her terror, it sounded to Eleanor almost as if she were scolding herself.

'Faith, you choose a strange moment to show yourself, madame.' Sir Percy was only a couple of feet away, but with Marie Antoinette's claw-like fingers so close to Eleanor's throat, he might as well have been a dozen yards distant in terms of what he could do to save her. 'What business do you have with us?'

'I believe we have interests in common,' Marie Antoinette said calmly. Her voice would have been the model of decorum and elegance, but there was a slight edge to it. Each breath came with an effort, drawn from a raw throat. 'Rest assured, I mean no harm to you or your League, or to this young woman.'

'In that case, you might let her go,' Charles suggested. In the flickering candlelight Eleanor could see the tight urgency of his eyes. Tony had one hand clamped on his shoulder, restraining him from any hasty action.

'I was afraid she might summon that light of hers and drive me away before we had the chance to speak. But since we are dealing with each other in a respectful fashion, perhaps she will give her word to refrain from anything like that?'

Eleanor swallowed. She sought Sir Percy's eyes, and he gave her a small affirming nod. 'I give my word not to take action against you,' she stammered, her voice higher than she'd have liked, 'unless you attack us first.'

'Excellent. See how perfectly we can manage when all parties are reasonable, honourable folk?' Marie Antoinette released her grip, and Eleanor took a hasty step away before she could change her mind, retreating towards Charles.

'It strikes me that not everyone down here is what one might describe as *reasonable, honourable folk*,' Sir Percy noted. 'Perhaps your interests are different, madame?'

'Perhaps they are,' Marie Antoinette agreed. In the dim light, far less illuminating than the prison room, her veil and gloves hid all traces of the damage inflicted on her face, and she might have been beautiful behind the black silk. 'I believe I've already given some proof of that.'

'You corroborated my lie earlier,' Charles agreed. 'I was . . . curious about that, madame. I imagine you have no reason to feel kindly towards us.'

That was one way of putting it, Eleanor reflected as she stood next to him. Marie Antoinette had hardly been rational at that point, but between them and the flowing waters of the Seine, as well as the wooden bullets of the Guard, she'd ended up like . . . this. How could anyone not hold a grudge?

'At the moment, you are the lesser of two evils,' Marie Antoinette said crisply. 'I am prepared to pardon your actions of last year. I was not fully informed as to the situation. Have no fear, I'm not asking passage to England. My intentions are more urgent. Your friend Saint-Just has no doubt told you what is at stake?'

319

'He has,' Sir Percy agreed. 'However, madame, you have little reason to love the Committee of Public Safety or even the National Convention, and every motive to wish the monarchy restored. Why would you stand against de Valois? He apparently holds the authority down here.'

'I am the Queen of France,' Marie Antoinette said firmly, her head poised with every fraction of superiority which Lady Marguerite had tried to drill into Eleanor. 'Charles de Valois was never more than a prince. What he does and does not wish is not my concern.' She turned her attention to Eleanor. 'You did such *excellent* work impersonating me, perhaps you know why I object to this turn of events?' The undertone of vinegar to her voice suggested that all might be pardoned, but was *not* forgiven and forgotten.

Yet Eleanor remembered the fury and desperation in Marie Antoinette's voice, that night in the sewers beneath Paris. *My son. Give me my son.* 'The Dauphin,' she blurted out. 'If this carries through, if the plot succeeds, then it will be Charles de Valois who has custody of your son.'

'But wouldn't you . . .' Charles started, then fell silent, probably following the same chain of reasoning as Eleanor. An ancient aristocrat from centuries ago, who hadn't been directly involved in the current politics, might be accepted by the people of Paris as a reasonable guardian for the Dauphin – even if he was a vampire. A few promises to stay out of the direct succession of power, some fellow guardians who could later be bent to his will . . . it could be done. But his mother, who'd already been put on public trial and had her character destroyed, who was now feared as a murderess stalking the streets of Paris, and whose face was so marred that she had to conceal it behind powder and a veil? Never.

People prefer vampires to look like living people, Anima agreed. *Not like the dead things which they are.*

Your thoughts on the situation? Eleanor asked.

If the vampires are fighting each other, we might as well make use of it. The same despair as earlier tainted Anima's words. *For what little gains we can achieve.*

Sir Percy had apparently followed the same train of thought, for he nodded slowly. 'Well then, madame, how can you assist us?'

'You truly believe that you can discover these explosives and prevent them from being detonated?' Marie Antoinette questioned. 'Just you few? There are more than a dozen vampires down here, and numerous servants who are extremely well paid to obey.'

Sir Percy twitched a shoulder in a fashionable shrug. 'I know at least one person above us who'll be glad to assist, and who can command significantly more support. The difficulty will be in locating the gunpowder, I suspect.'

'And there I can help you.' Marie Antoinette drew a thin packet of papers from the skirts of her dress. 'A plan showing the locations of the explosives.'

'Your price?'

Beneath the concealing silk of her veil, Marie Antoinette's mouth twisted in what might have been a smile. 'I require a hostage.'

'I'll do it, Chief,' Charles said, a moment before the other members of the League could speak. But Eleanor was silent. She'd felt Marie Antoinette's eyes on her. She knew who the vampire queen wanted.

'You will need all these brave comrades of yours,' Marie Antoinette said. 'The gunpowder is . . . defended. The girl will be safer with me. I give you my word as Queen of France that I will release her, safe and well, once this is over.'

'And why should you want a hostage?'

'It would be very convenient for you to flee, once you reach the surface. I'm certain you have little reason to save the current rulers of France from a well-deserved death. However, I want Charles de Valois thwarted. If one of you remains with me, then I will be . . . reassured as to your good faith.'

Sir Percy stroked his chin, then glanced to Eleanor. 'The decision is yours, m'dear.'

Of course he wouldn't question Marie Antoinette's word, Eleanor thought resentfully. All the noblemen and noble-women trusted each other – or claimed to, at least. No, he had to place the choice on *her* shoulders. 'You might need me with you, Chief,' she said, her lips numb with fear. 'If you need light—'

'Don't be a fool,' Marie Antoinette interrupted. 'I know what you're talking about. Charles de Valois already suspects, and his English conspirator even more so. If you confirm their suspicions, young woman, you will not leave Paris alive.'

I believe she's speaking the truth, Anima commented, abruptly interested, awakened from her despair. *I need to know more about this. Accept her offer.*

You want me to say yes? Eleanor asked disbelievingly.

It's no more foolish than when you went to that ball in London, Anima replied.

Eleanor nodded. 'I agree, then,' she said, trying not to think about what she'd just agreed to.

'If anything happens to her—' Charles began, taking a half-step forward.

Marie Antoinette stared him down. 'I have given my word, have I not?'

'You have indeed,' Sir Percy said cheerfully, his restraining hand falling on Charles's shoulder, 'and God forbid I should call your honour into question, madame. However, the given word is sadly no longer what it used to be in France, I fear, so I can only assure you that if any harm should come to

Eleanor, then you have *my* word that you will never see your son again, or see another dawn.' For a moment his levity slipped away, and the candlelight turned his eyes to blue ice.

'We are wasting time.' Marie Antoinette stepped forward to offer him the packet of papers. 'Here. The detonation is planned for midday. You have a few hours yet. I have marked an area on the map where we may meet afterwards. Now go. Except for you, young woman. Follow me.'

Eleanor reached out to take Charles's hand and squeeze it for a moment, but she couldn't bring herself to meet his eyes. Then she followed the vampire queen into the darkness.

Of course, Marie Antoinette didn't need light to navigate the cold rooms and corridors. But the absolute pitch blackness of Eleanor's surroundings left her confounded and stumbling. The vampire queen hissed in displeasure after a few of her missteps and placed Eleanor's hand on her wrist, leading her further and further away from the League and into a maze of turnings and dusty rooms. Eleanor tried to keep track of their route but was soon hopelessly lost. The only thing she *did* know was that they were moving towards a source of fresh air. The draught flickered faintly against her skin, brushing her face like a promise of freedom.

The glimmer of distant candles was like a thousand dawns all come at once after what felt like a never-ending night. Marie Antoinette shook off Eleanor's hand with a small noise of disdain, continuing to lead the way with the utmost confidence that Eleanor would follow her. They entered a set of rooms decorated in white and green, and a withered-looking elderly woman hastily rose from where she'd been sitting. She curtsied. 'Forgive me, Your Majesty, I had thought you were elsewhere . . .'

'I require privacy, Jeannine,' Marie Antoinette said. She

didn't even look at Eleanor, but Jeannine's glance was clear enough. The woman clearly thought that Eleanor was here to provide blood. 'I take it there are no messages for me?'

'No, Your Majesty.'

Marie Antoinette waved a hand in dismissal and Eleanor, again, could only marvel at the casual grace and certainty of her movements. She found herself studying the other woman as though she might need to impersonate her once more. A thought pricked at her mind. *If I were to impersonate a woman of quality, as Charles suggested, could I do this? Could I live like this?*

The door closed behind Jeannine, and Marie Antoinette seated herself on one of the dainty gilt chairs, her skirts pooling around her like shadows. 'You may sit,' she informed Eleanor, then paused at some flicker of expression crossing Eleanor's face. 'Why, what amuses you?'

Eleanor shook her head in apology, taking a seat on the chair which Jeannine had been using. 'Please forgive me, madame. It's a very stupid thing, and it's not something which can happen in any case, but I was just imagining my mother's expression if I ever told her that I'd been allowed to sit in the presence of royalty.'

For a moment, Marie Antoinette's own lips curved into a faint smile beneath her veil. 'I take it that your mother has no idea you are here in France, assisting the League of the Scarlet Pimpernel?'

'No, madame, but how did you know?'

'I truly cannot imagine any mother allowing her daughter to do so if she *did* know.' Marie Antoinette sighed. 'Then again, my own mother placed her daughters like pawns on the chessboard of Europe, and we hardly had any choice in the matter. She sent me to France, and . . .'

Eleanor racked her brain to remember anything about

Marie Antoinette's mother, the Empress Maria Theresa. The only thing she knew was that the woman had been Austrian – hardly enough material for a witty reply. She decided upon honesty. 'My mother was a housewife, rather than an empress, and married to a farmer, madame. But she too placed me where she thought it best. All my own hopes have been something which grew after that.'

'And what do you hope for?'

Eleanor spread her hands – dirty from the cells and the underground passages, calloused from the last few weeks, and sadly lacking in the softness and fineness suitable for embroidery. 'I want to be a seamstress, madame, and work in a modiste's shop. When all this is over . . .'

'That's all?' Marie Antoinette leaned forward, the silk of her veil rippling with the fierceness of the movement. 'That's *all*?'

'As I said, my mother wasn't an empress,' Eleanor said, a little bitterly, 'or even an aristocrat.'

'And yet you have power,' Marie Antoinette said softly. '*The* power.'

'How is it that you know about it, madame?' Eleanor demanded. It seemed pointless to claim innocence at this point. 'Nobody else does. Were you told by other vampires?'

'No, not at all. The younger vampires scoff at the idea, and the older vampires would prefer to conceal the matter and pretend humans never had the power to repel them. No . . . this is a case of royalty having certain advantages. There were books in my mother's library which were, shall we say, not for public consumption. I do not mean folly about Black Masses or witchcraft. I mean hidden histories, stories which were too important for common folk to know.'

And yet it's one of the common folk who inherited that power, Eleanor thought, but had the sense to keep those words behind her teeth. There were more important questions, and here was someone who might actually have *answers*. 'What did the books say?' she asked, Anima's impatience and urgency buzzing at the back of her mind.

'Shouldn't I be the one asking *you* about these things?' Marie Antoinette sounded surprised.

'I'm . . . undereducated,' Eleanor admitted. It sounded better than *completely ignorant except for the few facts which my teacher has seen fit to dole out to me from her own limited store.* 'And for all I know, madame, things were different in Austria.'

The vampire queen appeared to accept that. 'My birthplace was only a duchy of the Holy Roman Empire at the time, rather than the empire which it is today. It was created within the last fifty years or so by the Emperor Frederick. So it's hardly surprising that records are sparse. Yet it appears clear the rulers there and across Europe used to find mages to be convenient tools. They patronized them, paid for their books and studies, employed them to ensure the welfare of crops, the safety of their borders . . . What *wasn't* clear from the records was why the vampires disliked them. Vampires held a presence in society much like their present one in civilized lands.' Her tone suggested this didn't currently include France. 'The books mentioned accusations of witchcraft, much as with the Templars, trouble with the Church, the death of their particular patrons and supporters . . . Leopold the Virtuous was archduke in Austria, and one would have thought he would favour the mages, but the books spoke more about how he founded towns and fought against the infidels.'

'I'm sure the books didn't mention subjects such as what was done to Armand Saint-Just,' Eleanor said. 'That seems to be the deepest secret vampires keep.' One which they would kill to protect.

'Indeed they did not. But they spoke of how the mages

could conjure lights which caused pain to vampires. And when I remembered what you did to me, I could see no other explanation for what you are. So now, your turn, young woman. Do you represent some hidden college of mages? Are you about to take a part in worldly affairs once more? And how far do your plans for the future extend?'

Eleanor was taken by surprise. This didn't sound like the sort of conversation she'd been expecting, which would have ended with *scrub my floor* or *open your veins*. This was far more like a negotiation . . . with an equal. Or if not an equal, at least a representative of some force which deserved respect, and who was covered by the same mantle of dignity. 'There are a great many things I can't tell you, madame,' she defended herself.

'You show a commendable ability to keep your mouth shut.' Marie Antoinette paused for a moment. 'Why are you supporting the League of the Scarlet Pimpernel?'

Eleanor had no idea how to answer these questions. She felt as though she was dancing on a cliff-edge in ill-fitting shoes. 'Because I couldn't just stand by and see innocent people being killed, madame,' she tried.

'Is that what your superiors told you to say?' The older woman sounded world-weary, as though the very concept of *saving the innocent* had become a joke to be sneered at.

'To be honest, madame, usually they tell me that I'm putting myself at too much risk, then scold me for my folly, and say that I'm not paying enough attention to the world around me and the political implications.' *Don't you?* she asked Anima.

And with reason, Anima answered smugly. *It's a pity this woman was coaxed into becoming a vampire and damning herself. There's evidently more to her than the popular rumours suggested.*

'Mmm. And your plans for the future?'

'At this precise moment, they don't stretch far beyond hoping that my friends all survive the next few hours, madame,' Eleanor said. What would they be doing while she was sitting here in this dainty little chamber, making polite conversation? Were they all still safe? Were they all still *alive*? She'd had to sit and wait for news on other occasions before, but never one quite so dangerous.

Marie Antoinette sighed. 'I am being honest with you, young woman. I've preserved your secret. A *little* show of reciprocity would be appreciated. If you're not empowered to discuss alliances, then say as much now and we'll waste no more time on preliminaries. I'll merely give you a message to take to your superiors instead.'

'Alliances?' Eleanor faltered.

'Yes. Alliances.' The vampire rose to her feet and began to stalk up and down the chamber. 'Girl, I have had quite enough with being the game piece on someone else's board. Charles de Valois is a fool. I'm astonished that he's survived this long. He and his minions offered me the safety of my children in return for joining them as a vampire. They . . . failed. If my children *were* saved, it was because of your actions – you and your League – and believe me, I haven't forgotten that. Yet now they treat me as a token, a pawn, a threat to be trotted out to scare the people of Paris. I am given no voice in decisions or plans. Look at this room!'

Eleanor obeyed, trying to understand what she was supposed to see, and then it struck her. The room appeared pretty enough compared to the dark corridors beyond, but when one actually looked at it with the eye of a servant who'd dusted in truly stately homes, it was *flawed*. The furniture had nicks and dents. In the corners and near the floor, the paint and fresco on the walls showed signs of water damage. Thinking back, the maid had been, well, very old. The whole room was the sort of thing which one assigned to poor relations or unwanted guests, in the hope that they'd take the hint and leave as soon as possible.

Her expression must have told Marie Antoinette that she'd understood. 'When Charles de Valois falls,' Marie Antoinette said softly, 'matters will be different.'

CHAPTER TWENTY-THREE

'The best sort of alliance might be one where we both stay out of each other's way,' Eleanor offered timidly. She didn't need Anima's opinion on the subject. Common sense was enough to keep her well out of any vampire civil war. Soon she'd be back in England, and well away from all this. 'I'm sure my superiors would agree.'

Actually, I think it would probably be safer to kill her now, Anima muttered. *This vampire has plans. But the odds wouldn't be in our favour. Say whatever it takes to keep her happy until we can leave this nest of vipers.*

'For the moment, that would be acceptable,' Marie Antoinette agreed. 'But as for the future . . . you and your superiors might need to seek shelter. England is thoroughly permeated by my kind. What do you think will happen if they start hunting down mages again there?'

'Even if some of them might *suspect* that mages still exist,' Eleanor said carefully, 'and thank you, madame, for your assistance on that subject . . . I would still have thought they had more important matters with which to concern themselves. Revolutions, for example.' She remembered the salon which she'd attended with Lady Marguerite. It felt like years ago. 'There is a new spirit of change abroad in the world, not just in France.'

'One might have said as much five hundred years ago, and yet still they attempted to utterly erase your legacy and ensure that nobody remembered you.' Marie Antoinette gestured, and the candlelight threw the bones and hollows of her hand into stark relief, cruelly revealing the lines of scars beneath her silk glove. 'You may not fully appreciate such a thing, but believe me, only fear could have provoked such efforts. There must have been some secret which you mages knew, some vulnerability to which you had access. They – the vampires – had time on their side, after all. What *was* the secret, young woman?'

There was something, Anima snarled. *I know there was. And Bernard confirmed it. They had a plan. If only I could have reached them before I died . . . It must be to do with whatever is hidden beneath London. And now we have a possible further source of information, at Oxford . . . We must survive this. There is too much at stake.*

Eleanor looked up at the vampire queen, and her blood ran cold. Earlier this conversation had felt like one between two human beings, but now the mask of affability had come loose. Eleanor was in a room with somebody who could and would kill her if she felt like it, promise to Sir Percy or no promise. 'There are a great many things I haven't been told, madame,' she said, her lips numb with fear, 'and if you wish me to take a message back to my superiors, I will gladly do so. But it will be much harder for you to contact them without me.'

'You silly child!' Marie Antoinette patted her cheek. The vampire's flesh was icy cold. 'I have far more patience than to do anything hasty. Don't worry. You'll be going back with your friends.'

'But what will *you* do, madame?' Eleanor asked.

'Wait.' The word held the quality of patience which came from years of imprisonment, from howling mobs outside the window and insults in court, unjust judges and the shadow of the guillotine. 'This Revolution will not last. The people of France are already turning against their new masters. When the time comes, they will remember their proper loyalties to my son. He will reclaim power and the old order will be restored. Though we will not discard *all* the new laws. Some of them are rational, and I admit that there were . . . mistakes in the past. Certain people abused their positions. Well, they are gone, and a veil can be drawn over those matters. In the future, there will be no more revolutions.'

'Can you be so certain that the Revolution will not last, madame?' Eleanor thought of Madame and Monsieur Thiers, of Fleurette, of all the people who had plans for a *better* form of revolution. Did Marie Antoinette have a place in her kingdom for them? 'What if it simply changes France?'

Marie Antoinette shook her head. 'The Committee, or the vampires who control some of them, will ensure that it's brought to an end, and by their own hands. The more they attempt to enforce their new laws, the greater the depths to which their fear drives them, making it all the more certain that the people will eventually turn against them. The new law today is an example of this folly.'

She saw Eleanor's expression of confusion and condescended to explain. She seemed to be enjoying the chance to talk freely, even if it was to an English commoner. 'The new law will give the Revolutionary Tribunal new powers. It allows them to bring cases for the slightest things – slandering patriotism, discouraging others, bearing false news – and places an active obligation on all citizens to bring suspects to justice. Trials will be limited to three days at the maximum, and no witnesses or counsels for the defence will be allowed. The only permissible verdicts will be acquittal or death. What do *you* think will be the result of such a law?'

Eleanor didn't know a great deal about the laws of England, let alone France, but even she could appreciate how draconian this new proposal was. 'Everyone will be accusing his neighbour for fear that his neighbour will accuse him first,' she said in horror. 'It's bad enough already, but this . . .'

Marie Antoinette pointed a finger at her. 'You're a girl of no particular birth or education – no insult, young woman, you said as much yourself – and you show a far better grasp of legal and social matters than most of the Committee for Public Safety. The more laws such as this that are passed by the National Convention, the sooner the Republic will fall and proper rule will be destroyed.'

Eleanor wanted to agree. It made a great deal of sense. But it also sounded like the sort of treatment from a doctor which unfortunately killed the patient in the process. 'How long do you think it will take?' she asked.

Marie Antoinette shrugged. 'Years? Decades? I doubt it will be that long, but I can wait. I have time, now.'

Eleanor imagined the people she'd met in Paris – casual acquaintances, or even the ones she'd come to know – being reported under this law and facing a trial with no help, no witnesses, and no penalty except death. The woman she'd talked to on the street just yesterday. Citizen Camille, the old lady who'd unknowingly sheltered the Pimpernel and the League months ago, and who'd thought she was protecting runaway lovers. Even Louise and Adele from Chauvelin's household, where earlier Eleanor had scrubbed the floors as a maid.

How many blades of grass would fall from the merciless scythe of this new law, and others, before the people rose up

333

in a new revolt? How many deaths were *justified*, however good the end result might be?

'You aren't pleased by this prospect,' Marie Antoinette said. Eleanor's face must have betrayed her thoughts. 'But isn't this what you and your friends want? The end of the Revolution?'

'Yes, but . . . not at that price!'

'Sometimes the only way to teach a child the danger of fire is to let them pick up a live coal and burn their fingers,' Marie Antoinette said mildly. 'Do you think I should feel pity for the people who killed my husband and destroyed France?'

'But there are thousands who had nothing to do with that,' Eleanor tried arguing.

'Do you know who the Princesse de Lamballe was?' the vampire demanded.

'No?'

'She was a woman whose only crime was to be of noble birth. She was beaten to death by the mob, and since they knew she was my friend, they set her head on a pike and paraded it in the streets in front of the Temple prison where I was, because they wanted me to see it. The people of France who have "nothing to do" with the Revolution have called me whore and traitor, harlot, abuser of my son and betrayer of France. Let them *learn* what revolution brings them.'

Eleanor shook her head in denial, but Marie Antoinette's voice had a certainty to it which would not permit contradiction. 'But you were telling me that vampires control the Committee of Public Safety – aren't they the ones behind this?'

'No doubt. It seems they imagine they can control the forces which they have unleashed. I suppose when the Committee and the Convention fall, they will crawl back to us with excuses that they . . . were simply doing what we would have done in their position.'

Eleanor shivered. Thoughts were coming together in her mind, like a chain of dominoes falling one after another, and the final conclusion terrified her. If it was the vampires who controlled the Committee which had inspired this terrible new law, then perhaps, if the Committee were freed of their influence, the law might not be passed?

Should Eleanor accept Marie Antoinette's judgement and let the Revolution hasten its own end, or should she meddle? She wanted to ask the Chief, or Charles, or any of the League – she needed the opinion of someone wiser than her, more sensible, more knowledgeable. But she didn't *have* any of them. They were all elsewhere in the depths of Paris, trying to stop the plot de Valois had set in motion.

And she didn't have *time*. If the Committee proposed the law and the National Convention passed it, then there'd be no going back. She didn't pretend to know the details of how a law was agreed and written down in the lawbooks; that was the sort of thing Charles would have been able to explain. Yet she understood enough to know that nobody, man or woman, human or vampire, would wish to admit that they'd been *wrong* and retract their actions, once it was passed. She might only have a matter of mere hours, or minutes, to halt it.

'May I ask another few questions, madame?' she said as politely as she could.

'Certainly you may.' Marie Antoinette tilted her head curiously. 'What do you have in mind, young woman? It's quite clear that you want to persuade me to some course of action.'

Am I that obvious? Eleanor asked ruefully.

She may have had a reputation for frivolity and not caring about Court politics, but that doesn't mean she didn't understand them, Anima answered. *And once the Revolution struck, she would have had every motivation to hone her wits. Charles de Valois most probably thought he was acquiring a showpiece pet when he sent*

335

his servants to make her a vampire, but I believe he ended up with a lioness instead. *You're thinking of trying to cleanse the Committee of vampiric control, aren't you?*

Don't you agree that it would be a good thing?

I do. It's seldom that we agree quite so thoroughly, or have so obvious a target. But I also want you to remain alive afterwards, which could be more difficult.

'You spoke of wanting the Revolution to collapse,' Eleanor said. 'However, the vampires manipulating the Committee for Public Safety will do everything and anything to keep themselves in power.' Should that be *everything and anything* or *anything and everything*? Charles was the one who knew about figures of speech. 'Which means keeping the Committee in power, or at least *a* Committee.'

Marie Antoinette nodded. 'Ah. I believe I understand you now. You wish to persuade me that if you could remove their influence on the Committee, this would be to my advantage. As the Committee are only human, and would be certain to make more mistakes, or hold less power behind the scenes. Am I wrong?'

Eleanor saw her entire carefully reasoned argument punctured, with Marie Antoinette's wits as the needle. So much for her attempts to bring in evidence and build up to an emphatic conclusion. 'Well, no, madame, but am *I* wrong in suggesting this?'

For a moment Eleanor thought she saw a glint of interest in Marie Antoinette's eyes, then the vampire shook her head. 'I have given my word to return you safely to your League. You have far too much potential future value for me to place you at risk, or allow you to place *yourself* at risk, before you can say as much.'

'Yes, but . . .' Eleanor pleaded, trying to think of a way to convince her, 'if I'd dazzled you with a flash of light, then run away while you were distracted, and left a letter behind saying that I was doing it of my own free will, then surely you wouldn't be to blame in the eyes of the League?'

'It's a matter of honour,' Marie Antoinette said coldly, yet Eleanor heard – or was it just wishful thinking? – the echo of yearning in her voice. 'Besides, you would have no way of knowing where to go.'

'Don't you have maps of the Tuileries Palace?'

'Now why would I have such a thing?' The question felt more for show than genuine.

Eleanor shrugged. 'You have maps of other areas of interest – why not the Tuileries Palace as well? Charles de Valois must have maps of the Tuileries Palace too, if he's planted gunpowder below it. And if I could get there . . . well, nobody looks twice at a maid sweeping the floor, madame.'

'They might do, since Charlotte Corday. But then again . . .' She chewed on her lower lip, and Eleanor saw the flash of white fangs under her black silk veil. 'Would *you* keep your word of honour, young woman?'

'That depends on what you're asking me to give it for,' Eleanor replied guardedly.

'If I am to assist you with this foolish endeavour – for yes, I can see it would be to my advantage as well as yours, and without vampires to support them, the Revolution will collapse that much sooner – then I require a promise from you that if the situation becomes too dangerous, you will retreat. No ifs, no buts, no maybes, no considerations of possible second guesses or gambles. You will – what's the military term? – disengage. Return to the place where I will bring you, or take some other steps to preserve your life and rejoin your League later.'

Could she have won? Wild elation filled Eleanor, but was quickly frozen by the thought of exactly *what* she'd won. The chance to risk her life, again, for such a fragile hope. But Sir

Percy would understand. He *must* understand. If a law like this was passed, then even more people across France would suffer. Wasn't the whole reason for the League the protection of the innocent, and saving those who needed rescue? Wasn't this *precisely* the same thing?

It isn't, Anima said, her presence like a dash of cold water. *And while he'll be pleased with the end results if you succeed, I suspect he won't be best pleased with you personally. Still . . . he would understand. But I don't think you can expect things to be the same afterwards.*

Nothing's been the same since the Blakeneys came into my life, Eleanor answered. It had been less than a year, and look where she was – beneath the city of Paris, negotiating with a vampire queen, hoping to *save* the Committee of Public Safety rather than gloat over their downfall. *But I can't think on the same scale as Marie Antoinette. I won't let them pass a law like that just because it'll rouse the mob against them that much sooner. I can't and won't play that sort of game.*

Yes. It was a game between two groups of vampires. France was their chessboard, and the people on both sides were pawns to be drained of blood and discarded. Eleanor had not been this angry in a long time. Vampires existed, one could hardly argue the fact, and while she had expected some of them to be malicious – well, humans were too, one found both good and evil in every town and village – she'd never thought they were so entirely *corrupt.* Sir Percy had said, *We are not assassins.* Standing by and allowing this law to be passed, condoning it, would be just as bad.

With any luck, Sir Percy and the others would deal a blow to the plans of de Valois and his followers. And with a great deal of luck, perhaps she might do the same to their counterparts hiding behind the Committee.

'Yes,' she said to Marie Antoinette. 'I can give you my word on that.'

Elusive

Unless, perhaps – the thought hid behind other thoughts at the back of her mind – she had no other choice.

After all, she wasn't of noble blood.

CHAPTER TWENTY-FOUR

Eleanor emerged into the light blinking and rubbing her eyes. Even with good candles, the tunnels beneath Paris had a quality of darkness to them which no artificial illumination could entirely drive away. She made her way up the steps from the cellar cautiously – it would be the height of folly for her to trip at this point and sprain an ankle. Though she did suspect that Marie Antoinette might prefer it. She'd grown increasingly uneasy about their plan (well, Eleanor's plan) and although she'd led Eleanor to this exit from the secret tunnels, she'd released her with some reluctance.

The former queen had also pressed a gun on Eleanor – a muff pistol. An aristocrat's pretty toy, small enough to be hidden in a woman's muff or a man's overcoat pocket. It now sat in Eleanor's own pocket, hidden beneath her skirts, an incriminating lump worrying her every time it banged against her leg. She wished she'd had the courage to refuse it.

The exit led into a disused cellar, which in turn led up to a back alley, which led onto a street, and then across the Seine lay the Tuileries Palace.

Chauvelin would probably be pleased to have his worst fears confirmed about the tunnels which honeycombed the earth beneath Paris. He was one of those men who was always glad to have the world prove him correct in his cynicism.

Eleanor tweaked her dress (borrowed from Marie Antoinette's maid, poorly fitting but at least clean) into relative tidiness, patted the secret weapon which she was carrying under one arm (another donation from Marie Antoinette's maid) and shuffled forward to merge into the crowd on the street. It was mid-morning. They had left Marie Antoinette's chambers at just before ten o'clock by the dainty little clock on her mantelpiece. The National Convention were due to start their deliberations at twelve o'clock, and the Committee for Public Safety would certainly be in the chamber with them. She had no time to waste.

Which was a shame, because it was a glorious day. Perhaps it was because of her hours in the darkness below Paris, but the sunlight was that much more beautiful today. It played across the surface of the Seine and gilded every eddy and twist of current. It shone on the people in the street around her, bringing out the bright reds and blues of their tricolour rosettes, sashes and shawls, making them appear gay and cheerful. She wasn't the only one inspired by its brightness. Other men and women smiled at each other, exchanging cheerful words of greeting when they might have snarled demands or snapped complaints. There were even children singing. Singing the Carmagnole, admittedly, promising destruction to all the enemies of France, but the tune was pretty.

Eleanor joined the queue of people making their way across the bridge, and tried not to imagine the barrels of gunpowder which might be lurking directly beneath her every step. Of course, they should only be underneath the Tuileries Palace – but how far would an explosion extend?

Yet, strangely, her fear solidified her certainty that what she and the League were doing was *right*. A plan which depended on gunpowder beneath Paris and killing hundreds of innocent people could not by definition be a good plan. Equally, a plan which resulted in a law so draconian that it would drown all of France in bloodstained fear and, through its severity, turn the people against the lawmakers couldn't be a good plan either. It wasn't just a case of *things a gentleman didn't do* or *things an honourable man wouldn't do,* or even *things an Englishman ought not to do.* There were things nobody should do, because they were *wrong.* Attempts to dress the matter up in more complicated reasoning were unnecessary.

The Tuileries Palace lay in front of her. Once the possession of royalty, now, like so many things in France, the possession of the people. Or at least, some of the people – the members of the National Convention in particular. The gardens had been thrown open to the citizens of Paris. The Grande Galerie which ran along the side of the river, from the Tuileries Palace at one end to the Louvre at the other, was now a gallery where anyone could go to admire the art previously collected by kings. It was so *large* – four or five storeys high, running hundreds of yards along the side of the Seine, with glass windows spaced along it like gems in a necklace. How many paintings could such a place hold? Eleanor wished vainly for the opportunity to see what was inside.

A crowd surrounded the main entrance to the Tuileries Palace, and guards stood at either side of the main doors, letting only the worthy enter – members of the National Convention, their secretaries, their hangers-on, reporters for the newspapers and journals, caricaturists, bystanders and wastrels. The crowd might not know exactly what was going on, but there was a febrile buzz of conversation in the air, and Eleanor overheard more than one attempted bribe or plea for information. People were aware that something important was on the way.

Was it like this outside the Houses of Parliament in London? Another place that Eleanor had never seen. There was one difference, of course. She knew the Honourable Members of Parliament would be men of rank and wealth, probably landowners or their sons. How else would they have the money and education to be elected in the first place? Here, at least, the National Convention was more representative of the people as a whole. She knew it wasn't perfect, but she couldn't help thinking that, like the Revolution in general, there were ideas here worth further consideration.

She didn't even try the main entrance. Instead she followed the smaller stream of tradesmen, servants and beggars trudging briskly to the inevitable servants' entrance. Every palace had to let them in somehow. Probably even the Tower of London itself had a side doorway for whoever did the menial work that didn't involve standing around in fancy uniforms . . .

Her thoughts were frivolous, and she recognized that. Perhaps this was why Sir Percy and the League liked their frivolity in similar dangers. It made it easier not to brood on the masses of gunpowder which lay beneath her feet and which she was nearing with every passing second. It was better to fill her mind with petty things than to throw herself into a sweat by worrying about Charles, Sir Percy, Tony and Andrew and all the rest of them. They were the League of the Scarlet Pimpernel. They'd pulled off more dangerous capers than this before. Well . . . they must have done, surely? They were doing what only they could do. Now it was her job to do what only she could do.

There was a guard at the servants' side door, but he waved her in after checking her certificate of identity. (Fortunately Armand Saint-Just had been too gentlemanly to search her and strip her of her belongings when he'd drugged and kidnapped her.) She fell in behind a couple of other women whose conversation made it clear they were heading for the kitchens, then she shook out and donned her secret weapon.

343

An apron.

No doubt when royalty owned this palace, it had been the work of hundreds of servants to keep it clean. Even in these Republican days, when all men were equal before the law, someone – and usually a woman – had to sweep the floors, wash the clothing and cook the supper. This wasn't like the Temple prison, where they'd expected intruders and been on the alert for them. As long as Eleanor appeared busy with some task, any man from the National Convention who glanced in her direction would consider her no more important than a piece of furniture.

Marie Antoinette had agreed with this part of Eleanor's plan, though even through her veil it looked as though the vampire queen had bitten down on something unpleasant. Perhaps she was considering just how many times *she* had allowed herself to overlook her servants, and how they had eventually rebelled against her.

Eleanor had to fight against her growing sense of impatience to keep her gait at a casual pace, a saunter and a swing of the hips like any other woman here. The kitchens – huge rooms, big enough to have served a king and his court, now barely half full – might be busy, but they weren't *bustling*. She didn't want to catch anyone's eye by acting too briskly or with undue enthusiasm for her tasks. All she needed to do was calmly collect some dusters and make her way southwards, towards her target. She could do this. She'd reached every objective in her path so far, and everything was under control . . .

A heavy hand came down on her shoulder, and she squeaked in terror, cowering as she turned to see a guard standing behind her. He was bigger than her, almost as big as Sir Percy, to her nervous eyes, and had a good dose of pomade on his hair. 'Y-yes, citizen?' she gasped.

He leaned in, closer. He still had all his teeth, as his wide smile demonstrated. 'You're a pretty one,' he said. 'What time do you get off work, my little sweetheart?'

Eleanor realized he was one of the guards *off* duty who'd made their way to the kitchen for a drink and some food and were now loitering around till they had to go back to their posts. Still, if he should notice anything wrong, she'd be just as much in trouble. 'Not till this evening, citizen,' she said, lowering her eyes and batting her eyelashes.

'What a coincidence, me too.' His gaze lowered from her face to her bosom. 'I don't think I've seen you around here before. Perhaps we should have a little chat over a glass of wine and get to know one another?'

Eleanor glanced around desperately, but no other maids showed any signs of coming to her assistance. *So much for solidarity and the sisterhood of women.* 'I'd like that, citizen,' she said, forcing as much sincerity as she could into her voice. 'But I have to get back to work now, or—'

'You do that.' His hand slipped down her shoulder to pat her on the rear as he released her. 'I'll be watching for you. Ask for Jean-Claude Avisse. What's your name?'

'Anne Dupont, citizen.' Eleanor feigned a smile before ducking away. That was one thing to be said for the Blakeney household – the men there didn't feel they had some sort of God-given right to the company of the maids. She was conscious of Avisse's eyes on her back as she retreated. It was almost a relief – a smaller yet more immediate fear, rather than the greater one for herself, the League, and everyone in this building.

At least none of the other servants looked twice at her as she scurried away from the large guard. It was just one of those minor incidents in the great tapestry of their working life, and the less they were involved in it, the better for them. This was true in England as well as France.

The actual room in which the National Convention met

was at the north of the building. It had previously been a theatre, and it was large enough to hold the whole Convention, complete with inevitable observers and hangers-on. How nice it must be to be a king, and to be able to build a whole theatre inside your palace. Marie Antoinette had muttered something about King Louis XV dancing in a production there when he was monarch, over seventy years ago. Eleanor imagined her own king dancing there, and the thought of the elderly, bulky King George going up on tiptoes made her bite back a slightly crazed giggle.

If one went south from there, scuttling like a cockroach, and just as inconspicuously, along the wide elegant corridors of the palace, one came to the Pavillon de Flore. This stood looking out over the Seine, the corner-point for the Tuileries Palace from south to north and the Grande Galerie from west to east. It was spare and elegant, a square building five storeys high, with a roof which occupied two of the storeys and which slanted up like a nobleman's hat, festooned with spiking chimneys rising like cockades. Previously it had housed members and friends of the royal family, including Madame Élisabeth, whom Eleanor had met briefly during the rescue of the Dauphin last year, and the Princesse de Lamballe, who'd been Marie Antoinette's friend . . .

But now it was where the Committee for Public Safety held their private deliberations.

Eleanor had walked directly past the building, but hadn't tried to enter, even by the servants' entrance. She hadn't even dared look too closely at it. The guards by the door appeared far more competent and more interested in passers-by than the ones for the National Convention. She'd been told – and all Paris knew, apparently – that this was where the Committee would be meeting to discuss matters before joining the National Convention later.

For one brief shining moment Eleanor had imagined

herself breaking into the Committee's innermost meeting-room and cleansing them of vampiric influences. But common sense had pointed out the vast number of guards who would be in the way, and the likelihood that she'd be restrained and then dragged off for trial and execution – if she wasn't shot down first by some panicked sentinel who assumed she was an assassin, a vampire, or both. The image of herself striding in while the National Convention was in session was even less plausible. She wouldn't be allowed past the door.

However, Sir Percy had often mentioned *the journey between* as a weak spot when devising how best to pluck prisoners from their guards, or innocents from danger. The gaols at both the beginning and the end of a journey might be impregnable, but the passage from one to the other offered its own opportunities. And in this case, the Committee would have to walk from the Pavillon de Flore to the once-theatre where the National Convention would be in session, and this would take them through the corridors of the Tuileries Palace.

She chose a cloth from her selection and began dusting her way along the palace corridor, swiping smears off windowsills and cleaning dirt out of crevices in the gilding and ornamentation. Men walked past her swathed in airs of conscious importance, or hurried along with their arms full of documents and their eyes full of barely controlled panic. But nobody gave her more than a casual glance as she ran her cloth along a ledge, sweeping accumulated dust and dead flies into a neat pile. Hopefully someone else would be along with a broom at some point. This place really deserved better upkeep . . .

You're worrying about whether this palace will be cleaned properly? Anima asked, incredulous.

It's beautiful, Eleanor argued. She didn't have the education in architecture which some of the League possessed, but she'd swept enough elegant homes by now to recognize quality when she saw it. Some places were no more than gilt and New Money, but others had what Charles had called a Golden Mean (or something like that) of proportions and balance.

If I were you, I'd be more worried about what we're about to do, Anima scolded.

If I did that, Eleanor retorted, *I'd be panicking, and I wouldn't be able to give my full attention to dusting, and someone might notice. Besides, Sir Percy always says that we're fighting for the soul of France as much as for the innocents facing the guillotine . . .* That line of thought trailed off as she considered some of the people they'd rescued. Were they truly innocent, or were they all like Charles de Valois, willing to sacrifice as many living souls as necessary in order to claw their way back into power? And what about all the people they hadn't rescued?

You've rescued as many living humans as you have vampires, Anima said quietly. *What's more . . . I regret admitting it, but from my time with you and from your own experience, I'm forced to conclude that there are some vampires who are merely attempting to exist. That woman, Marie Antoinette, made a bad bargain and is trapped with the consequences, but when the only other option was to die under the guillotine's blade, perhaps she had very little choice. Though in a hundred years . . . still, I digress. I think the problem which lies at the heart of all this is that no vampire can remain virtuous. They may begin with the best of intentions, but nothing lasts. In the end, survival is all that matters. And the longer they survive, the more that becomes the cornerstone of their heart. It isn't the sinners I should have been blaming, it's the sin. I was almost as guilty as any of them when I tried to steal your body. The question is, what is the root of the sin?*

Eleanor turned that over in her mind as she left the corridor and entered the first of a set of interconnected rooms. Windows peered out into the courtyard beyond. Once a place for elegant strolls, decorated by ornamental trees and statues, it was now scarred by violence and trampling feet, empty and mutilated. *Have we been doing the right thing?* she asked softly, the thought barely articulated. She was afraid of what the answer might be.

You have. This time there was no doubt in Anima's voice. *You've saved lives. Whatever happens next, remember that. Hold to your beliefs, though perhaps not quite so strongly as I have done. You've managed to make me reconsider some of my opinions, and very few people have done that.*

Bells in the distance rang the half-hour. Eleanor frowned. *Is something the matter? You sound strange.* No, more than strange. Anima sounded . . . tired.

You aren't the only one contemplating your possible sins, Anima replied tartly. *And since I'm a great deal older than you are, I have that much more on my conscience.*

The sound of oncoming footsteps from the south roused them both from their conversation. Multiple footsteps, a group of men, not just those on their own like all the others who'd passed Eleanor. This must be the Committee. For a moment she felt sick with fear. A thousand reasons not to take action suddenly swam through her mind, urging her to keep her head bowed over her cleaning and reconsider her plan. *I could just say that it had been too dangerous to risk an attempt, and in any case the Chief never expected me to try it, and Charles wouldn't want me to dare such a thing . . .*

Except Charles *would* have expected her to make the attempt, if he'd known. He'd have done it himself, if God had gifted him with the abilities which had somehow come to Eleanor instead. Eleanor could do no less.

As the group of men finally entered the long room where she was dusting, Eleanor jumped in shock, squeaked, then ducked into a low curtsey. No more than they'd expect. Through her lowered eyelashes, she took in their faces. A few she recognized. Robespierre himself, seen previously at a distance (a great distance) at public events, and regularly portrayed or caricatured in half the city's papers; the other Saint-Just, cousin to Lady Marguerite and Armand; the condescendingly smiling Fouché, whom the papers called the Executioner of Lyon for how he'd suppressed the revolt there. And others, unknown to her, unidentifiable. The rulers of France. A bevy of secretaries followed at their heels, not so close that they might be accused of listening to their masters, but ready for the least word or signal that their services were required.

'The recent Festival of the Supreme Being,' Robespierre was saying to the man next to him, his voice light and fluid, 'proves just how much the people of Paris have taken the new thinking to their hearts. The social utility of the concept . . .' Behind him, two of the other men exchanged speaking glances, but made no comment.

Eleanor's heart was in her throat. There was no time left. They were almost level with her.

Now.

She found it easier to kindle the flame than she had done before. It had become quicker with practice, and would almost have been comfortable if she hadn't been so aware it was her own life she was burning. It leapt around her hands as she straightened, as though she was holding a necklace of lightning, each gem a point of fire, burning ferociously yellow, then blue-white, then pure white. Dust which had caked on her fingers cracked and burned away, falling in ashes.

Men started screaming, shouting words like 'Bomb!' or 'Arsonist' or 'Assassin!' but none of it was relevant. Her lightning filled the room with a brightness that surpassed the morning sunlight and threw shadows in long black streaks along the floor and walls. Her pulse thudded louder and louder, drowning out the voices, filling her head with its sound.

Some of the men collapsed. Not all the Committee did.

Equally, not all those who had collapsed were members of the Committee. Two of the secretaries. One of the guards.

Robespierre remained standing, his arm raised to shield his eyes. 'Woman!' he shouted at her. 'What are you doing?'

There will always be someone in the middle of a disaster who stands there demanding to be told what's going on, Sir Percy had once said, *or who refuses to be rescued until you sit down with them and fully explain your plan. In such cases, m'dear, I advise you to knock them firmly over the head and drag them away. Much faster.*

Eleanor ignored Robespierre. Perhaps the vampires had chosen not to control him because he was the man at the head of the Committee, and too obvious. But the fact that *others* were currently on their knees, or on the floor, shaking like men with the ague and clutching their chests, proved that everything Marie Antoinette had said was absolutely true. These men were afflicted by a group of vampires, forced to obey them and dance to their tune. The last little fraction of doubt in her mind vanished. She had to finish her job and cleanse them fully.

If she could.

Her strength was draining out of her with every passing moment. Every second of the burning light that was cleansing and healing these men was also coming closer to killing her. Without quite realizing how it had happened, she was down on one knee, then both knees, the skirts of her dress crumpled beneath her on the still-unswept floor. Each breath came with a greater effort, and she struggled to keep her eyes open. Tears ran down her cheeks, but dried before they could reach her jaw.

A bullet suddenly cracked against the wall behind her. Perhaps they couldn't see her well enough through the flame to shoot clearly, but if enough shots were fired, one of them was sure to hit her. And then what? She had to keep going, she had to maintain the fire long enough to be certain they were all cleansed, and then . . .

Then she was going to die.

What was worse was the sudden fear that she was going to die *before* she'd finished. She hadn't thought it would take so much more of her life's energy to cleanse a dozen men. With Armand, it had been a struggle. But now . . . it was a fight she couldn't hope to win. This might all have been for nothing.

Another bullet hit the wall behind her, closer this time.

I require your permission, Anima said, her voice suddenly abrupt, closer than it had been for weeks now, like thunder in Eleanor's head. *Do I have your permission?*

What did she want? Was it some desperate attempt to save Eleanor's life in order to preserve herself? *Why?*

I want to help, Anima said simply.

Eleanor teetered on the brink of refusal, goaded by memories of her own helplessness at Mont-Saint-Michel – but then she remembered Anima's apology afterwards, and Bernard's words. *She was not an evil woman.*

You have my permission, she thought, the last fragments of her power, her life, guttering around her hands.

Anima rose up and through her like a spring storm, bringing new strength to the flame. In its absolute light and utter ferocity, men writhed on the floor and vomited up black matter like congealed blood, soiling their smart clothes and smearing their tidy powdered hair with dust. Those who could still stand fired their pistols blindly or cried out for her to stop, unable to look at her.

A little of Eleanor's own strength returned as Anima shouldered the burden of the flame, but then she realized that Anima wasn't *stopping*. She streamed through Eleanor in a current of will, raising her to her feet again and shrouding her in lightnings. She spent herself without holding back, using the last fragment of power which had kept her bound to the living world and to Eleanor, and in another breath Eleanor knew she would be gone entirely.

I almost made the same mistake that they did, Anima said, her voice somehow doubled, tripled, resounding in Eleanor's head. *I would have sacrificed you to keep myself alive. But what is that if not the very thing every vampire does, once they decide they would rather drink blood than face true death and God's judgement? Neither of us has the strength to do this alone, and none of your friends are here to support you. Don't be afraid, Eleanor. I know what I'm doing.*

What are *you doing?* Eleanor screamed. She had no control over the power which Anima was expending, and she couldn't stop the old mage from doing what Eleanor herself had been about to do. She felt the decision, the commitment, behind Anima's words.

Completing your mission. And I leave my own mission for you to finish. Anima's voice was fainter now. *I thank God that he kept me from destroying you. You would have been the best of my apprentices. Seek out further training, Eleanor. I have faith that other mages survived. And . . . I will miss you.*

Don't leave me! It had been less than a year. It had been a partnership which Eleanor had never sought out in the first place, and which she'd regretted time and time again as the mage's ghost had scolded, criticized, and disapproved of her. She'd never truly accepted Anima's opinion that all vampires were evil either. Yet now, with Anima about to pass over the last frontier of death, she didn't want her to go. *Please!*

Run while you can, Anima said. *Finish my task. Into your hands, O Lord, I commend my spirit . . .*

A crack of thunder shook the room. Every window shattered, and those men who were still standing were knocked to their knees or left scrabbling on all fours. The fire vanished, and Anima with it.

There was only silence in Eleanor's head now. She called to Anima, but nobody answered.

Everything seemed to be moving at a snail's pace. It felt like the time, months ago, when she'd been near a keg of gunpowder as it exploded – the same numbness, the same stunned shock.

Eleanor wanted to collapse. She wanted to weep. But some fragment of sense, some tiny thread of rationality, held her together and kept her upright. She turned and ran, her head still spinning – the floor seeming to swing under her with every step like the deck of a ship at sea – and tears streaming down her face.

CHAPTER TWENTY-FIVE

Eleanor was trapped in enemy territory. Her mentor was gone, her powers were drained, and the Committee and all their minions had probably seen her closely enough that they could identify her, even among a group of other maid-servants.

There was only one thing she could think of to do.

'Help!' she screamed as she ran into the next room, waving her arms frantically. 'The Committee! Assassins! Vampires!' For a moment she was about to add *Counter-revolutionaries!*, but she was so dizzy she feared she wouldn't be able to pronounce it correctly.

There were a half-dozen men gathered there, already nervously eyeing the door through which she'd emerged. They must surely have heard something of the commotion as the Committee were cleansed, and definitely the final clap of thunder. It would be uncharitable to speculate why they hadn't already braved the dangerous noises to investigate. 'Where?' one of them demanded.

'There!' Eleanor gasped, pointing a shaking hand behind her. 'Oh mercy, I must tell the guards, I must raise the alarm . . .'

A number of guards came through the opposite door at a quick trot, two of them already unlimbering pistols from their belts. 'What's going on?' the one in the lead with the biggest tricolour rosette demanded.

'Assassins!' Eleanor repeated. She could feel the seconds slipping away. The back of her neck itched. Someone would come through the door behind her at any moment and shout, *Stop that woman!*

The loitering men joined the guards in a headlong rush, colliding with the Committee's own guards who had at just that moment managed to reach the door from the opposite direction. Eleanor heard the yell of 'Stop that woman!' as she continued her headlong flight.

Almost, *almost* she began to think that she might just get away.

And then a man caught her wrist and looked squarely into her face. 'Wait, what's this? You're the girl from Mont-Michel!'

Eleanor's heart stuttered in her chest as she recognized him in turn. It was the Warden from Mont-Saint-Michel, Duquesne, neatly dressed and with his hair smartly tied back. She tried to recoil and hide her face, but he had a firm grip on her. 'Citizen, someone just tried to assassinate the Committee . . .'

'I'm sure they did, if you were involved!' Other men started gathering around the two of them, blocking her way out, surrounding her, and Eleanor began to panic. A few moments ago she'd tasted power, but now she was a lamb at the centre of a ring of wolves. 'Looks as if we've fairly caught you this time, however! Fellow citizens, this little counter-revolutionary here is a sister to Charlotte Corday, and what's worse, she's collaborating with—'

The bells outside began to chime midday, and as they spoke the building *trembled*. Something in the earth deep down below shook, and everything aboveground responded. Lamps crashed from their hooks and vases toppled from their places. Everyone was shouting, screaming – it was deafening. People ran in all directions, those inside trying to get out of the building, those outside trying to get inside. Someone smashed a window and half a dozen people made a panicked attempt to scramble through it, though daggers of glass still clung to the edges of the frame, and it would have been far safer to use the doorway. All of them were now far more occupied with trying to save themselves from the perceived danger, and their attention was no longer on Eleanor. The stink of gunpowder hung in the air.

The League had been down there. Charles. Tony. Andrew. Sir Percy. *Charles* . . .

Eleanor stamped on Duquesne's foot, grateful that he was wearing elegant city shoes rather than the workmanlike boots he'd had on at Mont-Saint-Michel, and he yelped in pain. She wrenched her wrist out of his grip, twisting sideways at the gap between his thumb and fingers as Andrew had taught her. He grabbed for her again, and caught her sleeve, but it ripped as she pulled herself away. The crowd surged round them, as manic as any mob on its way to the scaffold to watch an execution.

She remembered what she'd promised Marie Antoinette, that she would retreat if she was in danger, but she'd also promised to *rejoin your League later*, hadn't she? She *had* to find out if the others were safe.

In the confusion, it was impossible for her to remember the maps that Marie Antoinette had shown her, pointing the way down to the cellars. But she could smell the gunpowder. If a breeze had carried that smell to her, then by God she could follow that breeze. Now she was paying attention to it, she could feel it like a thread tugging her northwards.

Rattled around like a billiard ball by shove after shove, she struggled to follow the scent, or the perception, whatever it was. Passing elbows left bruises on her arms and ribs. It took all her efforts to keep moving against the crowd rather than let the flow wash her towards the building's exit. But she was more slightly built than most of the men, and vestiges of manners kept them from pushing her as hard as they would each other. She forced her way through. At least with all the panic there were now other women in the crowd running and screaming, confusing anyone who might be on her trail. Other servants trying to escape, or visitors, or people here for some other purpose she didn't care to think about, and all of them panicking.

The door to the cellars was unobtrusive, at the back of a side room that was half partitioned off and used to store spare chairs and tables. Fragments of colourful porcelain lay splintered across the floor, the remnants of vases which had fallen in the shock. Eleanor picked her way through them carefully, not wanting to cut her shoes, and tried the door.

It was open.

Light gleamed from below. There must be lamps burning down there. She prepared to take a first step on the stairs . . .

. . . and then someone shoved her hard from behind.

Eleanor screamed in shock and terror, unable to catch herself – there was no banister, no rail, nothing – and went tumbling down the stone steps. She tried to throw up her arms to shield her head, but there hadn't been enough warning. A starburst of pain went through her skull as it rapped against the wall on her way down, and most of the rest of her found something to collide against as well. At the bottom she rolled over, moaning, trying to see clearly. Trying to think.

The door closed with a thud. Firm footsteps came down the stairs. A hand grabbed her by the front of her apron and hoisted her to her feet, shaking her. 'Well, citizen? Ready to talk?'

Eleanor's head flopped from side to side, her brains

joggling around inside her skull with every painful throb of her pulse. She tried to focus her eyes. Duquesne was holding her, casually straightening a lock of her hair with his free hand, pulling her close enough to stare into her face. 'Yes. The resemblance is there. Astonishing.'

'Resemblance?' Eleanor slurred. The part of her which had been trained by Andrew to assess situations, and know how to flee from them, was trying to grasp her current circumstances. This cellar was a storage room. Lamps burned near the stairs and near a far door, but otherwise it was just the two of them down here. (Though why would someone leave lamps burning with nobody to require the light?) The smell of gunpowder was stronger now, like a taint of malice in the air.

'To the Widow Capet. Still, nobody could say you look like her now she's truly a bloodsucking sanguinocrat, could they, ha ha!' His merry laugh raised echoes. It was even more annoying than Sir Percy's laugh at his most inane. That had to be a triumph for the ages. Eleanor was dimly conscious she should be thinking about more urgent things, such as the League, or her arrest or death, but she was having great difficulty focusing her eyes. 'What are you doing here?'

'Here as in the Tuileries, or here as in down here with you in these rather aromatic cellars? The answer to the first is that I have friends in the National Convention. Despite your best attempts, my girl.' His mask of good humour slipped for a moment, and Eleanor's vision was now clear enough to see the hardness of his eyes, the vicious snarl behind his smile. 'You and your friends caused me a great deal of inconvenience. Ruined my reputation. Stole my balloon!' He shook her again, then casually slapped her across the face before dropping her to the ground. 'How did she fly, by the way?'

Eleanor sat where she had been dropped, shaking her head

and trying to get her wits together. But also, and more importantly, she'd felt something hard through her skirts as she fell: the muff pistol which Marie Antoinette had given her. By some miracle, it hadn't gone off. It was her one trump card, though if Duquesne realized she was armed, he wouldn't bother playing with her like a cat with a mouse any longer. She had to try to distract his attention. 'You must have very good friends, citizen,' she mumbled, 'if they can somehow paper over the fact that you lost an entire fortress's worth of prisoners.'

'Naughty, naughty.' He sauntered towards her, and she shuffled backwards across the floor until she felt the wall bump against her back. 'So tell me, what *was* in Mont-Michel? Who was the stranger?'

'Which stranger?'

He raised his hand again, and Eleanor flinched back. 'Do I have to hit you again? When we were getting on so well? The old man, of course. The one in my study. We marched half the isle's population past him, and nobody recognized him, so he must have been an outsider. Old as he was, I'm surprised he could even walk across the causeway to reach the island. No, something was going on there, and I want to know what.'

'He was my uncle,' Eleanor said hopefully.

'Try again.' He loomed over her.

'He'd been hiding there!' she gasped. 'He . . . he was a counter-revolutionary and he thought nobody would look for him right in the middle of a gaol.'

'Better, but still not quite good enough. *How* did he hide?'

There was something about the way he asked the question which awakened Eleanor's own sense of suspicion. 'Why do you want to know?' she asked, in as surly a fashion as she could manage.

'Because I was sent to the place to look for secrets.' He

smirked. 'Certain people, far, *far* above your place in life, my girl, wanted me to conduct a full review of Mont-Michel. When the League turned up there, they became even more interested – after the fact, of course, but nothing's perfect. Not sure what they expected me to find, and I didn't find it in any case, but money is money and spends, doesn't it? Science is an expensive mistress.'

Certain people . . . Eleanor knew who he had to be talking about. Anima and Bernard had been right to be paranoid. Even now, hundreds of years afterwards, the vampires were still hunting them down. 'You're working for the vampires,' she breathed, the words coming out before she could stop them.

'Ah.' The tilt of his well-groomed head suggested satisfaction. She'd given herself away. 'So you *do* know about that, too. What a very interesting brain you have, my girl. I wonder what it'd take to look inside it.'

Appeals to Armand's better nature hadn't worked when he was controlled by the vampires, but perhaps this man's pride might prove a better lever. 'How can a man like you who believes in science work for them, citizen? Is that really going to lead to a future of . . . of optical telegraphs and inventions like that?'

He actually laughed at her. 'Why, you sweet naive little girl. It's nothing of the sort. Money, my dear, money. France is a large place. There's room enough for both them and me, and I have no objection to being paid for something I might have done in any case. I don't consider them in any way my *superiors*, merely the holders of the purse-strings. Men of science have had to endure worse before.'

Eleanor wasn't sure she could class what he'd done as right or wrong – after all, she'd served a vampire for pay. Perhaps the difference lay in what they'd both actually done for that pay. She'd only ever opened her *own* veins, after all.

He must be working for the faction of vampires which controlled the Committee, she realized. If he'd been working for the royalists, they'd surely have warned him not to come here today, for fear of losing a useful pawn. But this doubled her own peril. Once the Republican (well, Republican-controlling) group of vampires found out what she'd done to their pawns, and what she *could* do, then . . .

It had all seemed like such a *good* idea earlier.

He stroked his chin. 'I suppose I shouldn't be surprised that someone working for the League might know a little more about vampires than the average man on the street. Or woman, what? Still, it seems to me that you're suspiciously well informed. And then I wanted to see what you were up to, fleeing down here, and now I think I know. Collaboration with whoever's been playing with gunpowder beneath the palace. As if you didn't already have enough on your record to send you to the guillotine.' He shook his head mockingly. 'Who'd have thought that such a pretty young creature would be so old in sin!'

'I thought sin was an outdated concept these days,' Eleanor spat.

'You can't have a Supreme Being without sin, my girl. The names may have changed but the acts are still punished, whether we call it sin or counter-revolutionary activity.'

If he was only doing all this for money, then perhaps he'd listen to reason. 'We both know too much about each other, citizen,' she suggested. 'Perhaps it would be better if we both walked away? Who knows what I might say under interrogation if you hand me over.'

'Hand you over to the authorities? What rubbish. I'll be turning you over to people who'll find you a great deal more interesting, my dear girl.' She could practically see the thoughts sparking behind his eyes. 'Why, as a member of the League and involved in this explosion, they'll have all manner of things to ask you! And it's a benefit to all concerned. They might even keep you alive, which is a great deal more than the regular authorities will do for you. Play your cards right, and you could even come out of this with a purse of money to your name.' He rubbed his chin again thoughtfully. 'I wonder if I could claim a finder's fee? Now come along, and don't make a fuss.' He reached down and hooked his fingers into the pinned bulk of her braids, dragging her to her feet and ignoring her squeal of pain.

'I'll expose you!' Eleanor declared, but knew the threat was hollow. This wasn't a situation where she had any evidence to back up her claims. He'd wave a hand and pass them off as merely the panicked effusions of a traitor on her way to prison.

Duquesne knew it too, and he simply chuckled. 'Come along now, there's a good girl.' He tugged her forward, keeping his hand low so that she had to bend at the waist and stumble on her way, as though he was leading a farm animal.

Then a noise came from the far end of the cellar. A half-heard murmur of voices which were meant to be whispers but had carried further than they should. Words in *English*.

Duquesne's lips pursed in a silent whistle. He didn't say anything, but Eleanor could guess his train of thought. Quickening his pace to a stride, he began to drag her up the cellar steps towards the door.

Of course, he wants me out of here before I can call out to warn them. He's going to call the Guard, and the others will walk right into an ambush . . .

She had no power left to save herself. She was trapped in a cellar, just as she had been once before, and this time no ghost would appear to rescue her. She had only herself, her voice . . . and the gun which Marie Antoinette had given her.

If she screamed, the League would be warned. Duquesne

would hand her over to the Guard – or worse, whichever vampires were paying him – but the others would be safe.

If she pulled the trigger, then she'd be killing a man. A living human, not a vampire. And it would be only for her own sake, to keep herself safe. She'd threatened to pull the trigger before in order to save Charles, and she would have done it then, but did she have the right to do it now?

It's not just my own selfish desire to stay alive, she thought wildly. *It's for everyone connected to me, who wants me to survive, to fulfil my responsibilities. And even if it was just for myself, who says that my life is worth less than his? Who has the right to judge me?*

Both her hands had been on her head, trying to soften his punishing grip on her hair. She let her right hand drop to her side, and fumbled desperately in her skirts, reaching through the slit in the side, through the layers of skirt and shift, to find the hidden gun in her pocket.

Duquesne didn't even look at her as he reached for the door handle.

The gun flashed in the lamplight as Eleanor dragged it out of her inner pocket. It was a pretty thing, too pretty to be dangerous: chased with silver, inlaid with mother of pearl, with designs of lilies entwined across its butt. Duquesne's head began to turn as he heard her cock it, but he was too late. She brought it up and fired at him.

This close, she couldn't miss. The ball took Duquesne in the chest. He grunted as though a man had hit him, stumbling back against the door. His grip on her hair tightened and then relaxed. He tumbled down the stairs as she'd done earlier, coming to a halt at the bottom with his face against the floor. A slow trickle of blood began to ooze out from beneath him.

Was he moving? No. He wasn't.

For a long moment Eleanor stood there looking down at

him, the gun in her hand a weight heavy enough to drown her fathoms deep. The distant English voices had fallen silent: they must have heard the gunshot. But perhaps Duquesne wasn't actually dead. Maybe he was simply shamming, faking it, ready to jump up the moment she turned her back on him and grab her again . . .

Except she'd shot and killed him, hadn't she? *Thou shalt not kill. We are not assassins.* And it was no use telling herself that any of the League would have been ready to pull the trigger to save their lives, or to save each other. They weren't her and she wasn't them.

Anima would have told me that was bad logic and appalling grammar, she thought, then bit back a gulping sob. Anima had gone. It was just Eleanor now. And she had better pull herself together and take action, if all of this was to have been worthwhile.

She walked towards the far end of the cellar, from where she'd heard the voices. Once she'd rounded several stacks of crates and furniture, she saw a door in the wall standing half open. The door was obviously meant to be disguised: it was narrow and unobtrusive, painted to match the wall. Someone had shifted the crates from in front of it in haste, judging by the way they were piled up on either side.

The League? Or whatever reinforcements Sir Percy had managed to find? But there would be time to ask later. 'It's safe here for the moment,' she called, 'but we don't have long!'

A pause. 'Eleanor?' It was Charles's voice.

Which other woman would be standing around here calling to you in English? Yet her heart leapt to hear his voice: he was safe. 'Yes! But hurry!'

Andrew was the first to scramble through the doorway, looking to either side first before shouldering through, and the others soon followed. They'd all managed to acquire military uniforms from somewhere, and had muskets slung across their backs. Tony had his arm bound in a makeshift sling, and Sir Percy had a bloodied piece of bandage wound around his head. George and Jerry brought up the rear, with George limping.

'You're all safe,' she whispered, and then squeaked as Charles pulled her into a hug. The pistol dropped to the floor as she clung to him. He was warm. He was real. He was still alive.

'Your wit and percipience rivals that of Chauvelin, m'dear, and speaking of which, do shut that door and pull a few crates in front of it, George. The gentleman's a few minutes behind us, and our little truce in service of the greater good has run out, much to his pleasure.' Sir Percy took a deep breath and straightened, his shoulders cracking as he stretched. 'Faith, it's a pleasure to be out of those demned tunnels! A man can't breathe down there. I take it you have a good reason why you're not currently with the late Queen, Eleanor?'

'I do,' Eleanor said, resolutely putting off the day of explanations and reckoning, 'but there isn't time, Chief. The Tuileries Palace above is all confusion, but it won't last long. And, ah, it's possible there are some people looking for me up above, on the ground floor. Quite a few people, in fact.'

'Always good to focus on the essentials.' He waved them towards the exit. Charles released Eleanor from his embrace, but their hands somehow remained linked. 'In that case, we'll run the standard "arrested and taken in for questioning" gambit. Do your best to look miserable, m'dear. Once we're out of this building . . . well, I believe we may have made Paris a little too hot to hold us for the moment.' He paused as he caught sight of the fallen Duquesne. 'Is there something I should know?'

'I shot him,' Eleanor confessed.

Sir Percy looked at her. 'And no Englishwoman ever shoots

366

a man without good reason.' He patted her shoulder, but his eyes were troubled. 'Do your best to stay calm for the moment, m'dear. Think of my beloved Marguerite. The actress plays her part, and for the moment we're stalwart Republicans and you're a guilty prisoner. Are you sure you can do it?'

Why was he so concerned? Eleanor was quite calm. She curled her fingers into fists to stop herself from wiping them against her skirts. Just a little longer and they'd be out of here, and then they'd have *won*. She could endure as long as necessary and wasn't going to be the one who let everyone down. 'Quite sure, Chief,' she said, as firmly as she could.

'Then let's be on our way.'

CHAPTER TWENTY-SIX

The wind whined around the walls of the meagre cottage in which they were sheltering for the night. It was ostensibly the property of a local fisherman, but in practice rented out to smugglers, criminals, and the League of the Scarlet Pimpernel. Fortunately not all at the same time.

Andrew, Jerry and George were waiting down in the cove for Sir Percy's ship, the *Daydream*, to approach land, wrapped in cloaks to shield them from the worst of the weather and keep their lanterns dry. Tony had stepped along to the nearest village, a small hamlet as minimal as the cottage sheltering the League, in search of food and news. That left Sir Percy, Armand, Charles and Eleanor sharing the extremely confined space of the cottage. Sir Percy had the good grace to draw Armand into conversation, leaving Charles and Eleanor to huddle together in companionable silence.

Eleanor was morose. To be fair, they were all morose. Sir Percy had explained to her how somehow he'd located Chauvelin and persuaded him that a brace of royalist vampires with explosives in the hand was worth far more than a potential Pimpernel in the bush. With his assistance, and the additional men he'd been able to call upon, the League had managed to deal with the gunpowder beneath the Tuileries Palace, leaving Charles de Valois to retreat even deeper into the Catacombs. Yet it still didn't feel precisely like a *victory*. They'd saved lives, but the National Convention would be in session again before the day was out, and the Republic was unchanged. Eleanor had explained her own actions, as far as she could, and while Sir Percy had commended her for her bravery, he'd suggested that they should wait to see the final results.

The notorious Talleyrand had been discovered locked in a cell, and Chauvelin had taken him into custody on the spot. While Sir Percy would have liked to bring him along on their escape, the gunpowder had taken priority – and, he pointed out, being found as a hapless kidnapped prisoner of the royalist vampires was practically a signed endorsement of innocence. Or as close as one could get, these days.

At least Armand was safe. She'd fulfilled her promise to Lady Marguerite. Oh, perhaps he was having to flee to England with the League, but he was still alive, and that was one undiluted joy.

Charles had been tight-lipped ever since they'd left Paris. He haunted her side like a family ghost but fell silent whenever she attempted conversation. He appeared to be struggling with something which he was unwilling to share with either her or the others. Eleanor would have lost her temper with him if she hadn't felt so very guilty about running into such danger. Sir Percy and the others might have applauded her courage and her sense of duty, but Charles simply looked at her with those shadowed eyes which said, *I could have lost you*, and her heart twisted in her chest. She didn't want to do that to him ever again.

Eleanor wondered if Charlotte Corday had had brothers, or a lover, who'd known she was about to assassinate Marat, and argued with her about it. She'd stabbed the man in his bath and then gone to the guillotine for it, the papers had said. Had someone in the crowd looked at her with *those eyes*, the ones which reproached her for leaving them behind, and forced her to look away?

'There's nothing more I can tell you!' Armand said, raising his voice in the tone of a man repeating something he'd already been over more than once. 'I've told you everything I know.'

'And, sadly, told them,' Sir Percy remarked.

'If I had any way to apologize—'

'My dear fellow, heaven forbid I should suggest it was at all your fault! The problem is that it's placed all of us in a highly inconvenient situation. Eleanor in particular.' He glanced across at her and Charles. 'Which is why you won't be going back to France on any future mission, m'dear.'

'Then you agree!' Charles almost shone with relief. 'Thank you, Chief. I told you that—'

'You told him what?' Eleanor interrupted, suddenly wondering what the two of them had been saying behind her back. Nervous suspicion whispered that of *course* they'd been talking behind her back, but she suppressed it. She knew them better than that by now.

At least, she thought she did.

'I told him . . .' Charles's eyes flicked sideways to Sir Percy, and he amended his words. 'I *suggested* that it was quite simply unfair to continue dragging you into the League's business. Because, deuce take it, you have a great and noble heart, Eleanor, but it's not *right* for us to endanger you in . . . well, any of the ways in which we've been endangering you!'

'I thought we agreed I had the right to make that choice myself!' Eleanor argued.

'In a situation where nobody else could have done what you did!' They were practically shouting at each other now, even though they were sitting next to each other. 'Eleanor, you had to shoot a man! We should never have placed you in such a position. It was quite simply *wrong* of us.'

'My sister would box your ears if you said that to her,' Armand put in.

'Armand, my dear fellow, you're not helping.' Sir Percy sighed. 'Had I been allowed to finish what I was saying . . .' He gave Eleanor and Charles a moment to feel guilty before he continued. '*None* of us are returning to France for the near future. Yourself included, Armand. I fancy there's an arrest warrant with your name on it pinned to your door.'

There was dead silence for a moment. Then Charles and Eleanor broke in together. 'But, Chief—' 'But, Percy—'

'I fear the two of you haven't fully considered the crux of the matter,' Sir Percy said. 'The fact of it is, my dear friends, we have been revealed. Our carefully maintained curtain of secrecy has been snatched away. I believe the phrasing used in criminal circles is that we have had the gab blown on us. Eleanor?'

'I know nothing about criminal slang,' Eleanor said, offended, 'and I've been embroiled in far more criminal activity since joining the League than ever before in my life.'

Sir Percy laughed. 'No, no, m'dear, not that. I thought that you might want to put in a comment at this point, considering to *whom* we've been exposed.'

Eleanor realized what he meant, and blushed. 'You mean Lady Sophie, sir?'

'I do indeed mean my dear Sophie, Baroness of Basing for at least a couple of hundred years, and apparently far more deeply involved with the French royalist vampires than I'd ever suspected. I knew she suspected that Marguerite and I were involved in the League. Now she knows for sure. And there's also the minor matter of their desire to

371

use us as puppets, a subject which I think requires a great deal more investigation and explanation. It seems we should now turn our attention to England rather than France.'

Anima would have been glad to hear him talking like this, Eleanor thought bitterly. It would have been everything the old mage wanted – to know that someone with power and influence was motivated to look more deeply into the affairs of vampires. But . . . 'The problem is that Lady Sophie will know that we know, now,' she said.

The other problem, the one she hadn't mentioned to any of the League, was that she now felt the obligation of Anima's last request weighing upon her own shoulders. *I leave my own mission for you to finish*, Anima had said. And *Seek out further training*. How was she supposed to do any of that? Where did she *start*?

'She might assume we're all dead,' Charles suggested, bringing her back to reality.

'That will only last until we show ourselves in Society once more,' Sir Percy contradicted. 'The question is, how far does the rot go?'

'As in, how many vampires are involved in such a conspiracy?' Armand asked.

'Precisely. All of us here have known vampires who were honest, decent, straightforward fellows.' Sir Percy politely avoided saying that Eleanor had likely known far fewer vampires personally, or on anything other than the basis of providing blood for breakfast. 'I'm dashed if I'm going to risk starting some sort of panic! Things are bad enough as it is, with otherwise sensible gentlemen talking about barring our borders to France, and more than half the Members of Parliament seeing it as a quick dose to inflame the passions of their constituents. Can you imagine the reaction if a rumour about this reached the newspapers?'

'Yet there have already been rumours,' Charles said

thoughtfully. 'They were simply written off as Revolutionary hysteria.'

Eleanor didn't like the idea that had just come to her. She didn't want to say it aloud. But someone had to. 'Who owns the newspapers?' she asked.

'We're either giving this far too much consideration, or not enough,' Sir Percy opined, avoiding her question. 'Our next step is to return to England and review the situation. For the moment, France will have to take care of itself. You can't say we haven't done our bit to brighten the landscape—'

The door slammed open, interrupting him. Tony entered, shaking his hair off his face and pushing his cloak back from his shoulders. 'Sorry, chaps! Deuce of a blow out there. Hope I didn't frighten anyone.'

'The day you frighten someone, Tony, will be the day that Monsieur Chauvelin takes up growing turnips,' Sir Percy said. 'Any news?'

Tony's eyes flicked to Eleanor, then away again. 'Well, I have picked up some news that's just reached here from Paris. I'm afraid it's not the best . . .'

'Here, have some wine and tell us the worst,' Charles said, pouring him a cup of coarse red wine from the bottle they'd been sharing.

Eleanor felt her heart sink. The way he'd looked at her . . . No, perhaps she'd just been imagining things, perhaps she was simply fretting, but she feared the worst. Had something happened to Fleurette?

Tony took a careful seat on a rickety stool, accepted the wine, and then said, without looking up from his drink, 'They passed that law.'

'The one they'd been debating?' Eleanor demanded before she could stop herself. 'But – surely, Tony, you must be mistaken. Wouldn't they have realized what folly it was?'

Tony shook his head. 'I'm sorry, Eleanor, but I fear being

saved from peril has only persuaded them – Committee and Convention both – that they're in even greater peril and require every law they can forge in order to keep themselves safe and in power. It passed two days after we left Paris, but we were travelling so fast, the news has only just caught up with us. Couthon proposed it. He's the President of the Convention, goes around in a wheelchair. Halfway reasonable chap, but when it comes down to the point, everyone knows that Robespierre wrote it.'

Eleanor lowered her head into her hands. She'd done so much, they all had, and it *hadn't changed anything*. She'd lost Anima, she'd killed a man, the League had been recognized and now had to flee France, and it had all been for nothing. *Being saved from peril has only persuaded them that they're in even greater peril*. If anything, they'd made things worse. Tears leaked from her eyes. It wasn't messy noisy hysterics of the sort which would prompt a bucket of water or a slap, but she couldn't stop herself from crying.

'Eleanor?' Charles said. His arm went round her shoulders, warm and comforting, but the knowledge he was there, that she could turn to him, still did nothing to halt the growing cold inside her. *All of it for nothing. Why did we even bother trying?*

'Charles, dear fellow,' Sir Percy said, 'forgive me, but what Eleanor needs at this moment is someone to talk to her like a grandfather, not a lover, and as the oldest person here I intend to take that liberty. Yes, you may all go outside. And take your drinks with you. I'm not quite so cruel as all that.'

Charles hesitated, but Sir Percy leaned over to murmur something in his ear which Eleanor couldn't catch. He reluctantly rose to his feet and quitted the room with the others into the wind outside, leaving the two of them alone.

'There's a lot to be said for a reputation,' Sir Percy mused, 'but the fact of it is, reputations aren't always true. Here, Eleanor, you have more need of this than I do.'

Eleanor saw he was offering her a handkerchief. A miraculously clean white lawn handkerchief, still pressed into neat folds, and somehow unaffected by their journeys across France. 'Thank you,' she sniffled. Her fingers looked twice as dirty by comparison as she took it, and she tried to blot away her tears.

'We don't always win.' He'd leaned back in the pile of sacks he was using for a chair, but he wasn't playing the idle fool as he so often did. 'Truth is, Eleanor, we've frequently been lucky, but that's not always the case. I'm not just talking about the times when we've seen that a rescue was impossible and haven't even tried it – though, thank heavens, there have been few of those – but about the times when we've tried and failed. Perhaps the guards were just a shade too clever, or too wary, or even too stupid to take a bait. Or maybe the mob was too close, or Monsieur Chauvelin or others of his kind too hot on our heels. I snatch at every chance I can, but sometimes Dame Fortune is cruel. Gambling is sweet because of the risk of losing, but there are always times when we do lose.'

'But you're the Scarlet Pimpernel!' Eleanor cried out in despair. 'What we've been doing is important! We can't afford to lose.' Up till now she'd believed it could all be possible, because she'd believed in him. What was she to say now if he didn't even believe in himself?

'That's where you have it wrong,' Sir Percy said soberly. 'We – you, I, the League – *can* afford to lose. It's the people of France who can't. People like the ones you saved from Mont-Saint-Michel, who are going to march straight back into the mouth of danger to try to change the Revolution into something just and merciful, rather than the tyranny of the mob. Not one of them asked you to take them away to England, did they? The League helps those who can't help themselves, but there are many good Frenchmen – and women too, before you say it – who are helping themselves. And thank God for it, because France needs their work. They're confronting what's become of the Revolution, which so many of them initially supported. They had the highest of ideals, just like you or my beloved Marguerite, and . . . they have to live with how those ideals have been twisted. Yet in spite of it all, they haven't given up on their work.'

'But they didn't make it *worse*!' Eleanor had to choke back another sob. 'If I hadn't—'

'If *we* hadn't gone after that gunpowder,' Sir Percy said sharply, 'it would have exploded, and with a great deal more impact than the single cask which did go off. If *you* hadn't faced the Committee of Public Safety in an admittedly reckless, foolish, and ill-advised single-handed attempt to help them . . . Another handkerchief? No, very well then. Perhaps you shouldn't have taken that bait Marie Antoinette dangled in front of you, but I can't blame you for doing it.'

'Bait?' Eleanor said slowly.

'You think it was pure chance she happened to mention the proposed law in front of you, and then let you persuade her into allowing such a mission to prevent it? I'll warrant she took your measure within ten minutes and decided to use you to remove her enemies. I blame myself. I left you in her keeping. I'm as guilty as any other man here of assuming that the once-Queen of France was foolish or harmless.'

Eleanor felt as though she'd reached a new depth of despair. There was simply no room left for further tears. She'd just been used by yet *another* manipulator. 'That's *worse* than it all being for nothing, then . . .' *Like any supporter of the Revolution,* the words came to her. *Just one more person listening to the story they wanted to hear and following orders.*

'No!' Sir Percy's voice was like a pistol shot. 'If you hadn't done what you did, then they'd *still* have passed that demned law, but two days earlier. In the meantime, what you did

376

was the right thing. I'll give the Revolution this much credit – if vampires are exerting that sort of control, they must be stopped, and by any means available. But other than that . . . Sometimes there is no right answer, m'dear. Sometimes one only does what one can, taking the chances one can, and praying that Dame Fortune is listening. And sometimes . . . one is just unlucky.'

He sat up, leaning towards her. 'Tell me, Eleanor, did you ever wonder if all of the people we've saved have been, shall we say, quite as virtuous as they claimed to be when they were scrabbling for help to leave France?'

'You've said in the past that not all the aristocrats in France were innocent,' Eleanor said cautiously, 'and that some of them made matters worse. That they even provoked the Revolution.'

'Quite. Well, let's say there's been at least one . . . mistake, shall we call it? Among the people whom we saved and brought to England. It wasn't a vampire, so don't think that; they were living people. I'll not give you any names, but since then we've been a deuced sight more careful.'

Eleanor couldn't help but notice how very vague he was being when it came to what had happened, or how the situation had been resolved. She decided it was best not to ask.

Yet there was another matter which had been prodding at her conscience for a while now. 'How *do* you decide, then? Every time we've been in France, we've seen people in danger. To only pick and choose a few of them . . . it feels so very . . .' She sought for the right word. 'Entitled. Proud. Arrogant. Who made us the judges?'

'We made ourselves judges when we put ourselves in peril to do it,' Sir Percy said soberly. 'We do the best we can, and when we make mistakes or fail, we pick ourselves up and try again. That's the nub of it. I could quote you a dozen examples, but you know it's true just as well as I do. We *will* return to France, later. In the meantime, I believe there's important work for us to do in England. Do you agree?'

Somewhere in the talk, her tears had stopped. She scrubbed at her eyes with the handkerchief one last time, her throat dry. It was true. She had work to do in England. Anima had left her with a mission to complete, and one that might change the course of her entire life . . . again. If she was a mage, then what did that actually mean? What did it make her capable of doing? Would she, in time, be able to do everything which Anima had said was within her powers? She felt as if she stood on the edge of a cliff, with the sky stretching above her, and no idea of how to fly except by jumping off.

Sir Percy's words echoed in her head. *They haven't given up on their work.* Could she do any less?

She hadn't told anyone beside Charles and Tony about Bernard's words to her – *a secret hidden somewhere below London.* She had questions of her own to ask. Burning questions. And perhaps it was time for *her* to ask for help from the people she trusted, the people who'd risked their lives for her, just as she had for them. 'Yes, Chief. I agree.'

'Then—'

The door slammed open, and everyone else piled in on top of each other, crowding the small hut. 'Chief!' Andrew exclaimed, drowning out the others. 'The *Daydream*'s here, with news from England!'

Sir Percy rose to his feet, frowning. 'What news?'

'News of Lady Blakeney.' Andrew's face was like thunder. 'She's under arrest, Chief. As a French spy.'

ACKNOWLEDGEMENTS

I'd like to thank everyone who's contributed to this, whether as editors, publishers, agent, beta-readers, sounding walls which I bounced ideas off, and friends who encouraged me. Bella Pagan, Lucienne Diver, Rebecca Needes, Charlotte Tennant, Claire Baldwin, Sophie Robinson, Holly Domney; Charles Stross, Jamie-Lee Nardone, Elizabeth McCoy, Rachel McMillan, MJJ, Sarah McDonagh, Aliette de Bodard; my coworkers and my friends; my parents and my family; and everyone else who I should have remembered and mentioned here. Thank you all.

The protagonist has to change (and hopefully grow) during the course of a trilogy. Eleanor has become politically aware (perhaps the League shouldn't have given her such detailed history lessons about the Revolution in order to help her maintain her disguise) and started paying attention to the world around her. The problem with developing awareness and power, as has been said before in many places, is that with (great) power comes (great) responsibility. Or, as Granny Weatherwax put it in Terry Pratchett's *Maskerade*, 'The trouble is, you see, that if you do know Right from Wrong, you can't choose Wrong.' Or, vaguely remembered from an old school story, 'We've got a rather stiff run across country before us this term; but no one who can ride may shirk.'

While it's interesting to write from the perspective of

someone who is near the bottom of the social ladder and the hapless toy of fate and her superiors, it becomes even more interesting to explore what characters will do when given power and options. My thanks, again, to everyone who's helped and supported me in this.